Retinue: Defence of a Kingdom

Medieval England 1403

For more information about Graham Nolan
and his books visit:
www.grahamnolan.co.uk

GRAHAM NOLAN

Retinue
Defence of a Kingdom

Medieval England 1403

Three Crowns Publishing

This novel is entirely a work of fiction. The names, characters and incidents portrayed in it, while some are based on real historical figures and events, are the work of the author's imagination.

Copyright © Graham Nolan 2012

Graham Nolan asserts the moral right to be identified as the author of this work

www.grahamnolan.co.uk

ISBN: 978-0-9574694-0-2

Published by Three Crowns Publishing
Stone, Staffordshire, England

All rights reserved.
No part of this publication may be reproduced, stored in a retrieval system, or transmitted, in any form or by any means, without the prior permission in writing of the publisher, nor be otherwise circulated in any form or binding or cover other than that in which it is published and without a similar condition including this condition being imposed on the subsequent purchaser.

Cover Copyright © William Walker 2012

To my wife – you are truly my cinema!

Illustrations and Colours of Coats of Arms

King Henry IV, quartered, gules three lions passant guardiat and azure, three fleurs-de-lis or[1]

Owain Glyn Dwr, The four lions rampant, lion gules on or quarter and reversed[2]

Earl Edmund, 5th Earl of Stafford, chevron gules[2]

Ralph Fitz Warrin, quartered gules argent[2]

Sir Henry 'Hotspur' Percy, rampant lion and three fish, quartered azure and gules with cadency[3]

Sir Robert De Ferrers of Chartley, six sable horseshoes on argent[2]

Sir John Done of Utkington, barry of five, azure argent with three arrows in bend gules[2]

Sir Archibald Douglas, 4th Earl of Douglas, azure three mullets argent with heart, gules[2]

Images reproduced with the kind permission of:
1 Fleur-de-Lis Designs ©
2 Armourial Gold Heraldry ©
3 Bob Bonnington 2009 ©

MEDIEVAL COLOURS:
| Or: Yellow | Argent: White | Sable: Black |
| Gules: Red | Azure: Blue | Vert: Green |

Illustrations and Maps

Wales and the Welsh Marches

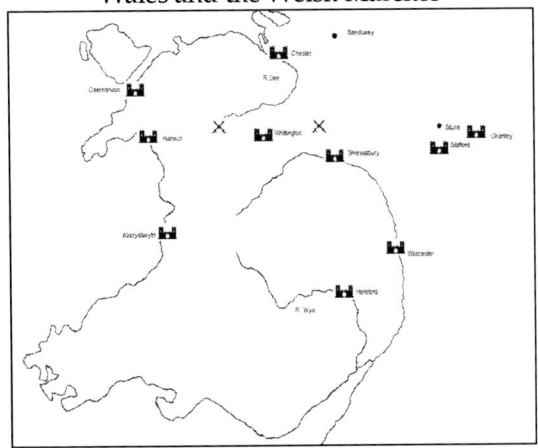

Ground Plan of Whittington Castle and Baileys

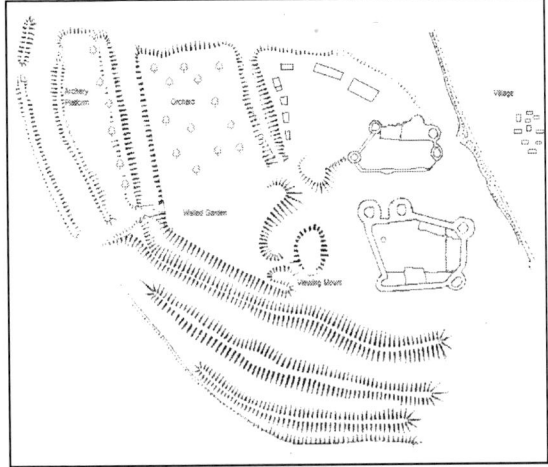

Based on a ground plan of Whittington Castle, Shropshire. Reproduced with the kind permission of Whittington Castle Preservation Trust © 2003: Whittington Castle Guidebook (Shrewsbury, 2003), p. 18.

CHAPTER ONE

Rowan pulled back the string at the same time as raising the bow. The tension caused his shoulders to ache as the steel-tipped arrow was drawn in a slow, practiced motion to nestle close to his ear. He was holding his breath just as he had been taught from an early age, his eyes fixed firmly on his target two hundred yards away, across the meadow. He had missed already and in his mind could not afford to miss again. Now, releasing his breath slowly, his fingers opened to allow the shaft to speed towards its target in a blur, the familiar snap as the string hit the leather bracer.

The news reached him even as he watched his tenth and final arrow fly wide, missing the target on the earth mound altogether and glancing off into the copse of trees behind. His exertions at the practice butts for most of the late afternoon after chores were taking their toll and the muscles in his arms and shoulders felt like they were on fire. He smiled as Eric ran down the single track, his long legs moving awkwardly, his urgency and excitement unmistakable.

It was not unusual to be disturbed by his childhood friend and Rowan was accustomed to his ever energetic willingness to share even the smallest news, from the latest adventures of one the local farmers' daughters to the news of the Earl's latest tax hike. However there was something that gave Eric's bearing even more energy than usual as he staggered over the last few yards of the dusty path. His breathing was heavy and resulted in a short fit of coughing before, taking off his usual red felt cloth hat to wipe away the few beads of sweat, he was able to stand upright and share his excitement.

Rowan listened silently as Eric relayed the news. He knew he should be grasping his friend by the arm, whooping with laughter and excitement but instead he just stood there; this was what he and his friends had spent numerous summer evenings talking about. It was what all the years of training had been for; the seemingly endless drawing of bows or swinging of swords that had been a part of everyday life as members of the Earl's retinue.

There was no mistaking Eric's mood as he grinned inanely at his friend. 'Don't just stand there like a dozy cow ready for slaughter. This is it!' Eric's excitement was infectious, and Rowan soon found himself reciprocating the grin. 'I don't believe it. The boys aren't going to believe this! Let's get down the Crown Tavern fast before they run out of ale!'

Quickly Rowan turned round, gathering his willow-framed arrow bag and russet cloak as his friend ran to collect the spent arrows embedded in the target. The arrow that had skidded off the earth mound was forgotten as they set off jogging along the narrow dirt path, leaving the Crown's Meadow behind as they made their way, between the youthful trunks of the trees, to the nearby market square of Stone Town.

The bells for vespers from the priory were just ringing out as they made their way along Adies Alley, which was alive with the news, noisy at the best of times with the bleating of livestock and people calling out their wares. Trading seemed to have been suspended as the townsfolk stood in groups chatting, arms waving as they spoke fervently, all absorbed in conversation.

Rowan and Eric approached almost unnoticed; unnoticed, that is, apart from Rowan's father who turned as though some unseen hand had touched his shoulder, sharing a half grin and a knowing look that said 'we'll speak later'. Rowan smiled almost imperceptibly and allowed himself to be dragged straight into the tavern.

Even before he ducked under the low doorway into the dim and smoke-filled room, he knew he was going to be assaulted by a cacophony of noise. Groups of men from the town were vying to be the loudest and ensure their boasts or insults were heard by all.

Nodding in greeting as he weaved his way past the familiar faces of the townsfolk, he arrived at the large table to the left of the big stone hearth just under the opening that faced out into the main street, his friends' favourite seating place. The fire had been lit to counter the slight chill of the early evening air that filtered in, the fenestral having been removed because of the fine weather. Sure enough, his friends, Martin, Daniel and Jerrard were waiting for him.

He could see that Martin's pale complexion under the mop of brown hair was already flushed either from the news, or more likely from drinking a couple of tankards of the brewer's strong ale. His friend, wearing his usual serious expression, was in deep conversation with Daniel, his dark eyes matching the shoulder length long black hair which women found so attractive.

'Eh up you two,' Jerrard welcomed them. Unlike the other two friends who had the same slim build as Rowan, Jerrard was thickset and proudly sported a thick beard despite being the same age. 'This is on Sid,' he said, glancing towards the bar and raising the jug he was holding in a toast to the smiling landlord, who was obviously happy at the unexpected extra early evening trade the news had brought. 'I took the liberty of asking for a couple of cups for you. Thought we might be celebrating,' he added, pushing two more of the wooden vessels across the table as Rowan and Eric sat down at the end of the benches.

'Too right,' said his friend as he reached over and poured ale from the jug, taking a deep gulp before he too raised his vessel towards the landlord. 'Here's to sorting the French out,' his toast was loud enough to cause many of the clusters of men to turn round and give an enthusiastic cheer.

Rowan wondered if he was the only one that was thinking too much over the implications of the news. Everyone else seemed to embrace the announcement that the Earl had called the retinue to arms with little concern or doubt over what it meant. 'What's brought all of this on then do you reckon?' he looked at Martin as he finished taking a drink of the dark brew which seemed less watered down than normal for this time of day. His friend was seen by the group as the one most up to date with affairs of the court and nobility, especially as his father was one of the town aldermen.

'I'm not sure, but the peace was never going to last with the French.' The uncomfortable standoff between the two antagonist nations had lasted nearly two years but England had been at war with France ever since the friends had been born and there was general agreement that peace would not last.

'Well that's good news for us then,' replied Jerrard, his eyes bright. 'It means we can get out of this place.' Despite his large build that made him well suited to helping out his father at the forge, he made no secret of his desire to leave the town.

'Your father will never let you go,' Eric chortled, refilling his tankard already.

'He won't have a choice, will he?' said Jerrard almost pleadingly, seeking confirmation from Martin.

'Well he can try, but you know as well as I do when the Earl calls us up, we go. Why else would we spend the time training?'

The group of friends, along with fifteen other men of varying ages from the town and outlying farms, spent two afternoons a month drilling at the Earl's castle at Stafford some ten miles away. They were armed, and trained with sword and buckler as well as bow, committed to the Earl who was, in turn, sworn to the new king.

The group had begun their training together more than four years ago now and considered themselves certainly able, although this was regularly scorned by the intimidating Master-at-Arms, Samuel Blacke. His constant insults drew amused looks from the few experienced men from the town, including Rowan's father who had been involved in the skirmishes with both the Scottish and the Welsh in recent years.

'I haven't even seen the call up notice. What's it say?' enquired Rowan.

'Well the soldiers who brought it read it out.' Daniel's statement underlined the fact that no-one in the group could read. 'It was a proclamation that the retinue was to be called up and that we should all attend the castle in a day's time ready to march,' replied Daniel.

'So it doesn't actually mention the French then?'

'Well, no, but apparently one of the lads from the Partridge farm spoke to some soldiers as they were going on to Yarnfield and they said it was definitely about sorting the French out. What else would it be?'

Rowan shrugged his shoulders. He had never really expected to be crossing the channel and fighting in a totally foreign land, especially when the threat from the Scots and the Welsh seemed much closer.

The group carried on talking for the rest of the night. They were the last to leave and were ushered out of the door by the yawning landlord, their not-so-whispered 'good nights' carrying across the darkness as they headed to their homes, swaying occasionally due to the effects of the ale which they had consumed as they discussed the night away.

The next morning Rowan awoke with a sour taste in his mouth and a hazy head. He rolled out from his straw-filled pallet, rubbing his eyes, and pulled on his thin woollen jersey before wandering into the main room where his mother was busy sweeping the old rushes from the floor.

'Morning mother, where's father?' he enquired.

'He's where you should be,' she grinned. 'For some reason he said he'd let you lie in today, probably listening to you stagger in last night. Was it a good night with the boys?' Her eyes, for a moment betrayed her concern.

'It was good but I'm paying for it now.' He didn't want to give his mother an opportunity to change the mood and quickly moved over to the bowl on the table and splashed water over his face, rubbing his eyes and then smoothing his brown hair with wet hands. 'I'll go and catch him up. See you later,' he said, pulling on his worn leather boots quickly before leaving.

He walked up to the top field, where he knew his father would be, mending the fence that had allowed some of the cows to stray into the woods the previous day. He breathed in the fresh air, enjoying the early morning sun as it filtered through the low clouds overhead. His mind wandered back to the news and what it would mean, reflecting on his reaction. Was it fear that had made him feel less enthusiastic than the others? No, he knew it wasn't fear. Maybe he was thinking about it too much? He had always considered himself a thinker, happy to allow other people to talk while he listened, so maybe that's what it was. With that in his mind he felt a lot better and his thoughts switched to the practicalities of what he needed to do next to prepare for the mustering the following day.

He thought about the clothes he needed and the food, and felt a pang of selfishness. He hadn't reflected on what it would mean for his mother with both he and his father leaving for goodness knew how long, and there was always the possibility that they may not be coming back. Sure, she'd waved his father off before when he'd gone off to fight and knew that it was part of their duty to the Earl; they had spent enough evenings talking about the possibility but, judging from the look she had given him this morning, she was obviously worried and was trying not to show it.

A welcoming shout shook him out of his sombre thoughts. 'About time, I've nearly done it now,' welcomed his father waving a mallet and standing by the previously broken section of fencing.

'Sorry, you should have woken me.'

'Oh it's alright, not a big job anyway, but you can hold this for me while I tie it in place,' he said, holding up a thick branch already affixed at one end. Rowan dutifully helped as his father tied the branch in place using some old rope.

As they worked his father raised the issue of the call-up. 'What do you think then, boy?'

'To be honest, I'm not sure. I'm looking forward to it I suppose, but I'm not really sure what to expect. At least I'll be with the lads,' Rowan replied a little uncertainly.

'Well, all I'd say is it won't be pleasant. Certainly Eric will have his eyes opened,' his father said, looking at his son, obviously rekindling some of his memories of campaigning. His father had several thick scars on his arms as well as a livid red burn scar on his neck partially hidden by his beard, reminders from previous sorties into enemy territory.

'Look boy, the truth is it's a bad business going to

war, whether it's the French, Scottish or Welsh. Either way I've seen too many good men, and women and children for that matter, with the bellies torn open. It's going to be hard and the best thing you can do is to keep your head down, listen to the sergeants and don't get all heroic.' His tone took on a serious note and his face adjusted into a look of concern for his son.

'Alright father, trust me, I won't get carried away,' Rowan reassured, although the seriousness of the words unnerved him.

They carried on working the top field all day, checking the fencing and baling the hay, knowing that although the elderly farmhands who remained would tend the crops and live stock, they would be stretched by the lack of men remaining.

That evening the five friends met up at the archery butts, the river Trent running close by, flowing slowly under the arched stone bridge to Walton. They'd agreed the previous night to meet here, to have a last practice before travelling to the castle the next day. All brought their longbows, each as tall as the friends who had practiced with the weapon ever since they were fourteen. Their bows varied slightly. All were made with strong English yew but, as the years of use had gone on, each had become personalised to its owner. Eric's rather predictably seemed to have suffered more from the wear and tear than the others.

Daniel had already set up a couple of targets made from white material pinned to the mounds. The boys greeted each other cheerfully and agreed to the rules of their normal competition.

Eric and Jerrard drew the first two short lots, causing a chuckle. Jerrard was by far the strongest of the archers, while Eric did well to draw his bow back fully despite the years of practice. Not only did this mean the arrows would cause greater damage when hitting their target but Eric also found it more difficult to keep pace with the regularity of volley fire.

'Well that's just great,' muttered Eric, as he and Jerrard pulled a dozen arrows from their drawstring bags and thrust their tips into the turf at their feet, before facing their respective targets about one hundred yards away.

Daniel began calling out the familiar command, 'loose,' as both archers let fly towards their targets. The last of the arrows were pulled from the ground less than a minute later, notched to the strings and released, much to Eric's obvious relief, although to his credit he had kept up with the commands. Both archers squinted towards their targets to see how many they had pierced. Jerrard had scored eight while Eric had only managed six.

'What a surprise!' Daniel laughed good naturedly as Eric pulled out his deeply embedded arrows - no easy thing thanks to the power of the bow.

Next up were Daniel and Rowan, although they were delayed as Rowan searched and retrieved the arrow he had so hastily left the previous evening. He, as with the others, thrust his arrows in the turf next to his right foot, quickly taking time to smooth some of the goose feathered flights that seemed to have got slightly crushed despite the frame in the arrow bag. He took his bow from its canvas cover before bending the top end away from him, using his foot as a block, feeling the yew stave bend satisfyingly until, with practised effort, he was able to hook the hemp bowstring over the top horn.

This time with Martin shouting out the commands it was a much closer contest, Daniel just beating Rowan, eight to seven. The competition went on until each archer had faced one another and the sun began to disappear for the evening. The victor was Jerrard. Having beaten Eric, he had gone on to beat both Rowan and Daniel, while drawing with Martin. This was not always the case with the victor changing regularly on these practice sessions so that each friend was chivalrous in defeat, although this did not stop the banter.

'Don't think the Frenchies are going to be worried about you.'

'When are you going to get that eye sorted?'

The good natured insults went on as they unstrung their bows, wrapping them in their cloth covers before making their way back to their respective homes for supper.

That night, Rowan picked out his clothes and weapons ready for the following morning's journey. He carefully laid out his thigh length mail shirt letting his fingers feel the gentle scrape of the small metal rings, proud to be one of the few archers who owned such a gift. Then he pulled out his quilted jacket which he would wear under the mailed shirt and was not surprised to see that a tear had recently been repaired by his mother. She was always there to wash, clean and sew. Again, he felt another pang of guilt but also a feeling of doubt. Would tomorrow be the last time he or his father said goodbye to her?

With that foreboding thought in mind he pulled out his straight bladed falchion almost reverently from its resting place under the bed, unsheathing it from the wooden cloth-covered scabbard. The three foot length of steel had a slightly dull gleam and its edge was keen. He wasn't too bad with the sword, or so he thought as he slowly turned the blade in his hand, knowing at the same time that he would much rather face any enemy with his bow.

The remaining items to take on his journey were three drawstrings, made from twisted and soaked strands of woven hemp; his rather tired looking open faced metal bascinet; a small and slightly battered buckler shield; a piece of flint and steel from which to light fires; a small tablet of wax for his bow stave; a light green travelling cloak, and a small wooden cross which he hung around his neck.

The charm wasn't because he was overly religious, though like all the villagers he attended church every Sunday and treated the local priest from the priory with deference. Most of the boys had a charm of some sort and relied on these whenever good luck was required, not that it always worked. The cross had been carved by his father, made out of red oak, with a textured touch, and a dovetail crosspiece joint. The cross was almost identical to his father's. It had been given to him, as it had by his father's father, to celebrate his fourteenth birthday, his transition from youth to adulthood.

The next morning he awoke after a fitful night's

sleep, his mind wondering about what the next few weeks, even months, would bring. The morning was bright, as it had been over the past few weeks, England was enjoying a hot summer and despite the interrupted sleep he felt wide awake and fresh as he tugged on his boots before stepping into the main room where both his mother and father were sitting at the wooden trestle table.

'Morning lad,' welcomed his father, 'how are you feeling?'

'Good, thanks,' said Rowan honestly, wondering how just a few hours ago he would have doubted the genuineness of his reply. 'What time are we leaving?' he asked, immediately regretting it as he glanced at his mother.

'Oh we've got plenty of time yet,' replied his father, apparently picking up on the concerns of his wife.

He sat down without another word and tucked into a breakfast of oatcakes and cheese, munching purposefully, focussing his senses as he absorbed the savoury taste in his mouth and using the food to avoid the worried eyes of his mother. Conversation was awkward, interspersed with periods of silence and it was with a sense of relief that he pushed the wooden plate away and scraped back his chair, excusing himself as he went back into his small room and collected his belongings.

Unlike many other noblemen, the Earl asked his men to bring their own weapons rather than provide them himself, though this, his father had reasoned, was offset by the retinue allowance of six shillings per day on campaign. It was still a sum of money he was unused to having and he looked forward to his relative wealth that he would undoubtedly spend with his friends in some tavern or other. He began his preparations for departure, sliding his bow into its protective canvas covering, tugging the string tight before securing the worn straps of the buckler through his leather belt and sheathing his sword and dagger.

Feeling the unfamiliar heaviness of the weapons at his waist and adjusting them slightly, he breathed deeply trying to calm the excitement and nervousness that was increasingly threatening to surge through his body. He returned to the kitchen where his mother offered him a small knapsack containing some food and ale. He took it with a smile and instinctively wrapped his arms around her, giving her a hug before slinging his canvas bow covering across his back. He glanced round and raised a hand in a smiling farewell, leaving his mother and father to say their own goodbyes as the door creaked closed behind him, the small iron latch clicking shut soundly.

Outside he gathered his horse from the nearby paddock adjacent to the house. Constance, a name that suited the cautious mare was a medium-sized light brown palfrey of some four years, not more than fifteen hands high. He smiled to himself as she nuzzled his open hand and he patted its firm neck familiarly. It wasn't a spectacular beast, especially when compared to any of the mounts possessed by the nobles, merchants or even wealthier farmers but he was proud to have such a horse, one of several that the Earl owned and had provided to the men of the retinue so that they could look after them.

Once he had strapped on the saddle and accompanying equipment, spare clothes and blanket, he rode slowly the three quarters of a mile towards the mill pond near the priory where the small retinue had agreed to meet before starting on their journey to Stafford. Sure enough, as he neared he saw the group of men standing around waiting for their companions. The air was full of excited chatter. His friends were already there, all similarly equipped, although Eric, true to type was still wearing his red felt cap flopped over his right ear.

With a self conscious grin, aware that others were watching him approach, he dismounted, giving Constance a reassuring pat as he was engulfed in the enthusiastic conversation around him.

Half an hour later his father, an experienced archer with the rank of vintenar, gave the order to mount up and start the journey to the castle where they would learn more about the call to arms.

The journey was uneventful and pleasant, partially due to the ongoing excitement and expectations and partly because of the increasing warmth of the sun. By mid morning they caught sight of the town and surrounding walls, the Earl's castle high on the ridge two miles further on.

Passing the ominous grey stone gaol to their left where thieves, tricksters and other villains had been committed, they rode through the shadow of the town's northern gatehouse and into the congested streets.

Rowan instinctively wrinkled his nose. He never got used to the smells of the large town and its tight streets filled with rotting food or worse, competing with sickly wafts from the tanneries and dyers.

As the small troop rode through, the townsfolk reluctantly made way, their haggling or journeys interrupted, while the young boys ran eagerly alongside. The sunlight was largely blocked out by the overhanging extensions of the crammed houses and stall fronts, their shutters open for business. The town was much more bustling and noisy than Stone with everything from tailors, shoemakers and armourers with their workshops behind their open fronted shops, to meat and vegetable sellers and hucksters selling their loaves of bread. The calls of the stall owners competed with the sounds of iron clad wheels of loaded carts and the clucking, honking and snorting of chicken, geese and pigs waiting to be sold, seemingly oblivious to the throng of people threading between them.

Leaving the main street and its shadowed, crooked side alleys for a moment, the troop entered the wide market square with its guild hall where richly dressed merchants in fur trimmed coats mixed among other freemen in similarly colourful thigh length tunics and hoses. Rowan spotted a few black cassocks of the Dominican friars as well as small huddles of women in their ground length kirtles who turned to watch the column of horsemen.

He immediately became more self conscious and directed his eyes forwards and straightened his back a little as he sensed the townspeople stopping their business to watch the small troop, their bodies bouncing rhythmically with the gait of their horses as they left the square behind, heading towards the south walls.

His eyes turned however as they passed Saint Chad's church. Rowan admired the ornate stone work and stained glass windows that stood out prominently against the wattle and daub homes and workshops either side. On the occasional visits into the town, whether to sell some of the family's livestock or to visit one of the annual fairs, he always found himself marvelling at the stone buildings within the walls.

'You'll catch flies in that mouth of yours,' Martin joked, spotting his friend staring at the church, his head turning as they rode past.

'You'll catch much more than that if you ever entered one of those places. The thought of becoming a monk doesn't really appeal to me,' Daniel joked.

With his glossy black hair, broad smile and ready charm he'd already had a lot of success with the local girls, causing him to get into trouble more than once, much to the disapproval of the local clergy.

The group's laughter mixed with the ongoing hustle and bustle of the town as they rode on towards the southern walls, leaving the intensity of the congested streets and townspeople behind and entering the cool shadow of the gatehouse. Their horses' hooves echoed loudly as they cantered over the stone bridge, the noise mixing with the jangle of harnesses and rattle of loose equipment, before they turned eastwards and rode past the water mill on the opposite bank beneath the town walls. The big wooden paddles turned slowly, dipping in and out of the river that flowed easily between the green reed beds as the riders headed towards the towers of the castle in the distance.

The ride continued to be pleasant enough, allowing Rowan to take in the familiar rolling countryside, occasionally passing villagers tending their fields, taking the opportunity to stretch their backs as they watched the troop pass, raising their arms briefly in acknowledgement.

Half an hour later they turned up the track that led through the heavily wooded slope towards the first of the two outer palisades ringing the imposing and formidable stone walls and turrets of the castle standing high on the hilltop overlooking the baileys.

Forming into a loose column once more, Rowan's father led the men up the slope to the first wooden gateway where the thick gates stood open, guarded by a couple of the Earl's household retinue. The helmeted guards, leaning on their evil looking halberds with their wide axe heads and pointed tips, nodded them through.

Inside the bailey he could see more activity than he and his friends usually experienced when they attended their regular drilling sessions.

People moved purposefully between the myriad of buildings, smoke drifting from their rooftops carrying sheaves of arrows, baskets of bread and other foodstuffs, preparations he assumed being made ready for their expedition. Some stopped and looked up briefly from their tasks before returning to their business as the troop made their way along the muddied main path that wound its way slowly upwards almost circling the hillside. Hens shrieked noisily, flapping out of the way of the small column as they continued through the second outer bailey. They were met by yet more activity, accompanied by the sounds of blacksmiths hammering out their fiery hot metals, the noise of dogs barking, and people shouting to each other. The noise only lessened as the men guided their horses up the final steep section overlooked by the crenellations of the castle walls.

An elderly herald greeted Rowan's father, asked that his men dismount, and gestured to some young stable hands who scampered forwards to take the horses. He then ushered the company upwards, towards the large castle gatehouse with its formidable flanking towers.

The invitation was unusual, only once before had he ventured into the courtyard, invited by his father to see close up the imposing keep within the walls. By the time he emerged through the cool shade of the gatehouse, his eyes taking in the suspended spikes of the iron tipped wooden portcullis as he did so, his thighs were aching from the climb and his breathing was laboured.

Within the high walls overlooked by the towers it seemed like the whole troop of retinue archers from surrounding towns had assembled, nearly eighty men. Greetings were made, hands shook and further questions about why they were here asked. Rowan saw his father make his way towards his former comrades in arms, also elevated in position to command their own companies who in turn surrounded the bear-like figure of Samuel Blacke.

Even as he watched, a messenger ran over to the Master-at-Arms who in turn called to the men. 'Fall in you lot. Hurry up.' His loud uncompromising voice rang out within the confines of the walls.

The courtyard turned briefly into mayhem as men

pushed past each other in their hurry to obey the command, seeking their familiar stations within their companies. Rowan, along with the rest of the company placed themselves on the right flank. Nudging between Jerrard and Daniel he glanced at his other two friends behind him, unable to prevent himself returning Eric's infectious grin that always seemed to indicate some mischievous act or other.

The ranks fell silent as the Master-at-Arms turned to face the heavy steel-banded oak door of the Keep which was already open. Castle guards in their livery of yellow tunics, belted at the waist with its distinctive red chevron, stood at the bottom of the short flight of steps leading to its dark interior.

The Earl appeared moments later, followed by a small entourage of three knights wearing their own variously coloured surcoats.

Despite his relative youthful age, being four years older than Rowan and his friends, the Earl made an impressive sight in his full armour with his helm under his arm, his face framed by a neatly trimmed short brown beard and bowl cut hair. The young noble stopped at the top of the steps and stared at the assembled men who looked at their lord in expectant silence.

'Men, I have called you all here in response to a request by our noble king.' The Earl's authoritative voice rang out after his examination of the men below, increasing in intensity as he spoke. 'Some of the Welsh continue to challenge our borders and raid across the Marches. His Royal Highness has commanded that we, the men of Stafford, lend our strength and march westwards. Knowing our history of loyal and ardent service, he has put his faith in us to teach them a lesson. I have assured him that I have some of the best archers in the country.' He paused, his eyes once more scanning the ranks of his retinue. 'I have no doubt of it. Are you willing to do your duty for King Henry and Saint George?'

His voice had reached a crescendo and the fervently asked question invited the resounding cheers from the assembled men, the cries for Saint George reverberating between the thick surrounding walls. For the moment the fact they were going to war on the Welsh and not the French was forgotten among Rowan and his friends as they joined in.

The Earl raised his hands and the cheering gradually subsided. 'Sir Robert,' he gestured towards a veteran knight of perhaps forty wearing an argent surcoat decorated with sable horseshoes, 'will be accompanying us as we deal with these enemies of our king. He too shares my judgement and will be similarly honoured to be marching with you.'

Rowan and his friends knew by sight Sir Robert De Ferrers, the lord of nearby Chartley Castle and it was plain to see that the two, who were related by marriage, were also good friends as they shared a brief look between themselves.

'To stop the gossiping among you,' The Earl continued, 'he has suggested I tell you exactly where we are marching and, though it may be against my better judgement, I can tell you we will be riding to the castle at Whittington, on the Welsh borders.' The comment and the Earl's obvious good humour brought some quiet chuckles among the ranks. 'We will set off within the hour so check your equipment and ready yourselves to do your duty. I have utmost faith in you.'

The Earl's last words struck a serious chord as he finished and, apparently satisfied with his simple message, turned and re-entered the hall with his entourage of knights, the metal plates of their armour scraping against the archway as they left.

As they dismissed and broke into respective groups there was real enthusiasm among the assembled retinue.

'Well done Eric,' chipped in Daniel, sarcastically, 'Wales, France, what's the difference?'

Eric took the comment with his natural good humour, 'Well, I was close,' he replied to the group's laughter.

'What's next then do you reckon?' enquired Jerrard to Rowan.

Rowan was aware that not only his friends but the whole company felt that because of the rank of his father he had some greater knowledge of what was going on, even more than Martin, usually the most thoughtful of the group.

'I don't know,' he genuinely replied with a shrug, 'but I guess we'd best sort ourselves out and be ready to march.'

His friends obviously agreed and they shuffled out through the gateway, following the rest of the troop who were all excitedly talking among themselves as they headed back down the slope beneath the walls.

Returning to the bailey they gathered and found themselves crowded into filing towards a number of large draught wagons on the small plateau. Rowan and Eric took the line on the right, while Jerrard, Daniel and Martin followed the one on the left, both lines roughly the same length. They could see men at the wagons laughing and chatting but couldn't get a clear view of what they were obviously collecting, and nor did the immediate men in front of them despite Eric's constant enquiries and craning of his neck. It was only until they got within twenty yards that they saw the slightly faded yellow and red halved surcoats being handed out with the badge showing the distinct three looped knot of Stafford on the right breast. When it was their turn they took them readily, Rowan lifting his up to the sky feeling a sense of pride at the simple uniform as he glanced at Eric and the rest of the group who all smiled excitedly back.

CHAPTER TWO

Forty minutes later, the troop were formed up and waiting for the order to march. Rowan looked down the line of men, nearly all wearing the livery of Stafford though a few wore the argent and sable colours of Sir Robert. At the head, the Earl sat on his big white destrier accompanied by his knight. Next to them was a similarly armoured Francis Courtney, a sombre looking esquire to the Earl who was similar in age to Rowan and his friends, and who was also appointed as protector of nearby Littywood Manor, according to Martin.

The banners of the Earl and his swallow-tailed standard with its cross of Saint George, Stafford knots and white swan, flapped lazily in the morning air. There were, to Rowan's reckoning, nearly one hundred and twenty fighting men, the vintenars and sergeants dotted along the side of the column next to their respective units. Behind the archers were forty or so similarly mounted men-at-arms, some with kite shaped shields slung on their backs and long swords at their sides. Their other equipment, the fearsome looking poll axes, halberds and heavy armour, would follow in the draught carts behind. Turning round he could see these heavy wagons, their teams of large oxen and the locked barrels containing extra bundles of arrows, arrow heads and other provisions that were piled high. Clearly visible on the leading wagon was the victualler, a massive man whose large frame was matched by his portly belly and who fiercely protected his supplies.

All in all, the column stretched about three hundred yards, the range of a longbow, the most impressive display of force ever seen by himself or his friends. In that moment Rowan felt no nervousness or trepidation at all, just a swelling in his heart as the order to march was given.

Martin had estimated it would take three days at most to reach the castle at Whittington, one of several built on the border Marches between England and Wales. It had stood for many years as a buttress against the disgruntled Welsh who continued to resist and threaten the King's rule, as they had done his predecessor King Richard, so recently usurped by Henry of Lancaster.

The Welsh, despite their defeats at the hand of the previous king, were showing increasing resentment and had united under the quartered lion banner and the personal golden dragon standard of Owain Glyn Dwr. It was this threat that had led to them and the rest of the retinue to be marching westwards.

The weather stayed mild for the remainder of the first day of the journey and the night was peaceful and pleasant for the men under the protection of their canvas tents. The five friends shared the rough material taken from one of the supply wagons, stretching it across simple frames made out of surrounding branches, making a cosy shelter that soon helped the friends to fall into a relaxed sleep.

The next day they leisurely broke fast before resuming their march. A relaxed atmosphere continued and pervaded through the column influenced by the lack of urgency from the knights who emerged from the large command tent well past sun up. The Earl was apparently in no rush which was probably a good thing Rowan had thought to himself, as he glanced back more than once during the day at the slow moving carts, their big heavy steel shod wheels lumbering along the dirt track. He and his friends spent most of the time leading their mounts and it was with some relish that they took their turn to leave the ponderous column and undertake scouting duties, listening with barely hidden enthusiasm as they were given their orders.

'Just remember, your job is to stay ahead of the column and warn about any potential ambush.' Rowan's father looked seriously at his son, then Eric and Jerrard who he had also called aside.

'You mean you don't want us to get to Whittington before you then?' Eric reflected the mood of the others; the force was large, the surroundings peaceful and the men felt at ease.

'Get off with you and don't let me down.' Rowan's father couldn't help but grin slightly before leaving the three friends to mount up and canter ahead of the column, Martin and Daniel watching along with the other members of the troop enviously.

It wasn't long after they had rather self consciously ridden past the nobles and left the force behind that Jerrard and Eric, buoyed by their separation from the column, entered into one of their usual bouts of banter, this time about the relative merits of ale versus wine.

'It doesn't half give you a sore head in the morning though,' argued Jerrard.

'Yeh but it will if you drink it like a bullock,' retorted Eric, 'at least you can only drink so much ale before you end up in the ditch!'

All three laughed out loud remembering the night before they had left the town when Eric had ended up falling in the ditch on his way home and sleeping in it for most of the night.

The laughter was complementary to the warm weather, the birdsongs and the sunlight that filtered through the canopy of trees that overhung the dirt path as they rode along.

Abruptly however, as Rowan turned back to his front, a flicker of movement halted his smile. His eyes registered something speed towards him wickedly from the trees ahead.

With a shriek of pain Constance reared up. Rowan, his arms previously resting across his lap and on his bow, grasped for the reins with his flailing hand, the other keeping hold of the bow. He missed the leather strap and he felt himself tumbling backwards.

The breath was punched out of him as he fell onto his side, his ribs taking the hard impact.

Anxiously he rolled away from his startled mount that bucked with pain and whose hooves stamped lethally on the ground threatening to smash into his body, before he scrambled from underneath on all fours to the trees on the right hand side of the track. Breathing heavily, he gratefully propped himself behind a largish oak tree, feeling the reassuring rough bark against his back and wondering what had happened for a moment.

He heard the whinnying of the other horses and the curses of their riders as they too strove to control their mounts. He could see his friends were struggling as their horses whirled round in confusion.

'Get off,' shouted Rowan, repeating himself loudly as Jerrard and Eric registered the shouts and unceremoniously slipped from their saddles just as more deadly arrows flew from the foliage.

The two friends scrambled into the protection of the trees on the opposite side of the track, their horses racing back the way they had come accompanied by his own palfrey, their hoof beats disappearing round a curve into the distance.

Rowan watched them go briefly before looking at his friends just ten yards away, slightly relieved to see that, like him, they had kept hold of their bows and were now standing with their backs pressed against wooden trunks and were busy placing an arrow each onto their strings. They both looked towards Rowan their faces flushed and showing both worry and fear.

He slid his back slowly up the tree so he too was standing, the bark snagging at his surcoat before pulling an arrow carefully from the bag on his belt, his fingers feeling the reassuring smoothness of the ash shaft as he notched it onto his bowstring.

Looking at his friends first he slowly edged himself to peer around the side of the trunk, his bow held low but ready.

It wasn't the best thing to do.

The still unseen attackers saw his movement and he caught sight of another blur before he heard and felt a solid thud, like a heavy axe blade biting deep into the trunk of the tree he was hiding behind. Hurriedly he pulled himself back, realising he wouldn't have been able to move quickly enough if the arrow had been on target.

Puffing out his cheeks and wincing at the thought that he could have been killed, he looked back at his friends and raised his eyes to the skies as a sign of relief. They grinned back nervously and, despite their predicament he felt a strange feeling of calm and resolve.

Motioning at his two friends he pointed for Eric to run back towards the column and warn them, though hopefully from the commotion and the riderless horses they would be aware something had happened.

His friend's face slowly registered the command with a mixture of emotions before nodding and patting his big friend on the back as he turned and ran through the thin undergrowth back towards the main column.

Watching him disappear among the trees he signalled to Jerrard that he was going to dash forward and that he should try to aim his bow towards any danger. Rowan had guessed the arrow's general place of origin, a large holly bush with its dense angled leaves providing ideal cover directly in front of him. Hopefully the fact that Jerrard was on the left hand side of the track may create a better shooting angle and the bowman or men would be exposed. His friend nodded, the grin now replaced by a look of concentration as he whipped his bow round seeking any movement in front. Rowan immediately launched himself forwards in a crouch until he breathlessly rammed his back against the reassuring bark of a trunk ten feet further on.

There was no speeding blur of another missile from the unknown attackers and he sensed rather than knew that his comrade hadn't released an arrow either.

Looking at Jerrard, he could see that he retained his focus on the bushes and trees ahead, using an enormous amount of strength to keep the string pulled back. He knew the supple wood of the stave would be creaking with resistance.

His friend despite his big build could only keep his bow tensed for so long before he let the hemp string relax and stood back behind the tree he was using as protection.

Rowan, his arrow still notched, now raised his bow, pulling the string back so his fingers brushed briefly against his ear. Then with a deep breath and learning from his original mistake whipped around the oak and searched for a target, his eyes quickly scanning the undergrowth and trees in front of him but always focussing back at the dense holly bush.

He saw nothing and though he knew he should retreat back behind the safety of the oak he dared himself to remain in his stance, matching his friend, remaining visible to attackers until his arm began to feel the strain, his chest muscles trembling until he too stepped back behind the protective oak tree.

'What do you reckon?' hissed Jerrard looking at Rowan, who now stood about ten yards in front on the opposite side of the track.

'Who knows?' he replied with a bit of a shrug trying to calm his heartbeat. 'Suppose we should just wait for Eric and the lads to come up,' though he wasn't convinced himself this was the right thing to do.

Then suddenly there was no time to think any longer.

He heard a guttural shout in a tongue he didn't know, responding growls from numerous men, the sharp snapping of twigs and branches, and the rustling of bushes being pushed aside that unmistakeably indicated the enemy were advancing on the two archers. Immediately glancing round the trunk he saw several attackers, weapons raised, rushing forwards from their hiding places among the trees less than fifty yards away, no distance for a bow. Instinctively he quickly drew the string back, briefly glancing down the length of the steel tipped arrow so its point aimed towards the chest of a cursing bearded attacker whose gleaming broad sword swept through the air above his head as he charged through the undergrowth. He let loose and reached for a second, realising almost immediately before his hand touched his belt that the rest of his arrows were still in his arrow bag.

The decision now was easy to make. He had no time to pull an arrow free so he turned and ran the way he had come, staying at the edges of the track where the foliage was least thick. At the same time he looked across at Jerrard. 'Run!' he screamed and was relieved to see his friend was already following suit needing no heeding, both men now in headlong retreat, crashing through the undergrowth and weaving between the trees, their hearts pounding.

Moments later, his breath now ragged and his legs beginning to slow his eyes registered with a sickening feeling a steadily advancing wall of men among the trees. With a fresh surge of fear he thought he had been outflanked before his feelings were replaced with relief as he recognised the familiar and reassuring colours of the Earl.

'Friend,' he shouted loudly repeating it twice in quick succession, concerned that he might find himself at the end of an over eager sword point or even a quickly released arrow. He halted in front of the men as they advanced warily until he was confident enough that his own gules and or surcoat had been recognised. It was only then that he put his hands on his knees, breathing heavily, and pushing the bascinet up from his forehead.

'What's going on then?' asked Samuel Blacke, the Master-at-Arms, pushing through the rank of archers and men at arms. He was no less intimidating when on campaign than on the drill square, that much was obvious to Rowan as he coughed first once, then twice before looking up at the hard uncompromising face, knowing as soon the words came out that he had a pretty pathetic answer.

'We were attacked by an enemy force,' he managed to utter before coughing once more.

'Who are they? How many?' came the inevitable questions in quick succession, his hands now on his hips and an underlying menace in his tone.

Standing up, Rowan was slightly taller than the sergeant at five foot ten inches but that didn't stop him faltering under the gaze of this hardened professional, aware that his answer would receive the scorn it deserved. 'I don't know. I think there were at least ten of them,' he answered too meekly for his own liking and feeling heat reach his face.

'Our Lord have mercy, you don't know! What sort of scout are you?' came the rhetorical rebuke. 'Oh forget it,' he said and putting a hand on Rowan's shoulder pushed him roughly towards the file of men. 'Go and make a report to the Earl, if you can call it that,' ordered the senior sergeant dismissively before turning back to the line of men who were now in various positions of rest, most leaning on their bows. The nearest, to Rowan's embarrassment, were listening in on the short conversation, 'Right, lets sort out these sons of whores,' roared the Master-at-Arms and the line once more began to march forwards through the woods towards where he and his friends had encountered the unknown enemy.

Rowan watched the uneven line tramp forwards through the undergrowth and for a moment felt at a bit at a loss despite his orders, knowing he had to relate what little information he had to the Earl, daunting enough at any time. He would much rather join the trampling line of men as they advanced through the sparse foliage beneath the trees, anything to avoid having to look foolish in front of the commander. Reluctantly acknowledging that he had no other option and with one more look towards the line of men that was by now partly hidden among the trees, Rowan headed back in the direction of the Earl. He could see the group of horseman, banners and surcoats visible twenty yards further on and broke into a jog towards them, bow in hand, and was relieved to see his friend already speaking directly to the noble, looking down at him listening silently on his large white destrier.

He slowed his approach hoping to be as unnoticed

as possible as he stepped forwards to stand behind Jerrard, a little to his left, trying to avert his eyes from staring at the Earl whose focus was on his friend. Rowan sensed the eyes of the knight and young esquire silently assessing him and he breathed in deeply in an attempt to steady his beating heart.

Rowan was hoping his friend could somehow provide more information than he could but that hope was dashed as Jerrard completed his report. 'There could have been more sire but we were taken by surprise,' he finished.

At this the Earl shifted his focus to Rowan and he felt himself shrink under the noble's stare that showed no emotion, or was there a hint of annoyance? 'Well, do you have anything to add?' The voice was surprisingly soft but nevertheless firm and impassive.

'No sire,' croaked Rowan, his mouth dry. He couldn't add anymore but felt he should do. Lamely he added, 'we were taken by surprise,' realising he was repeating his friend's words, his face once again felt hot and he looked at the ground.

'Let's see what we're up against.' The Earl turned to look at the chiselled strong features of Sir Robert, who in turn calmly assessed the hapless friends before pulling the reins so his warhorse turned its head with a snort and moved forwards. The esquire followed, an almost sympathetic look on his face which did little to make Rowan feel any better about his report.

Rowan immediately stepped to the side, as did Jerrard, and watched as the group trotted forward, horses tossing their heads as though similarly annoyed with the archers. The two friends looked at each other and ruefully shrugged, Rowan knowing that Jerrard must feel the same as him. They had not performed brilliantly in their role of scouts; they had met the enemy and were able to warn the column but had been feeble in finding out their strength or to whom they belonged. 'What else could they have done?' he thought to himself. If they had stayed surely they would have been hacked to death, but that thought didn't make him feel any better. What was clear in his head was that his first report to the Earl and his knights had not covered him in glory, in fact quite the reverse.

With a deep breath he cleared his mind and took Jerrard by the arm, 'I suppose we'd better find Eric and join the lads?'

'Yeh, why not?' agreed Jerrard as they turned and followed in the direction of the cantering horses.

'Well we made a right pile of bones of that,' his friend commented as they walked, trying to instil some levity back into both of their attitudes.

'Too right,' replied Rowan and immediately felt better for his friend's attempts to disperse the gloom. 'Come on, let's get back,' he said with refreshed enthusiasm and they broke into a jog through the woods towards their comrades.

It wasn't long until they caught up with the advancing men that had, by now, reached the point at which they had been attacked, yet there was no clamour or urgent sounds that signalled the enemy had been found. Both friends skirted behind the line and eventually recognised members of their company, nodding to their comrades in welcome and falling into step, twigs cracking under their feet as he pulled half a dozen arrows from his drawstring bag and tucked them individually into his belt, warily notching one on their bowstring like the rest of the archers.

As the line continued forward cautiously a commotion began off to his right and men craned their necks, peering across, their curiosity piqued, but their discipline maintained although the companies had now stopped.

'They've found one of the lads that attacked you,' the archer immediately to Rowan's right under a rather ill fitting bascinet explained as the reason was passed among the men.

For a moment he didn't know what to say and rather than relay the information as the men had done instead, he turned along with Jerrard towards where a small knot of men, including his father stood. As he approached his father turned. He was in mid conversation with the Master-at-Arms, his face devoid of any emotion as he came closer. Rowan could now see the attacker, the body prone upon the thick grass, his lifeless eyes staring out as conversation took place around him.

The man had a heavy dark moustache and beard with thick black tangled hair, his face starkly pale and strangely peaceful, somehow at odds with an obviously broken nose and several scars that spoke of a hard and brutal existence. He wore a thick red brigande jacket and a faded brown hose but with no badge of allegiance. A deep almost black stain had spread from the arrow shaft embedded in the middle of his chest.

'Christ's blood, well done, you must have kept both eyes open for once,' congratulated Jerrard, his enthusiasm plain as he slapped him on the back.

Rowan didn't really know what to say. This was the first man he had killed. In fact it was the first man he had shot at. He looked at the men standing around feeling their eyes on him and nervously smiled just as the Master-at-Arms barked the order to advance once more, the order relayed by the vintenars along the line, causing the men to pick up their bows.

An arm grasped his own and he turned to find his father looking at him intently, the trace of concern in his voice. 'Are you alright?'

'Yeh, I suppose so,' replied Rowan with a lack of conviction.

'Look, I know what it feels like to kill a man, and it's hard, even when he's trying to kill you,' his father said reassuringly. 'You'll get over it,' he continued, 'if you didn't kill him he would certainly have tried to do for you, and you did your job and warned the Earl.' Rowan didn't want to contradict him and go into how they had panicked and let their horses loose, forgetting their primary responsibility. 'Anyway best get back to the advance, I'll see you later,' and with that his father gave his arm a final reassuring squeeze before striding after the company that was tramping once again through the woods and leaving Rowan and Jerrard alone with the corpse.

'Well I suppose we'd better go with them,' suggested Jerrard who by now and slightly to Rowan's dismay was rifling through the dead man's clothes looking for anything of value. 'Typical. That lot must have already taken anything worthwhile,' he grumbled, indicating with a nod towards the outline of the soldiers. 'Well he won't be needing anything,' he reluctantly argued as he looked up at his friend and caught sight of Rowan's disapproving look.

The force advanced either side of the track for another ten minutes until they came to a large open field and the shouts of the vintenars relayed the order to halt. This allowed the men to once again rest either against trees or leaning on their bows until it was confirmed that they would make camp for the night. As the groups of men waited for the return of the horses and the supply carts that had followed behind as they had advanced on foot, they started collecting firewood. Rowan and Jerrard used the opportunity to search for their friends from whom they had become temporarily separated.

It took them a few minutes before they spotted Daniel and his distinctive tied-back short ponytail of black hair and the similarly built frame of Martin, who both greeted them with a brief hello and some good natured jeers which were picked up by the rest of the small company.

'Lost again boys?'

'Have you found your horses yet?'

The closeness of his friends provided comfort to Rowan, and he smiled as he and Jerrard wandered over and crouched down next to their friends, noticing one of their number missing.

'Where's Eric then?'

'Who knows,' replied Martin, 'we saw him running like his hose was on fire straight towards the Earl. By the saints' toes, he was lucky the knights never split him. In fact we thought he was just going to charge straight into his lordship. You know what he's like.' He chuckled. 'After that we were ordered to dismount and spread out. To be honest we don't know what happened to him then.'

'Knowing Eric he's probably asked to share a piece of chicken with the Earl and got himself thrown in gaol,' chipped in Daniel.

Accepting their friend's absence they settled down and began to relay recent events, Daniel and Martin wanting to know everything about the encounter, good naturedly echoing the same sentiments as the gruff Master-at-Arms earlier when their thinly embellished story that they had faced at least ten men had been seen through and they were forced to confess that they didn't know who, or how many, had attacked them.

It was a while later after the fire had been lit and the smouldering smoke from the dead branches had been replaced with crackling flames, that the horses were brought up and tethered a few yards away. Groans accompanied stretches as the men stood and went to brush down their mounts and take the saddles from their backs. Rowan was relieved to see Constance had not been seriously hurt by the arrow fired by the attackers and a farriers apprentice had applied a dark brown salve onto the wound. The heavy wagons followed soon after, rumbling along the track, their wooden planks creaking and harnesses jangling as the men continued to see to their mounts or, like Rowan and Jerrard, headed off to fetch tents and supplies. Their steps however faltered for a moment as they approached the high sided wagons and saw standing next to the heavily proportioned victualler on the driver's plank, the lanky figure of Eric grinning at them.

'What on this Godly land are you doing back here with the wagons?' asked Jerrard incredulously.

'You know me,' quipped Eric, 'why go chasing around when you can serve a better purpose by protecting the supplies?'

'More like the fact that you can be close to the food, and you don't have to walk,' grumbled back Jerrard.

'Well you can't have a go at a man for using his intelligence,' argued Eric, sharing a smile with the normally disgruntled victualler.

'Come on you two,' interrupted Rowan, enjoying the banter and sharing Eric's mischievous smile but nervous of the big driver's presence who he could see was preparing to harangue other approaching soldiers, his normal mask of disdain slipping readily across his face.

Having collected the canvas covers, cooking pots and small supply of vegetables the five soon set up their billet for the night and with the potage bubbling in a pot above the fire, the friends relaxed, enjoying the warmish night, thankful that it wasn't their turn to do guard duty and all lost in their own thoughts.

The summer was a warm one and the next morning they awoke to another welcoming dawn, though it was accompanied by a chill in the air making the men's breath visible. They packed their tents back on to the big wooden carts before mounting their horses and setting off once more along the worn track that took them more and more westwards into the green rolling hills of the Marches. There had been no incidents during the night but it seemed like the brief skirmish the previous day had stimulated the Earl into wanting to reach the castle at Whittington sooner than the pace of the previous day had indicated.

Despite their ordeal, Rowan was glad but surprised and nervous to hear from his father that their company was to leave the main column and accompany the Earl and Sir Robert to ride ahead directly to the castle, while the young esquire would follow with the rest of the men. There was relief among the company at the news that they would not have to trudge along with the rest of the column no matter how pleasant the countryside, though in truth Rowan was less relieved. Not so much about the threat of another skirmish, but of being in close proximity to the nobles who he felt he had let down.

The Earl sat astride his familiar white charger in its heavy trappings which pulled at its bridle impatiently as the twenty archers trotted past. He and Sir Robert had donned their full armour worn over chain mail vests that gleamed in the morning sun. Behind them, the heavy cloth banner of Stafford flew lazily. They looked very much as though they could ride straight into battle, thought Rowan, as he tried not to catch either of the nobles' eyes but almost inevitably a brief glance caught the forty year old knight's stare. He immediately looked down towards his saddle pommel but not before he could have sworn he saw a flicker of amusement pass across the veteran's face that did little to make Rowan feel better about his earlier report, and only served to prompt him to re-analyse once again the way he had reacted to his first engagement with an enemy. Urging his palfrey on with a sharp touch to its flanks he let out a deep breath as he passed by, still sensing that they were looking at him, the hairs on the back of his neck tingling as he kept his back as straight as possible.

Continuing down the track he couldn't help but keep thinking back to the skirmish that made him feel even more uncomfortable in front of the knights. He couldn't have helped the horse throwing him, and he had killed an enemy hadn't he? Having said that he was more than aware he had urged his friends to dismount rather than warn the column but, then again, they still wouldn't have known who the enemy were. His thoughts prompted him to turn round to Martin riding just behind Rowan. 'Do we have any idea who those swine were who attacked us?'

'No, but overhearing the vintenars this morning they reckon that they were probably brigands rather than Glyn Dwr's rebels.'

'Well, whoever they were I reckon they won't want to mess with us again,' Eric added confidently.

Rowan wished he felt like his friend who obviously, though he had shared the first experience of being attacked, was unconcerned and even bulled up by the brief skirmish.

They carried on enjoying the sunny morning although slightly tempered by the sweat caused by the thick jacks worn underneath their mail shirts. They stopped only occasionally to rest the horses, stretching their aching backs and making good progress as they rode on past midday.

It was as they were enjoying the green rolling hillsides and mountain slopes on either side that epitomised the area between central England and the Welsh border that their relative comfort was interrupted.

One of the scouts Rowan recognised as Beck, a plump twenty five year old with a round red face, came half jogging and half stumbling, dragging three palfreys behind him. His face was even redder than usual, showing the signs of too much exertion as he made directly for the nobles at the head of the column.

Sir Robert immediately raised his right arm in the air, followed by Rowan's father calling the small company to a halt. Pulling back the leather reins gently Rowan and the rest of the archers strained to listen as Beck reached the Earl who, together with Sir Robert, had rode to meet the returning scout. Out of earshot Rowan watched the bowman presumably give a report, pointing once towards the ridge four hundred yards in front, the noble's eyes following his arm before consulting for a moment and then turning their horses back towards the company and giving the order to dismount.

The command interrupted the men's mutterings and suppositions as they lifted themselves from their saddles, some easier than others. Rowan stretched his leg uncomfortably over the pommel before almost sliding down the horse's flank to the ground, somewhat gingerly bending his knees to relieve the ache. He knew he wasn't used to horses and wondered if he ever would be as he watched Eric share the same ungraceful ways of dismounting, holding onto his horse's neck before clumsily dropping to the floor.

The order to hobble the horses raised his anxiety further as he looped the thick piece of rope around each of the front legs of Constance before unhooking his arrow bag and then, fingers feeling like thumbs, threaded the spare bag through his belt, taking a deep breath as he did so.

The feeling of apprehension on Rowan's part was reinforced as the order to form up was given quietly.

The twenty men assembled in their familiar three rows, bows in hand, their protective covering having been removed and looking towards the two nobles and the standard bearer behind. They had also dismounted and looked at the gathered men before the Earl spoke in his calm, authoritative voice. There was no concern, just seriousness in his tone.

'Men, Whittington is just over the rise but our scouts,' he motioned towards Beck who now stood among the company, 'have seen a small group of men camped between us and the castle. We are going to advance and establish whether they're a threat, but for now were going to treat them like they are.' His eyes passed over the men before continuing. 'For many of you this will be your first encounter with a potential enemy. For some of you, you'll know what to expect.' Rowan could have sworn that the Earl glanced at him. 'Just remember your training and listen to the orders from your vintenar.' He then nodded to Rowan's father who ordered the men into single line abreast.

Rowan shared a grim smile with his friends to either

side as the order to fasten bowstrings was given before, with arrows not yet notched, they advanced warily across the rich green pasture towards the low lying ridge.

Nearing the crest, the Earl and his knight went down to a crouch and then on one knee. Rowan's father who was slightly behind the two knights turned and motioned for the line to halt and kneel, his arm horizontal and then descending downwards repeatedly.

As they waited, Rowan noticed that the two remaining scouts had not returned to the unit and must still be somewhere over the rise. His thoughts were confirmed when his father gathered the men round. 'Just over the rise is a track and then a copse of trees. The lads scouting are in the trees but there's a small chance we'll be seen cresting the ridge so we're going to have to make a run for it until we reach cover. Is that clear?' Rowan's father slowly looked across at each of the men's faces before, apparently satisfied, he ran back the few yards to the Earl and Sir Robert.

He saw his father give the nobles a nod before the two men raised themselves to a crouch and disappeared over the ridge. It certainly wasn't graceful or the kind of approach into battle Rowan had envisaged the Earl and his men taking. There were no unfurled banners, no cries about honour and death to the enemy, this was far more ignominious he thought, as his father gestured the men forwards to just below the ridge line.

'Ready?'

Rowan looked at his friends, his hands were clammy and he urgently wanted to wipe them on his surcoat.

'Keep low and go,' the urgent and whispered

command came.

Before he knew it he was following behind his comrades, running, trying to keep low as he crossed the ridge, his feet pounding across the uneven rutted track and dashing the remaining fifty yards down a steep slope before gratefully entering a line of thick and aged oak trees, panting and adrenaline-fuelled.

'God's wounds, I hope that was worth it,' Eric began to talk, betraying his nervous excitement.

He immediately raised his finger to his lips in a successful effort to hush his friend, his own breathing heavy as the next whispered order was communicated along the small line.

'Notch bodkins.'

Rowan reached into his bag nervously and drew out one of the steel tipped ash arrows, lethal at almost any distance and able to pierce through chainmail with ease. Notching it to his string, his fingers smoothing the goose feathered flight, the line of men advanced warily through the quiet copse of trees, the sunlight shining through the thin treetop cover. The low branches brushing and snagging at the men's shirts and mail, the light sound of leather soled footsteps was the only noise as the men advanced in silence, expecting a warning shout from an unseen sentry at any moment.

The dreaded alarm never came as the company halted after a short advance, still holding their partly drawn bows pointed towards the ground. Rowan could see the Earl now talking to the two scouts that had remained hidden among the trees, before turning to the line of archers and motioning them forward, right arm beckoning towards the edge of the tree line.

From the protective shade he and his friends could see a group of men and their mounts, a couple of coursers and some smaller palfreys tethered nearby, relaxed and seemingly enjoying the fine afternoon. The soldiers numbered just five and wore a variety of mail and jacks beneath gules and argent surcoats and despite their ease he noticed all had swords and long daggers in their belts. They were not being particularly watchful and it was only occasionally that they showed any interest in their surroundings. This was mostly focussed down the remainder of the slope towards the sturdy grey outline of high castle walls and towers a mile away. One, who Rowan guessed must be the senior by his armour and the full helm under his arm, was sitting talking to three men causing a ripple of laughter before glancing in the direction of a heavily built bowman who worryingly had picked up a bow and began making his way slowly towards the tree line off to their right.

As he watched, a scrape sounded nearby as the Earl slowly slid his sword from his scabbard ready to step out into the open and Rowan immediately felt the raised tension emanating among the group, his chest was tight and he felt slightly sick.

He braced himself to follow just as a loud shrieking shout pierced the air across the shallow hillside and a fair-haired boy ran full pelt from the trees like a startled deer down the slope angling straight towards the approaching bowman.

For a moment both groups of men were frozen all watching the youngster, but only for a moment and then the group below grabbed for their swords, looking worriedly towards the line of trees from where the boy had sprung while the bowman tugged an arrow from his belt, the lad now hiding behind him.

'Advance.' The Earl didn't wait to relay orders and loudly urged the men out of the cover of the trees.

'Come on lads, hurry, spread out and mark your targets.' The order was emphasised by Rowan's father pressing the men to move quickly.

There was no subtlety in their advance as they rushed out of cover. He could feel the sweat pricking his forehead as he raised his bow, drawing the string back towards his ear, instinctively aiming the needle-like point at the leader, avoiding the temptation to aim at the enemy bowman who was nearest but off to his right, covered by his comrades. The man in his sights was big, probably six foot tall with a thick beard complemented by curly hair that hung to his shoulders. His face was weather-beaten, showing a trace of disease, but Rowan could also see the resolve in his expression despite the rush of the twenty armed men from the woods.

'Put down your weapons,' came the steady voice of the Earl.

Both groups locked eyes, weapons held high. The tension in the air was palpable.

'Gladly, if you tell me who you are, my lord?' the man in armour replied, his thickly accented Welsh reflecting defiance, even contempt while his sword was unwavering in his hand.

'I do not think you are in a position to ask questions, but I will gladly tell you. I am Edmund, the seventh Earl of Stafford. Now, tell me who you are before one of my archers' arms tires and you find an arrow in your gullet.'

It wasn't too far from the truth, thought Rowan, as he felt the first aches start to emanate from his biceps.

'I am Bayard, sergeant to William de Movran who serves the Lord Fitz Warrin of Whittington,' the man replied, his belligerent attitude only lessening slightly.

'It seems we are on the same side, Sergeant Bayard, but I would ask you to lay down your arms for a moment.'

The Earl's request was met by a silent pause. The sergeant it seemed was still partly defiant and despite the odds seemed to be considering the order, his eyes narrowing.

It was the big bowman who was first to lay down his weapon on the ground, the movement causing a sneer from his commander, but the spell was broken and the rest of his men also slowly lowered their weapons, careful to avoid the sergeant's gaze who finally thrust his sword into the ground savagely.

No order was given for the archers to lower their bows as Rowan's father strode forward to collect the weapons, obviously not trusting the men despite their claims to be part of the garrison. Rowan would have taken the men at their word which made him briefly reflect on his own judgement. He still had a lot to learn, he mulled.

The men from the castle watched with emotions ranging from complete passiveness to barely disguised anger as their weapons were gathered and they were ordered to sit down in a tight group where they had stood. Rowan felt uncomfortable as he and Eric were tasked with keeping an eye on the sullen group, not that he felt that any of the men intended trying to escape. They were out in the open field and should the men flee down the hill towards the distant village and castle walls, they would be at the mercy of the archers' accuracy with the bow. The rest of the body of the Earl's men had made themselves comfortable between the tree line and the group of prisoners, apparently wary enough to keep a distance.

'Do you reckon they were telling the truth?' whispered Eric, gesturing with his head towards the captured group.

Rowan couldn't imagine they weren't from the castle. 'Yeh, they must be.'

'Well, let's hope they're not all as easy to surprise as these lot. I don't care much for their sentry skills,' responded Eric somewhat scathingly, apparently now confident of his own abilities. 'That lad will get a good hiding, no doubt,' he added.

Rowan glanced at the fair-haired young lad who sat cross-legged and had his head bent towards the ground seemingly trying to ignore the sergeant's harsh comments intently being hissed across the group at the bowman, obviously the boy's protector. He hadn't exactly done brilliantly himself he thought despite being about six years older than the boy who he guessed was thirteen. As he watched, the comments between the men become louder and suddenly the sergeant's hand flicked out and he cuffed the young lad aggressively around the head. Anger immediately flared through Rowan and he strode forward gripping his sword tightly, attracting the man's contemptuous gaze as the boy was wiped away tears from his eyes.

'Leave him alone,' Rowan said, trying to ignore the slight tremor in his own voice.

The response was a quick tirade of words that he couldn't understand, probably Welsh, as the man made to get up from his sitting position. Rowan instinctively pushed the man down so he sprawled on his back and then put the sword to his chest, effectively pinning the man to the ground.

'Leave him alone,' repeated Rowan as the man stared up at him, his expression of disdain replaced by a look of hatred.

'What in God's name is going on?' The shout from his father was harsh and clear as he marched towards him, a stern look on his face.

'I'm sorry sir. He was hitting the boy.'

'Well that's not your concern. Now move away, the Earl wants to see him.'

Rowan watched the sergeant followed by his father, walk up the slope. He was appalled at being admonished in front of the prisoners and his comrades and was still feeling sorry for himself by the time the horses were once again fetched up.

The afternoon by now was beginning to turn to early evening, the few wisps of cloud not enough to prevent a slight chill in the air and the Earl decided to seek the protection of the castle before night time fell, no doubt preferring the comfort of a warm bed that he would be surely offered. Not that Rowan could disagree, he too would welcome a night under a thatched roof rather than another night spent under canvas, no matter how pleasant an English summer.

The men formed two rough lines, riding their horses slowly towards the walls. The animosity and wariness of the men from Whittington began to dissipate as they travelled with their swords and bows which had been returned to them. In fact, Rowan observed, his father and the big archer were in keen conversation, although their apparent easiness was not totally shared as he felt the glare from the sergeant on the back of his neck. The man's mood was probably not made any better by Jerrard raising the young lad onto the back of his brown palfrey and letting him ride with him as they made their way down into the shallow valley towards Whittington.

CHAPTER THREE

William de Movran couldn't help the frown that crossed his forehead as he watched the column of men ride slowly down the slope. They rode along the beaten track that led through the surrounding marshlands, where the pools of water were still visible between clumps of grass despite the dry summer months, and on towards the castle. He glanced sideways at the Lord by his side who sensed the look and turned his slim frame, raising his eyes in silent acknowledgement of shared unhappiness.

Although commanding the Marcher castle he knew the Lord didn't welcome the unexpected visitors either, knowing each expedition had met with the same result. As well as there being extra mouths to feed, fruitless promises of payment, there would be months of misery with the enemy fading back into the hills as they tried unsuccessfully to bring them to battle, and each time after the King's men had retreated the rebels quickly returned.

It wasn't only that though that brought a sour taste to his mouth. It was not three years since Henry Bolingbroke had usurped King Richard. It still gnawed at him like a festering wound how he had been forced to distance himself from the former King and seek employ elsewhere and which had led him to where he now stood watching from the walls beside the Lord Fitz Warrin, who at least shared his caution towards the new holder of the throne.

The young noble had welcomed the offer of service from a soldier of his experience despite not having a retinue, happily giving him control of the patrols into the countryside outwardly dissuading Welsh ambitions. This did not mean they were unaware of the rebel movements or communicate with them in the borderland region. It was an uneasy arrangement and the arrival of the force threatened to upset their situation, he thought with bitterness, returning his stare back towards the approaching company.

From the stone battlements he could make out the colours of the unfurled banner though it was not known to him, nor was the surcoat of the knight who travelled behind the leader.

The small troop passed the village to their right, the doors firmly closed and windows shuttered, fearing the worst from the sudden appearance of soldiers. They rode on, following the track as it turned to run parallel to the moat and the main high castle walls.

Both men looked down from the northwest tower able to get a closer look at the approaching company and it intrigued the captain that they only numbered twenty and that there were no men at arms. Once more he scanned the slopes looking for the remainder of the force that would add to the two men's less than enthusiastic feelings.

'Is this all do you suppose?' The Lord asked, as if reading William de Movran's thoughts. He did not take his youthful eyes from the small column that was now approaching the barbican. Its thick oak drawbridge, framed by two large drum towers had been retracted and now stood resolutely closed.

He let the question go unanswered for a moment. 'If it is, my lord, then I'm sure we can accommodate them.'

The noble looked at him silently for a moment, no doubt wondering at the sincerity behind the words, his reluctance the same as his own. The young eyes searching his lined face, before turning to one of the men at arms standing on one of the gatehouse tower walls fifty yards away across the small moat that separated the main castle from the outer defences of the barbican.

'Lower the bridge.'

The call was passed down to the men in the courtyard below and with the snap of the brake and the rattle of steel links the heavy metal studded timber bridge slowly angled downwards to the waiting column of soldiers.

'We'd better go and greet our guests,' the downward curve of his mouth and resigned expression evident as the Lord turned and made his way to the stone steps that led to the inner courtyard below.

William de Movran stayed a moment, looking down at the unexpected company of soldiers who cantered across the bridge and into the shadows of the thick gateway walls leading to the outer courtyard, lost in his thoughts.

By the time he had descended the worn staircase he found the Lord had already made his way through the gateway of the inner bailey and out across the heavy drawbridge into the outer courtyard, his youthful energetic steps outpacing his own and he could see that his commander was in conversation with the two now dismounted knights.

He had little time for polite conversation and chose not to follow completely, deciding instead to wait on the lowered bridge connecting the two bastions, sensing the annoyance in his own facial expression and making a conscious effort to mask it. The rebellion in Wales had been building but there was no need for interference from the King, indeed he had been confident, after hearing how the royal coffers were constantly stretched by the ever continuing threat from Scotland and the French, that the likelihood of expeditions against the rebellion was unlikely.

Still scowling as Lord Fitz Warrin led the two knights towards him, he could see closer up that the leader was young and had the bearing of a noble, just like his Lord, while the other knight was well built and exuded the confidence of a veteran.

'Earl, this is William de Movran, commander of my garrison.' He bowed in deference, noting the calm confidence of the Earls stance, 'and this is Sir Robert.'

As he was introduced he stared into the knight's eyes. He had been right because this man showed the signs of someone who knew the battlefield. Both men nodded to each other.

'Shall we go to the main hall, I'm sure we have much to discuss.'

The nobles, oblivious to the two soldiers assessing each other led the way, passing under the archway of the inner gatehouse and across the hard pressed earth of the courtyard to the stone hall built against the eastern ramparts. Lord Fitz Warrin glanced at his man as he led the Earl towards the double wooden doors. He shrugged to himself. Whatever the implications, it would be interesting to hear what these men had to say.

The doors were opened as members of the household rushed about to accommodate the extra visitors. He was met by the heat exuded by a fire in the large stone hearth, the interior smoky despite the vent in the roof. The four men settled down on a slightly raised dias, where he caught the waft of warm bread and cooked chicken from the nearby kitchens. It was now late afternoon and his stomach stirred. The thought that the kitchen hands would be hurriedly trying to cook more food caused a flicker of irritation once more at the small company's arrival.

'So, Earl, you say the remainder of your company from Stafford should be arriving tomorrow?' His Lord's comments were not what William de Movran wanted to hear, more mouths to feed, and for what purpose?

'Yes, we thought it best to head here straight away following a brief encounter with, what we think were rebels. We can see now that there was no need to hurry.'

The soft conversation between the two leaders was interrupted by Sir Robert. 'Is that true sire? It would be a shame for us to march this way if there is no threat.'

The comment from the veteran knight immediately piqued Lord Fitz Warrins interest and he sensed an underlying reason behind the question, even a challenge. Either way he knew his Lord well enough to keep his mouth shut and let him answer the question.

'I need not repeat my comments to the good Earl

here but in the spirit of friendship I will, Sir Robert. We have no news of rebels and certainly do not feel under threat. There have been some rumours but we have sent out our mounted troops and have found nothing. Isn't that so?'

William de Movran paused while a young and attractive household maid poured some watered ale into the pewter cups, looking first into the keen face of the Earl and then the experienced eyes of the knight while he waited for her to depart. 'It is exactly so and though of course we have heard of Owain Glyn Dwr becoming braver, he has not troubled us.'

The Earl's face looked disappointed while his knight gave a simple nod of the head, apparently satisfied by the response.

'So what are your numbers?' The Earl enquired in a tone that lowered the intensity of the conversation.

'I have thirty men in my retinue in all, mostly archers while I have a dozen men-at-arms.'

'It's enough, especially as we have the castle here and we're able to constantly send out patrols,' William de Movran added, his arms gesturing towards the walls around them in response to the looks from the visitors.

'Certainly,' the Earl agreed.

'There's been no threat from the rebellion and the men have heard little.' He added sensing the angst he was in danger of causing with the Lord by his defensive tone.

'I'm reassured and hope you don't mind our imposition upon your hospitality' Once more the Earl offered a conciliatory comment.

It seemed that the conversation was turning into

pleasantries, much of it in William de Movran's mind superfluous and the entrance of the Earls archers, having stabled their horses, was a welcome distraction despite the irritation he felt by their presence. The sounds within the stone walls became increasing louder. Food and ale was brought out and the crackling fire cast flickering shadows as the night wore on.

He looked down at the company of archers, seated below, as they enjoyed the food and flirted with the young women who served them. Many of them were young and he guessed had little or no experience of battle. If they did indeed meet the rebels he wondered how they would fair, certainly from his limited dealings so far with Earl Edmund and Sir Robert they were confident in their ability. Time would probably tell he mused before being brought back into the conversation between the nobles.

***

As he and his friends rode through the shadowed gateway Rowan noticed that the impressive flanking towers showed signs of disrepair with the thick stone crumbling in places and vacant holes for mortar missing as they rode under the points of the raised portcullis. The iron shod hooves of the horses echoed beneath the arch and they dismounted once inside the tight confines of the barbican framed by two more towers opposite those of the gatehouse.

The column almost filled the courtyard and with the enclosing stone walls he felt hemmed in. The space was less than one hundred yards long and seventy yards wide, the high grey walls casting a shadow over the group of men. To his right there was a large whitewashed guardhouse with what Rowan presumed was a storehouse attached to it and directly ahead he could see an archway, smaller than the main castle entrance and leading out of the outer courtyard. To his left there was another archway leading to the main castle where the Earl had just greeted another youthful noble, who despite his smaller stature had the same inescapable bearing, probably the Lord of the castle he thought to himself as he looked down at his own dusty and worn surcoat.

He watched the two nobles share a brief conversation before the Earl and Sir Robert made their way across a sturdy drawbridge, met on their way by another well built and bearded knight.

As he gazed at the retiring nobility the order to dismiss was given and, following the rest of the men, he led his palfrey through the gateway in the southern wall to an open bailey, larger than the outer battlements from where they had come but not walled, instead surrounded by a large ditch of water forming an island. Rowan stood for a moment, holding the reins of Constance who waited obediently, patiently sniffing at the ground while her rider took in the land behind the barbican walls. He felt a tug at his sleeve as the lad, now lifted down from Jerrard's horse, sensing Rowan's interest in the grounds eagerly and with confidence described his local surroundings.

'This is the east outer bailey, the main island where the horses are kept' he said in a youthful but distinct Welsh accent. The last bit of information was not needed since dominating the buildings to his right were a large smithy and an impressively large two storey stable. The blacksmith, apparently oblivious to the new arrivals, continued to hammer a glowing strip of metal on the sides of his forge, the clanging sounding out in regular intervals across the open area. He saw that the bailey also accommodated some small wooden livestock folds that housed some noisy grunting pigs and clucking chickens that wandered happily around.

'That's the garden, the outer west bailey,' Rowan turned his head as the young boy pointed across a small wooden bridge to the left of the stalls and stables that apparently connected the main island to a second. He couldn't see much of the garden because it was surrounded by its own walls but what he saw looked large and well maintained with trees to its rear, 'and that's the mount.'

He had never seen the like and was impressed by the pavilion-like structure with its very own small moat almost parallel to the wooden bridge, which stood to his left, below the southern walls of the main castle. It was connected to the northern edge of the garden by another walkway and from here someone could enjoy the views of the garden, the outer baileys and the surrounding valley.

He was truly engaged with the layout and though from the little he had seen of the castle and the grounds, they were very different to that of Stafford, much smaller and in need of repair, he remained impressed. His reverie was broken as the boy, taking his local surroundings for granted took hold of the leather reins of his horse and led it to the large stable block where three other scruffily dressed lads of similar age began to brush down the companies' mounts, obviously hoping for a reward.

The men ambled back through the gateway, relaxed and somewhat excited, making their way inside the outer courtyard before going through the same entrance the Earl and Sir Robert had gone.

Rowan and the men's footsteps sounded loudly on the timber planks as they walked across the lowered crossing above the small defensive ditch, water flowing slowly below. They entered the polygonal courtyard where he saw a variety of buildings crammed against the enclosed circuit stone wall, smoke coming from kitchens as food was prepared and the fires lit in the hall despite the warm night air. A few men and women crossed the courtyard busily, some dragging heavy buckets from the stone well, water splashing over the sides, while sentries in the same gules and argent livery as the banner flying atop the battlements watched them curiously.

They followed the rest of the company through the heavy wooden doors that stood open and entered the large stone hall where a fire was alight in the big hearth at the far wall. Trestle tables and benches had been set up and to his left he saw the nobles in deep conversation. The benches scraped loudly on the stone floor despite the covering of fresh straw as Rowan and his four friends took their seats at one of the tables, their appetites raised by the sight of platters of bread, apples, cheese and meat waiting for them. Ripping the crust of a piece of bread and thrusting a piece into his mouth he looked up as he and his friends were served ale from earthenware jugs. He smiled sheepishly as a tallish girl with long black hair and pale skin reached over and filled the wooden cups on the table.

'Hello there, what's your name?' Daniel's smile was broad, his eyes focussed intently.

'Rosalind,' she blushed, wiping the table hurriedly and avoiding the friends' eyes who were now all staring at her.

'Doesn't that mean 'pretty rose?'

Rowan grinned. It was a trait he and the others knew well, while Martin was recognised among the friends as most knowledgeable, it was Daniel who seemed to know key things about the opposite sex.

The night wore on with the small company enjoying the heat of the fire, the food and drink, and the opportunity, particularly for Daniel to flirt with Rosalind who it appeared to Rowan seemed to increasingly enjoy his advances.

He saw Rosalind exchange giggles with an attractive slim blonde girl whose distinctive laugh seemed to fill the room as she shared her friend's glances towards the group of archers. Rowan smiled, hoping that she would catch his eye but was disappointed as seemingly ignorant to his looks she turned to continue gossiping with her friend.

Not for the first time he wished he had the same confidence as Daniel before, with an inward sigh, he decided to leave the smoky interior to seek some fresh air and wander the castle walls. This came as no surprise to his friends. His keenness to explore and look at buildings or countryside often opened him up to their teasing which was exactly what he got when he scraped back the bench and exited the warmth of the hall.

Once outside, taking a deep breath and trying to clear his head from the haze brought on from the atmosphere inside, he looked up at the high walls around him where light flickered through the lancets and above the battlements.

Keenly he made his way to the nearest tower and began to climb the dark circular staircase illuminated by torches that produced an uncoordinated dance of shadows on the walls. Rowan used his right hand to help steady his ascent against the tight curving walls, his breathing becoming heavier and echoing in the stone confines as he climbed upwards, making his way up past the inner wall walk and onto the battlements. There he was able to look over the marshlands and enjoy the clean and crisp air, though it was getting dark now and he could only dimly see the tree line on the horizon from where he and his friends had appeared earlier in the day.

The approaching outline of two men broke into his reverie and, as they neared, he recognised his father and the big archer whom they had surprised and captured earlier that morning.

'Had enough of Eric?' his father jokingly asked his son.

He returned the grin. Eric was often a source of innocent amusement for him and his childhood friend had, on more than one occasion caused his father to either double up laughing or throw up his arms in disbelief at the antics of the two friends.

'Rowan this is Leovald. Leovald this is my son, Rowan.'

'Good to meet you.' The Welshman had a weather-beaten but kind face and had the now familiar strong Welsh accent prevalent among the garrison. 'I noticed what you did for my son, Willard. I thank you for it, Bayard shouldn't have hit him but it wouldn't have been good for me to retaliate.'

'Thank you,' replied Rowan embarrassed, glancing at his father.

'You have though, made an enemy of Bayard, he holds a grudge, so be wary of him,' Leovald continued in a conspiring tone and holding out his right hand in thanks before nodding to Rowan's father and continuing on along the parapet.

'Well done lad,' his father also proffered his own hand.

It wasn't often he shook his father's hand. In fact the only time he could remember doing so was when he had won a village archery tournament, his one and only time. 'He's right, keep an eye on that Bayard,' he said seriously.

'I will,' he replied taking note of his father's tone.

'Anyway how are you feeling?' enquired his father trying to bring levity to the question.

They were always conscious of not crossing professional boundaries in front of the other men and it was the first time he had really been able to speak to his son individually since they had set off from Stafford.

'Okay,' replied Rowan simply.

'What about the man you killed?' His father persisted.

Rowan had at first thought about the dead man a lot following the discovery of the body, his mind slipping in short periods into a sort of melancholy as he asked himself who the man was, whether he had a wife, and where he might live. However he now realised that he had not thought about the pale bearded face staring into the sky since the encounter with Leovald's group. 'To be honest I haven't really thought about it.'

'That's good.' His father was probably relieved and keen not to push the issue further. 'There's likely going to be some more killing,' he continued. 'Once the rest of the column catches up we'll be looking to sort out the rebels,' he warned his son.

'Why? Can you tell me what's happening?'

The professionalism between father and son was not just shared in terms of their reaction to each other in front of the rest of the company but also in the sharing of information.

'Well, I'm sure that people will talk soon enough but it's safe to say that there are rumours that some of Glyn Dwr's forces are massing and that's why we're here. Mind you, from what I've gathered from Leovald, Lord Fitz Warrin will assure our Earl that it's just some minor renegades causing mischief rather than any serious threat.'

There was something that his father wasn't saying but he knew more than to try and press him and there was a pause as both fell into their own silent thoughts.

'You seem to be getting on well with Leovald?' Rowan broke the silence seeking to talk about something less serious that would not compromise his father's position.'

'Yes, he was part of the expedition last year with the Prince, as you know I was.'

His father rarely spoke of his battles and when he did it was a brief reference, but it was well known that the expedition last year had been one of misery and failure as the Welsh had avoided confrontation and retreated into the steep hills and valleys that so epitomised the country. 'He's part of the household guard here and seems a good man. In fact I think he will be good source of information for us. He doesn't normally take part in scouting duties but he's agreed to be a guide and join us which will help us immensely. I'll need to speak to the Master-at-Arms first so don't you go telling Eric and the rest of them.'

Rowan simply nodded, his father knew he wouldn't share his words even among his friends.

'Anyway, time to call it a day I think.' He grasped Rowan's shoulder, and with a curt nod made his way along the ramparts.

The night was really drawing in now and with a last glance out across the marshlands he decided he would turn in too, but as he took one last look over the battlements he could have sworn he saw a brief flicker of light. His curiosity piqued he stared for a bit longer, but saw no more illumination and then foolishly realised that the marshlands had lots of pools of water that would cause the moonlight to be reflected. He admonished himself for his wariness and realised he was maturing quickly, that the past few days had contained more excitement and emotion than he had experienced in his previous nineteen years. It sent a shiver of nervous excitement through his body and with that feeling he made his way back through the dark corridors, across the inner ditch and towards the temporary sleeping quarters.

The twenty men spent a comfortable night among the piles of straw on the first floor of the large stables. They woke the next morning accompanied, in many cases with involuntary groans as their bodies adjusted to the previous night's drinking and the cool morning air, complemented by the heavy sweet smell of the hay around them. There was no fire for obvious reasons and though it was summer there was still a morning chill.

Rowan pulled his blanket tighter up to his neck as he sat up, pinning the bottom of the material between his feet and the straw floor. He looked around at his friends, all in varying stages of wakefulness having come back the previous night to find all of his friends already asleep, encouraged by the alcohol and their full bellies.

'Morning.' Martin greeted him from his prone position on the floor. He too had his blanket covering his body like a second skin.

Martin probably drank the least out of the group of friends, but not by much and it was more down to his comparably poor ability to keep his drink down rather than any conscious desire on his part to maintain some sobriety. Jerrard, who was now rubbing his eyes with gusto often argued that was why Martin had the most intelligence out of the group.

'Good morning, he says,' croaked Jerrard, who then cleared his throat, turning his head to spit the contents against the angle of wooden floor and wall.

'You dirty sow,' muttered Eric, though he was used to the brash mannerisms of their friend.

'Can you lot shut up?' piped in the last of their friends to wake up. Daniel turned his body round reluctantly towards the group.

That was the only invite Eric needed. 'Don't take it out on us boys if you had to keep your breeches on last night,' he grinned mischievously. 'Now, if you had used one of my lines then she would have been more than happy to pay special attention to you.'

'More like she would have gone running to the lord of this castle and begged them to hang you from the highest tower as an example not to discredit the art of wooing!'

The group laughed good-naturedly.

'What happened then?' asked Rowan. 'Are you losing your touch?'

'No, Rosalind's not like that. Sure, we had a giggle but I wouldn't mind getting to know her better if we stay here for a while.'

Rowan could sense the seriousness in his friend's voice, maybe this expedition wasn't just about proving yourself on the battleground after all, he thought.

Their conversation was interrupted by his father, who had climbed the ladder up to the hayloft, his top half showing as he shouted to the men around the room. 'Come on archers, time to show the garrison what real soldiers can do. You've got three minutes to get fully dressed and fall in outside,' he said, before disappearing down the ladder as quickly as he had emerged.

The loft was soon a scene of chaos, men anxiously throwing their blankets off, tugging on boots, buckling belts, reaching for arrow bags. If anyone observed this pandemonium Rowan grinned to himself they would have fallen about laughing. His thoughts were further made real as he saw Eric, standing on one leg with half a boot on, hop backwards trying to stay upright before falling onto Jerrard, who responded by pushing him towards a small stack of bales where he finally lost his balance and tumbled onto the floor.

Once ready, the men assembled in front of the stables facing the rear wall of the barbican on top of which a couple of sentries lazily patrolled the ramparts. Rowan's father was standing in front of the company along with the standard bearer.

He found his place in the line next to Eric, tugging his belt as he did so, adjusting it so the heavy blade felt more comfortable against his leg. Like the rest of the men, he had put on his metal bascinet and the issued surcoats over his mail. The longbows were slung across their backs in their cloth cases, their bucklers attached to their belts and the men's hands rested on the pommel of their swords. As they settled down, Rowan's father ordered the men to attention.

All eyes faced forwards, glancing towards the stone archway that led from the outer courtyard. As Rowan waited he sensed someone staring down from one of the turrets and noticed Bayard. He could have sworn the sergeant was staring straight at him and he felt slightly unnerved, remembering the words of Leovald the night before. He instinctively averted his gaze and was grateful when the Earl emerged, Sir Robert as always beside his side together with the two nobles he had seen the day before.

'So these are your men dear earl? A strong looking bunch and eager no doubt to tackle some rebels,' the noble chuckled. In a little louder but softer tone he addressed the men directly. 'Welcome to you all. I look forward to providing you with comfort while you stay in my lands, though as I have told the Earl here you may be disappointed if you are seeking to make your fortune by capturing or plundering some rebels.'

Rowan could feel an inward groan from many of the men. Not so much from the potential lack of battle but the lure of plunder either from an enemy corpse or, much more valuable, a share in the ransom of a nobleman. It was a regular topic of conversation among the men that one good prisoner could change a whole family's fortunes for the rest of their lives.

'However, the good Earl has insisted that you men can help ensure that there really are no rebels up to any good.' He smiled at the Earl, who in turn returned the expression, inclining his head in acknowledgement before addressing his men.

'As the Lord Fitz Warrin says we will carry out the King's orders and ensure that we deal with any inkling of rebellion in these, the King's lands'.

He sensed some form of underlying verbal duel in the exchange of words but the reference to King Henry gave Rowan a surge of pride within. He straightened his back a little more.

'Sergeant,' he gestured to Rowans father, 'see that the men clean their weapons, look to their horses and keep them occupied.' With that he turned and headed back through the gateway, together with the lord of the castle.

The address over, Rowan dared himself to look back up to the tower and was somewhat relieved to see that Bayard was no longer there. He had thought he had been staring at him throughout.

After being dismissed, the company were given orders and he and his friends were directed to check their horses that now shared their stables with the bigger coursers of the garrison.

The group approached and Rowan immediately recognised the fair-haired lad, brushing down a light brown mare with an obvious lack of energy.

'You don't seem to be putting much effort into that,' he called, causing the boy to look round and give a sheepish grin that he returned. 'Where are our horses?'

The boy lowered the metal horse comb he was using, the loose rings jangling lightly as he pointed off to the left. 'They're over there sir,' before energetically falling into step with Rowan. 'I've made sure they're all fed and watered and I've brushed yours down this morning.'

'Good lad, you've done well,' he said approvingly patting the flank of Constance who shook her head contentedly, before reaching into his money bag and pulling out a sixpence.

'I understand your name is Willard from your father. Mine is Rowan,' he said, flicking the coin into the eager grubby hands that snatched expertly at the silver piece.

He found that Willard and the other youngsters had been tasked with looking after the mounts of the company. From what he saw, he was more than happy that the horses would receive good treatment in between the sorties that they would undoubtedly make following the Earl's comments.

The remainder of the day passed uneventfully but excitingly for Rowan, who was able to wander the grounds and get to know the layout of the castle buildings and lands surrounded by the steep sided moat.

He began his exploration by crossing the courtyard and climbing the stone stairs within the north east tower that overlooked the village and outer drawbridge. Shivers of expectation flowed through him as he looked through the deep arrow slits in the inner wall walks of the parapet or poked his head between the merlons on the curtain walls sensing a feeling of almost invincibility behind the rough stone. He could imagine a force assaulting the walls and in his mind drawing a bow letting an arrow speed downwards to the enemy below.

The towers above the connecting drawbridge overlooked the walls of the outer barbican and gave views towards the village and castle grounds. As Rowan turned round and looked back across the courtyard he could see the other main castle towers facing out across the wetlands of the valley and the tree lined horizon.

He was told more than once to 'haul his backside elsewhere' as he continued to explore the castle, wandering into the large hall where he and his friends had eaten on the first night, and into the kitchens with the smell of freshly baked bread. He explored the coolness of the chapel, the ordered chaos of the garrison quarters and the darkness of the under croft storerooms before making his way across the wooden drawbridge to the barbican and then to the outer baileys.

Trying to ignore the enquiring glances from some of the local garrison and villagers going about their business, he continued his wanderings.

Passing the happy cackle of chickens and rooting pigs, he stepped across the wooden bridge that provided access to the walled garden and found to his right a dense and colourful patch of trees. The large fruit orchard was hidden behind the blacksmiths, stables and stalls of the outer eastern bailey. Ripening red and green apples were temptingly visible against the duller green and brown of the trees, weighing down the branches from which they hung. He couldn't resist snapping of one of the plump fruits, taking a large bite and wiping the sour taste from his lips.

After a hundred yards or so along the worn track between the garden and the orchard he came across a second narrow bridge that seemed to lead to another mass of trees. As he carried on he found the copse gave way to a large cleared rectangle area of grass, forty foot wide which had, at one end, large round circlets of hay on wooden frames. He had come to the southernmost edge of the castle grounds protected by a wide moat of water and with a perfect view of the surrounding Whittington marshes. This third island, Rowan realised, provided a perfect practice range and the discovery excited not just himself but the rest of the men and it wasn't long before there was steady stream of archers from the company making their way to the platform.

That day and the next was enjoyable for Rowan and

the rest of the company as they developed friendships and an air of familiarity emerged between the company and the local population. Even the arrival of the Earl's main force seemed to cause little friction among the population of the small village. Soon the men were helping with the sentry duties on the outer gatehouse walls and carrying out their regular drills and bow practice, much as they would have done at Stafford castle.

During this time his father's friendship with Leovald grew and the two men would often be seen wandering across the courtyard, deep in conversation. This friendship was mirrored between the two respective sons and Rowan had longer conversations with Willard each morning and even started, along with his friends, including him in the regular practice sessions at the butts. Willard was definitely no natural, the arrows often shooting well wide of their mark from the shorter bow. He knew that only practice would ensure that Willard would gain the standard of the retinue bowmen and they continued to encourage the boy's ready enthusiasm.

The friendships did not stop there. Daniel had not lost any of his affection for Rosalind who, with her blonde haired friend who Rowan had learned was called Catin, was now sitting down watching the men practice. His friend was certainly enjoying himself from the sound of laughter coming from the small group and Rowan found himself wondering if they could be talking about him and self consciously held himself more upright focussing upon the butts at the end of the platform.

More than once Eric had pulled his leg sensing Rowan's attraction to Catin and he had sought unsuccessfully to bluster out his defiance at the suggestion, blushing as inwardly he hoped for an excuse to get to know the slim, blue eyed girl who seemed to infect happiness wherever she was. In fact, the only grating thing that made Rowan feel at all uncomfortable was the sergeant, Bayard, who obviously continued to retain a dislike of Rowan that manifested itself in contemptuous looks rather than open confrontation partly shared by some of the Welsh garrison. Perhaps not surprising, Rowan thought to himself, when you considered the Lord's men were now outnumbered by the Earl's force three to one.

Rowan and the company had not seen much of the Lord of the castle since their arrival, just occasional glimpses of him taking a walk along the battlements, accompanied by the stern looking garrison commander.

'They say he killed three on his own.' Willard had commented one day. 'They say that if it were not for him and his mounted sorties the rebels would have swept down and would have taken the castle months ago.'

'Not to be messed with then eh?' Rowan responded. That was not what he had wanted to hear especially as Bayard was one of his men.

It was on the fourth morning since the company had first arrived at the castle that the Earl ordered initial scouting missions be carried out by his men, though only with a view to returning by nightfall. These, though welcome by Rowan and his friends, proved uneventful - much as the Lord Fitz Warrin had predicted. The men rode across the vibrant green landscape that surrounded Whittington in all directions, trotting across clear fresh streams that flowed down from the hillsides and skirting the many large coppices that were a constant feature of the countryside.

The castle and small collection of buildings that formed the village rapidly became like home to Rowan and his friends, returning to the sight of wisps of smoke escaping through the vents in the thatched roofs, sheep grazing peacefully among the marshes, the smell of warm food from the communal oven and the waiting jugs of ale, and of course the chance for him to catch a glimpse of Catin.

Rosalind and Catin he had learned were childhood friends and it was clear that the two girls with their infectious laughs and mischievous remarks were well liked among the garrison and among the men of the newly arrived Earls force. Rowan often saw the girls in happy conversation and drawing admiring glances. However despite Daniels blossoming relationship with Rosalind, he had still only managed a few short and cumbersome words with her blonde haired friend despite her easy mannerism. Every time he looked into her sparkling eyes, a smile always threatening at the corners of her mouth, he could feel his cheeks blushing and would quickly make an excuse before retreating.

It was therefore with a touch of regret that he and the rest of his friends heard of rumours of Welsh forces gathering in the countryside, further than their patrols usually rode.

'Do you reckon the rumours that the Welsh are

massing are true?' His friend asked, taking a long gulp of ale and wiping his mouth with the back of his hand, the red felt cap sitting rakishly on his head.

Rowan was sharing a mug of watered ale with Eric at the only inn in the village following another ordinary but nevertheless enjoyable scouting trip. They were sat outside on a bench looking towards the castle walls, enjoying the early evening sun.

'It's hard to believe. I wouldn't discount a few bandits trying to make some shillings and the locals trying to get someone to do something about it,' responded Rowan, reflecting the settled mood of the garrison and expedition force. 'They've probably heard the Earl is here and want us to sort them. They know we won't march unless they say it's an army.'

'You're probably right,' said Eric grudgingly. He, like the friends, had got comfortable billeting at the castle but was still excited by any prospect of battle and when he glanced up from looking into his nearly empty mug recognised Leovald. 'Why don't you ask him? He'll know,' suggested Eric, knowing that through Rowan's friendship with Willard and the camaraderie with his father that the Welshman had become friendly with the men, probably more than any other in the garrison.

Leovald apparently had recognised the two anyway for he made his way along the dusty track to the table and greeted the friends. 'Fancy seeing you two here enjoying the sun and drinking the ale,' he smiled.

'Well you know how it is when you have had a hard day protecting the King's land,' came the banter from Rowan.

'Aye, I can see that,' chuckled Leovald. 'Room for one more?' He asked sitting down next to Eric without waiting for a reply. 'So what are you young fellows talking about then?' He said, not realising that this was exactly the question the pair had been wanting to ask.

'Well, Eric here, despite being the brilliant military strategist that he is, wants to know what you think about the rumours about a Welsh army gathering.' Rowan responded, keeping up the banter.

'I wouldn't take it lightly', Leovald said, a bit more seriously than Rowan would have expected. 'The Lord,' he leant his head forward towards the two who responded likewise, 'he and his men are dismissing the rumours but it's hard to think there is no truth at all to what the people are reporting.' He left a suspicion hanging.

Rowan was more than aware that any talk of the rebellion was quickly put down among the garrison and despite their friendship, Leovald had probably said more than enough to cause him to face some form of punishment.

Eric though, as was his character, didn't recognise this risk and pressed on. 'Surely the Lord knows the strength of the rebellion in his own lands and, if there is any he can easily send the men out to deal with them?'

His question was met with a slight raising of the eyebrows from the Welshman, who was obviously not prepared to say more. Instead he looked in the direction of the innkeeper who had just appeared in the doorway and ordered a jug of ale and an extra cup for the three to enjoy as the sun continued to disappear behind the thick stone walls of the castle. Rowan raised his cup to his lips and reflected that his earlier thoughts of ill founded rumours may not be so ill founded after all.

CHAPTER FOUR

'Come on lads, rub that sleep from your eyes and get outside,' his father ordered, waking the company from their slumber, now accustomed to the comfort and deep smell of their straw beds.

The sun was now emerging to light up the day and the animals began to make themselves heard as over a hundred men assembled below the barbican walls. This morning the Earl himself appeared, accompanied by Sir Robert and Esquire Courtney, all wearing their armour and holding their helmets under their arms.

Rowan could feel the added tension flow through the ranks as it did when their commander was addressing them. The eyes of each archer and man at arms watched him intently as he stopped and stared seriously across the ranks, from left to right, his eyes passing across the lines slowly and deliberately.

'Good morning men,' he began in the calm authoritative tone that they had now come to expect, his silent inspection finished. 'You may be aware that there have been some concerns that the enemy may be gathering in the region.'

So the rumours had reached the Earl, Rowan thought, reflecting on the friend's conversation the other day.

'As you are also aware that is why we have been sent here, by the god-blessed King Henry.' He let the royal reference hang in the air for a moment before continuing. 'It is now time for us to leave the comfort of Whittington, which I know some of you will be disappointed about, particularly those that have made friendships or like their home comforts.'

A few good natured assenting noises came back from the men and he knew that his friend Daniel would be thinking of Rosalind, while he continued to rue not having the confidence to speak to her friend more, especially now.

The slight smile the Earl had allowed himself was replaced as he continued. 'You will be ready to depart at midday. We will not be taking the baggage so gather your equipment and transportable supplies. If you have any questions speak to your sergeants.' The tone in his voice became harder. 'Make no mistake men, we may encounter the enemy.' He looked once more at the ranks before turning and making his way back into the outer courtyard.

Even before the Earl's figure had disappeared through the archway with his small entourage the assembly area erupted in a myriad of nervous conversations. It was only the interruption of Rowan's father that made him and his friends start to undertake the urgent business of collecting their belongings.

Rowan strode to the stables but the intensity of his thoughts were broken as he looked back at his friend, Eric. He looked like an overburdened donkey, two bags of arrows clutched in his right hand, a blanket and spare clothing stuck under his arm and his sword belt clutched in his right, his red cap perched precariously on top of his head. Somewhat inevitably as Rowan greeted Willard he heard an oath from his friend who juggled to keep his possessions from falling to the dirt floor.

'It's not funny,' grumbled Eric without humour, his mouth turned downward in disgust as both Rowan and Willard looked at each other laughing aloud. 'Hey!' Eric looked somewhat indignantly at Willard, 'do you want to help rather than laughing at your elders?'

Rowan pushed Willard in the back who happily ran to aid Eric as the rest of the men then started to strap their belongings onto their mounts.

As Rowan hefted the saddle over Constance's back with a grunt he reflected on how the youth and his friends had continued to look after their horses, clearing out the stables, ensuring the farrier re-shoed them, brushing down their coats. He would not relish having to care for his mount again while on the travels, despite his fondness for the young palfrey and reached into his small money bag.

At noon the company was formed up on the dirt road outside the front of the barbican gatehouse. The Earl's men however were not alone. Also formed up were twelve mounted men-at-arms, each carrying a ten foot lance, topped with Lord Fitz Warrins gules and argent pennant, shields strapped across their backs. They looked impressive, Rowan had to admit. Similar to the Earl's men-at-arms their limbs were protected by plate armour, and they wore breast and back plates and uniformly designed bascinets complete with leather aventails and metal cheek plates.

The head protection didn't prevent Rowan, much to his chagrin, from recognising that the man in charge of this force was Bayard sitting astride a heavy black charger. It must have been worth fifty pounds, thirteen hands high, nearly as large as the Earl's and certainly much bigger than any of his troops mounts, or for that matter any of the small palfreys the archers rode. Returning his gaze to the head of the column he could make out the Earl and knights, all in full suits of armour. Above, the Stafford banner and standard flew proudly.

The order to march was given and echoed down the column and soon the dust from the hoofs of over a hundred horses began to rise into the air from the dry track that ran parallel to the castle walls, before the company turned away and headed upwards towards the wooded crest. The men's departure was watched almost in silence by the russet clothed villagers and the remaining garrison on the battlements, many wondering how many of the retinue would be returning.

They part-rode and part-walked for the remainder of the day, the Earl's retinue of bowmen, apart from those scouting ahead and on the flanks, often marching alongside their horses because of the heavier armour and halberds carried by the mounts of the men-at-arms. The weather had still not let them down and there was a good feeling among the men as the sun continued to shine throughout the afternoon and into the early evening.

Rowan guessed that they had travelled nearly twenty miles before they made camp in a stretching shallow valley.

A small gurgling stream gave the men an opportunity to refill flasks and wash sweat from their faces before allowing the horses to greedily drink their fill. The only men now with canvas tents were the Earl and his knights, situated in the middle of the camp, but despite this Rowan and his friends were well at ease. The night was fine and any earlier concern about battle had dissipated as they rode among the rolling hillsides and wooded slopes. Nevertheless, pickets were allocated as the rest of the men gathered around the small fires that now pocketed the small valley casting a red glow into the darkening sky.

He and his friends were soon contentedly spooning mouthfuls of thick coney and potato pottage into their mouths. The Earl encouraged the men to practice their shooting whenever they had the opportunity and it was an unwritten agreement that any food obtained as part of this was split. The men of the company had shot six rabbit that afternoon, testament to the rich countryside through which they rode, and these now formed the basis of their dinner.

Rowan was savouring a gulp of the thick stew, revelling in its warmth as it slid down his throat, when he looked up to see the familiar figure of Leovald striding towards them who had attached himself to the Earl's men as a guide. However it wasn't the sight of the big Welshman that surprised Rowan, but the sight of Willard being guided along by a hand around the back of his neck.

'Hello boys,' Leovald's greeted the group loudly in his heavy accent. 'My young one here thought it would be a good idea to disobey me and follow us on campaign.' Willard kept his face down, his unruly hair covering any facial expression he was making.

'Angels of mercy, I wouldn't disobey, he's a braver man than me,' joked back Daniel.

'Well he's lucky the sentries are half asleep otherwise he would have an arrow in his rump as well as me to deal with,' replied his father.

Rowan could see that despite the firm grip on his son's neck and his stern words he was teasing him.

He looked at Rowan. 'Me and your father have been talking about what to do with him now he's here, and what punishment we should give him. We had thought about a good smacking, sending him home with no boots, but we thought in the end that the worst thing to do was put him with you lads and get him to do your chores.'

The suggestion was met with encouragement from the friends and even Willard looked up with an eager expression, though careful to keep his head down so his father couldn't see.

'I take it you lot would be happy with that?' enquired Leovald hearing the positive response.

'I think you can say that,' replied Rowan, 'we'll keep a good eye on him.'

'Yeh,' chirped in Eric good naturedly 'and if something goes wrong you can blame Rowan.'

'That's it then lad,' Leovald said turning his son to face him. 'You be good for these men and don't let me down.' He ruffled his sons hair before heading back to the campfire where Rowan's father and the other vintenars and seniors were crouched, looking up and laughing good heartedly as their comrade returned.

Willard proved himself a willing hand over the following three days, looking after the horses, gathering firewood and checking the archer's bags of arrows, making sure the goose feathers were not crushed or stuck together despite the wicker frames.

The column continued its peaceful routine, winding its way west, occasionally passing by a small hamlet where the villagers who had not had warning enough to disappear from the soldiers would stare. They looked on with wariness as they tramped past, largely ignoring any friendly comments from the men on horseback.

These were the only encounters as their sortie took them deeper into the Welsh countryside before, on the fourth day when the column was halted for the night, news started to filter among the clustered groups of men that a force was marching to meet them. The rumours passed rapidly among the soldiers and the sound of conversations increased around the campfires.

'Go and find out what's going on,' Jerrard urged Rowan. 'You've got more chance than any of us.'

Rowan was reluctant to go but his friends request was taken up by the rest of the group.

'Go on, Rowan, we need to know.' The encouragement continued and so he stood, feeling the back of his knees for a moment and rubbing the ache away. He glanced warily towards the centre of the camp where the tents of the nobles stood near to the silhouetted outlines of his father and the other sergeants surrounded by crackling sparks of the campfire.

As he approached, weaving his way through the

groups of fellow archers and men-at-arms he saw his father and his peers finish their conversation and begin moving purposefully, reaching for their sword belts and equipment. Self-consciously Rowan interrupted his father as he was pulling at his buckle, nervous that he was seeking preferential information, something he was always keen not to do.

'Can you tell me what's going on?'

His father glanced upwards, surprised at the appearance of his son, looking into his eyes for a moment. 'There's a rumour of Glyn Dwr's forces gathering but I can't really say. All I know is that Leovald got talking to the woodcutter who we passed earlier today and after a bit of encouragement he told him that a large body of men were in the area. I don't know any more than that for the moment, we're just off to see the Earl.' He gestured with his head towards his fellow vintenars who were heading towards the large command tent. 'It's either all or nothing so don't get too excited.' With a reassuring look he turned and followed his comrades into the tents interior, past the two men at arms and the banners that flapped occasionally in response to the slight wind outside.

Rowan's lack of confirmation was greeted with derision by his friends when he made his way back to their campfire but it wasn't long after that the sergeants emerged and against a backdrop of expectation by the waiting soldiers called their respective companies together.

'Sit down lads,' his father said, his calm manner at odds with the nervous chattering of the men from Stone. 'I know you'll have heard some rumours,' he glanced at Rowan. 'Well after further questioning,' for a moment Rowan wondered about the fate of the wood cutter but then focussed on his father's words, 'the Earl holds some credibility that those rumours may be true, and more to the point that the enemy may not be far away.'

That last comment brought a rush of conversation among the men and furtive looks as they wondered just how close the threat was and whether even now in the surrounding darkness an enemy host approached or waited silently ready to spring forwards among the resting men.

Rowan's father held up his arm to silence the chatter and once this had subsided, continued. 'Leovald is with the Earl and knights sharing his knowledge of the area, but for now we need to make best use of what light remains.' He continued, 'The men over there' he gestured to a troop of men from the village of Great Sandon, are going to start on the defensive ditch while you men can start felling some trees and making stakes.'

Rowan remembered how his father had once explained to him that on his campaigns it was normal activity to dyke and stake out camps when in hostile lands, and this rapidly felt as though it was becoming a hostile land.

Throughout the rest of the evening the men made their defensive preparations, using what few axes and wooden mallets they had brought with them. The work had been much harder than he imagined, even sharpening the ends of the stakes had been arduous, while the dryness of the land ensured the men were sweating heavily by the time each stake had been embedded in the earth to the satisfaction of the vintenars.

Three hours later the sound of men digging and hammering ceased, the valley now scarred with raised earthworks and stakes as darkness fell.

Despite the exhaustion from their efforts and the feeling of increased security Rowan was unable to sleep and along with Daniel and Martin carried on a hushed conversation into the night. Eric and Jerrard slumbered as though without a care in the world, a feeling enhanced by his bearded friends usual deep snoring.

It was with a start that Rowan awoke in the early hours of the morning just as dawn was breaking over the hillside to a kick to the sole of his boot.

'Wake up sleepy head,' chuckled Daniel, 'we're on the move.'

Rowan blinked and rubbed his eyes before throwing off his travelling cloak. 'Didn't think I'd get a bit of sleep last night,' he said still feeling somewhat dazed.

'I don't think we got much, I reckon we've only had four hours unlike Eric and Jerrard there,' Daniel pointed towards the two, who had also seemingly just been woken up judging by their blank expressions and excessive yawns.

Rowan, like the others, had slept partly dressed and while pulling on his mail shirt and surcoat over his jacket found the camp in a state of high activity. Horses whinnied as they were saddled, pots clattered as they were dropped, men argued about who carried what. There was an air of expectation and eagerness to be ready for what the day would bring and there was no doubt that the intention was to break camp despite the labours of the previous early evening.

The morning had started off colder and a mistiness persevered as the force was brought to order within the staked out camp.

'Where are we going then, do you think?' murmured Eric next to Rowan.

'Looks as though were going to find out,' he replied, as sergeants ushered the men inwards towards the Earl who was standing in front of where his tent was being disassembled.

'Men, we are going to ride onwards today and hope that we catch up with the enemy force, if it exists.' It was apparent the Earl wasn't totally convinced by the woodcutter's statement, even after further questioning. 'You men have trained for a long time and discipline will be crucial.' His words were calm and authoritative, with no mistaking the seriousness of his tone. 'I have given orders to your vintenars and I expect you to follow them'. He paused looking at the men's faces before gesturing to the stony faced Samuel Blacke to dismiss the men.

The men departed their hastily built camp shortly after. The earthworks were left to the elements while the newly honed stakes with nearly as much effort, and certainly as much cursing as when they were first planted, were dragged from the earth and strapped to the flanks of their mounts. At least Rowan, thought as Jerrard and Eric helped him fix the six foot sharpened stake to his palfrey, the effort of the previous night may have not been totally wasted.

An air of apprehension and almost silence hung over the column as they wound their way across lowland fields, men glanced warily to their flanks or ahead at the woodland that filled the hillsides, dense enough to hide hundreds of enemy soldiers. Despite the reservations of the Earl, Rowan and most of the men had no uncertainty over the gathering of an enemy force.

Their surety was justified as, just before midday he spotted the lead scouts racing their mounts back towards the Earl from a shallow rise ahead. Seeing the advancing riders a halt was called. The order was repeated down the column before a standard bearer cantered his horse along the line of now stationery horsemen to fetch Leovald who, with a snap of his reins rode to the front. The eyes of every man within the column watched him in nervous expectation.

It was an age later, or at least it felt like it to Rowan, that the column was ordered to resume their advance towards the shallow summit where they halted without an order being required. Ahead of them, down the gentle slope and across the valley leading to another ridge, stood the enemy.

Rowan stared at the force silently across the shallow valley, his horse snorted and he pulled at the bridle not taking his eyes from the opposite ridge line half a mile away, until his reverie was interrupted by the urgent orders coming from the respective vintenars. Tugging his reins but not averting his gaze he trotted after the rest of the troop towards the right flank where he dismounted, adjusted his steel bascinet and hurriedly untied the canvas cover that protected his bow and unhooked his arrow bags. He only half registered his father's orders to release the sharpened wooden stakes from their straps on the horse's flanks as his mind began to register the likelihood of battle. Likewise he hardly noticed Willard appear from nowhere and seemingly without the need for instruction pulled the skittish and reluctant horses back towards the crest of the rise.

With a longbow in one hand and the end of a stake grasped in the other, Rowan and his friends dragged the wooden defences between them forward to where his father indicated they should form up. The men shuffled into order and with relief dropped their cumbersome loads ahead of them so that they lay haphazardly in the calf high grass. Behind them the thin line of armoured men-at-arms two deep in their gules and or surcoats, spiked halberds across their shoulders began to form up.

He turned back to his front and strung his bow, bracing it against the outside of his foot, using his left hand to bend the stave and quickly hooking the string with effort over the horn nock at the top. Allowing the string to now take the tension, his muscles able to recover from the strain, he focussed once more at the unmoving enemy to his front and his surroundings.

On the right flank of the Earl's force, nearest to the men of Stone, the ground rose up towards a dense mass of thick oak trees less than a quarter of a mile distant. On the left flank was a much more definite and substantial hill that rose steeply and had blotches of bright grey scree of slate interposed along its slope. These natural features framed the two bodies of soldiers that were now assembled opposite each other with the valley between. Ahead he could see the enemy force. Ominous ranks of men showed against the skyline, a mixture of dull argent and gules, mail shirts and armour crowned by a glistening hedge of lances. In front, to the left of Rowan's place, a body of horsemen, armour shining bright and flying a large banner which stirred only occasionally in the brief wind, sat calmly watching the Earl's force assemble. Their calmness reflected the size of the enemy mass, it seemed to Rowan that they outnumbered the Stafford retinue by more than two to one

The tension in the air was palpable as the two bodies, almost five hundred men stood silently facing their enemy. Each temporarily settled as they assessed one another, the respective commanders apparently happy that their men were positioned at their desired places. Rowan found himself lost in his own thoughts, the only sounds now were the occasional snort from the nobles' destriers, their riding horses now with the rest of the men's on the reverse slope, and the nervous whispered comments among comrades.

'What are they up to then?' Rowans thoughts were broken by Eric, always the first to ask, standing behind him tapping his friend on the shoulder, indicating with an inclination of his head towards the armoured horsemen led by Bayard who were cantering behind the line, their hoofs pounding heavily on the ground beneath as they headed off towards the wooded slope on their right flank.

He didn't really care Rowan thought to himself,

grateful that, like the journey he had no dealings with the sergeant from Whittington whose obvious dislike of him showed no signs of abating.

'Do you reckon they've had enough already?' Eric joked half heartedly, ignoring his friend's silence.

Rowan thought he recognised a touch of nervousness.

'Must be making sure we won't be flanked,' he responded almost sullenly not even wishing to discuss Bayard and his small troop.

Despite dismissing the sergeant and his men he knew his explanation was logical. If the woods had enemy hidden within they could attack the Earl's force in the flank as they advanced towards the still stationery enemy. Rowan watched the men halt their horses at the tree line without incident before his attention was drawn back towards a movement to his front.

Three armoured horsemen had detached themselves from the group of mounted enemy soldiers and slowly trotted their horses down the slight incline towards the valley floor. Two squires followed behind one holding aloft a large sable banner, in its centre a rampant argent lion, the other four lions on gules and or quartered background.

Rowan turned and could see the Earl was already nudging his mount forwards, Sir Robert and Esquire Courtney who carried the square chevron banner following, the men-at-arms and archers shuffling aside to let them through.

As the two groups trotted slowly towards each other in the bright light of the early morning Rowan realised that he had been holding his breath and made an audible sound as he relaxed his lungs, releasing his trapped breath.

Looking left and right he could tell everyone else was totally focussed on the negotiation that was going on in the centre of the valley. It wasn't as if they could hear anything, even despite the still air, but nevertheless whatever they were discussing could mean either a peaceful end to the confrontation or something far bloodier and deadly. The realisation did nothing to avert his attention from the group exchanging words between the two opposing forces. Even as he watched he saw the Earl, easily noticeable on his distinctive white charger with his straight riding posture, pull on the reins and turn his mount back towards his subordinates and then towards his two lines of men.

The opposing leader did the same, turning his mount and heading towards the waiting mass of enemy soldiers on the slight crest opposite him and his friends. Unlike the Earl, the enemy leader raced back, his entourage not far behind. Rowan could see the man's long brown hair flying, his large frame, encased in armour, rising and falling easily with the canter of his mount, the large square banners flying behind, the beasts upon them clear for all to see. There was an exuberance about him as, arm held aloft Rowan heard, but could not interpret the words that galvanised the men on the rise into a frenzy of shouts, clashing of shields and raising of pikes.

His nerves became tauter and he altered his weight restlessly, he could tell his friends were also feeling uneasy as they shifted their postures, watching the enemy as they shouted their obvious challenges, no doubt laced with obscenities, the roar dulled by the distance. Rowan was thankful as the Earl, reaching the front ranks calmly halted his horse, seemingly oblivious to the baying of the enemy force behind him.

'It seems men that we are to do battle today.' His aristocratic voice carried across the two ranks of men even as he sought to calm his skittish mount. 'We have the joy of facing Rhys Gethin, one of Glyn Dwr's generals.'

Rowan glanced to look at his father standing to his front who shared a quick grin with Leovald, probably remembering the failed attempt to bring the Welsh commander to battle a year ago.

'Now is our chance to say we finally put paid to the rebels, through strong arms and good heart.' The Earl's voice rose as he spoke, his determination transferred and permeated through the ranks. 'We will face them head on. Stand strong for your friends. Stand strong for your King. As we are standing here, we will not be defeated!'

The roar of the men, Rowan included, was instantaneous. He found himself pumping his bow towards the sky repeatedly and grinning insanely, first at Jerrard and Daniel on either side, then the rest of his friends, the sickening feeling in his stomach temporarily forgotten.

Once the crescendo had reduced, Samuel Blacke gave the order for the men to ready themselves. The command was relayed across the line by the vintenars so each man was soon quiet, once more self consciously checking their armour and weapons.

The order was followed by Rowan's father's experienced advice. 'Ensure your bags are open, swords, daggers, mallets loose'.

Rowan ruefully thought back to the ambush in the woods all those weeks ago and his unpreparedness.

As the memory played on his mind the men readied themselves, clumsily pulling and tugging on their weapons or arrow bags. The order to advance came quicker than any of them wanted and he found himself walking forward in the ranks of bowmen, still adjusting his buckler anxiously so that it felt in the right position on his forearm should he need it. He was full of doubt, he had worn his small metal shield so many times but only now did he feel as though it wasn't quite right.

The men marched forward, their ranks mingling, stepping over the ragged line of dumped stakes and down the shallow slope. They tramped onwards almost in silence. The only sound was the breathing of the men and the soft tramp of feet made by the four companies of archers. Even the enemy were now ominously quiet. Rowan tried to keep his gaze lowered but could not help staring from under his heavy bascinet to the lines of the opposing forces that gradually became more and more distinguishable, the glistening blades unmistakeable.

'Halt.'

The order couldn't come soon enough for Rowan who felt as though he would be walking right up to the enemy ranks, unable to do anything as he was drawn forward in the midst of his comrades.

'Sort yourselves out. Give each other room.' The scornful shout came from Rowan's father, and similar rebukes could be heard from the other three vintenars.

The man in front of Rowan stepped slightly back, and he did likewise, shifting slightly to his right, so the front of the line across all four companies was straight.

'Make arrows ready.' The next order came, as Rowan now knew it would. He was now remembering the training, and he pulled out half a dozen of the ash shafts from the open bag and thrust the steel bodkin tips into the dry earth, just in front of his right foot.

He had to twist the steel points with some effort into the hard ground. No wonder they had not bothered to pitch the wooden stakes, he reflected, it would have taken hard work and besides there was little sign of enemy horsemen. They were nearly at the bottom of the gentle slope having advanced to three hundred yards of the enemy. Glancing round he could see the men-at-arms had followed the men slightly down the slope, and they now stood perhaps fifty yards behind the bowmen. The accompanying knights were still mounted and had placed themselves behind the men-at-arms in the centre.

The order to notch arrows carried across the lines and Rowan, his hand grasping one of the shafts just under the goose feathers tugged it free from the ground and easily, thanks to the years of practice felt the string slide into the thin notch of his arrow.

'First rank only' came the next command. 'That doesn't mean any of you scullions in the other ranks,' added Samuel Blacke in his normal hoarse and derisory tone. 'First rank only,' he repeated. 'Draw!'

To Rowan's front, the row of archers pulled their strings back, stretching them so they gradually came to their ears, the bow staves curving backwards taking the strain. He watched Bill Whitney in front, a middle aged labourer from Stone, with a medium build but with broad shoulders who appeared to pull the string back with as much ease as Jerrard, before raising the bow skywards. He and the rest of the first rank held their pose like that for a moment before the order to loose was given.

With a chorus of snaps, a sound like swathes of rotten twigs breaking, the line of dark arrow shafts shot high into the air at slightly different angles soaring towards the clouds, before starting to arc and speed earthwards. Rowan followed the almost graceful flight as they sped downwards and crashed into the enemy mass on the slope opposite.

The effect was obvious and new to Rowan. He saw the enemy force seem to shudder under the impact of the arrows, men were forced to the ground or knocked backwards despite their heavy armour and round shields lifted skywards in an effort to ward off the deadly points. Loud thwacks could be heard as the steel tips pierced deeply into the thick leather and wooden shields, metallic rings were heard as steel met steel and for those more fortunate slid off armour. For those less fortunate curses and cries of pain could be heard as the points either found some less protected area or simply pierced straight through padded gambesons. It seemed to Rowan that they had made a telling strike but then, like people awaking from slumber, the enemy mass stood again to face the men of Stafford, the cries of pain from the injured now completely absorbed by the shouts of rage and fury directed at the archers.

Trumpets blared out defiantly as he saw axes, swords and pikes pointed towards him and his comrades, enraged and contorted faces spitting out curses. The enemy still outnumbered the archers heavily and for a moment Rowan was unsure as to whether the wave of men would simply charge and overwhelm him and his friends, he glanced nervously to his rear in anticipation.

'All ranks, ten flights. Fire,' the shout brought him back from his worries. The Master-at-Arms was obviously happy with the range found by the first rank of archers and oblivious to Rowan's concerns was ready to inflict more damage upon the enemy.

The men around him with the experience gained by years of practice raised their bows and let loose. Quickly but slightly slower he drew his own string back, feeling the tension spread across his shoulders. With a last silent urge of effort he pulled back the last couple of inches, his elbow drawn right back before raising the bow skywards judging where the arrow would fall among the enemy ranks. It was with physical relief that he let the shaft slide from his grip shooting upwards with practised ease as the bow rolled forwards with the momentum, before he reached for a second arrow.

With a sudden ferocious force his head was abruptly snapped backwards, harshly pulling at his neck muscles, a loud metallic bang resounded in his head. He staggered for a moment, his hand no longer seeking the arrow as his balance failed him temporarily, his hand instinctively reaching towards his bascinet. With a shake of the head he pushed the steel helmet back from where it had fallen forwards over his eyes as he looked around stunned and bemused.

Around him he saw that the orderly ranks of men had been turned into chaos, the second volley of arrows forgotten, replaced by curses, screaming and the now too late warning shouts of 'arrows' from the men around him. In front Bill Whitney was on one knee, his bow lying discarded next to him, swearing loudly as he pulled at the dark shaft of an arrow that protruded from his lower leg.

The Welshmen must have had archers behind their front ranks, the bow as native to them as the English, sharing a rivalry with their abilities. He had seen for himself their accuracy both among the Earl's ranks and, most recently, from those within the garrison at Whittington. What was undeniable was that they had got the English force in their range, as the English had the Welsh.

It was the vintenars who quickly restored order with oaths and curses, roughly pushing the men and shouting at them to resume shooting, ignoring the injured and dead interspaced within the ranks. Looking down on his second arrow he had sought to grasp just seconds ago, Rowan lifted it to his bow, notching it quickly and loosing it towards the enemy. A desperate need took over to send as many shafts as possible towards the threat before more deadly arrows sought to maim and kill him and his friends.

He pulled and released rapidly, quickly tugging the arrows from the ground even as more missiles plunged down around him. A mix of sounds accompanied the barrage, dull thuds as the steel tipped shafts buried themselves deep into the dry grass, the thump of metal on metal as they hit plate, shields or bascinets and the yelps and cries as they struck men along the line.

Around him he could sense men falling and tried not to think of a lethal steel tip piercing his own mail.

'Withdraw, withdraw,' the cry was taken up.

Looking around he saw Daniel to his right staring worriedly towards the opposite slope. Following his gaze saw that the enemy were no longer content to stand where they were. The noise was swelling as the mass of men like a breaking dam began to detach themselves from their position and run headlong down the slope towards the line of bowmen. It was a few men at first but soon it was the whole force, banners and steel points held high above the charging ranks.

He left the few arrows still thrust in the ground and found himself running with the rest of the company, some helping their injured colleagues hobble quickly towards the men at arms that still stood in a firm line halfway down the English slope. Rowan lifted the arm of Bill Whitney, who was half knelt on the floor. 'C'mon we've got to get out of here quick,' he urged wrapping his arm round the man's waist and pulling him up.

With a grunt he helped take the archer's weight and together they stumbled backwards following the rest of their company. His heart was beating rapidly and he had no intention of wasting time and glancing back. He was focused on reaching the safety of the line of men at arms.

Retreating among the archers, Rowan and his injured comrade squeezed through the two ranks that made way for the panting bowmen. The foot soldiers hardly gave them a look, their stern and resolute faces beneath their helmets staring forwards, the Earl and his two knights calmly watching the advancing enemy.

'Form up you lot, injured to the rear. The rest get yourselves together.' The reassuring bellow from the Master-at-Arms helped steady Rowan and the rest of the company.

'You okay?' Rowan asked the now pale faced injured archer.

'Yeh, thanks,' he said in a deep Staffordshire voice, 'I'll be alright,' releasing himself from Rowans support. He also fell in about twenty yards behind the men at arms, hobbling gingerly and placing his weight on his good leg. There was no time now for anything but the barest medical treatment. The battle was beginning in earnest and Rowan and the archer knew it. To their front Rowan's father and Leovald were helping the men of Stone form up on the right flank, his father giving him an encouraging shove on the back of his left shoulder and a grin as Rowan took his place in line.

'Make arrows ready,' came the order over the roar of the rapidly advancing enemy, the sound increasing in intensity as they charged across the shallow valley towards the waiting defensive lines.

Rowan reached for his second arrow bag slung across his shoulder and again thrust the points of the arrows rapidly in the turf at his feet, keeping the last one and notching it against the string of his longbow. Planting his left foot forward and tensing his shoulders he drew his bow back before the order to fire came. He felt his training taking over as he angled his bow higher and loosed, judging the distance of the enemy between the armoured shoulders of the line of men at arms to his immediate front.

The enemy pounded across the grass, a mass of screaming men, with swords, lances and axes clearly visible, their faces contorted in rage. Arrows fell steeply towards the force that now filled the valley, throwing people to the ground, spinning them round in agony or buried themselves deep into the turf. Rowan though didn't wait to watch the flight of his arrows and instead he plucked another arrow from the ground, then another. It felt like moments before the enemy were too close to the defensive line for the bowmen to be effective. He had his sixth arrow notched and ready to draw but the distance was too close, the men-at-arms to the front in the way, preventing him from a clear shot.

'Archers, ready swords and bucklers,' his father shouted for the company to hear, still able to keep a calm tone in his voice.

In front he could hear the booming voice of Samuel Blacke shouting for the men-at-arms to steady themselves. 'Here they come, get ready to teach these whoresons a lesson.'

There was no mistaking the closeness of the enemy and with fingers that felt as thick as thumbs he clumsily grasped his blade and pulled it from its leather scabbard.

The charge met the Earl's line of men-at-arms within moments, a harsh crash of metal on metal. Many of the men in the second rank took an involuntary step back as the physical force of the enemy's charge impacted upon the front ranks. For a sickening moment Rowan thought the enemy would break straight through. He tensed, ready to run forward to reinforce the line.

'Hold yourselves.' As if sensing his thoughts his father's call was echoed by the other vintenars.

In front he could see the raising of swords and axes and the thrusting of shortened lances, some festooned with the colours of their enemy. His fingers tightened around the pommel of his sword as he watched the men-at-arms immediately in front of him battle with the enemy, the earlier loudness of curses only diminished slightly by the energy both sides were using as they swung their blades. Both masses of men were pushing and thrusting at each other, using their armoured bodies as much as their weapons. The second line of men-at-arms were as engaged as the first, using their fearsome halberds with their sharpened points to threaten the enemy, seeking a weak spot between their armour plate or thrusting it repeatedly towards the eyes of the enemy. Rowan watched with a sense of horror as a point managed to plunge home into the bearded face of a Welshman, too slow to dodge backwards. Blood and torn tissue covered the steel tip as it was withdrawn, a look of shock on the man's face as his blood spurted skywards and he tumbled to the ground. The two sets of men were seeking the smallest advantage that would enable their weapons to slash down the enemy.

The frenzy of battle was everywhere and Rowan saw to his left an enemy soldier, face contorted, fling himself towards a man-at-arms ignoring another of the enemy between them. He swung a heavy axe over his head, only succeeding in smashing it down into the armoured spaudler that protected his own comrade's shoulder. Then, before he could pull back his weapon, a sword was thrust into his belly by the man-at-arms he had tried to kill. Immediately in front of him, a Stafford man went down on one knee, whether from a wound or sheer pressure Rowan couldn't tell, and with no time to regain his balance he was seemingly swept away by the enemy who battered him further down to the ground. More men poured forward, snarling and cursing.

With resolve in his heart he prepared to throw himself forward just as another man-at-arms shoulder-charged into the group. The weight of his momentum and armour made them stumble backwards, creating space for the defender to swing his sword down with all his force, a cleaving strike that cut deep into the chain mail sleeve of the man's sword arm, almost severing it completely. The howl of pain was accompanied by a shower of bright red blood, the weapon dropped to the floor. Another blood-splattered man-at-arms joined in and Rowan recognised the squat figure of Samuel Blacke, smashing his hilt hard onto the bascinet of another enemy soldier, crushing the metal downwards and knocking the man's head sideways viciously before swinging his sword down into the torso of another. The enemy crumpled, his body bent inwards with the pain of the strike before being flung backwards by an armoured elbow jutted savagely into his face.

It went on, men throwing themselves forwards, swords and shields smashing against each other, blades cutting through cloth, mail and flesh, armour dented, gaps sought.

Still the archers of Stone watched with a sort of strange detachment, ready at any moment to charge into the melee, close enough to see every clash of shield and thrusts of swords, but held back by their steady commands.

'Keep holding lads, not our turn yet.' His father was still standing at the front of the company watching the conflict less than twenty yards away, keeping the men together.

Surely it wouldn't be long now, thought Rowan. He felt a bead of sweat trickle from beneath the leather padding of his now dented bascinet. Suddenly, off to the left he saw parts of the flank give way to the pressure of the enemy and a company of archers rushed forward to reinforce the line where the Earl's men were suffering badly. He glanced at his friends, returning their grim looks, there were no mischievous grins now, not even from Eric. They were all tense, ready to advance into the fray as the men at arms in front fought desperately, trying not to be overwhelmed.

A movement off to his right, near the tree line caught Rowans eye. He had forgotten about the horsemen who had stayed protecting the flank and he watched with relief as the line of horsemen with their gules and argent pennants flapping at their lance tips began to walk down the slope angled towards the melee below.

Rowan looked towards the opposite slope, over the heads of the desperately struggling men-at-arms, waiting for the moment that the rebel leaders would recognise the threat to their flank. Sure enough the movement drew the attention of the enemy leader and his small entourage of horsemen. To his disappointment the leader reacted calmly turning towards his men and issuing orders.

There was no urgency and Rowan started to feel a

sense of unease, as the enemy leaders retuned to watch the horsemen on the hillside. He followed their gaze, focussing upon Bayard, easily identifiable on his large black charger, his visor still up. Was he angling the line too far towards the Earl's flank? Surely not, the awful thought of betrayal was upon him like a punch to the stomach.

He turned to warn the commanders but saw that the deployment of horsemen had already caused urgent discussion among the knights while they tried to curb their excited mounts.

Increasingly Rowan was aware other men, picking up on his nervous glances, were staring towards the oncoming mounted men-at-arms, cantering down the hill, the archers' interest temporarily piqued away from the desperate hand-to-hand combat going on just a few yards away that was in the balance.

'What are they playing at?' asked Eric with not so much as a hint of the levity he had shown before the battle.

'It looks like the swine has shown his hand.' Leovald appearing among the ranks answered bitterly.

Rowan looked at his father's friend, he didn't sound surprised, but before he could give it further thought the urgent call of Sir Robert, picked up by his father rose above the sounds of battle.

'Form to your right.'

The line of horsemen was approaching down the hill, the trees at their back rapidly left behind. The sheer size and sense of power that came from the snorting horses was too easily apparent to the line of archers. For the moment the life and death struggles of the men-at-arms in front were pushed to the back of their minds.

'Move boys, quickly. Hurry up for pities sake.' His father's voice was loud and unerring but those last few words betrayed the urgency of their predicament.

Men rushed a few steps to realign themselves so they were facing diagonally up the hill towards the oncoming riders. Leovald and Rowan's father were pushing and dragging men so that the line was in some form of order ready to receive the impact of the heavy horses, although he still hoped fervently that the point of their charge was just to deceive the enemy.

They had no time to reach for their bows from their backs to shoot their deadly bodkin arrows. Instead men steadied themselves, their muscles taught, standing with just sword and buckler or in some cases heavy mallets ready to try to halt the armoured charge that would surely crash through them like a wave overcoming a small sandbank.

Rowan was under no illusions, having seen the devastating power and crushing impact of a lance point backed up by the weight of armoured horse, his mind pictured momentarily the wooden stakes they had so recently discarded. With a sick realisation and even knowing that most of the horses were lighter than the heavy destriers rode by the Earl and wealthier knights he knew they would be scattered like hay in a heavy wind. Even if they survived the initial charge they stood no chance preventing it biting deep into the Earl's embattled men-at-arms and turning the battle into a rout.

The horsemen were now within two hundred yards and Rowan could tell that the Bayard's men were having trouble keeping their mounts from springing forward and charging into the company who stood across the grass that slightly dipped and then rose at an angle.

He and his friends watched as an unseen order caused the horsemen to lower their visors, bring down their lances and let their beasts loose.

Fighting the temptation to run, he lifted his sword higher wondering if this was the best stance to try to combat a horseman riding full pelt towards him. If he had received training on this he forgot it now and stole a glance under the rim of his bascinet at his comrades to left and to right registering their looks of defiance, anger and fear.

'Steady men,' came the voice from his father. 'Steady and hold,' he repeated as the enemy horseman thundered across the slope, their strides lengthening, some surging ahead of others.

'Archers, shoot.' The unexpected order came from behind him and was immediately accompanied by the whistle of arrows past his ears causing him to flinch in alarm, his eyes picking up the blur of wood and feathers that flew from the company of archers who now stood to the rear of the men of Stone.

The arrows from the bows flew true, as far as Rowan could tell, unbelievingly missing their comrades and burying their sharp heads into the attackers, horses and men alike. Mounts reared in pain, their light armour and trappings unable to stop the force of the arrows, men held onto their reins struggling to remain saddled. One man was unhorsed while another simply tumbled to the floor, the horse oblivious to the arrow shaft deep in his master's throat. For a split second Rowan thought the confusion and whines of pain would stop the charge or at least slow it down.

He was wrong and the slightly more ragged line of horsemen continued their charge across the slope, pounding towards him and his friends. Rowan's knuckles turned white as he gripped his sword tighter, teeth gritted together, his mind wondering anxiously how he could somehow avoid the steel tipped lance points aimed at him and his friends.

'For King Henry!' the war cry sounded from Rowans right and daring to turn his gaze from the oncoming lances for a split second he caught sight of the Earl, on his distinct war horse, armour gleaming. Just behind him came his two similarly imposing knights, Sir Robert closely followed by the slighter figure of the esquire. All three spurred their horses forward, their visors down and charged to meet the enemy.

The three horsemen attracted the thundering lances and he saw Bayard alter the direction of his horse with a twist of his reins, his men following suit, no longer aiming at smashing through the thin line of archers but intent on killing or capturing any one of the nobles.

Within moments the two uneven forces crashed into each other. There was a smashing of lances on shields and armour, metal scraped off metal, and horses screamed with pain. The heavy horses of the nobles forced a path through the lighter coursers of the enemy who, despite their advantage in numbers, were unable to bring all their spear points to bear.

The nobles turned once through the initial charge. All were still saddled and apparently unhurt, including the Earl, who Rowan had seen deflected the lance point of Bayard with his shield but who at the same time was unable to unhorse the rebel sergeant.

Splintered lances were thrown to the ground as the three armoured knights dragged their long swords from their scabbards, turning their big destriers expertly with their knees to face their attackers once more. Two bodies lay crumpled on the ground, unmoving and ignored as the skirmish became an unorganised whirl. Horsemen smashed at each other with their swords and maces, shields and armour deflecting the lethal blows. The air was dense with the noise of battle. Rowan could see the Earl engaged in the middle of the mass of men, raising his sword left and right, battling with men on either side. He watched as his sword smashed against the pig snout helm of an enemy soldier, almost knocking the man from his mount before his charger took him towards another cursing attacker.

The numbers were against them, the momentum of the initial charge now gone, giving the enemy the opportunity to make their numbers tell. Even as he watched he saw the esquire feverishly swinging his sword to meet that of an enemy man-at-arms, before arching his back, reeling from pain as another of Bayard's horsemen, unseen smashed a mace into the back of his cuirass. The blow caused him to drop his guard and allowed the original attacker to once more swing his sword forward. This time he smashed into the knight's sword arm with such force that despite the steel gauntlet protecting his wrist the heavy blade fell to the ground. The young esquire swung his battered shield across his body, forcing the enemy away and giving himself a brief respite as he sought his spare weapons frantically as more of the horsemen closed around him.

Seeing the danger the knights were in, Rowan's father shouted over the sounds of battle coming from the clash of mounted soldiers and the line of foot soldiers. The Earl's men-at-arms were still fighting furiously to their left, desperately keeping the enemy from breaking through.

'To the Earl, to the Earl!' His father urged the archers forward into the melee, rushing forward with Leovald, followed by Rowan and the rest of the company, charging into the mass of men and horses.

Rowan ran forwards, sword raised high towards a mounted man-at-arms who was tugging his reins to turn his dark brown courser towards the attacking archers. The horse was nearly as high as his shoulder, a black mace sprouting lethal spikes swung ominously in the man's grip.

Despite the fear, Rowan kept running forwards hoping the man would keep his gaze from under his steel helm at the other members of the charging company. He swung his sword horizontally with all his effort, at the same time registering the blur of the heavy mace as it arched downwards towards another yelling archer. There was an explosion of blood, the weight smashing the man's helm into his skull as his own swing caught the edge of the metal shield which deflected the sword to scrape against the armoured fauld protecting the enemy's lower abdomen.

A shudder of pain shot through Rowan's wrist, the

blade sliding down the skirt as he was thrown to the ground, falling backwards to the turf as the horse was wrenched towards him. Sprawled on the ground, the heavy mount above him the eyes of the enemy briefly met his own and he felt time slow, expecting death.

The horsemen though didn't have time to lean from his saddle, having to turn and defend himself from more of the agile archers cutting and thrusting between the rearing horses.

Rowan's immediate danger wasn't gone though as the iron shod shoes of the enemy's horse stamped the ground around where he lay, threatening to smash his skull to pieces. Rolling to his left he scrambled to his feet, grabbing for his sword, dropping it once before successfully grasping the weighted pommel the second time as he stumbled away.

Looking round he saw the mounted enemy surrounded by more of the retinue, including the big figure of Jerrard, a mixture of fury and determination on his face that he had never seen before. Another enemy horseman brought his sword down with vicious force onto an archer's bascinet before Jerrard dragged the man from his saddle, smashing the pommel of his sword into the man's visor repeatedly before grabbing his helm in both hands and pounding it again and again into the hard ground. Rowan flinched at the savagery of it all. The company were desperately swinging their swords or else, like Jerrard using their bare hands to drag the enemy from their saddles so they could be set upon by their friends.

The Earl was still on horseback, his armour splattered with bright red smears of what could only be blood, his shield battered but his sword still swinging. He was hard pressed and fighting three enemy horsemen despite the efforts of his retinue to aid him. One of them was unmistakably Bayard who was swinging a heavy spiked war hammer backed with an evil looking falcon-like beak at the noble's shield. For a moment Rowan was transfixed by the personal battle just fifteen yards away in the centre of the whirling maelstrom of men and horses. It didn't seem as though the Earl would be able to keep the enemies at bay for much longer, his defensive moves of both sword and shield were slowing and his armour already bore the marks from the blows of Bayard's men.

The appearance of his father, even now followed by Leovald running forward and thrusting his sword into the neck of one of the enemy's horses came just in time. Rearing in agony the mount wrenched the sword out of his father's hand while the horseman struggled to keep seated. The distraction gave Leovald an opportunity which he took ruthlessly, ramming a short dagger into the man's groin between his metal plates causing a scream of anguish. The archer's attack instantaneously turned the Earl's personal battle that had looked indefensible to that point.

Bayard was the first to break from the conflict, turning the black destrier with a savage jerk of the reins leaving the last horsemen alone fighting the Earl, who on his much bigger warhorse swept his heavy sword downwards at the now disadvantaged enemy.

Rowan's brief sense of relief though was soon replaced by that of horror as he saw Bayard, having turned away from the initial fray shift his attentions instead to the two men on foot. He watched as almost in slow motion Leovald was thrown to the grass by the weight of the enemy's charger while Rowan's father, still without sword in hand tried in vain to avoid the swing of the heavy war hammer as the big destrier carried the enemy sergeant away.

Seeing their leader retreat, their hopes of capturing or killing the Earl disappearing, the remaining horsemen sought to break away. One moment they were viciously swinging their swords and thrusting their lances at the men on foot, the next they were urging their horses around from the clawing and vengeful archers. Some didn't make it as their horses were hamstrung and brought down while others were forcefully dragged from their mounts as they sought to retreat, despatched swiftly by sword or dagger.

Rowan was hardly aware of the change in the battles impetus, running as fast as he could towards his father lying unmoving among the other bodies that now littered the right flank. His mind was racing as he weaved through the surviving archers, not noticing how many had now let their arms fall by their side, dragged down by the weight of their weapons, breathing heavily and realising that they had managed to survive. Even the Earl and Sir Robert had no energy or desire to chase the retreating rebels.

Leovald was there already as he breathlessly reached his father's side, pushing a cloth against his shoulder in an effort to stem the flow of blood that was all too evidently flowing from the rent in his chain mail. His bascinet had been removed and his face was deathly pale, looking up as Rowan rushed to his side, attempting to give his son a smile, though it was more a grimace of pain.

'Damnation,' he said through gritted teeth, a cough causing tightness across his face.

Rowan wanted to reassure him and looked across at Leovald who sensed his loss for words.

'Here, help me sit him up,' the Welshman responded purposefully and together they slowly raised him to a sitting position but not without causing a cry of pain. 'We've got to stop the bleeding,' he explained as he unceremoniously tore a ragged strip from a bloodied surcoat belonging to one of the bodies lying close by, sensing Rowan's eyes watching him.

'Easy now, let's get this sorted and then you'll be as right as rain.' The reassuring words didn't seem to register on his father's face which had now gone even paler. Droplets of sweat could now be seen across his forehead as the Welshman finished tightening the makeshift bandage and then forming a sling.

'Don't worry he'll be sorted once we get him away from here,' he said in response to Rowan's worried look before glancing to his left with a frown.

Following the gaze he became once more aware of the sounds around him and he began to regain a sense of the battle that still raged a few feet away. To the centre he saw the men-at-arms were still embroiled in a bitter battle with the rebels. There was no longer a straight defensive line, but one that buckled and curved backwards on each flank, archers and men at arms now fighting together.

Without need of another word, Leovald took hold of his father's arm, raising it over his shoulder and lifted him to his feet. They walked him slowly back towards the top of the slope, past the lines of stakes piled on the grass that now seemed too easily discarded to where a number of wounded were now being treated. As Rowan approached he recognised Willard among the injured, helping an archer with what looked like a terrible cut to his leg swallow some water gratefully from a flask. All around survivors of the ongoing battle lay in agony, the rallying banner of the Earl firmly planted in the ground nearby.

Reaching the crest he glanced nervously back at the line of hacking and pushing men, the din of conflict still loud. The Earl galloped behind the battling soldiers, shouting words of encouragement, Sir Robert, now on foot, was in the thick of the fighting inflicting injury on the enemy to his front. For a moment Rowan was caught between the need to help his comrades fighting desperately less than a hundred yards away and to see his father safe.

'We're going to have to leave him here. Willard will look after him won't you boy?' Leovald had no such indecision.

His son nodded showing concern across his face as the Welshman lowered Rowan's father to the ground, accompanied by another moan of pain. 'Make sure he keeps his arm as still as possible and continues to put pressure on his wound.' He then slapped Rowan on the arm. 'Come on.'

'Go on, I'll be fine,' came the weak response from his father seeing his concerned glance, the words causing a short cough and pain once more flashed across his face.

He didn't want to leave but nevertheless allowed Leovald to steer him back down the slope. His feet moved almost unconsciously, his legs now feeing heavy, mentally still thinking of his father. It was almost surreal as he focussed his gaze back on the battle and at the scene that lay before him.

The two heaving lines of men still cursed and thrust weapons at each other. There had been some ground won by the rebels, the flanks pressed back on themselves compacting the Stafford force as the Earl continued to encourage his force from horseback in the centre of the line.

'Come on,' Leovald urged Rowan and although feeling weary he frantically looked for a discarded weapon to use. He still had his buckler strapped to his wrist but must have dropped his sword at some point, he couldn't remember when. So dragging the small shield from his arm and letting it fall to the ground he lifted his strung bow from his back reaching for one of the few arrows that remained in his belt. They ran to the right of the melee where he could see the men from his company now engaged in hand-to-hand combat. Shields deflected the steel tips of savagely thrust pikes, edges of swords smashed into chain mail or rand off plate armour. There was no order to the battle close up, everyone was fighting for their lives.

Stopping, Leovald next to him, his heart pounding rapidly and hoping the enemy would not turn their attentions on him, he notched an arrow. He aimed at a medium sized soldier who wore a coat of mail over a coarse dull vert tunic who was swinging a heavy sword at one of the archers. Without thinking he aimed the point of the arrow at the enemy's chest, he was not more than ten yards away, and let loose, not waiting to see the bodkin pierce the chain mail shirt, splitting the links easily to bury itself deep into the man's torso as he knew it would. Quickly tugging another arrow from his belt he continued sending shafts into the enemy ranks, not able to miss and continuing until his arrows were spent.

The deadly barrage from both men caused consternation among the enemy who began to shrink away from the flank, seeing their comrades falling to the lethal arrowheads and unable to break the stubborn resistance of the archers in front engaged in desperate combat. Rowan watched as the wing of the attack faltered and then broke. Rebels began straggling back towards the far slope from where they had begun their assault, some helping their wounded comrades.

Nearer the centre the fight continued. The Earl was still urging his men to kill the rebels even as Sir Robert just to his right, visor still closed, forced his way between two exhausted men-at-arms. His long sword arced down from left to right to smash into the mail aventail of a large bearded rebel. The enemy soldier was too focussed upon one of the men in front to see the swing that without his neck protection would have severed his head from his shoulders. He collapsed to the ground from the force, allowing the man he was attacking to viciously turn his poll axe and thrust its needle like point between the shoulder joint of his plate armour and bury deep into the man's flesh.

Rowan could hear the scream above the din of battle even as trumpet blasts rang out across the shallow valley, the repeated notes emanating from the opposite slope where the group of enemy horsemen, who to Rowan's weary anger now included Bayard alongside the broad bearded figure of Rhys Gethin stood.

The enemy foot soldiers, battered and breathing heavily but far from beaten and still numbering more than the Earl's began to step back from the conflict, holding their weapons warily, urged to fall back by their comrades and superiors.

'It looks like they're retreating, thank the Lord.' Leovald's voice was wary even as they watched the tableau below, too tired to join the fray.

The same went for the rest of the men. They let the enemy step back, exhausted and spent. There was little desire to pursue the retreating enemy. Even the Earl himself, visor now raised, was content to watch as the attackers continued to stream back to the opposite crest.

They left behind them a tidemark of bodies, many lifeless, others showing some movement signalling that despite being battered to the ground by the ferocity of the battle that they were still alive.

The mix of men-at-arms and archers, their line perilously close to breaking, began to look around, seeking friends, pushing shields and pikes aside as they searched faces, seeing if the men at their shoulders at the start of the battle were still the same men or whether they lay on the ground around them. The men gripped those friends who survived while others kneeled uncomfortably in their blood stained armour and surcoats tending the wounded where they could.

Rowan looked around him, the expanse of injured and dead were littered across the grassed slope, a couple of horses stood between the dead, well trained, patiently waiting for their masters who were lying on the ground either slain or badly injured. He saw Martin, sword hanging down by his side, a dazed expression on his face, his bascinet lost. Rowan gave him a weak smile. Walking over, he grasped his shoulder.

'We did it.' His friend said, almost disbelievingly, almost as much to himself as to his friend.

'We did that alright, and you've not even got a scratch.' Rowan tiredly replied.

Martin looked down at his body as though seeking reassurance from his own eyes to verify Rowan's words.

'You can trust me you know,' Rowan added, a deep sense of relief started to coarse through his own body despite the concern for his father.

Martin's expression too started to share the same feelings. 'I suppose so but I can tell you one of those big villeins nearly took my head off with one of those maces,' he muttered, with unusual deadpan humour.

Rowan's slight chuckle was interrupted by a shout from behind.

'Here lads.' Jerrard's gruff voice carried from twenty yards away where he was kneeling beside a prone figure, Eric standing by him.

With another lurch of his heart Rowan knew almost immediately that Daniel had been hurt.

Slowly at first and then quickening his pace, he followed Martin towards his friends, pulling up short as, sure enough, he looked down and saw Daniel lying on his back, his body inert on the flattened grass around him.

Jerrard had removed Daniel's bascinet slowly and revealed a savage mess of dried blood covering the right hand side of his face and hair.

'Is he dead?' Eric whispered to Jerrard but inadvertently loud enough for the friends to hear.

Rowan felt himself holding his breath.

'No, look he's breathing.'

Sure enough, Rowan could see the slight rise and fall of his friend's chest beneath the blood splattered surcoat.

'What happened?' Leovalds commanding voice was aimed at Jerrard.

'He was smashed on the head by one of those iron spikes a horseman was whirling around.' Eric replied before his friend could respond.

'A falconet, you mean,' Martin corrected him.

'Yeah, one of those, he fair flew through the air.'

The men would no doubt have laughed if the situation wasn't so serious.

'Good job he had his helmet on,' Jerrard lifted Daniel's bascinet. The side plate was a mangled mess, part of the thin metal actually torn and underneath was a mass of blood.

As Rowan stared at the crumpled steel, Daniel began to come round, moving his head slowly.

'Don't move,' Jerrard still kneeling pushed Daniel's shoulders gently back onto the grass.

Rowan looked around him as Jerrard stroked away their friend's long dark hair from the wound and spat on a torn piece of cloth to gently wipe the savage injury clean. The remaining men from Stafford were similarly tending their wounded colleagues or retrieving anything of value: weapons, coins, even foodstuffs from the bodies. He noticed however none ventured too far to where enemy bodies lay on the pasture between the forces, killed by the main volley of arrows fired by the archers what seemed an age ago. The enemy had retreated but had not disappeared from the summit of the opposite slope, reforming with shouts that carried across the battlefield.

It seemed the Earl was also watching the enemy because the vintenars soon began ordering the men to fall back up the slope. The men in turn hefted up their weapons wearily, many helping their wounded or simply exhausted comrades onto their feet as they headed up the low crest behind them.

Rowan watched as Jerrard and Leovald pulled Daniel to his feet and supported him between them. Eric and Martin quickly picked up any unspent and undamaged arrows they saw, making sure at the same time they shook the bodies nearby to ensure no comrades were left alive before retreating. With some dismay he could see scores of bodies lying unmoving and on the flank he recognised many of the men from his own company including, with a sickening sense of loss, the body of Bill Whitney, the snapped shaft of the arrow that had injured him earlier still stuck in his lower leg. Forcing himself out of his reverie for the dead he thought of his father and resolutely followed his friends, oblivious to the rising sound of jeers from the enemy that carried across the battlefield.

The force retreated over the summit. It was a distressing sight as the battered force assembled with sagging postures, stained armour and various tourniquets in evidence everywhere. It seemed to Rowan that the confident force that had ridden out just four days ago from Whittington had lost nearly a third of its men and those that were left were beaten. The seriously wounded had all been moved together and were lying or sitting clutching a variety of wounds. He saw Willard still crouched over his father and with some trepidation made his way towards them, kneeling down on one knee, his bow across his lap, relieved his father was still alive. His eyes were open and he was able to recognise his son. The bleeding had stopped although the cloth tied around his shoulder was now completely bloodied.

'What's happened?' his father tried a weak smile but his voice was painfully low.

'Don't worry, looks like both sides have had enough for now,' Rowan answered with as much confidence as he could muster. He was rewarded by a small acknowledging smile before his father closed his eyes, the wound taking its toll.

He stared at his face for a moment before looking round and seeing the Earl reverently walking beside a small group of soldiers who awkwardly carried on an improvised stretcher the body of the young esquire down the reverse slope towards the waiting men.

The noble passed his helm to one of his retinue, showing his brown hair matted against his head from the sweat and looked around his tired force who returned the gaze silently and expectantly. He paused for a moment looking at his men, a lack of emotion showing on the dirt streaked face. 'You fought well men and we've given the rebels a bloody nose, but for now we will head back to Whittington.'

The words had been spoken loudly for the majority of men to hear. There was a dull acceptance and relief among the survivors, Rowan knew in his own heart that there was no other choice. He would be grateful to get away from the blood-stained valley.

CHAPTER FIVE

The warning chimes of the steel triangle reverberated around the castle walls as the column emerged from the wooded hillside and the garrison stumbled hurriedly to their posts. William de Movran quickly climbed the dark and cold interior of the north tower as the dull metallic noise faded and he watched in silence, his gloved hand on the rough stone battlement as the column rode slowly down the track, passing the outlying marshland with its pools of water glinting in the late afternoon sun.

As the returning soldiers passed the collection of hamlets, the villagers halted their chores to watch the returning soldiers. William de Movran could tell that they had been in a fight. Even without the injured lying on the canvas litters beneath cloaks, the dark stained tunics and the bandaged faces, he could see from the way the men held their bodies that this was not a victorious home-coming. His hand tightened itself into a ball when he saw there was no sign of the gules and argent pennants, Bayard or the rest of his men and stared back towards the hillside wondering if they would appear. He stood there, his anger unabated as the column made their way in front of the walls and across the drawbridge. His eyes squinted towards the horizon as the sounds of the returning column now in the outer gatehouse began to reach him over the battlements and he could hear orders being given, cries of pain escaping from the mouths of the wounded and the clatter of armour and weapons as the men dismounted. He waited for a few more moments before wrapping his light cloak around him and descending the stairs determined to seek answers no matter what state the Earl and his men were in.

Emerging into the brightness of the courtyard he met the Earl just as he was striding towards Lord Fitz Warrin's chambers, his manner was purposeful, the dented plate armour, dark blood splatters on the dull metal, and dirt stained face all evidence of the fighting he had been involved in.

'You!' The words were aimed at William de Movran as he caught sight of the knight and halted in his tracks. He could feel the anger directed at him but was in no mood to placate the Earl, and could feel his own anger rushing upwards, feeling as though it would burst out of his mouth, a burning heat in his ears as the noble continued. 'My men died because of your mens treachery and as for there being no more rebels, you and your Lord must have been looking the wrong way.' The words were vehement and the soft tone had disappeared.

'I would ask that you consider your words sire.' The last word was said with some contempt for the younger man before him although he knew he would be reckless to openly challenge the noble. 'It seems I too have suffered and my men are no longer with you.'

'They are not with me de Movran because the

treacherous scullions turned sides and joined the rebels. Your men, under your command.' The accusation was clear and William de Movran found his fists clenched once more but before he could respond Lord Fitz Warrin, who had emerged from his chamber, interrupted.

'Earl Edmund, perhaps we should be having this conversation in my private chambers rather than here.' The Lord looked around the courtyard and at the few soldiers on its walls who were now looking down at the men.

'You are of course correct. I would indeed like to continue this conversation inside.' The Earl had quickly regained his composure and his speech had started to return to its normal considered tone, though William de Movran could tell he was far from finished.

As the Lord guided the Earl towards the stout oak door at the foot of the south eastern tower he caught his Lords warning glance before following them inside.

'Can I offer you a cup of wine?' Lord Fitz Warrin was immediately courteous and this, along with the fine surroundings, thick tapestries that adorned the wall, the fur rugs and small fire recently alight, seemed to help the Earl relax and avoid starting a confrontation immediately.

William de Movran took the opportunity, as he followed the men into the chamber to take a deep breath and compose himself, his mind still awhirl as to the fate of his soldiers and the battle that had taken place. Despite this, and taking notice of his Lord's gaze, he was careful not to prompt the Earl too quickly. Accepting a proffered cup of wine from his Lord he remained stood while they both sat themselves at a table by the fire.

'So Earl, I'm happy for your return but please tell me how you fared.' The enquiry was polite, ignoring the obvious state of the noble's armour and as William de Movran knew, the Lord's own resentment towards the continued presence of the Staffordshire force.

Finishing a large gulp of the watered wine and placing the cup on the table before stretching his neck left and then right, the Earl responded. 'We indeed met some rebels, many more than we anticipated.' For the moment he avoided repeating his accusatory insinuation. 'We were holding our own despite the numbers but then your mounted contingent turned sides and brought us to the brink of defeat.' As he spoke he stared at William de Movran standing behind his Lord.

Once again the knight felt a flush spread across his face. So his men, led by Bayard had defected and now he was being accused of knowing it. He stepped forward towards the Earl, his hand on the pommel of his sword, but the Lord had already read his reaction and raised a hand to silence him.

'I am shocked, truly I am. Certainly we had no idea of rebels in the area and the defection of my men is almost unbelievable if not heard from your own lips, isn't that so?' Lord Fitz Warrin addressed his question to William de Movran.

'It is.' growled William de Movran in response, consciously trying to keep from entering the conversation between the nobles. He knew he would be supported by his Lord who could argue much more eloquently than he could.

The Earl didn't seem totally convinced and he alternated his stare between the two men before with a deep sigh and seeming to make a decision continued, 'I think, my dear Lord, I am tired and if you do not mind would like to avail myself of your hospitality before possibly continuing this conversation later this evening?'

'Of course, I understand. Please let me know of anything more we can do.'

With that, the Earl raised himself nodded, first to William de Movran and then more slowly to Lord Fitz Warrin, looking into the eyes of the knight, searchingly. The Lord held the stare of the other young noble until he turned away without another word, lifting the iron latch of the door and making his way out into the courtyard beyond.

As soon as the thump of the door signalled the two men were alone William de Movran let go his spiel at his Lord. 'He has an audacity, he has brought this upon himself, bringing his men who too readily enjoy our hospitality and then of all things accusing us of treachery.' He threw his arms wide to emphasise his anger.

'I know, I know. I dislike them being here as much as you but we need not antagonise them.'

'Isn't that exactly what we must do?' The words came out of his mouth too quickly and he knew they were not considered.

'No.' The Lord despite his youth brought his authority to bear. 'For now we give them hospitality and allow them to do as they want.'

He simply nodded, admonished but inwardly fuming.

That night William de Movran walked through the castle gardens, he had dismissed his servant for he needed to think and the garden with its own low walls shutting out the sounds of the castle, the encroaching plants and the darkness helped his thought process. He sat upon one of the wooden seats and wondered, placing his head in the palm of his hands.

The English force had appeared unannounced, a surprise to Lord Fitz Warrin and himself and that had thrown his plans into confusion. Of course they knew that there was a large rebel detachment in the region and it was no surprise that they had been met in battle, the only problem was that even with the help of his men, Rhys Gethin had not managed to crush the royal force completely. Now all he had was a couple of his men-at-arms and Lord Fitz Warrin's garrison. He spat unconsciously onto the stone path, the white glob of phlegm disappearing into the darkness. Thinking back the unplanned appearance of the Earl's force had even prevented Bayard from killing the big Welsh sergeant when they first arrived, apparently one of the only people who the garrison may rally to if their loyalties lay elsewhere.

He looked up at the clear sky, seeking inspiration from the stars that were easily visible against the night time sky. The Earl's men, despite their losses, still outnumbered the garrison but in turn were, from what he had learned still largely outnumbered by Rhys

Gethin's force. It was a stalemate. The Lord was right. All they could do was wait and endure the presence of the Staffordshire force until they decided to retreat, for that was what they must surely do. He allowed himself a smile, it would just mean a matter of time before the original plan came to fruition.

He was just about to get up when the sound of light steps on the gravel path made his body tense and heightened his senses. For a moment he wondered if he had spoken out loud but just as quickly dismissed this thought. He waited, his hand automatically reaching for the rondel dagger at his side as he tried to slow his breathing.

The slight shape of a serving girl came into view. She was carrying a basket and started humming to herself, obviously enjoying the aroma from the flowers and the herbs, oblivious to William de Movran sitting on the bench. He watched the girl come closer, he could see that she had a slim figure despite the cloak wrapped around her. She was tall and had long hair that fell below her neck. He recognized her now from when she served the men and he pursed his lips, perhaps today's events weren't all bad. He waited until she was just yards away before standing up, causing the girl to let out a small cry, shocked by his sudden appearance.

***

Rowan and the rest of the company had passed the collection of wattle and daub homes in silence, the few villagers watching quietly as the troop rode past. Even the animals seemed to sense the nature of the column's return to Whittington and casually lifted their heads from rooting among the undergrowth to stare almost balefully at the men before returning to their search. The men rode between the two drum towers into the barbican courtyard, past the stares of the garrison on the gatehouse ramparts, emerging from the darkness of the thick stone archway where Rowan watched as the Earl strode straight across bridge into the inner bailey.

'He's in a hurry to tell him what a traitorous swines his soldiers are,' muttered Jerrard in Rowan's ear.

'He probably already knows,' responded Leovald in a hushed tone. Rowan's mind piqued.

'What do you mean by that?' the worry for his father was still raw.

'Oh nothing, don't mind me.'

'No, go on,' said Martin, joining in the conversation.

'I'm just being suspicious, think nothing of it.' Leovald didn't want to elaborate but that wasn't stopping the friends.

'When you think about it, they could be in it together.'

'What do you mean?' Eric had now joined in.

'Well he might be a sympathiser and might have a beneficial arrangement with that Glen, or whatever his name is.'

'Glyn Dwr you mean.' Rowan was keeping quiet, letting his friends explore their suspicion; a suspicion that was nagging away at him as he looked at Leovald.

His thoughts and their conversation were interrupted by the familiar growl of the Master-at-Arms. 'What do you think this is, a wench's washing day? Get the injured off those horses.' He turned to one of the garrison, his irritated tone continuing. 'How about some help here!' His tone making clear that it wasn't a request.

The wounded men were carried and supported through the inner courtyard and into the mustering hall while the body of the esquire was taken towards the Lord's own chapel. Leovald helped Rowan support his father while Jerrard and Martin helped Daniel, Eric walking quietly behind. Willard who had been ever-attentive, but quieter following the battle took the horses out towards the stables.

As they entered the hall, servants rushed about between the soldiers, arms full of fresh cloths or logs for the newly started fire that had already started to spew out thin tendrils of smoke. Others were already beginning to administer water or dressings to the wounded. Rowan together with Leovald, cautiously helped lower his father on to one of the pallets. There was little complaint, his pain having utterly exhausted him on the journey back to the castle.

Daniel had been laid down on a nearby pallet. His friends had managed to clean his wounds on the journey home in one of the streams, revealing a savage tear across his cheekbone down to his jaw, distorted by a massive bruise that was now beginning to show the tinge of yellow against the various hazes of purple. Rowan saw Rosalind rush over, her concern obvious. She knelt down next to his friend, her hand reaching to his dirty bandage across his face. Daniel attempted to turn his head away but Rosalind tenderly turned it back to face her. The moment was obviously private and as Jerrard and Martin moved away, so Rowan averted his eyes to see an elderly, slightly plump maid approach and without preamble start to mop his father's brow with a cloth, using water from a clay jug. She turned to Rowan and Leovald, ushering them away irritatingly with a wave of her arms, and glancing down at the bandage which had been applied and re-applied during the journey back to the castle with an obvious look of disdain for its application.

With a quick clench of his father's hand Rowan picked up his longbow and, alongside Leovald, followed Jerrard and Martin into the inner courtyard. Outside there were a few servants still rushing about but at the same time there was a weird sense of normality from the pain and bustle within the mustering hall.

The group crossed the small courtyard to some rough benches outside the kitchen where some of the other bowmen from the Earl's retinue were seated, their faces similarly strained and tired.

Taking a seat at one of the trestles a middle-aged woman, her long dark hair tied back, greeted them, her manner almost mothering. 'Here boys, have some broth. You look like you need it,' recognising the weariness and dirt streaked clothes, hands and faces, ignoring the caked blood on their armour and surcoats.

The men gratefully accepted the warm pottage of potatoes and carrots ladled out into the wooden bowls she had brought with her, thanking her as they took the proffered food and sat down eating hungrily. His appetite quickly responded to the warm smell, savouring the thick stew as it slid down his throat. They had eaten little on their retreat back through the hillsides, relying heavily on what rations remained and with no time to forage. The bowls were drained eagerly, husks of hard bread used to mop any morsel leftover.

Once finished he pulled his bow stave towards him, using the wax tablet from his pouch to rub its length slowly and methodically to protect the yew. The other men began to follow suit, either tending their own bows or unsheathing their swords and daggers and wiping them down using strips of cloths or simply using the edge of their surcoats. Silence among the friends was noticeable, much as on the march back, but eventually Eric broke the quietness.

'Do you think we'll have another go at the Welsh?' He spoke a lot less enthusiastically than before his first experience of battle, mused Rowan, and forgetting that most of the garrison were also Welsh.

'I doubt it. You saw how many of them there were and besides because of that treacherous swine, Bayard, we have even less men. It may even bring more soldiers to Glyn Dwr's cause.' Leovald ignored the Welsh reference but there was no hiding his concern.

Rowan looked at him intensely wondering about the loyalty of the garrison but before he could ask the big Welshman, Jerrard spoke up.

'If it wasn't for him and his horsemen we would have seen them off,' he said determinedly.

'Even then though, if we had planted those wooden stakes we would have stood a better chance,' offered Martin.

'Yeh should have used them, after carrying them half way across the countryside. You'd have thought the Earl would know better,' Jerrard continued grumpily.

'You forget though, how was the Earl supposed to know we would be betrayed? It wasn't as if they had horsemen at the start of the battle,' reminded Martin.

'Something similar happened at Pilleth a few years back,' Leovald added after a pause, probably unhappy at the reference to more treachery by his fellow countrymen.

Rowan now remembered the tale. The role of the archers, even though they were Welsh had caused some embarrassment and even some scuffles at Stafford castle over the following weeks when the news had first reached the garrison there. He could tell the reference to the defection still caused his friends, as well as himself to feel uncomfortable and it wasn't long before the conversation returned to tactics and the battle in an effort to gloss over the uncomfortable tale.

Rowan thought it was strange how, although they had plenty of time to reflect on their trek back to the castle, no one in the group had wanted to talk about it. It was as though the march back somehow hadn't closed the conflict and it was only when they were behind the protection of the stone walls that they could start analysing the events in the valley those few days ago.

Rowan put his tablet away as the group continued to talk, getting to his feet and stretching his arms. 'I'm off to see how my father is getting on.' With that, and the well wishes of his friends, he slung his bow and wandered back into the hall.

Inside the fires had done their job and warmed the interior, giving out a slightly acrid smell of smoke.

Servants and some soldiers continued to wander among the pallets or knelt next to the injured. As he made his way to his father's bed he saw that the plump, caring maid had moved on leaving his father's still figure lying underneath a blanket, unmoving. Immediately his heart began to quicken with concern.

'He's asleep,' came a quiet reassuring voice from his left. It was Rosalind, who still knelt next to Daniel, holding his hand.

Rowan smiled back, silently thanking her for her reassurance.

'How is he?' he asked, inclining his head towards his friend, who he could see was awake but appeared not to hear Rowan's question and remained staring blankly at the roof of the hall.

'He'll be fine,' Rosalind answered looking at Daniel caringly and stroking his long dark hair.

'Take care of him,' he replied unnecessarily and turned back to his father, putting his bow on the floor and unbuckling his sword belt before sitting down rather clumsily beside him on the reed covered floor.

Watching his father and the slow rise and fall of his chest he felt the stress of the previous days start to melt away, the warm fire contributing to his drowsiness as his eyelids started to close. Before he knew it he was asleep, head resting on his arms on the wooden frame of his father's pallet.

He awoke with a start; the darkness of the sky could be seen through the embrasures. The fire remained alight and the flickering candles provided illumination across the sleeping forms dotted around the hall which were largely silent. His father's face was still pale but was peaceful enough and with an inward groan he lifted himself from his knees before stretching, feeling the welcome relief of his back muscles and stifling a yawn before making his way into the clear night sky trying not to wake the sleeping forms around him.

He made his way through the castle and barbican grounds out towards the large barn where his friends were probably already asleep. It was as he was thinking of the fresh straw bedding awaiting him that he heard a faint cry coming out of the darkness.

Standing still for a moment, straining his ears, he thought it must have been a sound from one of the waterfowl in the marshes. He was ready to dismiss it just as another short but higher pitched noise permeated the darkness. It was no animal sound and Rowan felt a flash of concern sweep through him. His hand went to the pommel of his sword as he jogged across the small bridge towards the walled garden making sure his footsteps were loud on the wooden planks. There had been no more cries and his initial reaction to hurry towards the source of the sound was now tempered by the silent darkness, the shadows cast by the plants almost sinister.

He gripped the leather wrapped handle of his falchion tighter but didn't draw the blade.

He still wasn't convinced that he wouldn't end up looking foolish and that it would turn out to be a playful cry that he had heard, that he would more than likely be chastised for interrupting two lovers. His last thought appeared right for as he turned round the edge of the wall he caught the attention of two figures tightly embraced.

He was about to apologise but the words caught in his throat as he recognised the large bearded figure of William de Movran and crushed against his chest the much slighter figure of Rosalind who had hours earlier been at his friends side. His immediate reaction was one of embarrassment at finding Daniel's love in the arms of the knight who they had become suspicious of.

That soon changed though as he saw Rosalind scrape her shoe down the knight's shin, causing a curse of pain as she broke away, lifting the skirt of her dress in both hands and running straight past him, a shaken look in her face and tears in her eyes. There was no doubt the embrace had not been mutual as he looked back at the knight who had now recovered himself, reaching back to his full height after rubbing his shin.

'That'll teach me to underestimate a serving wench. Next time I'll have to teach her some manners.' There was coldness in the words and Rowan could see a smile spread across his face.

He didn't trust himself to reply and instead with as much composure as he could muster, turned and made his way back to the billet. The laughter from the knight followed him from the darkness.

Over the following days the castle, its inhabitants and the local population slowly started to return towards a feeling of normality. Weapons were cleaned and sharpened by the blacksmith, clothes darned and repaired by the seamstresses and ale consumed at the tavern outside the castle walls. The Earl didn't allow his men too much time to idle though, aware perhaps of the tension from their defeat and the lingering suspicion between his men and the garrison. There had already been a couple of brawls which had led to a stern lecture from Sir Robert and less formal though harsher warnings that left the men in no doubt of the consequences from the broad chested Master-at-Arms. Jerrard and more surprisingly to Rowan, Eric had already received their punishment for being involved in one brawl that had taken place in the mess hall, returning stinking and dirty from digging out cesspits outside the walls.

The butts at the edge of the castle grounds continued to provide a welcome focal point each day and Rowan and the rest of the archers looked forward to practising their skills, though he found himself drawn more and more into thinking about field tactics. This was an aspect of his learning that was new to him and he was keen to understand it more. He'd been practising with the longbow since the age of seven like the rest of his friends and boys across the country, but his first experience of battle had changed his perception on the importance of his own skill. He'd always felt that his life and the outcome of a battle would be down to the bravery and training of the men, but he now realised that as much depended upon the tactics of the commanders. So it was with a real hunger that he looked forward to the days when the men were marched out of the castle, to firmer pieces of land beyond the marshes to play out manoeuvres in preparation for more battles to come.

His father was getting better, but slowly, he had now been moved into a small temporary infirmary room to the right of the outer guardhouse at the foot of the western barbican tower along with two men-at-arms that had also suffered serious wounds. Three men had died from their injuries and the battle had now cost the lives of sixteen men-at-arms and twenty eight archers, including eleven from of his company.

Rowan would see his father each day to discuss the goings-on and share tactics that had been practised. He would often walk in and find Willard by his side like his own personal physician. He smiled to himself but it wasn't just the thought of Willard that lightened his mood because much as Rosalind had nursed Daniel, so too her friend, Catin had taken on the same role with his father.

Consciously he still found himself uncomfortable around the fair-haired serving girl and could manage nothing more than the briefest of courtesies that always ended with her leaving with the excuse of allowing him time on his own to speak to his father. He couldn't help himself looking into her blue eyes each time she spoke, inwardly gathering the courage to add something interesting but failing to utter any meaningful words before inevitably watching her slim body depart from the small room. More than once he was tempted to mention the near assault on her friend in the castle gardens but it was clear that, if she knew about it then it was a subject she did not wish to breach. He guessed this was partially because Daniel, though seemingly fully recovered physically from his wounds, still tended to sink into periods of depression despite her friends continued and open affection and Rowan did not want to risk impacting upon his mental state any further.

'You know you're a lucky man to have Rosalind looking after you. There's a lot of competition for her affections,' Rowan joked with Daniel one day as they sat on a small hillock waiting for their next turn at the practice butts, bows across their knees.

'I wouldn't blame her,' his sombre reply came as he felt the rough scarred tissue on the right hand side of his face.

Daniel's continued period of morose disturbed Rowan and his friends, so that when he wasn't present he would often be the topic of conversation, each friend wondering what they could do. It took Leovald however to stimulate the friends into more proactive action to help their friend.

'I hope you don't mind me saying but it seems that even though Rosalind hasn't talked about his mood with me, she can't help Daniel sort himself out.' He broached the subject one day while they were waiting for some of their clothes to be returned from the women who did the men's laundry for an allowance each month. 'Why don't you have a word with Catin?' He looked at Rowan, lifting his head up from the bundle of clean clothes just handed to him by a smiling elderly lady.

Rowan felt uncomfortable as the Welshman thanked the woman, reflecting on his previous failed attempts to broker conversations never mind talking about his friend in a manner which could be construed as behind his back. He looked appealingly at his friends for assistance.

'I'm not sure. I don't know her that well,' he said somewhat resignedly, almost knowing the answer.

'Oh and I suppose it's best if Eric or Jerrard speaks to her?' Leovald said with a bit of a wry smile.

Rowan couldn't help returning the smile, Eric would no doubt put his foot in it and Jerrard would in his own way get straight to the point and probably offend her.

'There's always, Martin, he's more likely to reason properly?' he suggested, not yet ready to accept the uncomfortable role that was being put to him.

'I grant you that but, as well as probably getting tongue twisted, he's probably too close.'

Out of all the friends, Martin had shown the most concern and worry for Daniel and while Rowan was uncomfortable with women, Martin was positively distressed.

'Okay, you're right. I'll have a word next chance I get.' He committed with a sigh and a slightly sickened feeling in his stomach.

The opportunity came soon and almost inevitably it was when he next visited his father in the small impromptu infirmary. His father was sitting up, his back against the rough stone wall and Catin gave a smile in greeting before starting to clear up the bandages she had just replaced with clean ones across his father's chest.

'How's the old man doing?' Rowan enquired, glancing at his father, all too aware of the effort he was making to enter into a longer dialogue with her than he normally did.

'The old man's fine you cheeky pup,' retorted his father, blissfully unaware of his attempt to engage more with Catin, who had now stood up and made to go off.

'Before you go can I have a word?' Rowan asked,

aware of his father's quizzical look.

'Of course,' she was no less enquiring in her look. Her clear, light blue eyes searched his own.

'Will you excuse us, father, I just want to have a quick word about Daniel?'

His father's expression turned to one of understanding as Rowan turned back to her and with his arm invited Catin out past the open oak door into the small outer courtyard. The sky above was grey and overcast as they headed towards the outer western bailey along the path that led across the small bridge. He wanted to find somewhere away from the hustle and bustle of castle life and with an inner resolve he led her behind the walled garden across another small bridge to the viewing mound below the rear castle walls.

He was nervous as he climbed the steps cut into the turf and waited for Catin to follow. Despite the dullness cast by the low lying clouds above, the viewing mound was peaceful and pleasant, giving panoramic views across the gardens and surrounding wetlands. Rowan had only ventured out once onto the mound despite his enquiring nature, preferring instead to keep to the gravel path between the walled garden and orchard which led to the archery butts.

As Catin arrived he hesitantly repeated the reason for asking her for her time. 'I just wanted to speak to you about Daniel.' She remained silent, waiting for him to explain further. 'My friends and I are worried about him and wondered if you had any thoughts?'

He was more than aware that he was sounding vague but he hadn't rehearsed what he was going to say and the friends truly didn't know what to do to break Daniels periods of melancholy. 'I know your friend Rosalind is worried too.'

Catin sat down on a wooden bench before replying, a sense of relief in her response. 'You're right, she does care for him but he keeps putting up a barrier. It's as though the scar has taken over his life.' Her hand went to her cheek, as though feeling his friends scar. 'She's tried to talk to him but doesn't know what to do either.'

It seemed that all parties were grappling with the issue though from the look on her face she was at least relieved to be able to talk about it. For a split second he wanted to take her hands in his but, as usual, his courage failed him.

'Rose told me about William de Movran.'

He followed her gaze towards the walled garden below as she continued.

'If it hadn't been for you God only knows what the man would have done.'

'Oh I just came along, it could have been anyone.' He could feel the flush spreading across his face.

'Either way you stopped that man and have kept quiet. Rose was wary you might mention it to Daniel.'

'I wouldn't, he's not himself and I don't know what he would do. He's depressed and we've tried to snap him out of it but with no joy. Everyone's noticed it.'

'I know I've watched him and when Rose takes her walks she says he hardly says a thing. She knows underneath there's the same man but he thinks everyone is looking at him and he's in danger of pushing her away. He thinks because of the scar she's with him out of pity.' There was obvious concern in her voice as she looked intently at him.

Without thought he took hold of her small hand and squeezed it, before quickly taking it away as he felt his face flush. To his relief she smiled, breathing deeply.

'Between us we'll be able to snap him out it, don't you worry.' Rowan stared into her deep eyes, seeking agreement, talking even as he felt heady from the touch of her hands. She nodded. 'Good, well I think the best thing we can do is show we're a merged force, what do you say?'

'I'd appreciate that, I really would.' Her face seemed to shine with relief as though a weight had been lifted.

The two kept talking for half an hour more, each sharing their concerns and as they did he could not help but register her smooth light brown skin and delicate neck. By the time they had finished they had reached an agreement to ensure they did everything in their power to help Daniel, but that was not the only reason for the broad smile on Rowans face and the pounding of his heart.

Sure enough, the following few weeks saw a lessening of Daniel's slides into depression as first Catin and then Rosalind became more and more part of the group. They gradually became more involved in their everyday chatter and activities, happily standing with the men as they practised at the butts, laughing at Jerrard's straight talking, holding discussions with Martin over some matter of justice or making sarcastic comments at Eric's shooting accuracy.

The next few weeks were a happy time, not just because of his shared glances with Catin but also his father's ongoing recuperation which continued to gather pace. He was soon a regular presence on the skyline of the castle walls supported by Willard at his side and he often greeted Rowan and the rest of the company as they returned from their resumed scouting duties in the surrounding countryside.

It was a vagary however in Rowan's mind that the men of Stafford had not been asked to provide guard duty since their return. This was despite the better relationships between most of the garrison and the Earl's men, although Lord Fitz Warrin and William de Movran remained aloof. Even Jerrard's mistrust had seemingly dissolved. The banter had resumed between the archers at the practice butts despite remaining competitive and the shouts of encouragement or derision for each arrow shot resonated across the platform in different accents. It seemed that Lord Fitz Warrin was adamant that responsibility for the castle remained firmly with the twenty or so men of the garrison. Once, when he had discussed it briefly with Leovald, Rowan came to understand how it made sense and that he couldn't argue with Lord Fitz Warrin's decision.

'One day you'll return back to Stafford so there would be no point.' The Welshman had replied when Rowan has asked him one day as they rode out to scout the surrounding countryside.

'Surely though it would give you less time to do guard duty, and besides I presume we won't return home until we try to deal with Glyn Dwr and his men?'

'I wouldn't be too sure. We'll need reinforcements and I can't see that happening too soon, bearing in mind the last couple of years, but I suppose you've got a point,' conceded Leovald. 'Mind you, I'd just be happy that you can keep snug in your beds at night time!' Rowan smiled at that. 'Seriously though, it's the Lord's castle and he's not exactly overjoyed at the success so far.'

Rowan nodded, his thoughts returning for a moment back to the battle in the shallow valley.

CHAPTER SIX

Almost a month had passed by since the battle with the rebel forces. Sorties had been dispatched from the castle but there was no news from the surrounding countryside. Despite this the Earl had also sent out messengers towards Shrewsbury seeking help from the garrison there.

According to Daniel the Earl's decision had not gone down well with Lord Fitz Warrin. 'He was apparently livid, throwing wine across the table when he heard, according to one of the girls,' he said glancing at Rosalind, as he and his friends shared a jug of ale after returning once more from manoeuvres outside the marshes.

'That's what Mary said,' Rosalind added almost defensively, before continuing, her tone lowered and glancing around the grounds, 'if anyone hears she'll get into serious trouble, the Lord doesn't like gossip coming out.'

Jerrard chortled. 'I wouldn't worry about that. Everyone knows he and the Earl don't agree on quite a lot of things'.

It was true. It often seemed the few times that the men had seen the Lord wandering the battlements or riding out through the outer gatehouse that he consciously tried to ignore the Earl's men. On the other hand their own commander had continued to talk to his garrison readily when passing, not showing any sort of conflict between him and the Lord.

'I wouldn't want to be one of his men,' said Jerrard. 'No offence, Leovald,' looking at the Welshman, he smiled, across the table.

'No offence taken,' Leovald replied in his strong Welsh accent with a genuine smile. 'Just remember who gave you boys the longbow.'

Everyone knew he could give banter back as good as he got and soon another jug of ale was ordered from the rather rotund owner of the village tavern, helping the friends continue their conversation long into the night.

The next morning, with the familiar taste of stale beer in his mouth and a hazy head, Rowan and his friends assembled. They jostled into position outside their comfortable straw billet though unusually this morning they were also greeted by Sir Robert.

'Attention,' Samuel Blacke's familiar but still commanding voice rang out.

Rowan and the rest of the force pulled their shoulders back, one arm on the hilt of their swords.

'Thank you Master Blacke,' Sir Robert's rumbling voice wasn't too dissimilar to the Master-at-Arms Rowan reflected. Though lower in volume, it nevertheless held a natural authoritative tone. Without preamble the knight continued. 'This morning the majority of you are going to ride to Shrewsbury with the Earl where hopefully reinforcements will be waiting to link with us. Some of you meanwhile will remain under my command. Your commanders have been advised.' Rowan glanced at his father who though not fully recovered had started to take his place on parade. 'That will be all.' The knight finished and nodding to the Master-at-Arms turned on his heels and left the bailey through the archway.

The information has been short and to the point.

'Silence.' The word crashed out in response to the murmurings that immediately started among the men, and was instantly obeyed. 'Right, you men from Stone have the honour of staying back to support Sir Robert's men-at-arms. The remaining men will pack up their gear.'

Rowan felt a tinge of disappointment that they weren't going with the Earl.

'I wouldn't have minded a nice few days in Shrewsbury,' grumbled Jerrard, sharing the same feeling aloud.

'I wouldn't be too disappointed,' replied Daniel, 'I went there once and it's only got enough alehouses and brothels to keep you going for a year or two.'

The change in his friend over the past few days had been remarkable, Rowan reflected. As the eager look in Jerrard's and Eric's faces and the levity of Daniel's comment was enough to get the rest of the friends laughing out loud as they followed Rowan's father to get more specific orders.

The column set off mid morning, just over fifty men-at-arms and archers, with the Earl's banner and standard at the head.

Rowan and his father watched from the drawbridge as they made their way parallel to the castle walls before heading up the track past the village and into the woods, a dust cloud surrounding them as hooves kicked up the dry dirt. His father had explained that the size of the Earl's force was large enough in case they encountered Rhys Gethin's force while the depleted company, the nine archers working with the Sir Robert's five men at arms remained to bolster the defences and continue their scouting duties in the nearby countryside.

It wasn't much, he thought, but almost doubled the remaining garrison so there were enough to defend the walls and, as he was to find out, the departure of their comrades brought an unanticipated benefit to Rowan and the remaining men from Staffordshire.

With less men crowding the fortress and the village, the small number of archers and men-at-arms enjoyed more banter with the local garrison and villagers, more time at the practice butts and a general feeling of contentment. During this period he relished the opportunity to get closer to Catin, though never able to push himself enough to make a more definite advance upon her affections despite an increasing urge to press his lips upon hers every time he spoke to her. How he longed to be like Daniel and Rosalind who now seemed to be closer than ever, happily holding hands as they spared time from their chores and wandered around the grounds. Even the memories of battle started to fade and it felt that the threat from the rebel forces had simply just melted away.

That was until one late afternoon when, as normal, Rowan and his friends had been sent out to scout the land, Leovald as he often did accompanied them.

It was a pleasant day despite the large patches of light grey cloud overhead and they were relishing their surroundings as they rode through the vibrant countryside. Their mood was helped by the half score of the numerous hares they had killed, the animals abundant and often seen hopping and sprinting across open spaces between coppices and woods surrounding Whittington.

They were walking their horses on the edge of one of these tree lines, around Babbins Wood in single file returning towards the castle when in the not too far distance a horseman came into view off to their right, racing along a part worn track made in the otherwise lush grass. There was something about the obvious urgency that made the men stop their individual discussions and banter, perhaps Rowan thought it was the contradiction between the man's haste and the calmness of their surroundings that made him and his friends halt their mounts. As the horseman came closer, hooves pounding along the track soon to ride past the small column, seemingly unnoticed, he recognised that it was not man but a youth and even more surprising, by the look of his attire and the blond straggly hair it looked like Willard. He glanced at Leovald enquiringly who was also studying the rider closely, probably with the same suspicions dawning upon him.

The boy had his head down and it was in doubt who was in control, for the horse despite obviously being one of the palfreys was proving too much for the rider, probably ten hands in height, pounding onwards across the meadow.

'That's my Willard,' Leovald's tone was indignant.

'Better hail him before he ends up in Stafford,' Rowan quipped.

'Hey!' Jerrard duly obliged testing the strength of his lungs and shouting at the top of his voice.

Around him Eric, Martin and Daniel cringed at the assault upon their ears even though it was at the second attempt that Jerrard's hail had the desired effect.

The boy's face almost touching the horse's neck, lifted slightly turning to his right, a look of surprise on his young face as the horse oblivious to the recognition between them galloped on. It was almost another fifty yards or so before Willard was able to slow it down, pulling frantically at the reins and eventually able to halt the sweating palfrey, its head rearing against the harsh tug.

'He'll be in trouble for taking that out of the stables,' laughed Eric, 'you watch what excuse he'll come up with.'

'He'll be cursing his small heart that he rode into us,' responded Daniel, 'not to mention you,' he added, turning to look at Leovald.

'Well if he's taken that horse without permission he'll soon know better.'

Rowan again chuckled, Willard's enthusiasm for everything and his honest nature made him a favourite of the company, not to mention Rowan's father who continued to receive his help while he recuperated from his wounds.

Willard had managed to turn the horse round but rather than walk the animal towards the group, had jumped off and was now running through the foot high grass towards the men at the tree line. They glanced at each other, their joviality pierced and a growing sense of concern as they dismounted.

'Found you,' the words though spoken through gulps of air only confirmed the sense of uneasiness that had swept upon the group.

'Slow down boy,' ordered Leovald, a hand upon his sons shoulder. 'Take your time and tell me, what's the rush?'

His concern, Rowan noted, meant that taking the horse was the last question he was going to ask. The men crowded round as Willard began to blurt out his story.

'Your father,' glancing at Rowan 'sent me to warn you. He and the rest of your men have been taken captive.'

No sooner than these words were out of his mouth than the rush of questions came from the friends. As usual Rowan preferred to stay silent for the moment gathering in the information as the flood of questions became too many for Willard to respond to in an ordered way and he just looked at each person dumbly.

'Leave the boy and your questions until he's got the whole story out,' ordered Leovald, his natural authority among the group taking over.

And so the story unfolded to the group's astonishment. The remaining men left at the castle, apart from the friends who had gone scouting had been rounded up and locked up by Lord Fitz Warrin. Straight away Rowan reflected it was a good thing the group had set off early in the morning in the expectation of a fine day and with added relief that it sounded that there was no bloodshed among the Earl's men.

'How did you get away?' he asked when Willard had finished telling what he knew, not usually the first to ask a question but his concern for his father pushing his normal reserve away.

'I was with your father, walking around the grounds as we've started to do before breaking fast when we caught sight of some of the garrison, armed and heading towards the stable block. Your father knew something was happening and so we crossed to the garden to get a better vantage point and that's when we saw your men being escorted out of their billets, arms on their heads.'

'What then?' asked Rowan anxiously as much for his father as for the fate of the men.

'I don't know, your father made me leave and try to warn you.'

What happened to him?' He tried to keep a calm tone but was inwardly anxious to know his father's fate.

'I don't know, I just ran and hid in the orchard. I waited a while.' He looked at Rowan, distress showing in his face. 'Your father never came so I crossed the bridge onto the platform and swam the ditch. I got the horse from one of the village paddocks.' Willard's words were now coming through sobs that he was unable to contain.

'Come on boy, you've done well. Let's sit down over there,' Leovald said reassuringly to his son, ushering him away from the group who watched silently, lost in their own thoughts.

'Do you think he could have got it wrong?' Daniel asked apparently still not able to accept this change of events in a hushed tone.

'You don't think he could have made this up surely? Just look at his face.' Martin as ever the considered member of the group replied.

'I can't believe we've been tricked again, the traitorous pigs need to be hung by their Welsh necks.' Jerrard's response wasn't surprising, maintaining his characteristic bluntness. 'I knew we shouldn't trust them after that Bayard turned traitor.'

'That's not strictly fair,' Martin countered, 'we've got on with most of the garrison, and besides, you wouldn't class Leovald as a traitor, I'd trust him with my life.' He kept his voice low looking over his shoulder to where the Welshman and his son were now sitting on the grass having led the sweat lathered horse that Willard had recently dismounted to the trees.

The men continued their discussion, Rowan maintaining his silence as the conversation moved from disbelief, to anger and then concern for their comrades. He thought of his father and hoped that Willard's words were right and he was unhurt while his chest tightened thinking about Catin and her safety. He prayed she would be unharmed, knowing that despite her closeness to the group, her humour was infectious among the soldiers and she was well liked among the garrison. He looked at Daniel and guessed he was concerned too. It was a good thing Rowan thought that he still didn't know about the episode with William de Movran in the castle gardens, a knowledge he wished he too was unaware of, especially at this moment.

As the conversation turned to the matter of their own survival and the risk that the garrison had sent men to seek them out, Leovald and his son returned to the group, the friends watching them approach expectantly.

'Willard here has told me all he knows and we've got a decision to make.'

'What do you mean. Hells teeth! Isn't it obvious? Let's get out of here and follow the Earl to Shrewsbury,' Eric interrupted quickly, his voice slightly higher than his normal pitch.

'Let me sit down and I'll tell you,' answered Leovald calmly, unperturbed by Eric's anxiety.

He ushered his son to sit beside him cross legged on the grass while the group of five friends shuffled round to make space so they were sat in a rough circle.

'It seems that we have a decision to make,' he repeated, glancing briefly at Eric. 'What my son said is true and it looks like for whatever reason the Lord has decided to imprison your men. The good news is that there's no sign that your men have been harmed. Your decision is whether to try and rescue your friends or, as I see it, make for the nearest friendly garrison, most probably Shrewsbury and seek help.'

The friends looked at each other. No one had the courage to be the first to speak and it was with reluctance that Rowan found himself offering his opinion first.

'Can we at least try to find out where they are held and see if we can rescue them? I don't like the idea of just leaving without knowing more.'

To his relief he was backed up by Martin. 'We need to find out a bit more before we just head to Shrewsbury, besides the Earl should be arriving in the next few days or so, so it might be better if we stayed around here and waited for the reinforcements to arrive.'

Jerrard and Daniel echoed their support, less rationally but with determination. Only Eric seemed less than enthusiastic putting forward his preference for the friends to leave.

'We can't do much when they're behind castle walls.' Even as he looked round he knew his argument was already lost.

Leovald brought the consensus of the group together. 'Looks like we should find out more about your friends predicament then,' he said with wryness in his expression. If Rowan didn't know better he'd have thought the big Welshman had expected such a response despite the dire situation. 'Willard says your men, when they were taken prisoner, were in their billet which thankfully places them outside the walls themselves. Obviously if the Lord wants to keep them outside the fortress, then that should make it easier for us.' He stared at each of the members of the small group to make sure they were paying attention. Satisfied they were he continued. 'Now, if we follow Willards example we can skirt round the castle and try to get into the grounds by the southern approaches, just past the parallel ditches and opposite the archery platform.' At the mention of the water defences Rowan glanced at Willard seeing the still damp clothes and wrinkling his nose at the stagnant smell that accompanied them. 'Hopefully we can then hide among the trees near the butts and try to find out what's happening.'

Martin agreed, 'There'll be less chance of us being

spotted from the walls going that way and besides they probably won't even expect us to know what's happened.'

'Or more likely they wouldn't expect half a dozen men to try and enter a castle secretly,' Eric grumbled, but Rowan could tell he was becoming less reticent about the decision.

'Exactly, and besides we're not entering the castle, we're just doing a bit of scouting and finding out what's happening to Rowan's father and our friends.'

'Including Rose,' Daniel added with a low voice, his face resolute.

'Right, let's agree the details.' Leovald brought their attention back to the task in hand and the group of archers was soon caught up in planning their incursion.

Their discussion continued into the late afternoon with the mood of the group one of determination and almost eagerness before the men lifted their bow casings across their backs. The mounts were readied, girth straps tightened, the remaining supplies stored in the canvas saddle bags. Taking up the reins some of the horses like Constance shook their heads as if reluctant to carry the six men and one young boy towards the castle.

They got within a mile of the walls before the small group consciously moved into the protection of trees, keeping on the reverse slope making sure there was no chance of being spotted by an alert sentry on one of the towers or any random scouting party. How things had changed, reflected Rowan, instead of going to support the castle they were now seeking to infiltrate it. He involuntarily shook his head at how things had turned.

By the time the men rested under the cover of the green canopy of trees the sun was going down. They looked across the open marshland towards the archery butts opposite, relieved to see no sign of any sentries.

'Looks like they're not expecting us,' Rowan whispered to Leovald, making conversation to cover the nervousness that was increasing minute by minute.

'It'll help,' answered the Welshman who was also lying on his front like Rowan.

They stared out across the wetland with its small islands of grass among the muddy pools of water, the distant practice range, the copse of trees behind and the backdrop of the high stone ramparts that rose menacingly into the darkening sky.

As if to heighten his anxiety and doubts over the wisdom of their simplistic plan, Leovald carried on. 'Remember we've got to get to the ditch in the first place so it's not exactly going to be quick going.' He knew the marshland surrounding the castle would be hard work never mind having to cross the moat, which despite the dry summer, still retained a level of dirty stagnant water. 'On the plus side we've got only one ditch to cross instead of the two to the east,' his Welsh humour coming out, not that it stopped Rowan thinking of the cold shallow waters, his weak smile did not reflect the wide grin of the Welshman.

The group were initially busy while they waited for the sun to disappear, and under the security of the trees, filled their horse's feed bags with fallen branches in preparation for their insurgency. As the task was completed the group became increasingly serious, self reflecting and more silent as the time dragged on, moving unnaturally slowly. The men remained a few yards into the wooded slope where Rowan sharpened his arrow heads, the rasp of the wet stone not too loud as he rhythmically honed the thin needle-like point of the bodkin tips while Jerrard and Eric seemed content to try to sleep. The rest stared around their surroundings, their backs leant against the rough bark of the tree trunks. He looked at Willard with a sense of envy for he, out of all the group, seemed the least affected as he casually whittled away at a piece of wood.

The plan had been agreed almost unanimously among the friends though some had been more reluctant than others. Willard would go back the way he had escaped, crossing into the grounds ahead of the group to find out what he could about the captives but foremost to keep watch for danger as the more conspicuous and heavily laden men attempted to cross the marshes and the butts. To Rowan's surprise, and possibly upon reflection, guilt, the strongest advocates of this tactic were Leovald and his son. During the ride towards the castle Rowan had discussed the decision with Martin, knowing he would have fully considered the risks, as he had with his earlier reaction to returning to the castle.

'It doesn't seem right putting him in danger again, he's done enough,' he suggested riding alongside his friend out of earshot of the others.

'You're probably right,' agreed his friend, as he twisted in his saddle to look at Rowan's concerned face, 'but he's definitely the least likely to be spotted out of us all, knows the lie of the land and his father knows that. Leovald and his son have lived here all their years, and don't forget he may not even be arrested even if he is spotted. He's a local.'

Rowan was dubious about the last point, since Willard as well as his father were seen by many now as part of the Earl's force, nevertheless he was clear on Martin's thoughts and the logic behind it. As they had sat round earlier in the afternoon and having made the decision to try and somehow seek to gain more intelligence about the rest of the company, it was Leovald himself who had first suggested that his son play a crucial role in helping the small group of friends.

'We'll have to wait until the light fades and then Willard here can go back in the way he came,' Leovald held his sons shoulder and looked round the group, an air of confidence about his statement that meant no one argued straight away at the proposal. 'Once he's crossed he can warn us of any danger.' The men had continued to discuss the plan but the decision had been made and whichever way they looked at it no one else could come up with an alternative that provided a better means of scouting their approach and keeping a lookout.

CHAPTER SEVEN

Rowan's nerves threatened to get the better of him as the sun disappeared altogether to be replaced by an increasing darkness and Leovald was satisfied enough to let his son rapidly make his way, crouching low, down the slope to the marshlands. Willard's silhouette became smaller, occasionally moving to the left and the right before being completely lost from the sight of the watching group.

'We'll give him a good two hours before we set off,' reaffirmed Leovald as they had previously agreed, and so the anxious wait continued.

The minutes passed and the darkness descended quickly. Rowan could still make out the grey stone walls of the castle, now illuminated by the torches on the battlements but the surrounding lands were hidden in blackness with visibility down to three hundred yards.

After half an hour he could contain his anxiety no more and turned to whisper to Leovald. 'If we wait much longer we'll have no chance of finding our way through the marsh and to the ditch at the right place.'

Leovald looked at the other friends pensively. It wasn't that long since Willard had made his way towards the fortress, certainly not as long ago as his father had planned. After a little more hesitation the Welshman agreed. 'You're right,' his tone hushed. I didn't think the night would draw in this fast.'

With an accompanying nod of agreement, the men shuffled backwards and gathered their kit. Rowan tightened his belt, checked the comfort of his sword and buckler, ensuring his arrow bag was pulled close, and his bowstrings were held securely within the protective waterproof canvas. He reluctantly left his bascinet and surcoat with his mount and picking up his bow in one hand and the improvised wood filled faggot in the other followed his companions back to the edge of the trees.

As the group halted Leovald turned briefly to his friends. 'Remember to keep a distance so we've less chance of being spotted,' and with not a further word he was off. There was no backward glance as he ran cumbersomely down the slope towards the marshes.

Rowan looked at his friends worriedly, they hadn't decided in which order to follow Leovald. 'Who's going next?' He whispered.

The men's faces, though hard to distinguish in the shadows looked at him dumbly. They obviously hadn't given it much thought either.

'Right then, I'll go last.' It wasn't that Rowan was being brave and his decisiveness took himself slightly by surprise, he usually waited for others to give their opinion, but he was now totally committed. 'Why don't you go next Martin. Then Jerrard, Daniel and then you Eric, in that order?'

'Sounds good enough to me,' answered Martin, followed by assenting nods from his friends.

'That's settled then.' Rowan looked back in the

direction that Leovald had set off in and was no longer visible. 'Better hurry. Ready Martin?'

Before his friend had chance to answer, Jerrard gave Martin a rough shove and found himself out in the open, looking back accusingly not seeing the funny side of things before hefting his bundle and setting off in a similar stumbling run towards the castle grounds, shrouded in darkness.

Rowan gave Jerrard a reproachful look but his friend, judging from the large grin across his face, his teeth bright in the darkness either didn't see it or take notice. To his left Eric stifled a guffaw. Then to his own horror, he found himself smiling too, a hand over his nostrils. A laugh choked in his throat threatening to spill out into the night time sky despite the deadly venture they were undertaking, remembering Martin's bemused face as he stood out in the open.

It took a few moments to regain their composure and with his eyes still glistening with tears, Rowan watched as his remaining friends set off disappearing one by one from sight into the darkness. The closer it came to his turn, the tighter his chest became, feeling the beating of his heart against his ribcage, the stifled laughter just a few minutes ago had been replaced by nervousness.

Barely a minute had passed between each friend leaving the protective cover of the trees but it had felt like an eternity. Drawing on his receding levels of resilience and with a deep breath he hefted his own bag and made in the direction of his friends who could no longer be seen.

The balancing act with his bow, arrow bag and faggot made his run as cumbersome as the rest, the ground becoming less firm and soggier. His leather boots began to splash into icy cold puddles of water and he was forced to slow his pace dramatically. His breathing became laboured and he had to pick up his feet to take a pace forward, focussing upon the ground immediately in front of him, seeking any reliable tufts of grass that would give him a firm footing and avoiding the sucking mud.

Occasionally he halted, allowing his breathing to slow, staring into the darkness trying to locate his position in relation to the platform of open grass, seeking to rendezvous at the earth rampart somewhere in the vicinity as his friends. As far as could tell he was probably no more than another eighty yards away, the darker silhouette of raised earth just visible. He was relieved that he had not strayed too far to his right, consciously trying to keep the tree line of the archery platform between him and the castle walls. With a deep breath he hefted his equipment once more and made the now arduous steps forward, the mud clinging heavily to his boots and breeches and it was relief when he was able to fall down, his back against the shallow earthen wall which provided a sense of safety among his friends.

Even as he leant against the bank and before he had managed to utter a word, the big frame of Leovald slithered over the top and disappeared from view. With a shiver Rowan heard the faint splash as the Welshman must have lowered himself into the moat on the other side of the rampart. The other friends followed suit, silently pulling their loads with them, tenseness permeating amongst the group. Then, before he knew it, he was once again alone, the night time sky increasing in its darkness, silence around him, pierced only by the croaking of a frog or honk of water fowl.

With conscious effort he rolled to his side, adjusting his grip on his equipment before pulling himself up and slithering over the mound, twisting himself round so his feet were the first to feel the coldness of the water in the ditch and letting his body slide down towards the unmoving dark liquid.

The water was harshly cold and his whole body tensed as it rose above his boots and then up towards his waist. With a start he found the water much shallower than he had thought and his feet started to sink into the thick mud at the bottom of the ditch. He found himself having to use the bank as support as he dragged his legs free from the mud's clinging grip before pushing the improvised buoyancy aid into the water, causing a few ripples as he did so, placing his bow and arrow bag on top in an effort to keep them as dry as possible.

Pushing forwards his breath was taken away by the coldness that quickly invaded his body. Involuntarily he puffed out his cheeks as he rapidly expelled air from his lungs, following this with a sharp intake of breath as his body struggled to adapt to the temperature. He kicked his legs frantically, making sure they remained under the water so no splash could be seen or heard but trying to make sure they didn't drop into the muddy bottom either which proved impossible because of the shallowness of the water. It was no more than three feet deep and he paddled forwards awkwardly, his arms either side of the buoyancy aid, his eyes focussed on the nearby bank.

Gratefully he felt the bundle nudge against the sloping earth and risking the clinging mud that sucked at his leather boots, threatening to strip them from his legs, he lifted his still dry weapons up the bank. The mud clung between his fingers as he dragged himself up the slope, turning over onto his back breathing heavily.

'Lord have mercy,' Eric offered, also lying on his back close to where his friend had emerged, his thin frame suffering from the wet earth and the cold.

'At least there's no more water,' Rowan answered encouragingly, letting his breathing calm down to a more regular rhythm. 'Time to go in a minute', he nudged his friend.

Eric responded with a groan. 'At least we know the rest of the boys are about.'

Rowan looked at his friend and following his eyes to see the dark outlines of the now discarded sodden bags of branches lying in a jumbled state along the slope, not too far from where they had emerged. He turned back to his front and lifted his head above the crest where he could discern the tree line fifty yards away.

'I can't see the rest but they must have already headed to the trees,' he whispered, turning to his friend who simply nodded. 'Okay, time to go' he said encouragingly but also more forcibly to his friend, sensing he would have been happy to wait there a while longer.

Lifting himself to his feet, the soaked clothes now hanging heavily, he picked up his arrow bag and bow and dragged himself over the crest of the earthwork. Crouching, and with his wet feet initially slipping on the grass, he ran towards the dark but welcoming orchard grove, fearing at any moment the cry from a sentry.

To his relief no sudden shout of alarm came and reaching the safety of the trees he slapped Eric on his back as they both took the opportunity to allow their breathing to recover, their hands on their knees.

'Alright boys,' Leovald's distinct accent pronounced as ever, came out of the darkness followed by his silhouette and that of Jerrard, Martin and Daniel.

'You took your time.'

'Funny,' Eric retorted, trying to stop himself from coughing from the exertion.

The friends' mood was less tense for the moment, happy to be in the cover of the trees, the night time sky dark around them. The only light came from the stars and the torches on the distant castle walls, the gnarled trees around them providing a sense of security as they sat together.

'What do we do now then?' asked Eric to no one in particular.

'Willard hopefully would have scouted from here to the east, hiding in the garden, making sure we weren't spotted or ambushed. Then he'll take a quick look towards the eastern bailey to see if he can spot anything of use before meeting us here,' Martin answered with a hint of exacerbation. They had discussed the plan numerous times.

'So we just wait?'

'Yes, we wait.' Leovald answered. At the mention of his son the tone was abrupt and brokered no further conversation.

A period of silence among the group followed as they waited, alert in the darkness, searching out any change in outline that showed Willard returning as planned.

Rowan began shivering despite the mild night and could not help but rub his arms as the time passed. The other friends too became restless either from their damp clothes or tenseness as Willard failed to appear, a concern he was beginning to share.

Each man was lost in their own thoughts as he judged midnight come and go, his own adrenaline and anxiety prevented him from feeling the least bit tired, helped by the distinctive smell from the stagnant water.

His nose rankled at the odour as he looked at the two friends who had already begun to succumb to sleep. Eric and Jerrard were again seemingly content despite enduring the same damp and smelly clothing, each curled on the ground beneath the trees while he and his friends continued to stare out in their discomfort towards the outer bailey and its orchard and walled garden.

In the silence Rowan's thoughts began to wander to how he and his friends could extricate themselves if Willard still did not appear before it became too light. The plan relied heavily upon not being seen and the more time went on the more he realised they were in danger of being captured or even worse. Despite their current relative safety, the trunks and calf-high grass would afford them little cover in daylight. The moat and marshlands, now at their rear, meant that if they were discovered evasion was unrealistic. One look at Leovald though made him keep his concern to himself. There was no way he would leave his son alone and that thought served to strengthen his own resolve.

'It's going to start becoming lighter soon,' he said turning to the rest who were still awake. We should be alright to stay here when it starts to get light. It's not as though they're going to do any archery practice today.'

His friends looked at him as though he was trying to make a bad joke, all but Leovald who was seemingly weighing him up, looking for the reasoning behind his comments. No one spoke, but seeing the look in their friend's face and noticing the Welshman's silence the others simply nodded their ascent, although Daniel and Martin were clearly disconcerted at the proposal and its inherent risks.

Seemingly committed, the group, with the exception of Leovald who stayed to keep a watch for his son returning, withdrew deeper into the copse of trees, edging backwards away from the small bridge that connected the archery butt platform to the main orchard and gardens opposite. They gently shook awake Eric and Jerrard. Daniel had his hand poised to cover his bearded friends mouth in case a loud oath erupted. He needn't have worried, for though it took a couple of hearty shakes, Jerrard opened his eyes, rubbed them and without so much as a groan, acknowledged the scarred face of his friend. Eric was a different matter, he didn't curse but he certainly groaned and Rowan could hear Daniel's hissed command for him to keep his noise to himself.

Their intentions to remain were shared as they looked round at the limited cover around them.

'Swear on a cross,' muttered Eric not usually known for his curses, but expressing his unhappiness at the group's decision to stay.

'It looks like we couldn't have done worse if we tried.' Jerrard added dourly.

The men knew they could easily find themselves in trouble. In the daylight it wouldn't take much to be spotted by anyone practicing at the butts.

'Whose great idea was this?' Eric wasn't about to let the opportunity for further pessimism to go unvoiced and Rowan was grateful when Martin intervened.

'With so few men they're not likely to practice archery are they? We've just got to hope no one wants to come picking fruits on this side of the ditch.'

Rowan looked up at the misshapen branches overhead, the distinct round shapes of apples hanging heavily.

'Besides,' Martin continued, 'if the worst came to the worst we can hide on the reverse slope of the moat.'

He hadn't thought about this option but suddenly remembered the discarded sacks of branches. 'The faggots!' It was his turn to swear.

'Might as well make myself useful.' Daniel, who had stayed silent during the conversation offered simply but readily.

Rowan reflected there was a sense of purpose about his friend. 'I'll go with you.' He looked round the group as he put himself forward, feeling a greater confidence within as he made the offer.

'You're fine, it doesn't take two of us.'

He didn't know whether to feel relieved or disappointed.

'There's more chance of two of us being spotted.' Daniels firm response stopped him from protesting further.

'Good luck,' he offered, not knowing what else to say. This was followed by similar wishes from the rest as Daniel silently handed his bow to Martin before setting off across the practice range, his shadow disappearing into the darkness.

The sky was soon showing off a myriad of red hues as dawn began to break. Daniel had returned dragging the six fodder bags, emptying their contents among the trees and Leovald had, with a dispirited gait, returned from his vigil at the edge of the orchard. There had been no sign of Willard, nor had there been any sort of commotion. The friends attempted to reassure the big Welshman that this was a good sign and though Leovald had made attempts to agree with them his worry was obvious. Even if they had not committed to remain, Rowan was sure Leovald would have stayed despite the very real chance of being spotted by the garrison.

Their surroundings were sparse and they set about making the best use of the cover afforded to them, lying by tree trunks and any grass that was high enough to shade the outline of their prone bodies. Rowan, his head resting on his crossed arms as he peered through the stalks of grass, was worried. If anyone looked with any purpose into the copse then the men would surely be spotted and Leovald's next words didn't help the increasingly sickening feeling in his stomach.

'We'll have to lay up in the orchard all day and see if anything happens. Hopefully if Willard's hiding he can get to us again in the late evening.'

'And if anyone comes in the meantime?' Eric asked.

'Then we remain here, retreat to the ditch, or if worst comes to the worst we'll have to deal with them.'

Rowan was anxious to evade rather than fight and his friend's last words caused him to close his eyes tightly and make a silent prayer that they would not be discovered. He then added a silent plea for the safety of his father before his thoughts returned to Catin, remembering her ready smile and slim figure.

'Rowan.' He recognised the hushed voice of Eric. 'Rowan, are you awake?'

The sharp sound of a cockerel from the nearby outer bailey accompanied his friend's voice and he realised with a start he had fallen into a brief sleep, the exertions and worry of the past few hours catching up on him, the sweet smelling grass providing a comfortable bed.

'I am now, but for pity's sake keep your voice down.' He was instantly aware of his surroundings and the situation they were in.

'By all that is Holy, it's freezing.' It was typical of Eric to be complaining but he agreed with his friend. Despite the relatively mild summer night and his short sleep, his boots, hose and jacket had still retained their dampness.

Scratching at his short stubble he yawned silently, the jaw muscles stretching to their limit before lifting his arms above his head, trying to rid the stiffness from his bones. 'Anything happened?'

The sky had lightened significantly so he could peer through the gnarled trunks towards the orchard opposite and the tops of the grey stone castle turrets above. His friend's manner was calm and his shake of the head meant that there was no immediate reason to worry.

Rowan rolled his shoulders and twisted his back to relieve the knots in his muscles, feeling with satisfaction the release of tension before picking up his bow stave and wiping away the dew. He then drew each arrow one by one from the protection of their canvas bag, hoping the wax covering had done its job. Checking the goose feathers were dry and that the bodkin heads remained jammed on tightly he pushed them through his belt. He then pulled out the spare bowstrings from the bottom of the bag dragging each through his fingers to make sure all three had also remained dry. Satisfied, he selected one and attached it to the horns at the bows tips, using the now empty arrow bag to wipe his sword blade and rub vigorously at the chain mail links of his shirt in an attempt to keep the rust away.

'What's the plan now then?' enquired Eric unnecessarily.

'We'll try to stay hidden and either hope that Willard had to lay low or if that's not happened wait until nightfall and find out what's happened to him ourselves.' The plan had not deviated but Rowan realised the question was probably asked more out of nervousness than not knowing.

Weapons now readied and the early morning daylight increasing the friends made themselves as comfortable as possible.

Leovald was adamant that he would take first watch, lying ten yards ahead of the group and off to their right, closer to the small wooden bridge. Rowan's senses remained heightened as the waiting continued. He felt as though he was constantly waiting to be discovered. There was some talking among the friends but not much, their perilous situation was another thing that hadn't changed since the previous night.

As the dawn spread the noises from more animals waking began to provide a faint backdrop to the silence the men had endured and he caught sight of Leovald as the castle began to come to life.

There was something wrong.

The Welshman was glancing hastily back towards where the small group of archers lay before slithering towards the men.

Rowan reached for his bow instinctively then unsheathed his blade, all too aware that the trees as well as affording the group some protection also meant by the time an enemy stumbled upon them there would be no time to stand up and draw their bows, it would be down to their steel blades. He gripped the handle, trying to shrink further into the ground but at the same time keeping his eyes focussed towards the low shape of Leovald who had momentarily halted, apparently waiting to see if the unseen threat continued towards them.

It had. The archer hastily resumed his retreat, keeping his belly to the floor.

'Quick,' he hissed, before he had even reached the friends' sides. 'Back to the earth-works, there's someone coming towards us.' He unceremoniously pulled at

Rowan's arm, lifting him from his prone position.

Once more he found himself running half crouched, fearing a shout at any moment, weaving between the few trees to the very edge of the ditch. He slid over the edge with no hesitation, his back pressed against the reverse slope and his feet precariously close to the cold water's edge. He was suddenly aware of how exposed he and his friends were. Anyone out on the marshes would have no difficulty spotting the men, never mind if they came to the edge. He glanced to either side at his friends who were all looking nervously upwards at the lip of the ditch, listening intently for any sound that would signal that they had been detected.

'Hello.'

They looked at each other. The call was faint but no one had expected a hushed and feminine voice.

'Is anyone there?'

There was no mistaking the soft tones, still hesitant and coming from the trees they had hastily left. Rowan looked at Leovald, who shook his head, nervousness pervaded the group.

'They must know we're here?' Martin hissed, looking at his friends for approval.

'That doesn't mean it's not a trap,' answered Jerrard abruptly.

'Sssshhh.' Rowan put his finger to his lips.

As if in response to his urge for his friends to be quiet, the voice called out again.

'Daniel.'

Instinctively the group looked at their friend whose scarred face was quickly beginning to show relief. 'It's got to be Rose.'

Without another word, and before anyone could grab him, he stretched himself up and peered over the edge.

He stared towards the tree line and then catching sight of his lover scrambled over the lip, his feet slipping briefly on the dirt bank. The rest quickly followed one-by-one leaving only Rowan.

With a sigh he found himself muttering to himself, 'one in, all in,' as he picked up his weapons and scrambled over the crest towards the copse of trees.

The friends watched self consciously as Daniel and Rosalind embraced each other, before she, sensing the group around her, slipped from the embrace and still holding Daniel's hand looked at Leovald.

'Willard's safe.'

'Thank God.'

Rowan could almost feel the big man's relief.

'What happened then?' Eric jumped in straight away. 'Why didn't he meet back up with us where he was supposed to?' his voice beginning to betray the stress he and the friends had been under throughout the night.

'What happened?' Daniel pulled at Rosalind's hand turning her back to face him, his voice coaxing and placating.

The story came out as the men sat at the edge of the orchard, their keenness to hear the tale overwhelming any thoughts about one of them standing lookout. Rowan himself quickly dismissed the thought as readily as the others.

'Willard crossed the ditch with no problem and was able to hide himself in the garden as you wanted him to,' she looked at Leovald, who nodded signalling her to carry on, 'but because there was no one likely to spot you approaching he decided to cross to the eastern bailey, below the walls.'

The men looked at each other with raised eyebrows.

'Anyway, he didn't get caught but apparently he couldn't make his way back because of the patrolling sentries. He hid in the hen house and it was just good fortune that it was my turn to collect the eggs this morning and he recognised me.' She completed the story quickly.

'Where is he now?' Leovald said as soon as she paused.

'He's still there. I couldn't do anything else and decided when he told me you were here to let you know. He was desperate to return.'

'Well what on God's earth do we do now?' asked Jerrard.

The morning was becoming lighter and Rowan could now make out the shape of Lord Fitz Warrin's banner hanging limply from above one of the grey circular towers. Despite the occasional sounds of animals coming from the crofts in the outer grounds, the bells of the small parish church in the village hadn't yet rung for morning prayers so Rowan guessed it was about five in the morning.

He looked at Rosalind and then Leovald. 'How long can Willard stay there undetected?'

'It depends, could be quite a few hours,' she replied.

'But not all day?' His question was met by a shake of the head.

He looked at their surroundings and remembered

his own panic as Rosalind had approached. A plan was beginning to form in his mind but was hesitant to share it.

'What are you thinking?' Martin asked, as if reading his mind.

'We have to try and get Willard now before everybody's awake, and possibly the rest of the lads.'

'You're mad,' responded Jerrard at once.

'We wouldn't stand a chance,' agreed Eric.

'Hang on though, we know we can't stay here and even if we do there's a good chance we'll be spotted.' Martin was once again in agreement with Rowan.

'And, besides, why else did we come?' Daniel added in support.

With Leovald's silence at the suggestion the argument was won.

'Okay, but despite agreeing I just want to put on record that I agree with Jerrard and that we're mad,' smiled Daniel.

The men quickly interrogated Rosalind for more information, aware that as every minute passed their chances of success receded. To his relief there was no mention of the captives being mistreated or of any harm to Catin as her friend continued her story.

The men had indeed been taken prisoner but their task only seemed to get harder as she explained that Lord Fitz Warrin had ordered the men locked within the walls of the barbican. They were held in the small guardhouse next to where the temporary infirmary had been set up, instead of the billet in the barn which Rowan and his friends and hoped for.

'The good news,' Leovald chipped in, 'is that they

won't be expecting us and Rosalind has said the gate leading from the outer courtyard is open.' She nodded in agreement before the Welshman turned to Rowan. 'What do you reckon, skirt round the back of the stables, along the rear wall and then through the archway?'

Feeling a swell of pride that he had been asked for his agreement ahead of the others, he thought for a moment before nodding. 'That's probably the best way and we can grab Willard on the way.'

'Okay?' Leovald looked at the rest of the friends who, with a mix of worry and determination, nodded their assent.

'Can I make a suggestion? Rosalind interrupted assuredly, glancing at Daniel. 'Those same sentries that stopped Willard will still be about, why don't I distract them? After all, they know I'll be out collecting eggs and fruit for the kitchens.'

Rowan realised he and his friends had completely forgotten about them and was thankful for her recollection.

'That will help. It'll be safer if you could.' Leovald immediately agreed.

'But what about you?' Daniel looked into her eyes, the concern obvious.

'I'll be alright, they'll know me, and besides Catin and I can meet you in a few days away from here. The confusion will also help Willard escape?'

At the mention of her friend's name Rowan felt a flutter in his heart, once more relieved at the confirmation that she had not been harmed.

'That's settled then. Willard is astute enough to meet

us on the road east so let's get on with it.' Leovald then lifted his bow and ended the discussion.

Rosalind and Daniel shared a quick embrace before she made her way back through the copse towards the western bailey. The men followed, waiting until she crossed the wooden bridge over the ditch, her footsteps light on the planks as she headed slowly along the track. They slithered across the small ditch, keeping parallel and using the orchard as cover, moving forward crouching in between the trees. Rosalind continued on the path to their right, towards the bridge that linked the two outer baileys where, sure enough, she had entered conversation with two men at arms, their gules and argent surcoats just discernible through the trees.

'Right boys, let's get to those barns,' whispered Leovald.

No one answered, everyone understanding the need for silence and nodding grimly before they quickly bore left, away from the now distracted sentries. Again, Rowan found himself following his friends, wading knee high through the muddy waters of the channel separating the wards, before clumsily climbing up the dirt bank to stand against the rear of one of the animal crofts.

Leovald led the group behind the two-storey stable and barns until they came to the stone corner tower at the rear of the barbican. Anxiously he glanced up expecting to see a guard peering over the stone battlements.

Thankfully all he could see was the dark cloudy morning sky which still retained the remnants of its reddish hue above the grey walls. Evidently Rosalind had succeeded in keeping the guards distracted from spotting them on the far side of the bridge.

Rowan could hear his own breathing now, heavy from his chest as he followed the Welshman, moving sideways, his back to the wall towards the archway. The rough stone work snagged at his mail links as he moved, still anxiously looking up. There could have been twenty men-at-arms on the walls above for all he knew, waiting to send deadly arrows and spears down on the five men beneath.

Even as the fear continued to invade his thoughts, Leovald stopped abruptly and Rowan found himself bumping against his broad shoulders. His friends were soon also packed closely together under the walls, no space between each of them as they sought to control their nerves.

'Ready?' Leovald looked first at him before leaning out and making sure the rest of the group were prepared. Apparently assured, he tentatively inclined his head so he could see through the archway, the solid oak door ajar.

Rowan watched anxiously as every second passed silently, urging his friend to withdraw his head before he was spotted.

'Right, there's two men on top of the gatehouse from what I can see, and two men outside the guardhouse,' the Welshman said eventually pulling his head back much to Rowan's relief.

He knew this is what he and his friends had expected although he had harboured the hope that his comrades wouldn't be guarded at all. He felt heat rising to his face as tension clutched at his chest.

'You ready, Jerrard?' Leovald asked.

It had been decided back in the woods as the men had waited for darkness that the two big men would overcome any guards in the courtyard. He and Daniel would try to keep any sentries on the battlements busy, while Martin would secure the archway leading to the inner castle and Eric would try to open the guardhouse door. Now he started to think that the plan was inherently flawed and he was powerless to do anything about it. He felt sick in his stomach.

Jerrard slid past him, keeping close to the walls, sharing a grim smile, a heavy mallet in hand. Rowan pulled an arrow from his belt and notched it, the string taught and bodkin head pointed to the floor. Daniel and Martin did the same.

All of a sudden, Leovald and Jerrard had gone. There was no time to worry anymore and he found himself rushing after them, pushing his back away from the security of the wall and under the thick stone lintel into the open courtyard with its high enclosing walls.

To his left he was already aware of figures struggling, their shapes distinct against the wattle and daub walls of the guardhouse while he quickly scanned the battlements above. He raised his bow and drew the string back in anticipation. Shifting his aim he caught sight of two sentries above the main gateway completely surprised by the sudden commotion below.

Pulling the string back a little further before opening his fingers he let his bodkin loose. The familiar thwack sounded as the tension was released. Instinctively he picked a second arrow from his belt. As he did so he kept his eyes on his target. His aim had been good and it had struck the man in the shoulder, easily piercing the chainmail links and flinging him back against the battlements. Martin's bow had sung out a moment after Rowan's. The second sentry, like his comrade was sent tumbling to the floor and disappeared below the stone works.

'To arms. To arms!' came the shout behind.

Rapidly turning round he caught a sight of another sentry in the gules and argent livery of the garrison, running across the battlements to their rear, bow in hand. He followed the figure for a moment and let another arrow fly. It missed, speeding through the air just behind the man.

'Satan's curse' he swore to himself. He knew even as he drew the next bodkin that the sentry had reached the relative safety of the south eastern tower of the barbican.

He kept his aim, waiting for a figure to appear between the stone merlons until his arm began to ache.

Still the enemy did not reappear.

He chanced a glance around him. Martin to his left still held his bow drawn, searching for any more threats from the walls above while against the guardhouse wall, a dazed man-at-arms, his helm lying close, a hand over a bloody wound to his head, was watched over by Jerrard brandishing his heavy mallet. Against the same wall Leovald held a dagger across the throat of the second sentry.

'We need a key,' Eric shouted urgently across to the Welshman, crouched by the locked door.

There was now no need to keep silent. Rowan could

hear the alarm call echoing within the main castle, calling men to arms. Already they would be donning their armour and rushing along the stone passageways or out into the castle courtyard.

'Keep the walls covered,' he shouted to Martin as he ran the few steps back to the archway from where they had sprung, for the moment the archer above forgotten. He slammed the thick door shut as he saw the sentries that Rosalind had distracted running across the outer bailey towards him. Looking quickly around he saw the locking bar leaning against the wall. Letting go of his bow he hefted the thick piece of timber and dropped it into the two iron cradles with a reassuring solid thump.

Breathing heavily, adrenaline coursing through his body, he picked up his bow. 'How are we doing?' he called urgently to Daniel who was standing by the archway leading to the main castle.

'So far, so good, but I'm not sure how long that will last,' and as if to confirm his words an arrow splintered against the stonework beside him.

Even as he heard his friends curse from the near miss, the locking bar shook and rattled as the men from the outer bailey banged their weapons against the thick door, the dull thumps adding to the urgency of the situation.

Eric was now rifling through the pockets of the man who lay on the floor in front of Jerrard before snatching up a set of heavy keys and frantically started trying them in the lock. With a cry of success he turned the mechanism but, just as he did, an arrow smacked into his torso.

Rowan saw the blur of the arrow just moments

before it plunged into his friend from across the courtyard.

As he heard the cry of pain from his friend he knew the missile had been shot from the tower, from the sentry he had missed earlier.

Shouldering his bow he drew his blade and made for the turret entrance. He quickly lifted the latch and threw open the door before entering the dimly lit interior. Taking in the worn stone stairs that wound upwards, he switched his blade unfamiliarly to his left hand, his right hand helping him keep balance against the central pillar as he made his way rapidly towards the top. He half fell into the guard space due to his momentum, an arrow slit helping to illuminate the first floor as he looked around anxiously knowing he was lucky no-one had been waiting for him.

Taking a breath he became more cautious. Above him the wooden hatch was shut and though he couldn't hear anything he sensed the sentry on the battlements.

The light from the embrasure allowed him to search the room but there was nothing of use, just a couple of stools, a table and a few empty mugs. He undid his buckler from his belt glancing up once more at the hatch above him as he did so. Rowan knew the enemy sentry had every advantage and that he could have his bow trained at the opening waiting for him to come through or ready to thrust the point of a lance into his body. He knew sickeningly he couldn't just walk away, the injury to his friend raw.

With knees tensed on the last few steps below the hatch, his buckler raised above his head, he thrust forward with his sword arm, flinging the wooden hatch cover up and over. It was heavier than he thought as he put his full force behind it. Even as the door crashed against the stone floor he saw the tip of the arrow pointing directly at him. Time seemed to slow as he gazed into the man's eyes. All of a sudden his buckler was smashed backwards and his arm wrenched violently, his body spun sideways. He hadn't even seen the arrow released but realised he must have instinctively thrown up his shield just in time.

'God's Holy cross!' He was yelling now, rage taking over. He slammed his sword arm onto the turret floor to keep his balance and then to lever himself up, rolling to his left as he did so. His left arm was ringing from the shock, the leather straps of the buckler amazingly unbroken. 'Christ in heaven, you whore's son,' the curses were coming thick and fast out of his mouth now.

Snarling, he turned to his attacker, rising to his feet. He faced his enemy with sword and shield in hand. The man was about his build and age, wearing a thick gambeson under his surcoat and an ill fitting bascinet, his bow now discarded in favour of a heavy steel blade.

Even in his rage Rowan recognised his face from the small garrison, not that it mattered at that moment as he launched himself forward, swinging his falchion from right to left and using the buckler to protect his body. The man brought his sword upwards blocking the steel but was forced to take a step backwards. Again Rowan repeated the swing with the same outcome, the sharp ring as the edges met piercing the early morning air. He swung again and then again until the man had his back to the battlements, both men breathing heavily.

Lord Fitz Warrin's man desperately countered and swung his sword in a horizontal arc immediately after parrying his last battering stroke, making Rowan thrust his buckler forward to meet it. Again he felt his arm jar at the impact but it allowed him space to smash his own sword hard into the soldier's bascinet. A duller sound rang out as the blow harshly jerked the man's head sideways, a large dent in the metal. The man staggered, disorientated, which allowed Rowan to smash his sword against his opponent's. It clanged to the floor and he pushed the sharp tip against the man's breast, threatening to split the thick padding of his gambeson.

Rowan was sweating profoundly, his breathing painful as each gasp of air hurt his throat. His enemy stood still, all fight had disappeared from his face and was replaced by worry, as the metal tip threatened to sink into his chest and pierce his heart. Kicking the man's sword away, Rowan looked over the crenallation to the courtyard below where he could see a crowd of archers now freed from their captivity.

His brief sense of relief was interrupted by a sharp shout of warning from the sentry who despite the sword at his chest threw himself into a crouch onto the turret floor. Looking down he was momentarily confused before he heard and saw a brief blur as an arrow whistled past his head, a matter of inches away. The shaft continued speeding into the distance even as Rowan threw himself to the floor, realising it had come from the walls of the castle.

'Get down,' Rowan shouted and hastily gestured at the man to move towards the steps.

The unarmed sentry was more than happy to obey

the order, crawling across the stone floor to the opening and scrambling down the steps.

Rowan followed closely behind, his head bent low expecting another arrow at any moment. He gave a silent prayer as he safely entered the shade of the inside of the tower, not bothering to pull the hatch shut as he turned round to find the sentry waiting on the floor below. The soldier appeared to have no intention of running and silently waited for Rowan to follow him down the winding stairs inside the dull turret interior until they both emerged into the outer courtyard.

'I wondered where you'd got to,' Jerrard joked with relief as he saw Rowan appear. 'What have you got here?' he inclined his head towards Rowan's prisoner.

'You don't want to know,' he replied feeling suddenly tired.

'You might as well put him in the guardhouse with the others,' indicating with his head the building that so recently had held the Earl's men captive.

The man went readily enough and, once he was inside, and the door secured behind him, Rowan asked, 'what's going on?'

Around him men were urgently managing to arm themselves from the small arsenal kept by the gatehouse. To his relief he saw his father, Leovald and to his surprise Sir Robert having an urgent discussion.

Jerrard saw his confusion. 'They locked Sir Robert in the room your father recuperated in. I don't think it's what he's used to but I bet he's happy now.'

The friends had expected the knight to be imprisoned in one of the chambers of the castle befitting his status.

'I suppose we'd better leave them to it,' Rowan said watching the group in deep conversation for a few moments more before realising Jerrard had hurried to the archway separating themselves from the inner drawbridge. 'Hang on a minute Jerrard.' Rowan ran after his friend feeling guilty. 'How's Eric?' He had, for the moment, forgotten about his friend, relieved that his father was safe.

'Oh he should be alright I reckon, it went straight through his side, and I mean straight through. The point was out the other end. We had to snap it off. I don't know how they managed to miss anything within that skinny frame. Mind you it must have hurt,' he said grudgingly. He's over there', Jerrard gestured with his thumb to where a rather forlorn looking Eric was sitting, his back to the wall beside the main gateway, his ribcage wrapped in a tight bandage.

Rowan raised a hand in greeting which Eric spotted and returned, unable to hide a brief flicker of pain as he did so.

'What's happening?' he asked Daniel, making sure he followed his friend's example and stayed either side of the archway leading to the castle.

'Well they haven't raised the bridge yet but I can see a lot of running about inside and the more of them are climbing the battlements, so keep your head down'.

Taking a chance Rowan peered round the archway to see the helmets of half a dozen men already on the gatehouse walls and towers. He looked across at the archway, there was no sign of them pulling up the bridge which meant they could counter attack at any time. He involuntarily gulped - just so long as they didn't organise an assault he hoped they would be able to successfully complete their plan and extract their friends.

That thought started to disappear as, looking back towards the centre of the small cobbled courtyard. He watched as Sir Robert having finished his rapid discussion with his subordinates strode purposefully into the middle of the rag-tag mixture of archers and men-at-arms. Just behind him, Rowan's father returned a smile and nod as he saw him.

'We're going over that bridge and heading straight for Lord Fitz Warrin's chamber. We go fast and direct, before they gather their wits and raise the drawbridge, and batter our way right through to the chambers.' The knight's strong and determined voice carried so every man could hear, including Rowan still standing by the archway, the same archway that Sir Robert was talking about charging through, right under the bows of the archers, now ready above the ramparts. Rowan was still taking in that thought as the knight looked round at each face before speaking. 'Ready?'

***

The sudden appearance of the charging men from the shadows of the stone archway not more than a hundred feet away took William de Movran by surprise. He had been looking around as the men of the garrison and his three remaining men-at-arms manned the stone walls and the small gateway beneath. His intention to pursue the prisoners, who would surely try to make good their escape suddenly wiped away.

'They're coming!' The unneeded cry came from one of the garrison archers to his left.

William de Movran's disdainful glance at the Welshman was brief as he quickly stared towards the tide of men who began to pound across the bridge.

'Then kill them, for God's grace kill them!' he urged, just as bowmen appeared from the archway opposite.

They emerged behind the small group of charging soldiers inevitably led by Sir Robert. There was no mistaking the bearded figure despite his lack of armour as he raced towards the gateway below. William de Movran had no time to wonder how he had managed to escape as a small but lethal shower of arrows were released. They sped upwards towards him and the rest of the men on the battlements. He ducked instinctively, the order forgotten as metal tips struck the stonework around him.

A cry of pain rang out from his left but he was unconcerned. Judging that the brief barrage was over he lifted his eyes above the parapet. Beneath, the small force of charging men had nearly all crossed the bridge, their feet pounding on the wooden planks. From the cries and clash of metal some were already forcing their way into the courtyard below.

War cries of 'Fitz Warrin, Fitz Warrin' mixed with the clash of steel, echoing in the confines of the inner gateway. Wiliam de Movran cursed himself for not ordering the drawbridge raised despite the confusion and hoped his men beneath would hold the attackers while he could gather the rest of the garrison. Even as those thoughts ran through his mind the Staffordshire archers opposite rushed to reinforce their comrades battling beneath the gatehouse.

'Get down there and crush them.' His frustration welled within him. The first counter volley from the garrison had smacked harmlessly against the stonework of the archway before the enemy charged across the bridge. He angrily pushed one of his men-at-arms across towards the doorway to the turret that led down towards the main courtyard below. Plate armour scraped against the rough stone walls as his feet and those of his men rushed down the winding staircase, past the guard room level and into the daylight of the courtyard.

In the confines of the inner castle, with walls rising around them, the harsh clash of steel against steel and the duller sound of metal against shield accompanied by the curse of men rang out clearly. He could see bodies already lying on the dusty floor. In some cases small pools of blood formed around the crumpled figures as men continued to battle around them.

Immediately to his front his few remaining men-at-arms stepped forwards, visors down and their shields forwards. Unlike the enemy they wore their armour and moved with the assurance that this gave them. They knew that their heavy blades would easily cut through the thin jackets of the attackers who he realised seemed to be just the Earl's men. He saw no surcoats or badges of others which gave him renewed heart.

Sure enough, he watched as the recently released captives fought back desperately but nevertheless fell back as his men in disciplined formation stepped forward, forging onwards among the chaos of fighting men around them. One of the enemy, a soldier of perhaps thirty with a heavily lined face that showed years of service, was too slow and he watched as the keen edge of a long sword sliced across his belly. The cry of pain was followed by the man slumping to the floor, no longer concerned with resistance but keeping his entrails in. Both hands clasped the wound, his sword clattering to the floor, his face looking up at his attacker with a mixture of surprise and shock.

His men continued forward as the enemy closed up in a desperate defence. Around him William de Movran could tell the larger numbers of men from the garrison and his few men at arms were now in the ascendency and that they would surely slaughter the small force of archers and men-at-arms.

There was no feeling of satisfaction however. Instead his head was full of anxiety as he saw a few of the attackers reach Lord Fitz Warrin's chambers only thirty yards away.

'Kill them, kill them!' The words came out of his mouth with urgency before he slammed down the metal visor of his own helm.

He was already breathing heavily as he swung his long sword over his head and pushed himself forward in between his men-at-arms. He swung his shield to the left to deflect a sword blow while throwing his own sword forwards towards an enemy who stumbled backwards as it struck home. He relied upon his men-at-arms at either side to protect his flanks as he forged forwards in the middle of the swirling mass of men, the sounds of battle all around him.

And then his men were stepping back, the intensity of the fight slackening, the noise seeming to fade. Blades were no longer swung with such ferocity and he could see men pausing. Panning his head sideways he could see the cause of the sudden lull through the horizontal slit of his visor.

Lord Fitz Warrin had emerged beside Sir Robert. The Lord still commanded the castle and, with his arms aloft made the men of his garrison pause.

Inwardly he cursed vehemently. He had been lax. How had he allowed this to happen? The turnaround in fortunes would be quick and he realised the precariousness of his position. He nudged the man-at-arms to his right, backing towards the gateway from where the attackers had charged.

'Halt your fighting.' Lord Fitz Warrin's voice rang out as he and his men-at-arms reached the bodies lying in and around the gateway.

He knew the garrison would obey. The battle had irrecoverably turned and he didn't want to stay around and watch the outcome. The Lord of the castle continued speaking but William de Movran was no longer concerned with any of his words, only that he was able to extricate himself from within the castle walls that would quickly become a trap.

Entering the shade of the gateway arch and then striding across the wooden bridge, ignoring the arrow shafts that sprouted from the boards like stalks of wild grass, he lifted his helm from his head. The sweat stung his eyes and did nothing to assuage his seething anger inside. Everything had been going so well. The departure of the Earl of Stafford and most of his force had been unexpected but an opportunity to gain control of the castle. He had even captured Sir Robert and his men. The approaching Rhys Gethin would have been impressed and he could have expected a substantial ransom. Instead he now had to leave Whittington, his life in danger, his allegiance to the rebellion now known.

'God's teeth.' He ignored the side long glances from his loyal men-at-arms and continued across the courtyard towards the outer gatehouse. He still held his heavy sword in his hand, his helm in his left as he approached the main outer gatehouse. To his right, a wounded bowman was propped up against the side of the drum tower, watching him. He could swear there was a slight smile on the young man's face as if silently mocking him and he felt no remorse as he coldly stepped forwards and quickly pushed the tip of his sword against the man's chest. The material of his jacket resisted for a moment but with a bit more effort the cold steel slid through the cloth and into the man's flesh. He looked into the man's eyes below the mop of light brown, almost blond hair who now stared back at him almost uncomprehendingly as the blade slid deeper and deeper. There was no mocking now in the young lads' eyes as they slowly glazed over.

His anger and frustration was only slightly satisfied as he drew his sword out of the man's torso with some difficulty, using his foot as leverage as he pulled the blade from the sucking flesh. Glancing back towards the archway leading to the inner castle there was no sign of pursuit. The swine were probably patting each other on the back he thought bitterly. Well, he would do his damndest to make sure their congratulations were short lived and with that in his mind, he strode across the drawbridge followed by his remaining men-at-arms, determined to have his revenge.

CHAPTER EIGHT

Rowan, breathing heavily, saw that he and his friends could easily have been slaughtered by the garrison who stood in the courtyard and along the surrounding battlements. Sweat pricked his forehead as he looked at their faces, most of the garrison familiar to the small remaining group of attackers who could still stand. The garrison looked confused, unsure of what to do. The emergence of their Lord, the battle cries for Fitz Warrin from their attackers, the retreat of William de Movran and the fact that they had so recently been allies, even friends, held them in a sort of paralysis.

It was Leovald who broke the inertia and the sudden silence between the two forces. Arms raised he walked out into the courtyard's centre. 'We're on the same side, lads,' his loud voice carried around the walls. With no helm, his face framed by his shoulder length hair, the big Welshman was easily recognisable and Rowan watched, and then followed suit as first, Sir Robert and then the remaining attackers lowered their weapons.

'Thank you, sergeant,' he heard the youthful Lord say, striding forward from beside the knight to stand by Leovald. He was seemingly unconcerned by the garrison around him, most of whom still held their weapons warily. 'Get the men to tend the wounded and re-assemble in twenty minutes.'

Then, as if remembering his men in the courtyard and high upon the battlements he silently looked around as if gauging their loyalty.

With a look of almost disappointment and a renewed sense of purpose, he turned on his heels and returned to his chambers, followed once more by Sir Robert who quickly spoke to Rowans father as he passed, 'Get our men to help. Like he said, we're on the same side.'

Hesitantly the men began to tend the wounded. There was an inevitable tenseness between the two groups, both wary that only moments before they had been trying to kill each other.

Rowan felt a deep sadness looking at the bodies lying unmoving on the packed earth of the courtyard and under the gateway where Sir Robert had literally battered through the defenders.

Two bodies, one with the gules and argent surcoat of the garrison and the other in a plain tunic that belonged to one of the company, were lying haphazardly beneath the shadows of the gatehouse. In the courtyard a blanket of darkening blood lay beneath a man-at-arms, his face upturned and his lifeless eyes staring into the sky. Another attacker lay close by, his blood-smeared hands and arms fruitlessly clutched at a savage wound in his belly, his eyes similarly fixed in death. A third was propped against a comrade, an arrow shaft protruding from his unprotected back, his breathing already desperately shallow, a bubble of bright red blood accompanying his painful coughs.

Looking round as he made his way towards the

inner drawbridge Rowan could see many others had suffered wounds to their heads and torsos, a couple of obviously broken noses, gashes and what would become large purple bruises evident. Avoiding the bodies lying against the curved walls, he stepped across the timber boards, walking between numerous embedded arrow shafts sprouting from the timber, shot from the gateway above.

Their stealthy approach and the assault so rapidly turning from rescue to desperate attack now seemed an age ago. His mind was awhirl as he wandered through the archway into the outer courtyard where more casualties lay among discarded equipment. It was then his mind slowly registered the sight of the body against the gatehouse wall. His heart dropped, a feeling of sickness sweeping through him. The dressings were still tied tightly around Eric's torso but there was a fresh stain of blood in his midriff, his body lolled to the right, his eyes staring unseeing.

'God's bones,' Jerrard shared his familiar comment with the friends as they sat outside the inn straight after their friend's burial in the small cemetery of the village church a few hours later. There had been no sense in delaying the burials, each mound of freshly dug earth topped by a simple wooden cross, testament to the death of friends and comrades.

The sense of loss hung heavily over the group despite the efforts of Rowan's father and Leovald, their words doing little to lessen the despondency that covered the group of friends.

It had not taken much to arrive at the conclusion that

William de Movran or one of his men had thrust a sword into their friend's undefended chest as they fled the castle. Every time Rowan thought about the callousness of the action he felt sick, especially when he thought of Eric's ready smile, his eagerness and clumsiness. Even the unspoken relief when Catin appeared, unharmed, her friend jumping straight into Daniel's arms or the sheepish smile from Willard behind them, did little to add purpose as Rowan looked into the dregs of ale remaining at the bottom of his wooden cup.

The heavy atmosphere was not helped either by the revelation that William de Movran had boastfully told the Lord of the castle in his confinement that Rhys Gethin and his force was approaching, now expecting the castle to be open to the advancing rebels.

Since the assault the friends had been told by Leovald that the Lord had been locked in his chamber and the garrison informed he was ill. It seemed that though many of the Lord's men had been uneasy at the imprisonment of the Earl's troops, their ingrained obedience to his second in command held sway. The understanding of what had happened did not help lift Rowan and his friend's gloom around Eric's death.

'If that louse ridden pig decides to come back I'll rip his heart out,' continued Jerrard, brimming with hate.

'Do you think they'll still come, now that we have the castle back?' Daniel asked in an effort not to encourage Jerrard's fury and the anger among the group

'I would if I knew there were little over two dozen men,' answered Rowan, 'and that's obviously what Sir

Robert and Lord Fitz Warrin think,' he said watching an elderly woman carrying a large basket of grain along the path towards the gatehouse.

Sir Robert was preparing for a siege. At least with the provisions the villagers were bringing in and the livestock in the castle grounds they had enough victuals so that they wouldn't starve, he thought ruefully, looking up at the gules and argent banner flying above the south east tower. It would be the lack of men that could be their undoing.

'Let's hope the Earl returns soon,' Martin's interjection interrupted his thoughts.

'Yeh, but when will that be though?' replied Jerrard unhappily, his fit of anger subsiding as his attention moved to the present predicament.

It had been only two days since the Earl had set off to Shrewsbury and there was no guarantee that a force was ready to march immediately. He knew the noble wouldn't be aware of the aggressive advance of some of Glyn Dwr's forces or the precariousness of the castle's defences following William de Movran's treachery.

'Probably four days,' Martin said a little unconvincingly.

The conversation was in danger of becoming even more downbeat and was saved by the appearance of Rowan's father, with Willard as usual by his side.

Rowan hadn't spoken much to him since the rescue and the desperate charge into the inner castle but he and his friends had received his thanks, as well as the gratitude of Sir Robert and the Lord, normally something that would bring them much pride but which was greatly lessened by the death of their friend.

'Sorry to do this to you, lads.' His father knew the loss the group was feeling and shared a fondness for Eric. 'We need everyone to help prepare in case they go through with the attack.' His father certainly wasn't discounting the chance that the rebels would continue and advance on Whittington, whether forewarned by William de Movran or not. 'I need you to go and collect all the arrows the bowyer has finished and then get whatever materials or help he needs to make more.'

The men without a grumble got to their feet, Rowan draining his remaining ale, and set off to help in the defensive preparations. There would have to be time for more grieving later it seemed.

The preparations came to an abrupt halt the next day as an archer from the garrison despatched to keep watch came galloping down the track, throwing up clouds of dust in his wake and causing soldiers and villagers alike to pause in their duties. If they were like Rowan they also kept half an eye open on the hills and forest surrounding the castle looking for the first sign of the enemy approaching.

Standing upon the battlements he watched the rider come to a halt just before the drawbridge, greeted by the easily recognisable figure of Leovald who took hold of the bridle of the sweating horse, its white lathered flanks clearly visible. Seeing Willard's father brought a smile to Rowan's face as he remembered, much to his and his friends' pleasure that Lord Fitz Warrin had recognised the respect his soldiers had for the big Welshman and the role he had played in his release and so promoted him to act as Master-at-Arms of the remaining garrison.

After a cursory conversation between the two men, the rider dismounted while the Welshman headed back through the gatehouse and straight towards the inner castle to report to the nobles who, he guessed, were continuing their planning in the Lord's chambers. He turned and watched from above as Leovald emerged from the inner gatehouse and went straight to the oak door of the tower that so recently had been the focal point of the desperate assault.

The warning chimes came soon after, calling the garrison to assembly. The metallic ringing of the triangle was clear and urgent, reverberating between the stone walls and added to by the calls of Leovald and his father.

Archers and men-at-arms quickly put down their loads, stopped their discussions or halted sharpening their swords and ran to their designated places in the ranks, lining up in the main courtyard, while the women and children looked on worriedly at the departure of their men folk.

Rowan, as with the other men on watch duty, remained where he was, able to peer down on his comrades from his vantage point on the wide battlements. Below, he watched as the men straightened their posture as the Lord and Sir Robert emerged from the doorway. Leovald had taken position in front of the remaining garrison, reflecting his new status as the men listened in expectation.

'It seems the rebel forces of Glyn Dwr are marching on us,' the Lord spoke. His voice was calm, still retaining its authoritative tone. There was no hint of anxiety, almost in a matter of fact way as though it was no different from a comment about the weather. The Lord let his words sink in, looking across the assembled force, seemingly taking in each face. 'We expect them to appear in three to four hours, so finish your business and attend to your posts, you all know what to do.'

Rowan and the rest of the garrison had been told of their duties in case the rebels did attack, something they had all suspected but had hoped would not happen. Even as he reminded himself of his responsibilities it seemed that the address was already over. Though the words had been calm and confident, the Lord wasn't much for encouraging the men or providing detail he reflected, unlike Sir Robert who finished the assembly.

'Before you get arses moving like a whore with the pox remember that these rebels are exactly that, rebels. We're fighting for King Henry and Earl Edmund. Whatever happens, we do not let this castle fall.' Rowan felt himself physically stiffen, a shiver of determination running up his spine, the hairs on his arm pricking. 'Now dismissed.'

It felt like an eternity until the enemy vanguard was spotted on the skyline two hours later.

At first it was a small group of horsemen, hard to discern from the two or so miles away, but gradually he could see them joined by more and more men, the group slowly but steadily beginning to move down towards the village outside the castle walls, like an invading colony of ants.

Rowan watched from his allotted space on top of the outer gatehouse battlements. All around him on the barbican walls, within the flanking towers and in the courtyard beneath the defenders wore the same livery. It had been decided that the men of Stafford would hold the outer walls while the remaining garrison troops protected the main castle.

The Earl's archers, some sporting bloodied bandages from their earlier conflict, had equipped themselves with extra sheaves of arrows lying in anticipation against the parapets, their bows strung ready. In the courtyard below, the small number of men-at-arms stood with their freshly burnished shields or sharpened halberds at the ready. The gateway to their front was dark, the heavy steel portcullis was already down, the drawbridge ratcheted up so that Rowan could see directly below him to the twelve metre wide water filled ditch. Despite the strength of the defences he couldn't help but feel trepidation as the outlines of men inexorably filed down towards the village. There must have been three times the men they had faced in the shallow valley all those days ago.

'Well, it looks like we'll have a fight on our hands,' Sir Robert said to Rowan's father, loud enough for the nearby archers to hear. The knight slapped his father on the back cheerfully and turned to make his way down the steps in the tower. Rowan, not for the first time, marvelled at the calmness and surety that nobles such as Sir Robert could share among their men.

The enemy must have numbered over five hundred, facing the twenty five men behind the walls of the castle. Not good odds, he mused. The garrison had finished their preparations as much as possible and he now just stood and stared, unconsciously sharpening his needle point arrow heads unenthusiastically with his wet stone.

The enemy mass threatened to spill from the track to become an encircling tide but he could see how, after only a few steps either side, men's legs sunk into the marsh, bringing curses as they strained to rid themselves from the sucking mud and water. Relentlessly though the ominous column continued forward, battle banners flapping in the slight breeze and the now recognisable figures of Rhys Gethin and his captains at its head. But it wasn't those leaders that brought bile rising to Rowan's throat, it was the sight of William de Movran. His allegiance and that of his now reformed household troops, Bayard included, was evident for all to see sas they sat easily beneath the lazily flying banners of the Welsh army.

The tide of men halted just north of the collection of buildings, resisting the temptation to enter the now empty dwellings to their right, their small front garden tofts eerily empty of animals and playing children. Most of the villagers had sought safety in the surrounding Babbins Wood, while a few, like Rosalind and Catin, had remained in the castle to support the garrison.

The massed column stood silent, menacingly.

Rowan could make out there was some order to the enemy organisation. The men were dressed in a variety of plate armour, chain mail, brigandine jackets and metal helmets. They stood in groups ranging from ten to fifty men separated by a few feet with different banners of their liege lords in their centre.

As he cast his eyes over the still column a herald trotted his horse forwards from the mounted men-at-arms at the front. He was not as gaudily dressed as Rowan had often seen at tournaments, more dressed for war with the glint of armour beneath his surcoat.

The man guided his horse slowly forwards. His eyes were averted from the watching garrison as he reached the corner of the track and followed it parallel to the castle walls towards the barbican gatehouse. Fitz Warrin's soldiers, stationed on the main castle battlements and peering out of the arrow slots in the inner wall walk, watched in silence as he rode within lethal arrow range of the defenders. The focus of nearly every man was fixed upon this one single figure.

Rowan's attention was only distracted as the Lord, accompanied by Sir Robert, made his way into the outer courtyard and towards the nearest gatehouse tower. He realised he would have a privileged position to witness proceedings.

Sure enough, by the time the herald had halted his horse in front of the two drum towers framing the firmly shut drawbridge, Rowan saw the two men appear on the tower. The Lord, though less burly than Sir Robert, emitted the same sort of power and authority, his bright armour making his frame seem more formidable, unadorned like the knight in his argent surcoat with its sable horseshoes as he looked down upon the lone horseman.

'My Lord, Rhys Gethin, knight to Lord Owain Glyn Dwr, the rightful Prince of Wales seeks the fellowship of Lord Fitz Warrin in pursuing the rightful independence of Wales and ownership by its legitimate rulers.' The herald took a deep breath and perhaps an opportunity to remember the message he had to deliver. 'My commander is aware of your lack of numbers and requests your immediate response before instructing to take the castle by force if necessary.' He swept his right arm round to indicate the mass of men behind him, leaving the ultimatum hanging in the air.

As heraldry went it couldn't have got much shorter, thought Rowan, having endured what seemed like hours of preamble at tournaments as similar messengers spoke. It was clear that William de Movran had happily relayed the poor state of the defenders and therefore was not prepared to give them time to delay their surrender. At least Rhys Gethin was happy to try diplomacy first. It was strange he thought, that just a few days ago Rowan would have been worried at Lord Fitz Warrin's response to the offer, but despite his apparent reluctance to hear or take any note of any rebellion in his lands, neither was he part of the uprising. He glanced once again to his right where the Lord stood commandingly, his breastplate catching the early morning sunlight.

For a moment, silence hung in the air. Rowan could feel his comrades on the gatehouse walls and further to his right, the men of the garrison holding their breath and straining their ears for the response, but like all well trained soldiers they remained observant of their station keeping their eyes locked forward.

'You can tell your pretender that Prince Henry is the legitimately appointed Prince of Wales and that these gates will remain barred.' The words were firm and clear, delivered with the assured authority of nobility that Rowan could still only wonder at.

The Lord had delivered his verdict. The herald did not seek to return the response back to the waiting knights, waiting below their banners to the north of the village. Instead he paused a moment, tugging at the reins of his horse which impatiently shook its head. 'My Lord has no option but to declare that he will take the castle by force, though he will spare any within who would join him before we attack.'

That last remark, obviously intended for as many of the garrison to hear as possible, along with the haughty manner in the way it was delivered, caused an explosion within Sir Robert. 'God's teeth, you traitorous scum! You can try but it will be your poxy heads upon my lance point.'

Rowan could see the man visibly shrink in his saddle, before Fitz Warrin took the knight's arm. 'I think what Sir Robert is saying', he glanced at Sir Robert whose face was a bright red, 'is that we must decline the offer.' It was good fortune the herald wasn't within striking distance of his heavy sword, thought Rowan, for he would have surely used it to take the man's head from his shoulders.

The Lord's words spoken loudly down from the walls brought a sense of decorum back to the proceedings and even levity among the defenders and once more Rowan felt a sense of awe and even loyalty to the young noble.

'I shall inform my lord,' and with significantly less confidence than before, the messenger slowly turned his brown steed and trotted back up the track where Glyn Dwr's knights waited with their force of men-at-arms.

'Scum.' Sir Robert's anger had hardly abated, 'We don't let them in James,' he said determinedly to Rowan's father.

This was the first time Rowan had heard the knight address his father on familiar terms and it brought home to him the small nature of the force and their reliance upon each other.

'Sire.' Rowan's father answered simply as the knight turned and accompanied the Lord back down the steps.

He knew there was no more talking to be done, the next time the enemy approached the walls Rowan would be fighting for his life and the lives of his comrades.

'They'd better stand.' The insinuation from Jerrard wasn't surprising especially since all that they had undergone, he thought, though Rowan had no such doubts at the resilience and loyalty of the remaining garrison.

'Let's have none of that,' Rowan's father had overheard the comment and the look towards Fitz Warrin's men on the castle walls. 'We'll need to rely on each other before this thing is over.'

***

William de Movran was not surprised by the response from the garrison. He almost found himself sneering at the grey walls and the few archers spaced along its battlements. He would take the castle, perhaps not as he had intended those few days ago but either way he would take control and make sure those that had dented his pride would pay. For a moment he imagined the ransom he could hope to achieve from the nobles and, for those with no worth he would make examples of some of them. They would learn quickly enough to respect him once more.

His ignominious retreat from these same walls just a few days ago caused a wave of anger within him and he could feel his chest tighten remembering his stumbling exit from the castle, glancing backwards nervously, waiting to see the sudden appearance of pursuing horsemen from the gateway as they hurried along the dirt track towards the comparative safety of the trees that surrounded the valley.

He had felt like a fugitive. Sweat across his brow, his armour dirty and with just two men-at-arms he had staggered gratefully into the cover of the shaded green canopy. Let them have their moment he had thought to himself as he allowed his breathing to slow, holding a branch away with one hand, turning to peer down at the village and fortress in the marshlands below. His lot was well and truly thrown in now and he knew that, whatever happened, his hope now lay in victory or at the very least a negotiated peace for the rebellion. That had been two days ago and now here he was, his banner flying alongside the rampant lions of Glyn Dwr's rebellion.

His thoughts were brought back to the present as Rhys Gethin turned to him and the rest of the mounted nobles and commented almost cheerfully in his broad Welsh accent, 'well we have our answer, much as we were expecting, eh?'

That brought a short cheerful chorus of derision

from his knights who were obviously used to the stubbornness of the garrisons, not that William de Movran felt the same relish for the assault ahead or indeed the same motives. All he wanted was to expunge his earlier failure with a swift and deadly recapture of the castle.

As if sensing his separate feelings, Rhys Gethin turned to look at William de Movran. 'What say you then William de Movran? You must be keen to finish the job you started?'

He felt the words were insinuating but nevertheless he contained his temper. 'Of course my lord, it would be an honour to say the least to capture the castle that has been a thorn in the side of the Welsh.'

His repost was dangerous, almost tempting Glyn Dwr's knight into open confrontation. He could see the tension in his face for a moment, the glare of his eyes beneath his thick bushy hair, before the muscles relaxed and the moment passed.

'I trust you are right. Do not fret. Your efforts in our cause will not be forgotten or unrewarded.' Rhys Gethin left the words hanging in the air as he turned his horse and began issuing orders for the deployment of his troops around the walls of the castle.

William de Movran knew his die was cast but nevertheless felt stung by the reminder as he glanced back at his sergeant from astride his destrier, feeling to his chagrin an undervalued part of the Welsh force.

It had been two days earlier that he had been reunited with Bayard and his remaining men who had been among the advancing column of Rhys Gethin's forces. Emerging from a coppice with his two men at arms retaining as much dignity as he could muster he had virtually bit the head off the scout who challenged him. The chastened soldier had then apologetically led him and his men back towards the approaching column.

He and his men-at-arms had stood in silence on a small hillock as the Welsh force, hundreds of trampling feet mingling with the hoof beats and jangling harnesses of horsemen approached.

Coming into view the riders on their heavy horses had rode under the rampant lion of Rhys Gethin, many wearing his sable and or colours accompanied by the quartered banner of Glyn Dwr. As more and more men appeared behind the mounted knights, this time on foot, William de Movran had been impressed by the size of the force and the way they held themselves. He recognised that this was no rabble.

The horsemen halted at the raised hand of the leader and he found himself staring at the hardened faces of the Welsh knights. It was not in his nature to be cowed however and as the scout introduced him to the nobles he met their eyes without fear.

'I am pleased to meet you William de Movran. We already have the honour of some of your men with us.' Rhys Gethin indicated down the column.

At that he had glanced along the long lines of soldiers, through the dust that still mingled in the air kicked up by the tramp of feet, to where he could see Bayard and some of his men at arms, no longer wearing the livery of Fitz Warrin, noting that their place near the rear did little to respect his decision to support the rebellion.

'It is truly my honour and I look forward to developing our alliance.' He responded cordially, determined to keep his composure in front of the watching knights.

'As do I, but now is not the time for talk. We will continue our journey, there is much daylight left and I'm sure you can understand our desire to continue our advance.'

Without waiting for a response, Rhys Gethin put his spurs to the flanks of his horse and headed onwards leaving William de Movran standing on the hillock watching the force march past with more than a few quizzical looks from the men, their pikes, javelins and halberds slung across their shoulders.

He had been irked by the short and dismissive greeting from the Welsh leader and had sought an audience in his tent on the first night they made camp. Approaching the bearded commander who must have been fifty and was sat on a fur lined campaign chair issuing an order to one of his messengers, he sat down opposite, uninvited to do so. His deliberate manner caused Glyn Dwr's captain to look up dismissing the messenger before locking his hard brown eyes with his own, using a small knife to slice a piece from a dull red apple before popping it into his mouth.

He forced himself to remain silent as he allowed the leader to study him while he also sought to get the measure of his ally. What he saw was the hard face of a veteran lined by years of fighting, a broad chest and thick arms. A competent commander he thought.

'I welcome you and your aid, William de Movran. It

is only disappointing that we were not able to carry out the plan brokered by our mutual friend, Sir John Done.' The leader of the rebel forces had obviously finished his own assessment and his thickly accented words were much more welcoming than his initial greeting but nevertheless challenging.

'Indeed, my Lord Gethin, the appearance of Earl Edmund was unfortunate to say the least.'

After several urgent messages the original plan had changed with the arrival of the Earl's force. The agreed assault on Whittington helped by William de Movran on the inside had been delayed in favour of open battle.

William de Movran had convinced Lord Fitz Warrin of the need to send a mounted contingent in support of the Earl's troops. The Lord had been nervous of upsetting the delicate balance he had struck with the rebels in the area but he was also loyal to the King and agreed. The Lord was unaware the horsemen were chosen because they were loyal to William de Movran or shared allegiance to the Welsh rebel cause.

Despite this the altered plan had not been successful. The report from Bayard had been less than enthusiastic of the encounter between the two forces in the hills of north Powys. He had no doubt his sergeant was probably covering his own back but he could tell the genuine frustration in his voice when he spoke of the failure to push forward the assault despite their numerical superiority. It seemed Rhys Gethin had apparently chosen instead to wait for the return of his horsemen who had, with disastrous timing, rode to meet up with the reinforcements that had been sent from Owain Glyn Dwr.

His subordinate had described to him nervously how, as agreed, he had chosen the moment to turn the mounted men-at-arms against the Earl's force. They had charged into the flank hoping to decisively turn the tide of battle and deal the English force a mortal blow which would force them to retreat all the way back to Stafford. Instead, Bayard had explained how the attack had been thwarted, how many of his men had been killed, and how Rhys Gethin had left him with no choice but to watch the remainder of the Earl's force retreat to safety.

William de Movran had listened angrily, clenching his teeth together. Now, in front of the Welsh commander, he was partially tempted to launch into a verbal attack for the loss of his men and the failure to destroy the Stafford force.

He consciously took a deep breath. He knew that he needed the men under Rhys Gethin's command more than the Welsh knight needed him at this moment, though inwardly he vowed that this would not always be the case.

'However all is not lost. The appearance of your force has sent the Earl scampering back towards Shrewsbury leaving only a small garrison at Whittington and we are still able to take the castle,' William de Movran replied focussing back on the present, his voice calm and determined not to reveal the temper he felt within.

'That is probably so, but it would have been so much easier had you been inside.'

Again he felt like the comment was barbed and he didn't know how long he would be able to maintain his passiveness, but the look on the Welshman's face opposite was devoid of mischief as he sliced another piece of apple and slipped it into his mouth. He realised, not for the first time, it was his own inner feeling of failure that was causing him to feel defensive and he tapped his fingers on the arm of the chair, giving him time to think of a suitable reply. His own gamble had not paid off and he was sure the knight was astute enough to know he had made his move hoping for a large ransom for the captured Lord and a victory that would have given him ownership of the castle, a strong bargaining position.

'Again a cruel twist of misfortune, however I have no doubt we will have little trouble taking the walls as agreed.' William de Movran's eyes once more locked on those of the man opposite.

'I am reassured by your judgement.'

For a moment he thought Rhys Gethin was mocking him but the genial manner of the veteran remained and his next comment was welcome.

'And though the Earl's forces have indeed been an unexpected turn of events the overall plan remains the same.'

He felt like blowing out a breath of air in relief. The hundreds of armoured men would continue towards Whittington where he would be able to exact retribution for the stubbornness of the Earl's force and garrison. Already he started to feel a sense of satisfaction, imagining already striding along the battlements looking down upon the beaten defenders below.

Since that point he had endured rather than enjoyed a courteous relationship with Rhys Gethin, sharing only but the most cursory of acknowledgements as the armoured column had wound its way between the hills and mountains towards the castle and village of Whittington. Now, staring across at the walls, the undercurrent between him and the Welsh commander was forgotten. It was time for him to take back the fortress and position himself as an invaluable member of the rebellion that was gathering like a storm cloud ready to unleash its force against King Henry. With his mood lightened at the prospect he turned his attention back to Rhys Gethin and the other knights around him as orders were being given for commencement of the siege and preparations for the assault to take place.

CHAPTER NINE

To Rowan's surprise the enemy seemed content for the moment to keep watch outside the castle walls. Only a few maintained a vigilant eye in case there was any attempt at a sally, not that it was likely, he thought grimly. Perhaps a quarter of the besiegers, still easily outnumbering the defenders, could be seen. Most wandered between the village buildings that now acted as their billet, fruitlessly searching the empty homes or making fire pits. The rest had been despatched back up the track no doubt to begin preparations for an assault, using the plentiful timber from the surrounding woods to construct siege equipment.

He looked over the parapet once more, down the rough stone walls to the small grass redoubt and the wide ditch and its shallow murky water. He wondered at the willingness of the enemy to attempt such an assault.

'They're going to have a devils own job.' Daniel too was peering downwards, the livid red scar appearing to stretch his skin giving his comment an accompanying savagery, matched probably by his friend's thought of revenge for the injury. His bitterness had now resurfaced with the sight of the enemy.

Neither Rowan nor the two young women had yet

mentioned the incident with William de Movran in the gardens, either to each other or to Daniel. In Rowan's mind it would serve no purpose other than to cause greater anger. The sight of the besieging enemy and the tension it provoked was already palpable among the garrison despite the reassurances of Leovald and Rowan's father.

Of Sir Robert and Lord Fitz Warrin there had been little sign other than the occasional walk across the courtyard or the cursory inspection on the northern battlements. It seemed that they at least were happy and perhaps experienced enough not to want to keep a personal lookout on the enemy, relying upon their troops to do so. He for one found it hard to ignore the besiegers below the castle walls.

His earlier anxiety began to lessen slightly towards the late afternoon as the sky began to darken. He was less convinced now that the enemy would suddenly charge from the buildings and assault the walls. That confidence however didn't stop him losing his appetite for the pork and bread brought up from the kitchens, utterly at odds with Jerrard who, as usual, wolfed his down seemingly without a care in the world. Rowan had to push his wooden plate away as he sat with his back against the battlements, his stomach feeling tight, his hand ineffectually trying to rub away the sense of sickness.

Martin looked at the plate as it scraped on the stone floor. 'Not hungry?'

'Not really', Rowan replied honestly.

'Me neither,' his friend responded with a slight smile, 'I think I'll be happier when they attack, rather than just waiting.'

'You're right,' he said simply. He wasn't sure if that was true, but the waiting coupled with the exertions of the last few days and then the death of Eric were beginning to take their toll.

There was hardly any banter now between the friends and the anticipation of an assault made the knot in his stomach feel like a perpetual illness.

Their waiting went on throughout the first night, the friends taking it in turn as lookouts high on the gatehouse turrets allowing each other to sleep in the rooms below. Rowan was largely unable to take the opportunity to sleep, only managing to take brief naps before anxiety woke him. Instead he wandered up onto the battlements once more or peered through the arrow slits where flames from the enemy fires illuminated the many shadows of the enemy and where confident laughter mixed with bawdy war songs could be heard.

Looking behind him across the outer courtyard Rowan wondered, not for the first time, about the security of the wall to their rear through which the friends had managed to launch their surprise rescue, worried despite the dark outlines of his fellow archers on the battlements opposite.

At least the iron bound oak door below had been barred, something that would have changed their whole situation he thought to himself ruefully, perhaps for the better as he returned his stare towards the buildings of the village below that housed the besieging force.

His melancholy grew as the night continued to pass uneventfully if not comfortably. The occasional howl from a wolf in the surrounding woods replaced the noise of soldiers as his eyelids drooped once more in search of sleep.

It was not until the next morning that the main enemy host returned to the valley. They appeared unhurried as the lightness of the sun began to shine through the thin banks of cloud, which though casting a dull overcoat over the land weren't dense enough to preclude a cloudy day. Rowan moved his shoulders round to loosen his muscles and stretched his neck from side to side, watching as the mass of men slowly flowed down the track continuing towards the village. He recognised with a sense of foreboding that they ominously carried among them scores of scaling ladders and wide wicker mantlets that would act as large shields to protect the assaulting archers.

The advance stirred those in the garrison who had managed somehow to catch some sleep. The sounds from within the inner and outer defences increased as men scrambled up onto the battlements or peered through the narrow arrow embrasures to stare once more at the enemy.

Looking round at the courtyard below Rowan saw his father, the ever willing Willard by his side, enter the chambers to inform the nobles of the emergence of Rhys Gethin's forces from the surrounding woods. Rowan realised with even more certainty that this day would test his and his friends' courage as well as their skills with bow and sword.

Adding to his tenseness the next couple of hours passed inexorably slowly as the enemy began to assemble in full view of the defenders just north of the village. Muffled shouts could be heard as vintenars and sergeants-at-arms ordered the men into formation before the commanders emerged from the local inn.

A frown crossed Rowan's brow at the seriousness of the situation and the fact that one of the men was unmistakeably William de Movran.

The group of enemy knights, in full battle gear, armoured plate over chainmail, their heavy blades sheathed in their scabbard, war hammers hanging from their belts or across their backs gathered together for a few moments before turning to their own retinues and companies, taking their place in front of their men.

Rowan stared towards William de Movran. The hard face was easily recognisable framed by his long dark hair, his helm under his arm as he stood in front of a group of perhaps fifty spearmen and men at arms. He watched as Bayard stepped forward to greet his lord accompanied by another soldier with a distinctive ponytail and wearing a kettle helmet and cuirass. Seeing the men in conversation his thoughts immediately returned to the battle in the steep sided Welsh valley, the deaths of his comrades, the injury to his father and the treachery that had nearly ended in defeat for the Earl's force. His eyes hardened reflecting his thoughts within as he saw William de Movran gesture irritably to the tall ponytailed soldier who, judging by his bearing and armour, must have some authority among the spearmen. He continued watching, sensing the rest of his friends doing likewise. The bitter feelings on behalf of their dead friend had not dissipated.

The rest of the enemy force were marshalling

themselves in a slow and almost unhurried way into companies, assembling beneath the standards of their commanders. The men of the garrison watched silently checking the spacing of their feathered flights perhaps for the third or fourth time, pulling at their bow strings or fingering the hilts of their swords as the enemy force continued to assemble.

Rowan watched as William de Movran led the mixture of men-at-arms and spearmen to the east, crossing the track into the marshland. He watched as the fifty or so rebels soon became disorganised, struggling across the marshlands, some encumbered by ladders seeking to plant their footing on firm pieces of grass, much as he and his friends had done nearly a week ago. Often it was in vain as saw their leather and metal clad feet sinking into the stagnated water and sucking mud. Those with ladders suffered even more and Rowan could imagine the curses that were being uttered. If it hadn't been for the seriousness of their situation he may have been tempted to mock the slow moving force. As it was, he recognised that the enemy were encircling the walls to cause an even greater threat, resurrecting Rowan's concern about the rearward battlements.

'The devil won't even give us a chance to shoot an arrow into his gullet.' Jerrard spat on the floor in disgust.

'I wouldn't worry too much about it, I've got a feeling there'll be more than enough to take his place,' Martin responded, staring back at the assembled lines of men formed up directly in front of the castle walls.

'That's not the point and you know it. That evil

whore has got to get what's coming to him.' Of the four, Jerrard was most taken up with the death of their cheerful friend.

'It'll come, don't you worry. Just like that Bayard.' Daniel was much calmer but in a dangerously resolute way. His friend unconsciously reached to the side of his face, brushing his hair aside and touching the softer scar tissue with his fingertips as if reminding himself of the injury, a movement that had now become part of his friend's everyday mannerisms.

Rowan listened silently to his friends as he watched the enemy group that had stoked their anger slowly disappear from his line of sight. He wondered if ever a battle could become personal, certainly he felt as though this was and that it would be deadly with no quarter given.

The group disappeared behind the north east tower, moving slowly, and still struggling as they made their way across the boggy ground, flanking the castle walls. Rowan looked once more towards the rear outer gatehouse and the barred entrance beneath.

'Watch your front. The enemy are making their way round.' The call came from his father and was aimed at the three archers guarding the southern barbican wall.

It wasn't the words of caution that made Rowan wince but the harsh coughing fit of his father that the effort brought on. The pain across his face clearly revealed he had still not fully recovered from his wound. Likewise the look of concern on his own face must have been clear to his friends as Martin sought to lighten the mood which had descended upon the group.

'At least we know they're not very subtle. There's no

need for a lookout with that lot.'

He attempted a smile at his friend's comment but as he did so his attention was drawn to Leovald. The big archer was ushering all of Lord Fitz Warrin's remaining archers to the east wall opposite the enfilading force, the furthest jogging along the battlements, their sheaves of arrows in hand. He and his friends watched as the bowmen settled themselves in order, giving themselves space, filling the length of the battlements, waiting for their comrades to be in position before feeding the notches of their arrows onto the strings. For a moment there was a pause and then, at a distant order that reached across the castle walls from the Welshman, the garrison troops seemed to turn their bodies a quarter to the right, pulling their strings back while at the same time angling their bows skywards. Like a flock of startled starlings the arrows were released and streaked into the light blue morning sky.

Rowan realised that the flanking force must have come within the range of the archers and the newly promoted Leovald had taken the opportunity to sting their enemy.

There was a sense of satisfaction mixed with disappointment that he couldn't see any real damage inflicted on the enemy soldiers struggling through the marshland.

His thoughts however were tempered somewhat after the garrison, able to release one more volley, lowered their bows and excitedly began chattering with each other, jeering out over the walls and some slapping each other on the back. From their manner he guessed the steel tipped shafts plunging downwards must have inflicted some casualties among the spearmen as they struggled across the wetlands. He easily remembered the force of the arrows and the terrible wounds that the deadly bodkins could cause, especially against lightly armoured men, and imagined them ripping into the bodies, arms and legs of the encircling force.

'Looks like first blood to us then,' Jerrard commented, obviously annoyed not to have the opportunity to take first blood. 'I hope they at least killed some of the poxed scum.'

'I think we'll get our turn soon enough, Jerrard.' Martin tried to encourage his friend, looking once more to their front, the action to the east of the castle walls seemingly of no consequence to the enemy mass in front as they patiently waited.

Not that Jerrard was looking in their direction, his eyes remained fixed on the men stationed on the inner castle walls still congratulating themselves. 'At least we know we're all on the same side.' His distrust of the garrison was still not fully abated.

No one responded, knowing their friend would soon snap out of his mood.

Rowan knew Martin was right, and he too looked at the arrayed ranks of men in front of the walls, nearly five hundred in number, weapons in hand, siege equipment at their feet. Their lines stretched from the left hand side of the village, where the marsh prevented further encirclement, across to the track that rolled down towards the castle and its defenders. The homes in front reminded Rowan of stones on a dry river bed which, with one order, would be engulfed by a tide of men who would flow around them and throw themselves at the walls of the defenders.

He and the rest of the men waited for the order that never seemed to come. Many of the enemy had now sat down and the commanders had once more gathered together. It seemed that they would endure more waiting, all the time the tension flowing through their bodies. The sun began to shine with increasing ferocity down upon the waiting forces, sparing neither side from its heat, with only the occasional cloud providing a brief respite. Rowan found himself taking his bascinet off and tugging at the neck of his mail shirt, wiping away his sweat while below the enemy greedily drank from communal buckets passed across their lines, their officers enjoying the shade of the village buildings.

'They're waiting for the force to encircle us so they can attack at the same time.' Rowan's father had answered knowingly as he had passed from man to man encouraging them while they waited, trying to reassure them as the late morning passed into afternoon.

As Rowan gratefully slaked his thirst from a bucket of cool clear water from the well he could not help himself glancing once again across to the walls to the rear. A further two archers had been sent across to reinforce the wall but he couldn't help a nagging concern despite the mass of enemy in front. Perhaps it was because it was the way they had infiltrated into the castle those few days ago. Not for the first time he wondered if they should just abandon the barbican but he knew instinctively that order would not come.

He tried to push his worries away, picking at the loose mortar between the solid stones of the wall embrasures, scraping it away with his fingernails, the lime colouring the tips white. It provided a distraction for a short while before he found his eyes once more looking towards the enemy assembled to his front.

The attack eventually came at the height of the afternoon, signalled by the shrill blast of a trumpet followed by others, their sounds piercing through the calm air and causing the friends to stare at each other in a mixture of surprise and worry despite the seemingly endless waiting.

'This is it lads,' Rowan's father's voice promptly shook the men's temporary inertia away.

All about him he could see and hear men on the battlements running to their positions. Below, in the outer courtyard, the few men-at-arms were shouting at each other, the scrape of metal distinct as the wickedly sharpened points and blades of the halberds were picked up from their resting places against the stone walls. Rowan quickly reached for his bascinet and rammed it upon his head, adjusting it slightly before picking up his bow from its resting place against the side of one of the embrasures.

'Only loose on my order.' Sir Robert had appeared on the tower to his right, Rowan's father by his side and to his surprise the much smaller form of Willard.

Rowan wondered briefly if Leovald knew that his son was putting himself in harm's way yet again, but knew he would be too pre occupied with the defence of the inner walls.

'Here they come,' Daniel's now determined voice dismissed any further thoughts he had of Willard.

The two friends looked from their vantage point on the left hand turret while Jerrard and Martin stood slightly below on the curtain wall above the drawbridge at the approaching host. The enemy, with an accompanying roar began to pour through the village and down the track towards the castle, swords and lances thrust high into the air, their faces contorted as they shouted out their battle cries. With alarming speed the attackers surged forwards into lethal arrow range.

Taking a deep breath, and along with the men on the battlements whose numbers felt pathetically small he notched his arrow onto the string and began to pull back against the tension of the bow stave, his shoulder and arm muscles beginning to feel the strain.

'Steady.' Once again Rowan heard his father's calm voice, holding the men from letting loose an arrow too soon.

His muscles began to twinge as the mass of men emerged from the outskirts of the village and poured towards the moat and castle walls. He altered his aim, looking over the stone crenellation and aiming just slightly above the broad rimmed kettle helmet of a charging man at arms who had appeared between two thatched buildings, he could see an unintelligible curse coming from his mouth.

'Loose.'

The order took a split second to register in his mind before his fingers opened and he felt the release of tension from his muscles and the slight whip against his bracer as the arrow flew towards its intended target. Instinctively he reached for one of the stack of arrows leant against the stonework, not looking at whether his first arrow had managed to pierce the enemy's plate armour.

'Now fire at will! Kill them!' The roar of Sir Robert's voice from the opposite turret was reassuring and straightforward.

Quickly notching his second arrow he felt a rush of adrenaline pumping through his body.

This time he focussed at an enemy bowman in the process of pulling his drawstring back and once again his fingers relaxed and the arrow flew from the battlements down towards the enemy.

All around him he could see the thin streaks of arrows flying down from the walls into the mass of men. For the moment they couldn't miss.

'Son's of whores!' The curse from Jerrard and then the thwack of steel-tipped arrows and the splintering of shafts on the stone walls showed that the enemy bowmen had managed to plant their protective mantlets in the dirt and were beginning to fire back. He crouched as he notched his next arrow, now cautious of the enemy barrage.

'Keep firing, for God's sake. Don't let them across the moat!' The cry against the crescendo of shouts from the enemy below, the nearby curses of his friends and the spatter of metal on stone was even now becoming desperate.

Rowan took a deep breath and peered over the embrasure.

'Get those with the ladders.' The cry of his father came from his right who, ignoring the enemy's arrows was pointing down towards groups of men who were managing to carry their long unwieldy assault equipment towards the moat under cover of their archer's fire.

Even as Rowan took in the scene, an arrow smashed into the side of the embrasure making him snatch his head away, the chipped stone pinging against the side of his bascinet. 'Hell and damnation!' His curse came out involuntarily and looking to his left he caught a look from Daniel who had obviously heard his friend's cry.

'They're as bad as a shot as you are!' His friend grinned, as though enjoying himself, before stepping forward and letting loose his arrow. He pulled back quickly behind the stonework, crouching slightly and plucking another arrow from the floor.

Looking past Daniel, Rowan could see that his two other friends on the wall directly above the drawbridge were continuing their fire, despite the almost ceaseless barrage of enemy arrows flying upwards from the archers behind their large wicker shields.

He still had his arrow notched and, with a deep breath and a silent prayer to himself he pulled the string back taking a step forward so he could see the enemy below.

Quickly focussing on the nearest group, he picked out a man-at-arms, both hands occupied as they carried the ladder forwards intent on the escalade. The arrow sped downwards as he hastily dodged behind the stone protection.

Having braved the enemy fire he regained his composure and the years of practice began to take over. He notched, drew back, aimed and let loose, not waiting to see the damage he and his friends caused, just continuing to reach for the depleting pile of arrows and firing into the mass of men below.

He switched his aim between those throwing themselves into the moat and those firing up to the battlements, each time pulling his head back from the counter-fire.

He and his friends were now firing rapidly like they had been trained to do, arrow after arrow being loosed.

Dead and injured littered the ground and waters below.

Still the enemy came on. Many were struggling across the thigh deep water, fighting against the mud as it slowed them down making them a ready target for the archers on the walls.

With heightened anxiety Rowan saw a ladder now being passed forwards above the lifeless bodies littering the dark waters, feathered shafts sticking from corpses as men held the rungs high from the water as they carried it nearer and nearer to the walls.

He let go another arrow at the men below, leaning over the parapet to see if they had managed to clamber upon the narrow strip of earth below the gatehouse.

The urgency amongst the defenders increased.

More arrows continued to fly into the surrounding enemy. Men grasped at arrow shafts as their steel tipped points pierced their throats, arms and legs or slid through padded gambesons and chain mail almost effortlessly to puncture deep into their flesh. Curses and shouts continued to sound out as the enemy pushed against each other waiting to throw themselves against the walls.

'Keep firing. For God's sake, don't let them get

across.' Despite the encouragement from the constant shouts of his father and Sir Robert, Rowan knew the enemy were too numerous. His muscles were aching; his fingers now raw.

He rested for a moment, his back to the parapet and beads of sweat immediately forming on his forehead. Glancing at an angle between the rough stone blocks he could see that more ladders were being passed forwards. It would only be a matter of time before they were raised against the gatehouse walls where he and his friends desperately sought to push them back.

The garrison on the northwest walls were providing enfilading fire, adding their arrows against the determined attackers. More and more bodies floated in the moat staining the shallow water a dark red. The increased barrage only seemed to anger the enemy who were now almost fighting each other to enter the water and reach the foot of the walls, urged forwards by the knights and their sergeants, all the while cursing the defenders.

He tugged free one of the last dozen arrows from his belt; the arrows that had just minutes ago seemed so plentiful lying against the wall now exhausted.

Rowan took aim and let loose.

The point buried itself deep into a man's chest. The enemy's struggles against the muddied bottom forgotten as he dropped his hold on a ladder and clutched at the shaft in vain. A look of surprise showed on his face before, almost in slow motion, he slid backwards into the water, blood already beginning to surround his body.

'Well done, men.' The shout came from the turret

opposite to his right. 'A shilling to the next man who topples another ladder.' Sir Robert's voice carried clear, his visor lifted briefly, goading the men into even greater efforts.

Rowan felt a surge of pride, for a moment overcoming the anxiety of the assault around him.

'Got him!' Jerrard soon shouted out, grinning to his friends, wounding another of the enemy who was trying to pick up the ladder that had just fallen into the water.

Rowan looked down from the barbican tower and returned the smile just as, with a sickening metallic ring Jerrard's head was snatched backwards and he tumbled to the floor of the battlement.

Martin reacted quickly, dropping his bow and slithering across to his friend who was lying on his back. The force and shock of the enemy's arrow making Jerrard's legs give way.

'Give over will you, you idiot.' Jerrard's familiar gruffness came as a relief to his friends as he tried to push Martin away, tugging off his bascinet and rubbing the side of his head.

Rowan and Daniel continued to fire at the enemy below, ducking quickly behind the stonework as soon as their arrows were released, before notching another.

As Rowan aimed between the thick ramparts he could see more and more men reaching for the ladders floating between the bodies, while on the track more troops were hefting their wooden burdens forward. The enemy were determined to reach the walls under cover of the arrows that continued to smack against the sides of the embrasures.

'Don't stop! Keep shooting, for pity's sake.' The defenders sensed the increased momentum behind the escalade and ignored their raw fingers and aching muscles as they snatched arrows from their belts and let fly at the enemy below.

Another arrow took a ladder carrier in the throat as he waded forwards and this time it was grabbed by a knight from among the Welsh ranks, distinct in his full helm, the pointed visor pulled down wearing a dirty vert and argent surcoat. Despite the treacherous footing underneath the knight waded on, grabbing one end of the ladder with his gauntleted hands before striding forwards, pushing aside the bodies that floated in his way.

Rowan altered his aim, the point of the arrow now aligned to the knight's chest. He let go, pausing for a moment despite the counter fire and watched the arrow as the bodkin smacked somewhere between the man's gard brace and the pauldron protecting his left shoulder. Though his aim had not been true, the man still staggered backwards, threatening to topple into the bloody waters as the armour deflected the arrow. Rowan could sense the man's curse as he sought to stand his ground, the mud underfoot probably helping him before, almost in slow motion, the knight staggered on resolutely towards the foot of the gatehouse with the ladder still in one armoured glove.

The noble attracted the aim of the other archers on the battlements and more arrows sped towards the armoured figure.

Some missed, others similarly bounced off the man's armour but one took him in the thigh just above the waterline, causing him to stumble. Once more the knight recovered his footing and continued on.

Too quickly he was below the gatehouse walls and dragging his burden up the slippery slope of the moat.

Rowan ducked as another arrow smacked against the stonework, a sudden flurry of missiles quickly dissuading him from leaning over the battlements.

The roar from the enemy increased, the knight's bravery and determination spreading among the attackers as they poured forwards to aid him and carrying more ladders as they came.

'There at the walls!' he cried out unnecessarily, looking instinctively to his father and Sir Robert on the opposite tower, using the walls as protection, peering down at an angle to watch the assaulting men below.

He wasn't sure if his father had heard his shout but Rowan could see him directing fire from the men across on the castle walls into the flanks of the attackers. He grasped another arrow and let fly. There wasn't anything he could do about the men directly beneath but he could still aim at the enemy who hadn't crossed the moat yet.

'Stop more of them getting across,' he shouted urgently, sensing Jerrard had at least partially recovered from his near miss and along with Martin on the curtain wall were resuming their fire at the enemy mass as they came on.

The defenders continued to fire despite the barrage that still assaulted them from the enemy archers behind their wicker mantlets in front of the village.

It was easy to find targets among the attackers but despite the arrows from the towers and battlements continuing to punch through padded gambesons, mail shirts and armour, the enemy relentlessly advanced, wading across the moat to mass beneath the walls.

The sweat was beginning to drip past his eyebrows down into his eyes and he managed to cuff it quickly in between grasping for another arrow. 'Get them,' he was talking to himself, his words lost against the cacophony of shouts and curses from defenders and attackers alike.

'They're climbing,' the shout from Martin accompanied the sudden appearance of ladders against the gatehouse walls.

Without thinking, Rowan quickly hung his bow across his back, the bowstring tight across his chest. He quickly undid the buckler from his belt, thrusting his arm through the leather straps before reaching for the handle of his sword, scraping it free as more ladders appeared. One ladder smacked against the stonework almost directly in front of him between the stone merlons.

The time for arrows had passed as his friends also grasped for their swords. Arrows still flew up at the defenders, stopping him from going too close to the edge where the wooden rungs now shook with the weight of men climbing upwards.

'What on God's earth do we do now?' At his side Daniel's anxiety was obvious.

'We kill the wort-ridden dogs.' Rowan was surprised by his own cursing reply. It could have so easily come from the mouths of Sir Robert or his friend, Jerrard.

Looking down across at his big bearded friend he watched as now un-helmeted and seemingly oblivious to the arrows firing up at him he grabbed both uprights of a ladder in his fists. With a grunt of effort Jerrard pushed the struts outwards, his face going red as he exerted all his strength so that the top of the ladder slowly moved away from the battlements, the timber bending. Momentum was with his friend now but he couldn't push the ladders further and so twisted the struts so it began to fall sideways accompanied by shrieks from the enemy desperately holding onto the rungs below.

Jerrard turned to his friends, a big grin on his face. 'That's how to do it!' before stepping back hastily hearing yet another thwack as an arrow splintered against the stonework. 'Satan's hairy-arse,' yet another curse left Jerrard's mouth and Rowan couldn't help a tired grin to himself as his friend suddenly seemed to remember the threat he had so recently ignored.

Not that his smile lasted long as a sword point appeared above the ladder in front of him, followed by a raised shield with the device of a red dragon emblazoned upon it.

Rowan instinctively smashed down hard on the kite shaped shield with his falchion but was rewarded only with a dull thud as the metal struck the hardened leather and a shudder passed along his own arm. The shield angled slightly from the blow but not enough to expose the attacker to a second strike and the enemy took another step upwards on the ladder.

'Kill him, for God's sake', Daniel for the moment had no one in front of him though he too was warily watching as a second ladder shook with the weight of men climbing.

Rowan swung again with his full force behind it but

his effort met with the same effect. The impact caused more pain to lance along his sword arm while the shield resolutely stayed in place protecting the enemy behind even as the man started to clamber between the embrasure. Now however the leather shield proved an encumbrance and it caught against one of the stone sides for a moment giving Rowan a glimpse of the man's moustached face now almost level with his own. He felt time unnaturally slow for a moment as his eyes locked onto those of his adversary. His mind was racing, a mixture of fear and energy coursed through him as he thrust the point of his sword into the man's neck before he could react. There was brief resistance and then with a sickening feeling he felt the steel rip through into the man's windpipe. The man let out a brief gurgling sound, his eyes still locked on Rowan's almost accusingly as he toppled backwards, the blade sliding out accompanied by a tide of bright red blood along its steel edge.

Rowan's heart was pumping. Around him he could hear his friends grappling with more attackers as they sought to clamber over the battlements. Next to him, Daniel's sword clashed for the first time against that of another enemy soldier seeking to gain the turret they defended.

Another helmeted face appeared in front of Rowan, no shield this time but the sharp point of a pike thrust forwards in an attempt to push him back. He slashed his sword at the point, the force of the blow almost knocking the enemy from his perch as he clung onto his weapon. The man took another step upwards, thrusting viciously at his face, and he involuntarily took a slight step back. It allowed the man to reach out with his free hand to the sides of the embrasure to give him some purchase as he sought to pull himself through the gap. Rowan instinctively changed aim mid swing and brought his now bloodied blade down to slice into the man's hand grasping the stonework taking his fingers clean off. The man's cries of anger turned into screams of pain before he too, with the aid of a push into his face from Rowan's buckler followed his comrade to smash heavily into the thronging enemy below.

And so they came on, Rowan was having trouble breathing and longed to rid himself of his bascinet, its lining soaked so that it seemed to encourage the sweat to sting his eyes and threaten more than once to force him back from the wall to clear his vision. All along the gatehouse walls his friends were fighting furiously. The din of battle rang in his ears, steel on steel, a deflected blow, a missed swipe, steel on stone, a curse or a shriek of pain were all around. Next to him, almost standing back to back with Rowan, Daniel was cursing savagely, using every effort to stop the enemy getting a foothold on the battlements which would enable more of the attackers to spill over and take control.

To their right, Jerrard and Martin were taking it in turns to batter at the enemy, Jerrard having decided to discard his sword and using his heavy mallet to smash into the attackers, denting plate armour and breaking bones as he and his friend sought to stem the stream of attackers. Further across, ladders had also reached the opposite gatehouse tower and he caught sight of his father and Sir Robert, both as heavily engaged as Rowan and his friends, their swords catching the sun as they swung down through the air thrusting and blocking as they fought off the enemy.

'We're not going to be able to hold them,' Daniel gasped as he sent another of the enemy tumbling through the air as a further attacker appeared in front of Rowan.

He knew his friend was right. His arms were aching and he was exhausted but all too aware that once the enemy gained a foothold their defeat would be inescapable. He was too tired to reply but, taking a deep breath and with determination in his heart he raised his sword and swung it at the man-at-arms who was trying to clamber over the parapet.

The first enemy success was accompanied by a roar from the turret to his right.

Risking a quick glance Rowan saw with trepidation the broad figure of a man-at-arms who had somehow managed to clamber over the wall and with unmistakable savagery was now swinging his long handled mace horizontally at the two defenders. Sir Robert stepped back from the lethal swing, allowing the heavy metal spiked head to pass harmlessly in front of him before confidently taking a long step forward and using his shoulder to smash into the similarly armoured chest of his attacker. The man toppled backwards, he was now against the stone embrasure as the knight brought his sword up two handed aiming a blow at the man's neck. The man raised his mace to block the blow and he could have swore he heard the clash of the two weapons meeting and then in the same move, almost too quick for his eyes, the knight smashed his helm into that of the enemy, into metal and face alike before the figure crumpled to the floor disappearing below Rowan's eye line.

But the damage had been done. The felled man had acted like the first stone pulled from a wall. Suddenly it allowed two more of the attackers to gain space on the rampart and behind them more attackers appeared. He watched as his father and the knight now gave ground as weapons were thrust towards them, Willard was behind the two warriors as they defended desperately unable to turn back the tide.

'By the virgin, there's too many of the swag bellied swine,' Jerrard cursed loudly, indicating that he too was aware that the bulwark provided by the stone bastion of the gatehouse walls was beginning to break.

Rowan knew there was little he and his friends could do as they struggled to force back the incessant tide of enemy soldiers climbing up the scaling ladders. At least the storm of arrows had now ceased for fear of hitting their own men but that was of little comfort as they fought hand to hand desperately protecting their section of wall but knowing to their right the enemy were threatening to finally overcome the defenders.

He allowed the next attacker, this time wearing a mailed shirt, to raise his head and upper body above the stonework and with what was now almost becoming a practised manoeuvre stepped forward, thrusting his sword at the enemy's face. The man frantically raised his own sword to protect himself, using much of his strength to hold onto the ladder with his remaining hand, allowing Rowan in the same movement to smash his buckler forwards behind the blocked thrust of his sword. The bossed centre hit the enemy with a force and momentum that jerked his head savagely backwards. Despite the pain of his obviously broken nose the man held on for a moment before Rowan smashed his buckler once more into the now blood-splattered face and the man fell shrieking to the ground below. He quickly glanced below into the bailey of the barbican. They needed reinforcements quickly if they were going to hold on.

'Get some men up here and repel them,' he cried out, but even as the last words left his mouth he registered for the first time the clash of steel from the rearward walls.

Like themselves, the archers on the southern walls had now come under sudden attack and were faring as badly. With a feeling of dread he could sense the coordinated attack was working. Enemy men-at-arms who had circumvented the walls were now engaged in hand-to-hand combat with the defenders, who had similarly discarded their bows to parry at their attackers with sword and buckler. Even as he watched, one of the archers went down, an enemy lance piercing his leg and before he could recover, he was physically forced from the parapet, falling with a sickening thud onto the dirt floor of the outer bailey.

Below Sir Robert's men-at-arms were obviously torn between maintaining their stations and rushing to the aid of the archers up the stone stairways of the turrets. Then there was no decision to make as the figure of another archer appeared at the foot of the south west tower. One arm was hanging limply by his side, a dark smear spread across his faded vert surcoat, his sword held out defensively as he backed out of the dark interior of the turret doorway. A spear tip appeared out of the gloom followed by the dark gules uniformed figure of an attacker who rushed forwards, seemingly intent on finishing the archer off as soon as possible. Once, twice, the archer parried, trying to protect his left hand side which was exposed by his wounded arm. It seemed that his strength would fail him and leave him to his death but then one of Sir Robert's men rushed forwards. He swung his halberd horizontally at the enemy who, though registering the threat, could do little to avoid the blow as the full weight of the steel blade smashed heavily into his body, cutting through the protective layers of his gambeson to bury itself deep into his innards. His feet almost left the dirt floor with the force and he was already dead by the time the boot was placed on his chest to lever out the blade.

'They're coming over the back.' Rowan's shout was almost a scream as he swung his now dulled and chipped blade at the next attacker clambering upwards. It was clear to him that the enemy were now moments from cutting off their retreat.

'Fall back, fall back!' The call was taken up by the few men on the battlements.

'Back boys, they'll be following,' he could hear Jerrard urging Martin as they stepped towards the stone-framed entrance to the tower's interior which Rowan and Daniel still defended for the moment.

Even as they retreated he saw enemy soldiers begin to pour over the now undefended rampart. It was time to go. He swung his sword one last time at the enemy, ineffectively smashing his blade so it glanced off the stonework. The man ducked below the parapet giving

Rowan a few precious seconds to hastily follow Daniel down the open staircase, his bow scraping on the stone sides. He took one last look at the dark outline of enemy soldiers, who now yelled with victory as they pulled themselves between the stone embrasures. Rowan slammed the hatch door firmly shut and with fumbling hands slid the locking bar, thrust to him by Daniel, through the metal hoops.

The sudden dullness inside the tower and protection afforded by the solid door allowed Rowan and his friends a brief respite. Both were breathing heavily from their sudden retreat and the efforts in trying to thwart the assault.

'Christ on the cross, that was close,' Martin was leaning against the circular inner wall. 'I don't think we could have held out much longer.'

The two friends had also managed to bar the door to the battlements but even as he made his comment the loud thudding of metal pommels against the thick oak door started.

'God almighty!' Daniel said involuntarily as he flinched at the noise. 'We'd best get out of here.'

'I'm with you on that one,' Rowan responded and, with suddenly weary legs raised himself from the stone steps where he had recovered his breath.

He followed his friends down the winding staircase partially illuminated by the sunlight through the narrow lancet. Peering through the deep arrow loop as he passed his heart sank as he saw the massed number of rebels seemingly undiminished by the efforts of the defenders.

The echoing of metal thumping against the barred

doors above followed them as they scrambled down the stone staircase and its worn steps, past the gatehouse armoury into the courtyard. Despite the heavy portcullis now firmly in place behind the raised drawbridge, the courtyard was beginning to fill with battling men. The attackers had managed to overcome the soldiers on the rearward wall and were now pressing the small group of Sir Robert's men-at-arms and remaining archers. The odds were not in the defenders' favour as they retreated step by step forming into a defensive wall of shields, swords and halberds shifting backwards towards the archway leading to the main castle.

Instinctively Rowan and his friends rushed to the right flank of the defensive line, knowing that the enemy from the front walls would soon lend their blades to the melee and took his place alongside one of the men-at-arms with a large battered shield.

'There'll soon be too many of 'em,' came the broad Staffordshire accent from the man next to him as the enemy temporarily stepped back, waiting for more of their comrades to appear. Both groups of men breathed heavily, their hands holding tightly to their weapons, a matter of mere feet from each other.

'What in the Lord's name are you waiting for then?' came the gruff taunt from Jerrard, his heavy mallet held ready in his large fist.

Rowan wished his friend would keep quiet, not wanting to encourage the enemy to press home their attack which no doubt would come soon enough.

His thoughts were interrupted as first his father and then Sir Robert burst out from the shadows of the nearest tower entrance.

The knight was holding his sword level, pointing at some as yet unseen enemy, keeping them at bay for the moment. His father carried the limp form of an injured comrade, the dark shaft of an arrow tipped by grey feathers embedded in the un-armoured torso. With a sick feeling that turned his stomach he realised from the size, the garb and blond shoulder-length hair that it could only be Willard.

At that moment more men charged from the doorway from where he and his friends had retreated, the men having somehow managed to break through one of the strong wooden doors. Their appearance, coupled with the sight of Sir Robert battling his attackers, seemed to release the pent up eagerness of the enemy to throw their bodies at the small wall of defenders.

With a refreshed wave of curses the enemy leapt forward, their weapons smashing downwards ringing against raised shields or swords. The line seemed to stagger from the weight of the charge and Rowan found he was forced backwards. A man-at-arms swiped with a broad-bladed axe at him, splintering his hastily raised buckler. Even as the man's momentum carried him forwards causing Rowan to lose his balance, he thrust his sword forwards and was rewarded as he felt the steel tip, aided by the man's weight split through the man's leather jerkin. With a cry of fear and pain the man felt the steel pierce his body but was unable to stop his charge and took the blade with him to the dirt floor beneath.

With a grunt of effort Rowan tried desperately to

retrieve his weapon but even as he did so glanced up to see the contorted face of another of the enemy men-at-arms who had his lance aimed at the centre of his chest. In that moment he could see clearly the man's features, the few remaining black stained teeth below the large drooping moustache and the frenzied eyes baying for blood, knowing he could not avoid the point.

The blur of steel came from his right, deflecting the lance so it ended up ripping across the front of his surcoat and gashing his arm. Rowan was already throwing himself to the floor expecting the thrust of the steel tip, his hand letting go of the pommel of his sword which was still embedded in the corpse. Above him his father followed up his defensive blow with a second swipe of his sword at the enemy forcing him backwards.

'In all the saints names get up,' his father urged without taking his eyes from his front, and then louder for the rest of the men to hear, 'fall back, fall back!'

Rowan hurriedly reached forward and with effort dragged the sword towards him, wriggling his arm free from the remnants of the smashed buckler before getting to his feet and backing towards the archway and the drawbridge beyond.

The men funnelled backwards encouraged by Sir Robert, his visor now up. 'Come on men, quickly now.' The knight was now watching the men fall back from the drawbridge below the castle gatehouse. Despite having to shout above the surrounding mayhem his voice was calm and encouraging.

More and more attackers came over the walls to reinforce their comrades as they continued to swing their weapons at the depleted defenders who stepped back pressing against into each other in the confines of the stone archway.

Behind, Rowan could hear the sound of men's heavy footsteps as they retreated across the wooden planks of the drawbridge. He realised it was his turn as the press of men behind him lessened and he was able to stumble across the crossing, anxious to get away from the now possessed attackers. The enemy still came at the defenders but by now they had fallen back under the shadows of the archway, the narrow front helping keep the enemy at bay. The clash of steel still continued, accompanied by the curses of men but Rowan only had thoughts of safety as he staggered under the inner gatehouse and into the castle courtyard beyond.

The men so recently engaged in battle were in various states of relief within the inner walls. Many were gulping in air, their weapons heavy in their arms while some were being tended by the few women remaining who were binding wounds. Among them he saw Willard lying on a cloak by the side of the stone well, Catin by the young boy's side mopping his brow with a dark piece of cloth.

'Get that drawbridge up.'

Rowan's brief reverie was broken. The battle was far from over and the enemy were still pressing forwards. The harsh ring of steel could still be heard as a few defenders still fought a rear guard action. Rowan glanced to his left where three men-at-arms were hastily beginning to turn the metal arms of the windlass controlling the drawbridge.

'Put your backs into it!' The call was coming from

the battlements above and, glancing up, Rowan could see Lord Fitz Warrin urging the men in their efforts.

With aching muscles he stepped back towards the drawbridge where he could see two remaining defenders doggedly defending the outer archway, giving the garrison the time they needed to raise the bridge. A man-at-arms, his surcoat ripped and torn revealing the dull gleam of an armoured plate was wearily raising his shield as an unseen attacker smashed again and again at the protection. The man's shield arm was visibly getting slower to redress the shield's positioning but it was the sight of his father next to him that brought a sense of dread.

His father had now discarded his bascinet, or perhaps had lost it in the melee and was thrusting his sword forward and then back with frenzied urgency, occasionally raising it to block a strike. Behind him, Rowan registered the cranking of the metal chains showing that the efforts of the men at the windlass were beginning to take effect. He saw the first shudder of movement as the tip of the tough drawbridge was raised from its resting place not more than eight feet from the two defenders.

'No!' His cry came out instinctively as he ran towards his father, his mind in turmoil as he began to register what was beginning to happen. But his rush through the gateway was abruptly halted by the strong arm of Sir Robert. Rowan's immediate reaction was to throw the noble's arm away but the knight stood firm and his efforts to get past his heavy build were thwarted.

'Leave him. He's doing it for us. There's nothing you

or I can do if we don't want the enemy to overrun us'.

The logic in his words did nothing to relieve Rowan's feeling of horror as the drawbridge began to rise. Even as he watched he saw the man-at-arms at his father's side succumb to a heavy blow to his helm, the body toppling against the sides of the archway and giving the enemy more space to bring their weapons to bear. He watched as his father took a step backwards, throwing his sword upwards in a desperate parry but was unable to prevent a lance pierce beneath his guard. His body doubled over, seeking to retreat from the wound but this only exposed his neck and with sickening ferocity a sword slashed down causing a spurt of blood to fly into the air.

He knew his father was dead even before the drawbridge managed to block out the faces of the attackers who now were being assailed by the arrows of the defenders on the ramparts above, their effect and retribution not registering amongst Rowan's grief.

'He was a brave man, your father.'

He turned to look into the hardened face of Sir Robert, his blue eyes filled with concern.

'Without his bravery we'd even now be fighting for our lives.' The knight's hand briefly rested on his shoulder even as the heavy drawbridge thudded shut, blocking out the light within the archway. 'I wish I had more time to share your sorrow but we have to defend the castle.' As he hurried away he added meaningfully, 'your father wouldn't had wanted his death to be in vain either.'

As he watched Sir Robert turn and leave, ordering the men still recovering in the bailey onto their feet he registered the ongoing sounds of battle around him, dulled by the barred gatehouse and walls rising above. He realised the background noise of men cursing and shouting had now become almost as natural to his ears now as wind in the trees. It had only been a couple of hours since the enemy had moved against the castle but it felt like a lifetime. Jaded he sheathed his sword and lifted his bow from his back following behind the knight who hurried to organise the defenders against the enemy who poured into the captured outer castle.

In the confines of the courtyard the remaining six men-at-arms had taken their bascinets off, the skull caps beneath dark with sweat. Some retained their halberds while others had just their long swords in their hands, all of their blades were bloody and their surcoats, mail and armour showed the effects of battle. They were assembled just behind the barred gatehouse, the last defensive line should the enemy find a way to breach the raised drawbridge. The few surviving archers from the barbican, including his three friends, were collecting sheaves of arrows that had been made and stored in the days before on a couple of covered wooden carts left just outside the Lord's chapel.

Daniel turned as he thrust some loose arrows through his belt and caught sight of his friend, his scarred face showing concern as he saw Rowan's face. 'You alright?'

Rowan realised his friends in the heat of the retreat might not know of his father's fate and resolutely decided the news could wait. Sir Robert was right, he thought to himself, grieving could happen later. Right now he wanted to fight and kill the men that were responsible for his grief. 'Yeh, fine,' and then he remembered the prone figure of Willard, surely not him too he thought to himself. 'How's Willard?'

'Rose says Catin is looking after him but he looked bad when Jerrard took him from your father.' Rowan mentally despaired at the mention of his father but Daniel didn't seem to notice. 'He's been taken inside the hall,' he jerked his thumb towards the eastern building.

'Right let me get some arrows and we'll get up on those battlements.' Rowan didn't want to speak any more and, though weary, could hear the increasing noise from the attackers who were obviously intent on taking the walls.

His two other friends welcomed him as he replenished first his arrow bag and then grabbing a further sheaf in his left hand hurried to the gatehouse tower. The leather soles of his boots scuffed on the stone steps as they wound up the dark interior betraying his tiredness, his thighs were aching as he brushed past the garrison archer who fired through the narrow arrow loop on the first floor.

As the man reached for another arrow he caught sight of the friends. 'Watch out for the archers when you get up to the top. They're accurate swine.' As if to reinforce the warning the loud smack from a couple of steel arrow points bracketed the edges of the loophole. 'Christ's bones.' An inevitable curse came from the archer's lips heavily tinged with a Welsh accent before he drew back his bow, leaning into the embrasure to let another arrow fly at the enemy outside the castle walls.

The scene that met Rowan's eyes as he raised his

head from the trapdoor was chaotic, made even more so by the sight of both Sir Robert and Lord Fitz Warrin with their backs to the merlons protecting them from the enemy fire.

'Keep your heads down,' Sir Robert didn't let his previous encounter with Rowan show, his focus now firmly on the situation at hand. Arrows streaked past or smashed against the stonework that protected the heads of the nobles and the few archers on the ramparts directly above the drawbridge. 'They're on the opposite battlements as well as down below. For now I need you here.' His voice was raised against the noise emanating from the enemy.

Rowan half crawled to the wall and took a quick glance across, seeing the figures of the enemy firing arrows furiously not more than twenty yards away. Fortunately the walls of the outer castle were lower than the height of the inner walls behind which the remaining garrison sheltered giving them an advantage. He looked at his friends now similarly crouched on the floor of the turret before turning to Sir Robert. 'They're only keeping us down by their weight of numbers, sire. We can deal with that?'

Sir Robert considered Rowan's offer for a moment before deferring to Lord Fitz Warrin to his left. The Lord gazed into Rowan's eyes for a moment before calmly agreeing.

'Right lads,' Rowan said with outward confidence he didn't necessarily feel but seething with anger at the death of his father. 'Jerrard and Martin go to the battlements and the north tower and let them know we're going to let the enemy have a few volleys,' he indicated the tower fifty feet away. As well as commanding the approach to the outer drawbridge and the village, men on the tower and were able to lend their fire on the enemy facing them on the barbican walls. 'Get whatever men we have on the walls to shoot as soon as I do and keep on firing.'

The two crouching men simply nodded, accepting their friend's leadership and quickly made their way down on to the battlements connecting the towers.

The same orders were passed down to the two archers directly above the drawbridge before he and Daniel leant their arrows against the walls of the tower. He could feel the gaze of the nobles upon him and swallowed his nervousness, peering at an angle through the gap at the enemy opposite for a half a minute before judging he had waited long enough. He switched his gaze towards the other tower seeing the two familiar figures now in position.

His breathing was quickening and he braced himself, knees bent, and nodded to Daniel. 'Now!'

The men rose to their feet, pulling their arrows to their ears in a well practised motion. The bow staves creaked as they bent to the pressure exerted by the pull of the men's shoulders.

Immediately Rowan's eyes focussed upon an enemy who was in the process of drawing his own bow. There was no time to flinch and the arrow left the string, its tension released and his right hand quickly grasped the next arrow in his belt.

He heard one of the garrison archers give a cry of pain but he was now moving instinctively, the grief and anger being released in the frenzy of his shooting.

Again and again he reached, drew and let loose the steel tipped arrows and was hardly aware of the enemy either dead, injured or seeking shelter from the incessant barrage from his comrades, the smack of arrow tips on masonry like the heavy patter of rain.

All of a sudden there were no more enemies as he shifted his aim, the steel tipped arrow in his eye line, across the walls opposite in a fruitless search for more of the enemy.

'Well done men,' came the enthusiastic voice of Sir Robert, now able to stand up along with Lord Fitz Warrin, temporarily confident enough to raise their visors once more. 'That should hold them for a while.'

For a moment longer Rowan stared opposite, his bow held taught until he was satisfied that the enemy archers had decided not to contest the fight before glancing downwards. His eyes were drawn to the bodies at the outer bailey archway. Sure enough he could see among the corpses the heavily stained mail and surcoat of his father a short distance away across from the inner ditch.

'Rowan, I'm sorry, we didn't realise,' the words came softly and heartfelt from Daniel by his side who sensed what had unfolded below and following his friend's eyes also recognised the prone body on the floor.

There was a silent pause. He wanted to say it didn't matter, that his father had died bravely, but it did matter to him. Why was it his father that had died? Surely he could have been saved? Surely he could have done more?

Once again Sir Robert seemed to read the situation,

interrupting his thoughts. 'While these swine are sorting themselves out one of you had best move him.' He indicated the dead archer on the ramparts just below who had received an arrow neatly through his chest. Rowan could see how his now unmoving hands had vainly clutched around the shaft seeking to stop the flow of blood that had spilled copiously across his chest and was now becoming a darker shade of red as it dried in the afternoon sun. Rowan realised it must have been his cry he had heard as he launched the first of his arrows at the enemy on the opposite battlements.

'Rowan,' it was the first time Sir Robert had used his name. He wasn't even aware he knew it. 'Go and see that Welsh sergeant and see how he's faring.'

Before he had chance to acknowledge the command an arrow smacked against the stonework signalling that the enemy had not altogether sought safety. 'Quick now,' Sir Robert urged as he crouched once more behind the stone work snapping his visor down as an arrow flew upwards missing them and soaring on into the now almost cloudless blue sky.

Rowan half crawled to the open hatchway and slid down, making his way past the archer at the embrasure who was too preoccupied staring outwards to notice him exit through the doorway onto the battlements.

Glancing out he could see one archer tending a wounded comrade shot in the arm. The lifeless bodies of two others, one sitting, his back to the wall staring sightlessly upwards, while another lay with one arm hanging over the ramparts, dangling over the courtyard below. Further along, another man in the Lord's livery was trying to restring his bow and a sixth cautiously peered out across the short distance at the enemy held walls.

He pushed himself away from the stone doorway and ran, head crouched, his bow held low past the embrasures, expecting an arrow to be sent in his direction at any time.

The man having his arm tended to looked up briefly, his face pale from the pain. His comrade was too intent on tightly wrapping the bandage around his friend's forearm to look up as he passed. Similarly the man stringing his bow also showed little interest, his face betraying a look of weariness as Rowan stopped, making sure the walls protected him from any arrows even though for now there had been no resurrection in the barrage.

'Have you seen Leovald?' he asked grasping the man's arm, taking the time to take a breath.

'He went that way after we finished, said he'd just check on the other men,' the soldier pointed his thumb towards the tower entrance.

There were no more arrows as he continued towards the safety of the narrow doorway. It seemed that the defenders sudden volley had had the desired impact and he felt a brief sense of satisfaction.

Entering the cool of the interior and resisting the temptation to climb the stairs to see how his two friends had fared he made his way to the east wall where he could see the big Welshman with another member of Fitz Warrin's garrison staring out between the merlons keeping a watch on the enemy below.

'Leovald,' he called, gesturing to his friend, for some unknown reason keeping his voice low.

The Welshman showed a brief look of surprise and then curiosity before, taking one last look over the walls and ordering the two archers on the south eastern turret to continue to keep a lookout, came half crouching over to meet him.

Rowan was pulled roughly to the ground as Leovald reached him, 'Are you looking to get an arrow in that head of yours?' he exclaimed loudly in his broad accent.

'Sir Robert wanted me to ask about the situation.' A cough tickled at his throat as he spoke.

'Well we're fair short of men which you've seen. I've spread them as well as I can.' Rowan's eyes followed Leovald's inclination of his neck towards the two archers behind him, there were none at all on the southern wall. 'I'll probably even have to pull these men when they attack so we'll have no one watching that approach but for now I think they're content not to press on.' The Welshman recognised the same slackening of the battle as each side took a pause in their efforts.

'You may have to do it sooner than that now the enemy have got the outer gatehouse. We'll need all our arrows to stop them from forcing their way through and bringing more reinforcements across the village.'

Leovald listened to him in silence, apparently at ease with Rowan's assessment of the situation. 'You're right, I'll just have to leave one of the least injured lads. Mind you I'm not sure how long the arrows will last us.'

At this, Rowan looked down into the courtyard below where sure enough the once highly stacked carts holding the supply of arrows had probably less than fifteen sheaves remaining in each, only just more than twenty four arrows per man, but it wasn't this thought that made his heart feel like breaking for the second time that day. Below was the blue clothed figure of Catin who had just emerged from the hall, her cloak was now stained, her blond hair ragged, but what concerned him more was her tear-streaked face. She must have sensed Rowan looking down at her because at that moment her moist eyes stared up at the battlements, first at Rowan and then at Leovald who mercifully had returned his gaze back towards the surrounding countryside.

'Looks like the buggers have had enough for now,' but the lack of response from Rowan caused Leovald to turn his attention from the attackers to his friend. 'What's up?' he asked seeing the concern in Rowan's face before noticing Catin below.

For a moment nothing was said, Leovalds face was enquiring at first and then slowly registered that whatever it was concerned him. Then it hit him as surely as a punch into his midriff. He grabbed Rowan's arm. 'Willard?' he asked quietly, dreading the response.

Rowan couldn't speak and slowly nodded, feeling sick to his stomach. He watched his friend as the confirmation sunk in slowly, his arm now beginning to feel the pressure from Leovald's grip.

'Watch the walls,' and with that command the big Welshman hurriedly stepped into the turret and down the steps to see his son.

CHAPTER TEN

William de Movran couldn't help feel frustrated that they had been unable to carry on the assault into the main castle, despite the relative success of the attack. He knew more than Rhys Gethin and the rest of his knights the difficulty that the thick grey walls and the ditches of water presented any attacker. Once more he inwardly cursed that he hadn't himself raised the drawbridge a few days earlier. It would have changed everything.

He had spent over two years at the castle, having pledged his service to Lord Fitz Warrin but secretly hoping someday King Richard would be reinstated to the throne. More recently he had contented himself by plotting with Sir John Done who had visited the castle the previous summer and who had sensed his loyalty to the old King.

Over those first few days and subsequent visits his hope and ambitions were reignited as Sir John had assured him that although he, like so many of Richard's other followers, had dissipated in the face of Henry's overwhelming forces he would be rewarded for his continued loyalty. The only uncomfortable arrangement was that he would also be throwing in his lot with Glyn Dwr's rebellion but for that he had decided his reward would be Whittington Castle, made all the easier if he captured the walls that he had so briefly held and now faced.

In the months and years he had grown to understand the strength of the castle, its water and stone defences and had encouraged Lord Fitz Warrin to pursue a course of inaction, arguing that it was better not to aggravate the Welsh rebels even though the support for Glyn Dwr continued to grow. At the same time he had been happy to gather the support of like-minded men from within the garrison. These were people like Bayard who were not necessarily loyal to Richard but wanted power and others, including several archers from Cheshire, who had served Richard previously and were happy to throw in their lot.

He now realised this inaction had probably precipitated the arrival of the Earl's force as more than once the Lord Fitz Warrin had been forced to explain to Prince Henry his lack of vigour towards the Welsh rebellion.

He sighed to himself, it was no good going over old ground. Instead he brushed ineffectually at the dried mud from the marshes that still clung to his armour and mail beneath. It was apparent that the attack had stalled. The Welsh commander was in no mood to push onwards during the late afternoon and early evening, the sudden counter barrage following the raising of the drawbridge had been enough to see to that.

Still he was satisfied in the role he had played up to this point and knew he had earned some respect among the other knights. His assurance about the merits of assaulting the rearward walls of the outer bailey had been proved right and he allowed himself a slight smile as he sat in the comfort of the village inn, his legs stretched forwards, holding a liberated cup of wine poured by his sergeant who was sitting opposite him on the wooden winged chairs. The rest of the inn was populated by other knights who despite their grudging respect largely ignored him, not that it mattered he thought to himself.

With a sense of satisfaction he knew his advice and subsequent circuit in full view of the garrison had been successful, the unceremonious and arduous clamber across the mud almost forgotten. In fact his assault had been aided when the ponytailed Welsh knight commanding the spearmen and, who had resented his command, had been one of the soldiers that had lost their lives to the arrows of the defenders as they had struggled across the wetlands. He could visualise the armoured body even now lying spread-eagled and mud-splattered amongst the sodden clumps of grass, a look of incomprehension on his face as he slowly choked on his own blood.

He took a large swallow of the harsh wine. Yes it had been fortunate, the knight would have resisted him as he waited in safety even as his comrades perished in the main frontal assault despite the signal from the trumpet. Not one of his remaining men at arms had been killed while almost half of the Welsh spearmen allocated to him had perished or had been fatally wounded, a result of him sending them first against the walls.

The wine and the warm atmosphere with the backdrop of hearty chatter among the soldiers helped him remain calm. He still felt some anger and frustration that he and his men-at-arms had strode through the gateway too late to prevent the enemy retreating behind the fortress walls. By the time the locking bar had been scraped free, the enemy had hastily fallen back towards the inner castle. They had desperately fended off the attackers who were now flowing over the walls, the bravery or stupidity of two of the defenders preventing them getting inside the castle before the drawbridge was raised.

Although he had been challenged in the immediate aftermath by Rhys Gethin he had been stout in his defence, blaming the dead knight put under his command for the failure to make a diversionary attack at the same time as the frontal assault.

'So what are we going to do now then, my lord?' Bayard asked, his manner almost as relaxed as his own. Despite the casualties before the walls of the castle they still outnumbered the defenders massively.

'We wait. I suppose Rhys Gethin will have ordered more work gangs to the forest and within a day or two we'll be able to bring siege engines to bear. Don't worry, we'll soon have Whittington under our control.'

'And what of the Welsh, my lord, will they stand by their original agreement?' Bayard looked round furtively, keeping his voice low.

'They will, they need all the allies they can get and, by God, it's part of the agreement.' The question threatened to displace his good mood.

'I'm sure you are right, my lord, and I will look forward to meting out some revenge.' Bayard knew how to placate him and the mention of retribution make him feel better.

To have victory snatched from him four days ago was galling and he still smarted from the failure of his impromptu plan. 'Quite right sergeant, let us toast to success once more.' He smiled as he acknowledged Bayard's raised cup with his own. Inwardly though he was thinking of his subordinate's failures. Maybe it was time to get rid of him, but dismissed the thought almost immediately. His retinue was small enough as it was and besides, Bayard had proved his loyalty and was still useful to him.

His thoughts were interrupted by the opening of the inn door as the Welsh leader entered with his small entourage in full armour, helms under their arms.

The laughter and banter slowly died away as the broad figure stood in the doorway, for a moment looking round at his commanders waiting for conversations to cease. His men's eyes were slowly drawn to the doorway where Rhys Gethin examined each of his soldiers in turn.

'My friends, we have done well this day.' This was accompanied by a slapping of backs and an increase in noise between the nobles.

William de Movran watched in silence, noting the drinking amongst his allies was already beginning to take effect.

Rhys Gethin raised his hand to silence his commanders once more. 'There's little more we can do for now and the few garrison remaining are now trapped behind their walls. Isn't that so William de Movran?'

The faces of over twenty knights followed their leader and looked towards him.

He lifted his chin returning the inquisitive stares obstinately. The Welsh accent grated upon him but not as much as the fact that once again he was being singled out as aligned to the rebellion.

'That is quite so my lord, there can now be but a few of the garrison and the Earl's men left.' He lowered his head in reluctant deference.

'Well then, now that we know we can sleep safely I bid you men good night. Make the most of the hospitality afforded to us and I hope your heads are not too hazy in the morning.' His last comments brought laughter and he gestured to William de Movran to follow him outside as the conversation among the men resumed.

Leaving Bayard behind he followed the noble out into the warm night, the stars even now beginning to appear. He walked for a moment in silence beside the thickly bearded commander as the flames from the fires lit within the buildings caused shadows to flicker against the wattle and daub sides of the homes.

'I have to admit to you that I am not all together happy about the situation.' The commander let the comment hang in the air as they continued along the narrow street.

William de Movran remained silent, not rising to the insinuation he suspected lay beneath the comment.

'The fact that Fitz Warrin has been able to hole up behind those walls isn't the success I was truly hoping for but nevertheless it is what we're faced with. To this end I want you to work with my engineer and come up with an assault plan. You know the castle?' The Lord stopped and looked at the knight studiously, waiting for a response.

'I do and would be happy to guide your engineer's preparations.' He was wary now. Not from the fact that the Lord was right in that he knew most about the castle but that the emphasis upon success seemed to be placed upon his shoulders.

'Good, that's settled then. I will await your reports and leave you to your deliberations.'

With that, the Lord turned away, silently dismissing him even as he thought about the responsibility, deciding it was a good thing. After all, having the credit for the capture of the castle would surely help to strengthen his case for ownership of the stronghold. He looked to his left at the walls discernible against the backdrop of fires, the ramparts similarly lit by the occasional watch fire, the sparks floating lazily into the dark sky. Though imposing he knew he would conquer them.

The next day he awoke with a renewed vigour. Without any squires to call upon he shouted for Bayard to assemble the men and bring him a bowl of water to dispel the early morning sleepiness.

Refreshed, icy water dripping from his beard and only bothering to pull on his thigh length hauberk and breeches he made his way outside into the fresh morning air where his sergeant was dutifully holding the reins of his black destrier. He could tell from the lack of sound that most of the besiegers were still asleep. The night had passed off peacefully. That is, if you ignored the occasional curses and fights from the men who had let the drink inhibit their senses. There had been no noise from within the castle walls that sat now isolated, surrounded by the smoking fires of the Welsh army.

Galloping up the main dirt track towards Babbins Wood, the walls of the castle at his back, it wasn't long before he reached the heavy carts newly arrived and the tents of the men sent to cut down timber. A dishevelled man wearing an often repaired shirt was despatched from his task of lighting a fire to locate the engineer who appeared a few minutes later.

The engineer looked as unkempt as the man who located him but, unlike the messenger, seemed happy and pleased to see the now dismounted knight. He was a squat barrel-chested man, almost completely bald and had a confidence about him as, with one hand, he rubbed the sleep from his eyes. 'My lord?' The man touched his forehead in respect.

'Rhys Gethin has sent me to oversee your progress.'

The man looked at him almost dumbly, and feeling as though he needed to explain himself further he added. 'I am William de Movran and know the castle well.' As soon as the words were out of his mouth he felt as though somehow he was justifying himself to the broad face in front of him.

'I welcome your direction, sire.' The broad Irish accent was surprising while his beaming face showed that he was indeed happy to meet him and appeared not at all affronted that the knight would be providing him guidance. The engineer rubbed his hands on the thick tanned leather apron he wore as though trying to rid his rough scarred hands of the dirt and grease that were now ingrained over the years of apprenticeship and employment in workshops and on campaign.

The man cheerfully introduced himself as Seamus O'Breen and invited him to follow to where a group of perhaps forty men were busy with axes, hatchets and two-handled bow saws. The sounds of felling trees and hewing timber, the thud of iron blades on trunks and the rasp of metal teeth against the tough wooden fibres filled the clearing.

'Wood is what's needed so I've got the lads pulling down timber but I would welcome your thoughts, my lord. The ladders were a bit rushed never mind basic. I didn't even have time to add iron hooks or points to the struts but they seemed to work alright from what I'm told?' Again the professionalism came out, focussed upon the performance of his work rather than the blood and death of the escalade against the stone walls.

William de Movran found himself taking an instant liking to this man despite his down-to-earth demeanour.

'They did work but now we they're locked behind the walls of the castle and we need to prise them out.'

'I thought that would be the case, hence the work.' The man's words were interrupted as over the backdrop of axes and saws a thick trunk came crashing down a few yards away accompanied by the harsh splintering of the wood, branches snapping, leaves crushed and the massive thud of the fallen tree. 'Watch yourselves you God forsaken son's of horse thieves,' he shouted at the men who were already reaching for water to slake their thirst after their success and who grinned back at their engineer. 'These boys know how to chop a tree down but I'm amazed one hasn't fallen on their heads yet.'

'You were saying?' William de Movran was keen to listen to the plans. The recklessness of the Welsh labourers was not a concern and his pre occupation translated itself to the jovial engineer.

'Oh yes. Well from what I saw yesterday afternoon, the main problem is crossing the moat surrounding the walls.' He swept away some dirt and loose undergrowth with his foot, wiping his hands on his apron, a habit William de Movran would get used to before crouching down to draw the outline of the castle with a broken stick. 'We could build some catapults, even trebuchet but I couldn't guarantee the walls would fall into the moat to give us a crossing and besides I understand we want the castle as intact as possible?'

'That's true,' crouching beside the Irishman as he pointed to the roughly drawn outline. 'The key is the drawbridge across the moat. It's not big, perhaps forty feet at the most, but it's enough and although the water's shallow, the ditch is still a pig.'

'Nothing is insurmountable as my good daddy would say, bless his soul, but it's a bit of a test so it is.' The man was rubbing his chin thoughtfully. 'Ordinarily I'd just say fill the ditch with rubble but looking round I think we'd be hard pressed to find any unless we tore down the village buildings or we sent the wagons back to search for them.'

The engineer was obviously talking to himself so William de Movran let him continue.

'There may be another way, but it's nothing I've tried before although I've heard of it?' He looked into the knight's face, his eyes were almost twinkling and William de Movran could tell he was excited by what he would be proposing.

'Go on.'

The engineer tapped his nose repeatedly with his finger and then entered into his proposal.

The excitement of the engineer was infectious. 'You sure you could do this?'

'Oh yes, don't you go worrying yourself. It's sound in principle. There'll be problems but nothing a good honest Irishman can't overcome.'

'How long?'

'I'll have the plans to you by the afternoon. It will perhaps take a day or two at the most to build.'

He could tell the engineer was already drawing up plans in his head. 'Go on then and I will wait on your proposal.' He almost slapped the engineer on the back as he stood up such was the confidence inherent in the conversation.

'Let's go and leave the man to it.' He turned to Bayard and almost humming to himself he wandered back to the tethered horses. If the engineer was right, he would be within the castle walls in a matter of days.

In fact the squat engineer was better than his word and after enthusing over his plans, he shared them with Rhys Gethin in his temporary quarters now set up in the carpenter's house. The sweet smell of wood chippings and wood smoke hung heavily in the air.

'You are sure this will enable us to break the defences?' The Welshman studied the series of intricate drawings made on parchment, peering closely on more than one occasion to understand one aspect or other.

William de Movran let the engineer answer. He had

been convinced when he had earlier raised some questions of his own and was confident in the man's certainty.

'Yes my lord, the basics are simple really. Simple is often the way, so it is, and though not often used I have heard of its employ.'

'And you say that it can be completed in a matter of days?'

At this the man's eyes lit up and not just because of the insinuated endorsement. 'Better than that my lord, we have nearly all the timber required and I've already got the furnace roaring a fair old treat. With a few more men and materials we can have it ready for tomorrow.'

When the engineer had first raised the prospect of being ready for an assault the next evening William de Movran had been excited. He could tell that this piece of news swung it for the Welsh leader who had raised his concern more than once of the need to take the castle in the next few days.

'Very well, you shall have the men and materials you need. I suggest you get on with your work while William de Movran and I continue with our discussions. You seem to be proving your worth.'

That last comment brought a smile to the engineer's face as he eagerly pulled together the rolls of parchment in his big stained hands from the table and nodding to both nobles hurried out of the doorway.

'He certainly enjoys his work.' At the same time Rhys gethin gestured for William de Movran to take a seat. 'Now we have the opportunity to plan our attack.'

'Indeed sire.' It seemed to him, as he took a proffered cup of wine, that everything was coming together.

***

Rowan and the remaining garrison waited pensively for the remainder of the first day of the assault, four full hours of sunlight slowly drifted into evening while the enemy were seemingly content to regroup.

During this time there was the intermittent call to arms as a sentry spotted movement either from the village or across in the barbican archway and ramparts. Each time the anxious alarm amounted to nothing and the defenders soon resumed their preparations. The men sought any spent enemy arrows that weren't too badly damaged to replenish their stocks, repaired dented arrowheads, honed blades dulled against armour and cauterised wounds and applied salves to deep gashes, mostly in silent contemplation.

Leovald had appeared from the hall, the look of anguish confirming what Catin had told the friends in between sobs of grief; Willard had died from an arrow through his young chest.

The friends had consciously left the big Welshman alone as they watched him wander across the courtyard to Lord Fitz Warrin's chambers where the defence preparations were being coordinated.

Rowan saw him enter as he chewed on a piece of tough bread, taking a break from preparations. He was still trying to reconcile his own grief and seeing Leovald somehow made him feel more resolute. Perhaps because his father, and for that matter, Eric had died as soldiers, and that Willard was just a boy it made his death more harsh. Even as he was thinking it, his chest felt tight. Maybe it was true, but all three deaths had been caused by William de Movran and his sergeant. Both their images came into his mind and at that moment his heart filled with bitterness, that there was no longer time to grieve. Swallowing the last crust of bread he picked up the sheaf of arrows and made his way up the stone stairs of the gatehouse turret.

It was in the darkest hours of the night, while Rowan was on sentry duty, straining his eyes and ears across from the gatehouse turret walls for any sign of movement that he spoke to Leovald. He couldn't discern his friend's face, although his outline was silhouetted by the flickering light cast by the fires on the castle walls.

'Is everything okay Rowan?' Leovald enquired, his Welsh tone steady, 'Looks like the treacherous swine are going to stay then. It's like a hundred fireflies,' he added. It was a flat statement without any hint of humour.

Rowan let his eyes wander around the countryside. To his right, fires from the village illuminated the low night time sky, while to his left there were campfires in the garden, orchard and even the outer eastern bailey. For a moment he didn't respond, taking in the background sounds of the surrounding army and the subtle noises from the sleeping garrison who were dotted along the battlements, woollen cloaks keeping out any chill from the clear night air.

'I'm sorry about Willard,' he eventually said softly, hoping that it didn't sound meaningless, but not sure what else to say.

'Thank you. He was a brave lad and I'm proud of him,' Leovald paused before continuing, 'and I'm sorry about your father'. He left the comment hanging in the air.

Rowan didn't want to respond for a moment feeling a rush of sadness and instead focussed on the gatehouse walls opposite, seeing the regular horizontal outline of the merlons just a stone throw away.

'You know, Sir Robert said that if it hadn't been for your father the enemy could have slaughtered all of us?'

Rowan took a deep breath, despite recognising to himself that Willard's death was much more tragic, Leovald's thoughtful words still pained him.

'Sir Robert also said that your father's wounds had opened up again and that he was amazed that he was able to carry my son to safety, never mind protect the retreat.'

Rowan felt tears rising within him, a mixture of pride and sadness. All of a sudden, despite his surroundings, the death of his father, the death of Eric and the savagery of battle caught up with him. He couldn't stop the tears from first welling up and then slipping down his dirt encrusted cheek. It was all he could do to stop a sob coming from his mouth. Leovald's arm came round his shoulder and though he heard words of consolation they didn't register. The act of compassion just made it worse and his chest was as a tight as a drawn bow as he desperately tried to keep from crying out, instead focusing his mind to overcome the emotion that threatened to overrun him.

With a deep breath from the very depth of his lungs he cuffed the tears from his eyes, wiping the dirty rivulets from his cheeks and stepped backwards.

'I'm alright. It's just, you know...'

'Yes lad, I know. We've just got to keep it together. It's no good me and you letting their deaths be in vain.' The words were delivered calmly with steeliness in his voice.

Rowan nodded taking a couple of deep breaths.

'They'll find it hard to assault us now the drawbridge is up, even though we've got so few men and speaking to Lord Fitz Warrin he won't give up the castle easily,' he continued, moving the conversation on to their present predicament.

Rowan remembered Martin telling him and his friends as they had been practising on the archery platform of the long history between the Fitz Warrins and the castle. After the recent events and now the unburdening of his some of his grief he felt similar resolve about defending its walls.

'You think we'll be able to hold out then?' testing Leovald's view to see if he was just saying the words out of encouragement as he looked once more over the myriad of campfires surrounding the walls.

'Aye, we'll do that alright. The best chance they'll have is by starving us out and we've got plenty of food in the cellars. The Earl will return with reinforcements well before then.'

There was no sign of false encouragement and Rowan felt a lot easier as well as determined. The Welshman left him shortly afterwards, both parties consciously avoiding any more talk of the deaths of their kin or their friend Eric.

The gradual increase of noise caused by men and animals stirring and the morning sun beginning to shine through the turrets thin lancet caused Rowan to open his eyes slowly. His sentry duty had lasted until two in the morning and he yawned loudly before pushing his arms and legs from beneath the blanket, straining his muscles as though he was on some form of rack, resulting in a groan of satisfaction.

'Looks like someone enjoyed their night's sleep,' said Martin, glancing back from staring out from one of the other narrow arrow loops in the north turret. 'How are you feeling?'

'Not great I have to admit,' he replied standing up and brushing the thin layer of straw from a gambeson that he had used as a makeshift mattress against the hard stone floor. For a brief moment he felt guilty as he registered the dark red blood stains on the front of the jacket from its previous owner, but only for a moment. He reflected on how much more insensitive he had become to the killing around him.

'No sign of them then?' Rowan added. He had decided, like the rest of the small garrison, to forego the comfort of the pallets made up in the main hall in case the enemy launched a sudden attack. Fortunately their precaution and his uncomfortable night had not been rewarded as he picked up his bow.

'No, looks like they're happy to just to break their fast, I can see loads of them in the village and they've got the fires going.'

Rowan could imagine the smoke coming from the holes in the thatch roofs and his stomach began to pang with sudden hunger. 'I'll go and get some breakfast,' he volunteered, 'want some?'

'No, you're okay. I had some an hour ago while you were catching your beauty sleep. Mind you, you can get Daniel to come and take his share of the watch. You'll find him with Rosalind, surprise, surprise,' he said good-naturedly.

Making his way down the circular turret steps he found Daniel sure enough at the entrance to the kitchen, leaning against the daubed walls, watching the dark haired Rosalind inside busily preparing platters of ham to pass to the garrison.

'Martin told me you'd be here,' he joked walking across the courtyard. He was also conscious of Catin her slim back to him as she shaped some dough and made sure his voice was loud enough to carry, hoping it would attract her attention.

His friend returned the grin, seemingly oblivious to his split attentions. 'Well there's no better view than from where I'm standing,' he glanced into the interior of the kitchen which emitted the smell of warm bread.

'That's because he knows how lucky he is and, believe me, he's lucky to have me!' His friend's reply too had been loud enough for Rosalind to hear and was immediately answered by her brisk retort from inside.

To his happiness her response was accompanied by Catin's distinct laugh, though she did not turn her head towards the doorway.

The atmosphere was pleasant, even jovial and it seemed that the horror of yesterday and their current predicament had been put aside or, rather Rowan thought, avoided for now.

'Where's Jerrard?' He tried to keep his eyes from

wandering back to the inside of the kitchen wondering whether a set of blue eyes were looking at him.

'Oh he's about. He's like a bear with a sore head though and just wants to have a go at the enemy. If it wasn't for the men-at-arms at the gate I'd swear he'd knock the pins out of the chains and charge across the drawbridge.'

Rowan could picture their friend, his mallet in hand taking on the whole of the attackers. He could be grumpy at the best of times but now he was also constantly angry, like a burning furnace.

The morning continued uneventfully. He and his friends were charged with manning the north wall and turret facing the village and track approaching the outer barbican gatehouse while Leovald and his remaining nine archers packed the walls facing the captured archway. The archers who were too injured to do much more than act as lookouts kept watch over the rest of the walls. The four men-at-arms, each carrying one injury or another, Sir Robert with them, rested in the courtyard below, able to rush to wherever help was needed.

Rowan looked around him, the morning was now coming to an end. The clouds, unlike the previous day, had not dissipated but had instead increased so the sky above was a dullish light grey. There was little the defenders could do now but wait. Their preparations were done and it was now down to the besiegers.

The enemy across from the walls however showed no inclination to attack, although Rowan could see soldiers wandering between the buildings and the surrounding baileys or quickly traversing between the village and gatehouse over the drawbridge. This journey was well within an arrow's range but it was as though some unarranged ceasefire existed between the two forces, neither wanting to antagonise the other.

It was in the late afternoon when he caught sight of William de Movran, Bayard and a short broad-set man by his side as they looked across from one of the towers of the captured gatehouse.

The sight brought a murmur among the garrison and Rowan felt anger course through his body, for the death of his father and friends and the role the knight and his sergeant had played.

Despite orders to conserve arrows he reached for one of the wooden shafts from his belt, his eyes never leaving the figures of his enemies just a little more than a hundred feet away. Drawing back his string, he aimed the tip of the bodkin at the knight.

As if emphasising the knight's disrespect for life, William de Movran wore no helm.

Rowan took his time, the steel tip in his eye line wavering slightly before he let go, not seeking another from his belt, his whole focus was on the trajectory of the arrow as it sped towards his target.

The aim was true but at the last moment the rapidly raised shield came up and the needle like point pierced the leathered covered metal with a dull thud.

The three men flinched, shocked by the sudden missile, crouched low looking across at their assailant. Then, William de Movran raised himself and tilted his head in mocking acknowledgement as if goading Rowan, who felt his face flush with anger.

'Dogs,' Rowan hissed under his breath.

'You'll get another chance,' Daniel was by his side, holding his arm and stopping him reaching for another arrow.

Rowan didn't respond as he watched the rebels descend out of sight. Bayard, followed William de Movran's example and waved his arms in an elaborate motion at the defenders, before he too disappeared from sight.

The overcast day dragged onwards as the noise from hundreds of men continued to float across from the surrounding enemy camp. At one point Rowan was rebuked gently by Leovald, the Lord of the castle having seen the shot at the enemy against his orders. The reminder of the need to conserve arrows was not issued in a belligerent way, the young noble knowing of his loss. Rowan reflected on his original assessment of the Lord as he looked once again over the battlements.

Shifting his gaze to look downwards at the still shallow waters below, he thought once more of Leovald's assessment of their situation. Although besieged and with the enemy so close he still couldn't see how they could hope to overcome the muddy water-filled ditches and the thick stone walls. True they had managed to capture the barbican and its walls but the defenders had been forced to spread their men thinly while the enemy had been able to attack from two sides, one that hadn't been protected by the water defences. They would try again, he supposed, looking down at the archway opposite, but he knew this was where they would concentrate their defensive fire. If they did come again they would be ready, he vowed to himself.

That readiness was tested when darkness descended and the men's nerves were at their highest. Eyes stared out intensely into the shadows towards the village where many of the campfires, unlike the previous night, ominously remained unlit. The men within the walls stirred as the sentries pointed and whispered to each other, refastening the buckles on their gambesons or lifted their bascinets from their heads to hear better.

Rowan listened intently, his eyes searching for any movement in the darkness. For the moment he was relieved, perhaps anxiety had got to the look outs. Then he heard a sound, or rather sounds. It was the noise of wheels that rumbled forwards heavily on the dirt track towards the enemy-held barbican. As the noise increased he could discern tramping feet, the rasp of metal armour and the occasional low voice. There was no mistaking that something was going on outside the extent of their vision.

'To arms, men.' The whispered command was passed from man to man and soon enough every man of the small garrison had grasped their weapons and were, like the sentries, transfixed as they stared into the night towards the village edge. Only the few lit fires from the village and those from the castle battlements were alive and giving out a minimal glow.

'What in heaven's grace is going on?' Martin whispered nervously.

'Don't know, but whatever they're doing they're up to no good.' Jerrard's gruff voice retorted.

'Put your poxed helmet back on.' The unmistakable Welsh lilt of Leovald called out as he strode along the wall angled towards the outer drawbridge and village, looking up towards the four friends on the north tower.

Jerrard now admonished quickly rammed his bascinet back upon his head.

'You're to put some fire arrows into the village,' Leovald continued, half whispering to the men above as well as to the men on the curtain walls. 'We need to find out what those sorry heathen's are up to.'

Rowan reflected on the order for a moment. The men had been warned that they might have to do this if a night attack was attempted, but it still felt disconcerting that they would deliberately set one of the village buildings alight.

Daniel silently distributed the specially prepared arrows, their shafts wound with tow impregnated with pitch.

Rowan, like the others, notched his arrow before carefully pushing the arrow tip towards the flames, waiting for it to catch hold. He had never fired a flaming arrow before and was nervous as he pulled the bow away. Turning to his left, he aimed the arrow out into the blackness judging where the weaver's home stood, it was the nearest building to the castle, just across the track and he visualised its tightly packed thatch roof.

The rippling blue and orange flames from the arrow flickered in his eyesight as he elevated the bow, resisting the urge to let the burning missile go immediately as he pulled the string back as far as he could. To his left and right he saw the luminous streaks of flames fly high into the night sky as they left his friend's bows with a snap, almost majestically rising and then reaching their zenith before falling steeply towards the village below.

He waited for a heartbeat, determined despite his hands feeling the heat from the flames less than three feet away to allow his friends' arrows to act as an aiming mark, illuminating the buildings before letting loose.

Many arrows fell harmlessly to bury themselves into the track or crofts while others, one to Rowan's satisfaction his own, embedded themselves in the thick thatch of the nearest buildings.

He watched for a moment while the others reached for more fire arrows as the flames were seemingly extinguished in the thatch. He wondered whether the arrows had pierced straight through the roof but was slowly rewarded by the dull reddish glow and then the distinguishable flicker of flame illuminating the shadows of men advancing towards the castle.

'Christ on heaven,' Jerrard swore as he saw them, 'they're up to it again.'

'Good lads,' Leovald congratulated the friends from the rampart below. 'Now shoot the heathens.'

The light of the flames spurred the enemy onwards. They had been spotted and silence was no longer a concern. The night time suddenly was full of curses and cheers from both defenders and attackers alike.

Rowan was tempted to seek more tow wrapped arrows but the sheer size of the enemy threw that thought from his mind. Now was the time to use his years of practice and fire arrow after arrow towards the approaching force.

Frantically he and his friends plucked the arrows, first from against the stone walls and then from their belts, sending them into the mass of silhouettes that flickered against the backdrop of the dark sky and the crackling, shimmering flames which had now taken hold in the thatch.

The effect was rewarding as, despite the darkness, men screamed and cursed. Rowan aimed, let loose, aimed and let loose again, frantically trying to prevent the enemy crossing from the village to the drawbridge. His fingers were quickly red and raw having not fully repaired themselves from the first onslaught.

Again the enemy came forwards with their wicker mantlets providing their archers with protection as the defenders' arrows embedded themselves deeply in the wooden frames. Many more sought out those attackers not offered the protection. A man screamed as Rowan's arrow punched into his chest, piercing straight through his chainmail, the dying man collapsing in the dirt.

Still the shadows of the attackers came on.

The friends concentrated on the men trying to cross the drawbridge into the outer barbican gatehouse, even now the sound of running feet on the strengthened wood audible against the noise of the swearing enemy. Against the light of the battlements and the flames now casting sparks into the night time sky he could see more men falling to the friends' arrows, some toppling into the moat, others crawling away wounded. Many made it through while others carried forwards more mantlets to protect their comrades.

Soon, the one sided barrage had changed into a

ferocious exchange. Arrows flew from either side or above the wicker shields while the enemy archers on the captured walls also lent supporting fire to their comrades. An arrow slapped into a rebel, his mouth wide open shouting some incoherent curse, the force physically throwing him backwards to lie on the earth writhing in pain as he clutched at the embedded missile.

'Got him,' came the satisfied comment from Daniel. 'Mind you, there's plenty more of the swines,' his voice now dry and rasping, reflecting his exertions.

Rowan too was beginning to feel the effort, his shoulders aching. 'Keep shooting,' he urged, more for his own benefit than anyone else's.

Two more men lifting their wooden defensive shield into position were struck by arrows before the return fire forced Rowan to crouch behind the stone work. The weight of the enemy fire was now beginning to tell as more and more arrows flew upwards, some alight and making an orange trail in the night time sky but many unseen in the darkness, their clattering impact upon the stonework now feeling like the irregular fall of heavy hail stones though much more lethal.

'By the virgin herself and all her handmaids this is now too much,' shouted Jerrard, he too had his back against the wall like his friends.

All of a sudden he reacted to his friend's dead-pan curses and found himself grinning.

'What the Hell's teeth is wrong with you?' The comment from Jerrard made him break into a tired laugh.

It was infectious, first a chuckle from Daniel next to

him, similarly with his back to the battlements, sheltering from the deadly arrows that flew up at him.

'This is ridiculous,' Jerrard grumbled.

It was too much and Rowan saw Martin and Daniel begin laughing. For a few seconds their desperate predicament was ignored, overcome by their close friendship.

The rumble of the heavy wheels on the dirt path brought them back to their plight.

The unmistakeable sound of a siege engine approached the outer drawbridge accompanied by the occasional screech from one of the axles and the sound of scores of men heaving and pushing. The noise caused Rowan to wipe his eyes quickly with the back of his hand, the laughter immediately gone as he peered around the stone merlon.

He recognised that the defenders, largely shadows in the darkness, seemed content not to press an attack. Instead they were happy to keep up their barrage of arrows on the men high up on the battlements, protecting the wheeled machine as it made its way slowly across the drawbridge like a mythical beast protected now by a wall of mantlets accompanied by men carrying lengths of timber.

Even as the realisation came that there was little they could do to prevent the advance into the captured outer bailey there was a roar of flames to his left, towards the gatehouse.

Rowan's ears registered increasingly urgent shouts among the archers above the inner gatehouse walls as the fire glowed brightly illuminating the enemy-held archway opposite.

With a quick look once more to his front, he cautiously used the walls to protect himself from the continuing arrows. He glanced at the enemy milling on the other side of the moat, still illuminated but only partially by the flickering fires of the thatch behind them, and decided in a split second to find out what was happening. Rising to a crouch, one hand keeping his arrow bag close by his side and the other grasping his bow, he made his way quickly towards the inner gatehouse.

'Where for heaven's sake are you off to?' Jerrard asked, watching his friend, crouching past him on the cramped turret battlements.

'Just going to have a quick look at what's going on,' he answered urgently, patting his friend's shoulder before heading to the hatch on the floor. 'They're not going to get across here and I'll be back before you know it.' Rowan felt as confident as the words he spoke, realising the assault was provoking an inner strength and calmness he hadn't before experienced.

Hastily he clambered down the steps and then out onto the curtain wall. He ran as fast as he could to the gatehouse tower along the battlements, keeping low in an effort to avoid the arrows that continued incessantly to smack against the thick protective walls.

Gasping he found himself in the protective circular confines of the eastern gatehouse tower almost tripping over the body of one of Lord Fitz Warrin's archers.

The gloominess of the interior was lit by the flickering flames coming from outside so he could see that the man was on his back, an arrow protruding prominently from his face. It must have been one heck of a fluke Rowan thought to himself, crouching down beside the body. He could see the arrow was firmly embedded, the blood-stained hand of the man against his face while the other was reaching for something unseen, bent upwards against the curve of the wall.

His breathing slowing, Rowan raised himself up and peered through the arrow loop knowing that the dead body beside him had done the same thing perhaps just a few moments ago.

Through the framed embrasure facing the archway opposite he saw liquid filled bags tossed over the ditch towards the foot of the drawbridge where flames greedily embraced the timbers, igniting the oil within causing more bright flashes to illuminate the ditch between the two forces and a rush of heat. The whoosh was followed by an increase of cheering from the enemy opposite as the oil sought to take hold of the drawbridge causing consternation on the battlements above.

'Water. Throw water!' The calls were taken up as men grabbed whatever buckets they had nearby and threw their contents over the ramparts in an effort to quench the flames below. Others were already running towards the well and making for the steps below Rowan.

'Get a poxy line going. Stop running round like headless chickens!' He could hear the distinct roar from Sir Robert down below in the courtyard as he began to take charge, forming a line quickly of his men-at-arms to pass buckets from hand to hand up to the battlements.

Rowan stepped to the turret archway to peer along

the wall where still the arrows continued to fire at the defenders, now illuminated above the flames. One man screamed as an arrow buried itself in his neck despite the mail hauberk, the wooden bucket clattering to the floor of the battlements as he reeled backwards and tumbled into the inner bailey.

'Someone pick that up.' This time it was the distinct calm voice of the young Lord of the castle from above who was staring across at the enemy from his position on the gatehouse tower.

Rowan instinctively pushed past another archer, grabbing the bucket before tossing it carefully to a man-at-arms in the courtyard below where he could now see that the women and the wounded were now helping pass the buckets of water up towards the walls.

Turning, he grabbed an outstretched handle from the shadows of the tower he had emerged from and heaved its contents over the wall, trying to keep his head hidden behind the protective stonework remembering his predecessor's fate.

His efforts were quickly rewarded as the ferocity of the fire was tempered. He continued to receive the buckets thrust towards him, hurling the water over the embrasure to splash down on the flames below.

But the chain was slow, the buckets too few and the amounts too small and he could tell from the surging heat and brightening flames reflecting in the moat below that they were losing the fight to stop the fire taking hold.

Still he and the rest of the defenders continued their desperate efforts, their arms were aching, shoulders tight while the enemy incessantly sought to kill them with their arrows until eventually and inevitably the call came to cease their efforts.

'Enough, enough. There's little more we can do about the fire.' The familiar voice of Leovald gave the order.

The command was accompanied by an acknowledging nod to Rowan. 'That fire's taken hold and there's not a lot we can do about it,' he continued grimly, 'and we're just going to lose more men.'

The Welshman remained crouched beneath the parapet as the barrage continued. 'Forget that water up here now boys. Concentrate on keeping the inside of the wood damp,' shouting down at the men and women below who were passing buckets from hand to hand from the well and back.

'You'd better conserve your arrows too,' he spoke to his friend, 'looks like you'll need them in the morning.'

His tone was grim but Rowan was too tired to think about it. His body was sweating heavily under his mail, his throat suddenly parched as he allowed himself to slump to the floor his back to the battlements, the empty water bucket clattering to the floor beside him. He could hear the crackling of wood and sparks as the flames cast dancing shadows around the defenders on the parapet.

The timber continued to burn over the next couple of hours, spreading the acrid smell of smoke over the walls as Rowan and the rest of the garrison re-gathered their strength.

The enemy occasionally continued to throw bags of oil across the ditch causing blasts of flame and stimulating the fire that had now adopted a blue-red hue as the wood continued to bubble and burn.

The mood among the men was determined but resigned, sensing this very deliberate and latest move was just another pragmatic step to the eventual capture of the castle and the undecided fate of its defenders. Even the continued dousing of the drawbridge from inside had now stopped as the men went about making further preparations for the enemy's next onslaught against the walls of the stronghold. In front of the drawbridge, men were now hammering extra pieces of timber across the gateway, others were busy collecting what weapons and missiles remained, fixing bodkin heads to undamaged arrow shafts or sharpening their blades.

Despite the fatigue the men remained awake and the remainder of the night passed slowly as the flames from the drawbridge continued to cast their fiery glow above the stone ramparts.

CHAPTER ELEVEN

It was as the morning sun was beginning to lighten the sky that Jerrard reappeared to join his friends as they leant exhausted against the chapel walls.

'Hello there lads. It's nice to see your miserable faces again,' he said mockingly. 'Thank all the good Saints, we've hardly got any arrows left,' he added, indicating his arm in the improvised sling. Their friend had taken yet another injury. This time an arrow in his arm but, like before, seemed proud if not a little annoyed by his luck.

'That'll teach you to keep your big hairy arse out of the firing line,' Daniel tried to respond to Jerrard's levity.

'Why would I do that Dan? It's almost worth getting an arrow in my shoulder to get services off your Rosalind.' His face brightened at his own mischievousness.

'You keep your hands to yourself,' Daniel responded happily. 'I'll have to go and make sure she's not too distressed from treating you!'

The men chuckled, causing a few stares from the weary men around them, the events of the night all too real in their memories with an impending assault almost imminent. Well, at least the friends could attempt to joke with each other, thought Rowan tiredly as he watched Daniel with effort raise himself from the wall and, rubbing his hands free of dirt, make his way to the hall.

He watched his friend go, tempted to follow him in the hope of seeing Catin when Jerrard's tone changed back again. 'We're in trouble aren't we?'

There was a moment's pause. He didn't know if it was because of his own tiredness or the truth of the comment. 'You could say that,' he eventually replied. 'There's not many of us left. I reckon less than twenty archers including us and just four of Sir Robert's men-at-arms, and that's counting the walking wounded.'

As he spoke, Martin and Rowan watched Sir Robert striding towards the group, his helm under his arm. Their silence and efforts to rise up alerted Jerrard who turned round.

'You've done well men.' Then seeing Jerrard's arm he asked, 'how's the injury?'

Jerrard faltered under the question from the knight. None of them were used to being addressed directly. 'It's nothing, sire.' He managed to put together a few words, adopting an accent much to Rowan's inner amusement.

Not noticing the effect of his question on the big archer, the knight nodded and continued, 'I've just spoke to Lord Fitz Warrin and he wants you men back on the north walls. His vintenar,' he indicated in the direction of Leovald, 'and archers will be on gatehouse walls again. I don't think the enemy will be in a hurry to attack but we know they won't want their efforts last night to go to waste. So get yourselves on the battlements and make sure you're ready. My men and I will protect the gateway.' He gestured with his head to where the men-at-arms were stood ready should the enemy somehow succeed in pulling down or destroying the drawbridge.

The men nodded seriously, conscious of the social difference between the man facing them in his blood-caked armour and themselves. The noble stepped forwards and grasped Rowan's shoulder, looking round at the three friends. 'Whatever happens we make the enemy pay for their treachery.' The stare was hard and focussed, his words giving the friends renewed resilience and determination.

Rowan could still feel the gauntleted hand on his shoulder and felt a sense of pride as he and his two friends picked up their bows and made their way deliberately to the tower opposite, before climbing up the worn stone steps, its interior dark despite the morning light outside. The flames which had illuminated the confines of the rough stone circular walls the previous night had now ceased, leaving behind charred and blackened timbers of the drawbridge.

The group each found a place on the wall, expecting at any time to be the target of a flurry of missiles which thankfully never came, before placing down a few spare arrows within easy reach. Wary of enemy archers Rowan looked to his left at the short stretch of moat that separated the two bastions, knowing this was where the next assault would come. For now there was no aggressive movement from the enemy, though the friends could tell they too were wide awake as the sight and noise of hundreds of soldiers, their commands, conversations, clatter of pots and metal permeated the still morning air.

Daniel had now followed the three friends up onto the battlements and sensed their mood immediately, despite being in relatively high spirits having recently seen Rosalind.

'What's up?'

'Oh nothing,' Martin responded. 'It's just going to be a long day, I suppose.'

Jerrard was much more to the point. 'It's not just going to be a long day, it'll be a bloody day. Mark my words.' His comment stopped any further enquiries from Daniel who, knowing his friend's mood, shared an understanding look with Rowan.

Rowan returned his friend's expression before asking, 'How's Rosalind?'

'Fine, just fine. She's coping, though some of the wounds she's tending look pretty gruesome.'

'And Catin?' he tried not to let his anxiety show though it was obvious from his friend's look he was unsuccessful.

'Oh she's fine. In fact between her and Rose they're managing to keep spirits up.'

'I bet they are!' Jerrard broke back into the conversation, his grim mood immediately forgotten.

Rowan could see by his big wide grin that he was teasing him. He looked at Martin and could tell that his thoughts about Catin were now known. He kept quiet, feeling his face go red as the men chuckled good naturedly.

'Alright you boys,' Leovald had appeared from the

shadows of the gatehouse turret. 'Anyone would think that we're not surrounded by thousands of the enemy trying to batter down the walls.' The men looked, their smiles quickly extinguished as they could see their Welsh friend shared no such merriment. 'I need a volunteer to keep an eye out on the other battlements and seeing as you're injured, Jerrard, and can't draw a bow I think it should be you.'

Rowan could see his friend was disappointed but he obviously realised that there was no point in arguing and, with a sullen look, and brief farewell made his way to the north east tower. This part of the castle gave a panoramic view of the approaches to Whittington and the surrounding marshlands so it was possible to watch for an unexpected assault from those quarters or, as discussed often among the defenders, the possible return of the Earl of Stafford with reinforcements. That thought heartened Rowan for a moment before he glanced down to the men in the courtyard and then back across at the enemy held walls and village, his mood instantly more much sober.

The defenders on the gatehouse towers were now assembled and Rowan could see the shorter figure of Lord Fitz Warrin with the burly figure of Leovald by his side. Below Sir Robert was in conversation with his few men-at-arms who were obviously waiting for a more immediate threat before picking up their shields and putting on their heavy helmets.

As they waited, the three friends checked their arrows. Despite their efforts to make good the spent missiles, they had found they had just half a dozen arrows each, their spare supply and arrow bags having been exhausted. It seemed the other archers on the gatehouse walls fared little better when Martin went to see if they could share any. Knowing this and seeing the preparations of the enemy, many of them now in clear view as they assembled in the village, the outer baileys and barbican walls, the tension among the friends increased.

Rowan felt like he had permanent indigestion and took a deep breath, letting it out slowly in an effort to calm himself. This seemed to work for a short while, allowing his heartbeat to slow before the feeling returned.

As the morning wore on there was a distinct increase in men moving towards the captured courtyard. More of the enemy were climbing onto the battlements opposite and trumpets began to sound as a wave of men from the village buildings rushed forwards to huddle behind the various mantlets left behind from the previous night. The hairs on the back of Rowan's neck stood up. There was a no doubting what the increase in activity meant.

'They haven't been idle have they?' Martin responded to the sight grimly. The friends knew that the massing of the enemy signalled that an assault was imminent. 'At least they know that there'll be more arrows coming their way,' he half heartily chuckled to himself.

Along their own battlements men were preparing themselves, shifting nervously. Sir Robert's men-at-arms in the courtyard were putting on their helmets, tightening their arming straps, picking up their lethal halberds and loosening their swords.

The resumption of the enemy arrows came a few moments later, first from the men down on the track and then almost immediately from the men on the walls opposite. Commands were now being shouted as captains and sergeants encouraged their men to unleash a continuous storm of arrows. It seemed to Rowan that the barrage was more intense that any that had gone on before.

'Christ almighty, how many?' The curse from Daniel came as all three crouched behind the battlements.

Even if they had enough arrows to fire back, Rowan knew it would surely mean they would be hit by one of the seemingly endless number that whistled through the air around them.

'Here they come!' The cry came from the defenders on the gatehouse as enemy troops now appeared under the opposite archway.

Carefully, conscious of the deadly arrows speeding upwards towards him and the other archers, Rowan looked across to see enemy soldiers manhandling what looked like some sort of giant ladder through the archway. As he watched the men began to raise the cumbersome structure vertically into the air. Two men fell despite some of their comrades trying to protect them with shields, arrows striking them down and sending them spinning into the moat below as the defenders braved the enemy arrows and returned fire. Urgent orders were being shouted from both sides but were hardly discernible against the backdrop of war cries'.

What was clear though was this was a precursor to

the assault on the main gates. Realising he couldn't just watch in comparative safety, Rowan reached for an arrow, calling to his two comrades at the same time to fire at the small knot of men exposed below the archway. As he aimed, using the tip of the steel point as his mark, he registered the men on top of the enemy-held gatehouse helping to heave up the two lengths of the device with ropes. They were perhaps a foot thick, crafted so that they each seemed to be made of two lengths at right angles to each other. Their tips were mounted with heavy iron claws and thick cross pieces kept the two lengths parallel to each other. There was no time for curiosity as he let his arrow loose and it flew straight and true, slamming into the back of one of the men helping raise the structure, as he quickly reached for another.

More and more desperate arrows were being fired at the attackers despite the counter fire and both sides were taking casualties, judging from the curses and cries of pain. More than once he heard the smack of an arrow tip or the whistle of a flight as they missed him by less than a couple of inches.

The attackers below the archway had been decimated by the defenders' fire and now numbered less than five, their comrades lying unmoving either in the shallow waters below or against the steep sides of the slope. Despite their losses however Rowan watched with fascination as the structure toppled forwards, accompanied by a loud cheer from the attackers on top of the walls as it thudded heavily into the thin stretch of ground at the foot of the blackened drawbridge, the iron claws embedding themselves deeply in the dry earth bank.

For a moment there was a unnatural pause as Rowan and the rest of the defenders wondered what the attackers had actually achieved. The smooth lengths of timbers looked like some kind of wrongly oversized ladder but it would be difficult for men to balance across. Then slowly emerging out of the archway the thick ominous nose of a siege engine emerged and the ingenuity of the enemy engineers dawned on him. He could see now that a portable bridge had been built, protected by a stout flat timber penthouse covered with fresh hides and under-slung with a huge tree trunk shod with iron. The wheels fitted neatly on the wooden lengths of timber so recently toppled forward which he now realised were angled to act as runners.

'I don't believe it.' Martin whispered showing he too had understood what was happening. 'Christ's bones, what do we do?'

It was clear the enemy were making their move as the wheels inexorably trundled forwards, the chains holding the ram rattling beneath, accompanied by the loud rhythmical chants as they pushed the device forwards. Those chants filled the air as the length of the covered bridge unerringly emerged from underneath the archway.

The defenders had no answer for the moment and were conserving their arrows, both forces focussed on the siege engine as it traversed the ditch and inevitably reached the blackened timbers. More cheering and cursing assaulted the ears of the defenders. Desperately the men on the gatehouse walls threw earthenware pots filled with flaming animal fat onto the wooden roof, causing pools of fire to engulf the protective hides but it did little to deter the attackers who charged forwards onto the bridge to grab hold of the battering ram.

As the swing of the heavy trunk with its iron-shod point crunched for the first time against the now fragile drawbridge Rowan realised that only he and the men along his wall could see the attackers, the sides of the structure remaining unprotected apart from a few struts. Like his comrades he raised his bow once more. The ragged volley of arrows struck the enemy, causing cries of anguish as they buried into their gambesons or more lightly protected torsos. Some arrows deflected or scraped off armour while others embedded themselves in the portable bridge.

Still the ram swung, pounding against the wooden barrier, the timbers already splintering.

The men's arrows now attracted resumed attention from the enemy archers and a hail of steel-tipped points peppered the wall, making the defenders snatch themselves backwards, flinching from the barrage that flew around them. One tore at Rowan's surcoat and mail causing a flicker of panic as it scored his side while Martin was less lucky and received an arrow through his hand causing him to drop his bow and cry out.

Immediately he and Daniel scurried across the floor of the ramparts. 'Hold still,' Rowan shouted, as he grabbed Martin's left wrist with both hands, trying to keep the injured hand still. The arrow was embedded halfway through, blood streaked from its steel head and down the wooden shaft. 'Snap the thing off.'

The words acted like a slap in the face to his friend who looked first at him and then Daniel, his curses halted as he registered what was about to happen, his face almost pleading.

'Go on,' Rowan urged his friend. 'Quick!' for he was more than aware of the cheers of the attackers below.

Martin let out a sharp cry of pain as the top half of the shaft was snapped despite Rowan's efforts to keep the hand still. Rowan then pulled the remaining shaft through the hand, the flesh sucking at the wood as he did so until it released suddenly and he could throw it discarded to the stone floor. Quickly Rowan then tore at the bottom of his jacket, wrapping the dirty cloth around the bloody hole.

'You'll be alright,' Rowan encouraged his friend, whose face was now as pale as new daub.

The distinct crunch and splintering of timbers grabbed their attention back, knowing immediately that the drawbridge had been breached.

Hastily they picked up their bows again and, like the rest of the men, notched their arrows as a wave of enemy came on, heavy axes in their hands.

He and his friends let loose despite the counter fire and the first volley of arrows smacked into the leading men in their gules gambesons and coats of mail. Some tumbled to the floor, bodies and weapons slipping into the ditch below even as more men poured across the bridge intent on reaching the fortress gates.

The men reached for their few remaining arrows and rapidly let loose, taking advantage of the fact that the enemy archers were focussing their attention towards the gatehouse. The enemy fired arrow after arrow at their comrades directly above the drawbridge who Rowan guessed must be suffering terribly. There was no question of saving the small stock of arrows now. Rowan knew that once the attackers had penetrated through the gates, their sheer numbers would overwhelm the remaining force. He let his last arrow go, flying into the mass of men that now pushed against each other, eager to gain entry as the broad axe blades started to bite deep into the weakened timbers of the drawbridge. The thuds resonated loudly and consistently as they sought to capitalise on the breach made by the heavy ram.

'God in heaven!' He said involuntarily as he glanced downwards. Already it seemed that the enemy were almost through the wooden defences; thick splinters of wood stood out at angles as the wide blades hacked down again and again. The roar increased among the armoured men that now filled the length of the bridge.

He ran quickly knowing that the defenders had little time before the enemy breached the gate, instinctively reaching down and dragging two unspent arrows from the belt of a dead archer who he recognised as a wagon maker from Yarnfield, before stepping over the body and hastily running down the tower steps. Now was not the time for sentiment.

Breathlessly he emerged into the courtyard and could already see the body of an enemy soldier lying half through the broken timbers and being dragged out of the way by the attackers. Two of the men-at-arms had abandoned the small line of defenders for the moment and were hacking at any man that tried to get through the gap made by the heavy axes. The needle like points of the halberds were repeatedly thrust forwards, dissuading any more attackers from coming through the initial breach.

'Steady men, steady. There'll be enough of the swine soon enough.' Sir Robert stood with his men-at-arms, Lord Fitz Warrin and the remaining bowmen now alongside. They, like Rowan and his friends, had been drawn from the battlements to the desperate defence of the gateway. Even the seriously injured had stumbled and crawled from the infirmary.

Among the dozen or so remaining men Rowan saw Leovald by his Lord's side, a heavy blade in his hand and off to his left Jerrard who grinned back half-heartedly at his friends, having been drawn from his isolated sentry post. Rowan knew there was no need to keep watch over the rest of the walls. If the castle was to fall it would be here. He notched one of his last two remaining arrows.

More shafts of light were coming through the blackened wood as chunks were now being stripped away remorselessly by the blows.

'Ready men,' Sir Robert called, his voice trying to steady the nervous and desperate defenders.

The two men-at-arms were still holding their own, causing cries of pain as they continued to thrust their points at the arms and legs of the enemy that got too close, but now the unseen attackers were able to fight back. The gap was becoming large enough for the enemy soldiers to make their own counter thrusts, causing the two men to step back which in turn enabled the axemen to get much closer. Within what seemed like moments the ragged hole was quickly enlarged so Rowan could see between the men in front of him the triumphant enemy waiting beyond.

'Step back.' The knight shouted at his two men to retreat into line just as one was caught by the point of a pike that scraped down his thigh armour and somehow managed to pierce his lower leg. He fell with a curse but was dragged backwards by his comrades away from the cheering attackers.

'If any of you archers has any arrows left, use them now,' the knight commanded as the first of the enemy squeezed through the gap, a large pockmarked shield to his front.

More than one arrow slammed into the shield but three took the man, two in the leg and one in the face, killing him instantly. The soldier dropped to the floor without a cry, his shield clattering to the cobblestones. Behind, a man wearing plate armour immediately took his place, while the timbers shook with the continued axe blows that still landed against the drawbridge and reinforcing wood.

Rowan pulled his bow back, looking between the shoulders of the men-at-arms, aiming the tip at the man's face. He hadn't fired at the first attacker. The arrows that had killed him had been loosed quickly, before he had aimed properly. He wanted to make the two arrows taken from the body of the wagon maker count. He breathed deeply as he opened his fingers and watched his arrow fly the short space, no more than twenty feet and pierce the second man's chest plate, before he too fell to the ground on top of the first attacker.

It seemed that before the man had even hit the ground another came through, this time able to take a step into the courtyard, his armour providing him with a few more precious moments of life. Crucially his body protected the men coming through behind him.

Rowan snatched his last arrow from his belt and let loose, swearing as his arrow spun away, deflected by the man's armour plate this time. He was immediately relieved as another arrow from an unseen defender managed to pierce the man's groin despite his mail skirt causing the enemy man-at-arms to fall to the ground in agony. His screams added to the swearing and cursing of defenders and attackers alike.

With no more arrows to fire he discarded his bow and drew his sword as more enemies charged over their fallen comrades, one or two losing balance as they did so, others falling to the last few arrows of the archers before they too drew their swords.

'At them!' and with those two words the defenders charged forwards into the enemy who had managed to clamber through the charred opening into the courtyard.

In those first moments the men-at-arms and archers outnumbered the attackers and he was able to watch as Sir Robert, slamming his face plate down after giving the order, smashed his shoulder into an enemy soldier who flew backwards despite his shield into his comrades behind him. The knight swung his sword in a cleaving strike against the man's chest plate, knocking him to the floor with vicious force before swinging his body so his armour took the force of a blow from another enemy soldier who in turn was lethally chopped down by a man-at-arms. The defenders battered at the attackers, who cursed and bled but who were also taking a toll especially among the lighter armoured archers who were less used to using their blades. Men from both sides were now being wounded and killed in equal measure and bodies piled up around the gateway.

Rowan found himself screaming as he rushed forwards at a heavily armoured man-at-arms with a vert quartered surcoat who had emerged through the confusion of the melee, his scarred face framed by the side plates of his helmet. The man swung his sword at him, snarling all the while and shouting some intelligible curse. Flinching, Rowan dived under the swing bringing his own blade up but only succeeding in scoring the man's thigh armour. He rolled quickly away from the enemy's immediate reach who in turn switched his attention to a nearby archer, slicing straight through his arm before despatching him with a thrust into his belly, even as the defender stared in disbelief at the stump.

All around men were embroiled in their personal battles and, though the defenders had initially pushed the enemy backwards, the trickle of reinforcements were gathering pace as they now began to turn the tide on the garrison. Many were hacking their way towards the distinct figures of Sir Robert and Lord Fitz Warrin who stood with the last three men-at-arms, a tide of bodies around them, their armour blood stained. Not for the first time Rowan wished he had some more arrows in his belt and glanced backwards towards the big cart that had held what had seemed at the time a plentiful number of sheaves.

A thought crossed his mind even as he parried an enemy pike, sucking in his stomach and turning side-on in an effort to avoid the lethal point. The point went past him but tore at his mail, scoring the links as the enemy swung it sideways at the same time as retracting it. 'Goat herder!' he found himself cursing more in fear than as a threat and, stepping forwards, swung his sword down so that it cut at the man's fingers at the same time biting into the dark wood of the pike shaft. The man dropped his weapon, reeling away in shock just as Daniel thrust his sword point into the man's belly, the force easily piercing through the padded gambeson. There was no time for thanks as his friend then avoided a swing from the dead man's comrade and Rowan smashed the buckler upwards into the man's chin snapping the head backwards. It allowed his friend to throw himself forward, knocking the man from his feet and grappling with him on the ground before somehow managing to thrust a dagger dragged from his belt into the man's throat.

Rowan grabbed Daniel from the ground and pulled him backwards as the melee continued around them.

'Come on, I need you.'

His friend, his face and mail shirt now almost completely covered in fresh blood, stared at him with wide eyes for a moment, the frenzy of the battle well and truly upon him. Rowan had to physically grab his arm and pull him back from the gatehouse.

'Help me get this wagon moving for Christ's sake!'

Still his friend looked at him dumbly until he saw Rowan take hold of the back of the cart and try to push it forwards.

The wheels didn't budge despite his efforts.

Daniel, now out of his trance-like state, put his

weight behind him and the two friends strained their backs against the large back boards, their feet seeking purchase in the packed earth. Two injured men saw their efforts and lent what strength they had.

They pushed with all their might and there was the slightest motion.

'Push!' Rowan urged through gritted teeth determined to gain momentum.

The heavy wheels moved slightly and then more.

The wagon rolled forwards, increasing in pace, men at arms and archers stepping aside even as they continued their frenzied combat.

The wheels now rolled rapidly, Rowan and Daniel continuing to push forwards with all their might, the weight of the wagon crushing the bodies beneath. With a splintering of wood, it slammed into the stone archway, wedging itself against the sides and once more blocking the gateway.

The sound and realisation that they were temporarily cut off from their comrades began to dawn on the attackers. They nervously glanced back at the new barrier even as they parried against the defenders who, with renewed heart, swung and thrust their heavy blades. They were encouraged by the curses of Sir Robert who had once again lifted his faceplate and whose calls were taken up by the now almost snarling garrison. The attackers were stepping backwards and calls for pardon started to be heard amongst the ringing of weapons, many unheeded as men were chopped down mercilessly, the blood lust in full flow. A few were spared but not many and soon the courtyard looked like a slaughterhouse, the remaining men covered in blood, bodies and discarded weapons; helmets and shields littered the floor.

The men looked at each other, incredulous for the moment. The shouts of the enemy still roared from behind the new barricade but many of the heavy axes used in the initial assault now lay on the floor of the courtyard, their owners beside them.

'Hell's curses, that was well done,' Daniel patted his friend on the back as they both got their breath back, hands on their thighs. 'But now what do we do?' Although there was temporary respite there was no mistaking the threat from behind the improvised barricade that meant they would soon be battling for their lives again within minutes.

'It's that swine of a bridge. As long as that's still in place we're done for.' Rowan said, as much to himself as to his friend. 'We need to burn the thing, that's what we've got to do.'

'They tried that though and it didn't work.'

'Well, we'll have to try again otherwise we're done for. We just need to try something different.' His words trailed off. 'What if?' he muttered, before again silently thinking about the idea that was forming in his mind.

'What if, what?' But if his friend was looking for an explanation he was disappointed as Rowan ran to the two nobles who were already encouraging the remaining soldiers to defend the new bastion.

'My lords.' Both men looked round. The bloodied dented armour of both showed that their plates had deflected more than one sword thrust. 'I think I have an idea how to destroy the bridge.' He had got both of the men's attention now.

'God's teeth, I hope you have, boy.' There was a crust of blood across the right eye of Sir Robert that made him even more intimidating.

'We can try and burn it.'

'Is that your plan? The Lord here tried that already, even poured oil on the devil, isn't that so? He turned to Lord Fitz Warrin who nodded, as usual not entering the discussion unless he felt necessary. Instead he stared at the young archer before him with quizzical eyes.

'Yes, sire, but there could be another way.' He went on to explain hurriedly, encouraged by the silence of the knights.

'It might just work.' The Lord was the first to speak up after he had finished, glancing towards the noise from the attackers just a few feet away. The enemy were trying to get close enough to get at the improvised barricade, the remaining defenders pushing against them, threatening them with halberds and captured pikes.

That was enough for Rowan as he looked across to the most seriously injured who were no longer capable of holding their own as part of the defensive line. Amongst them was Catin who was now tending the wounded as best she could in the courtyard. There was now no time or spare men to bring them inside the hall.

'Catin!' he shouted. She looked up without a trace of surprise at the sound of her name, her blond hair now streaked with dried blood and tied back. 'I need oil, lots of it, and a firebrand.'

She nodded, pushing wisps of hair away from her face with the back of her hand and with a reassuring smile to the injured bowman finished tying the dressing around his torn leg, before picking up her skirts and running back to the kitchens.

Rowan sprinted up the winding stairway, Daniel and three injured archers behind as they left the nobles and what seemed to be a pathetic few soldiers to defend the archway.

He emerged onto the battlements above the attacking force and kept his head low, relieved his appearance seemed to go unnoticed. No arrows flew from the opposite walls and he prayed that would remain the case as he rammed his blade between the stone merlons, chipping away frantically. Soon he was joined by the injured archers and a gasping man-at-arms who worked with him, two kneeling and one on his back as they began to hack at the elderly mortar of an adjacent stone, ignoring their various wounds hidden beneath blood soaked bandages.

It was hard work and all the time the sound of splintering wood and the cry of the enemy was increasing below. Even though the mortar was in poor repair he was relieved as Leovald appeared, heavily limping from a deep cut to his leg to lend his effort, pounding at the hardened pale sand and lime mix with a dulled broad-bladed dagger.

'Heave!'

The stone shifted a little and, encouraged, their arms no longer weary because of their urgency they pushed again. This time there was a discernible movement and when they heaved once more, their muscles straining, the large piece of stone fell smashing directly down into the flat penthouse roof. The weight of the masonry caused a splintering of timbers but the protective covering held, despite the roar from the enemy beneath that showed they had at least caused some panic among the attackers.

A second stone was pushed from the ramparts by the other injured soldiers and crashed similarly into the hide covered roof with the same result.

Rowan cursed just as the enemy archers having decided the defenders had abandoned the battlements began to race back up onto the barbican walls to resume their counter fire.

'Quick! They're coming back. Hurry before they start shooting! Take the whole section down!' His words were frantic now as the men began ramming their steel points and chipping away once more at the crumbling mortar.

'Come on! Push, one, two, three!' and the men lent all their weight, this time to the section of wall of seven or eight stone blocks having weakened the lime mortar mixture.

For a moment the wall didn't seem to shift.

'Come on! Again!' he urged desperately now, listening to the ongoing clamour of the attackers below. The men once more shoved with all their might.

Their efforts were rewarded by a slight movement and grating of stone as the blocks began to give way. Suddenly momentum was with the small group and the whole section hurtled down onto the siege engine, smashing through the roof and tearing the covering inwards. The masonry crashed onto the timbered floor, causing consternation among the men below and no doubt breaking the bones of some, their assault temporarily forgotten as their roars of anger and now pain filled the air.

'That'll hurt,' Leovald smiled scrambling to the protection of the remaining battlements as one of the wounded archers gurgled horribly as an arrow pierced his neck, fighting briefly to stop the flow of blood before collapsing slowly to the floor as arrows began to fly from the enemy opposite.

Rowan too dived to the cover of the remaining wall but couldn't help himself peering down to see what damage the mass of masonry had caused before he was unceremoniously pulled back behind the remaining battlement. 'It's a robust swine but I hope this'll work.'

He saw the anxiety still in the faces of his friends, not knowing how successful they had been in deterring the enemy as Catin and Rosalind arrived, carrying one of the large washing tubs between them.

'Stay there, for Christ's sake,' Daniel cried out seeing them about to step out of the tower and, ducking, scampered to join them, Rowan just behind him.

'You've got it,' Rowan said, staring into Catin's eyes gratefully before taking the handle of the tub while his friend took the other.

The thick heated oil gave off a sickening stench as they dragged the tub across the floor, its bottom scraping on stone until they had reached the gap in the wall with part of the remaining rampart providing cover.

'Let's hope they haven't protected the floor,' he said, breathing heavily, feeling this was their last chance.

'Come on, let me help.' Leovald crawled towards the two men, their backs to the wall now either side of the reduced rampart. 'I'll give you a hand' and crawling so he could get his big hands under the bottom of the tub Leovald lifted it up while Rowan and Daniel raised the handles.

'Now!' He felt like every second was a minute as they poured the contents over the dismantled embrasures.

Arrows thwacked against the remaining stonework and one smashed into the tub, sending it reeling backwards despite the men's grip, but not before the foul liquid had splashed downwards onto the siege engine beneath.

Frantically he looked back towards the tower and gratefully saw that Catin had remembered the firebrand and was already holding it forward having lit it from the brazier inside. Slithering backwards he took it from her hands, immediately feeling the heat from the burning wood as he held it in front of him. The heat was now intense as he pulled himself up with his free hand, fearful of the enemy arrows, and dropped the burning torch to land in the pool of animal fat beneath the broken roof of the siege engine.

Arrows flew at him, one amazingly passing between him and the side of the embrasure he had leant from. He could almost hear the tickle of the goose flight against his face as it whistled past and he ducked back behind the parapet hoping to God that his plan had worked. The shouts, curses and screams from the enemy below showed that they had made an impact but how serious that was no one was prepared to put their head above the walls to find out.

Rowan feeling utterly exhausted, slumped back

against the ramparts, his fingers unwittingly rubbing the smooth oak of the cross about his neck.

A shout came from one of the girls within the gatehouse tower but the call was muffled. For a moment he wanted to shout back but felt too weary. If they had not succeeded then surely the castle would fall and they would be left to fate.

'It's worked! You beautiful boy!' The excited shout from Leovald accompanied the screams from the attackers below and, sure enough, smoke soon began to swirl up into the sky and the smell of burning wood and hides assailed their nostrils.

The relief swept through the garrison as the enemy could only watch from the captured barbican walls. The smoke from the burning bridge now accompanied by the snap of burning timbers rose high while the enemy force camped and waiting for victory in the surrounding orchard and village knew that they would have to wait a little longer.

Rowan and his friends clambered down from the ramparts, exhausted from their exploits. In the courtyard the injured were being treated while others were moving among the dead checking for life, either dispatching those that were dying slowly from their wounds or helping carry them to the makeshift infirmary in the hall. He noticed there were precious few survivors, with less than a score of defenders able to even partly swing a sword, the nobles included.

Sweat had plastered his hair to his skull as he took off his bascinet, wincing with pain from the blisters on his right hand and heading straight for the well. He watched as a man-at-arms let his comrade unfasten his breastplate, grimacing with pain while with relief he saw Martin by Jerrard's side. The big man had inevitably taken another wound, this time a gash to his side, and Martin was having trouble persuading his friend to remove his hand so he could see the extent of the injury.

'Well done lads. That's given them a bloody nose and bought us some time.' Rowan watched as Sir Robert wandered among the men, his words provoking a grin here and there despite their obvious strain and fatigue.

The knight caught sight of Rowan and headed for the young archer. 'Well done, sir, it was some good thinking up there, never mind with the wagon.'

Rowan gave a smile despite his tiredness and the pain now throbbing from the cut to his side and blisters on his hand, his embarrassment preventing him from uttering a reply.

Sir Robert sensing how uncomfortable he was with the praise said no more. Instead the knight turned to give encouragement to a man-at-arms who could hardly stand but nevertheless was trying to retrieve weapons from the dead.

Rowan returned his gaze to the devastation around him and then, letting his eyes rest on the banner of Fitz Warrin still hanging from the battlement tower, gratefully slaked his thirst from a ladle of cool, crisp water drawn from the well, allowing the liquid to dribble unabated down the stubble of his chin. He was proud of the part he had played in defending the castle and felt a competence he had never really known before, but with this came a feeling of weary acceptance as his eyes switched back to look at the broken gateway. The wagon had now been pulled back so as not to catch the crackling flames from the bridge and he knew that they were almost defenceless. If the enemy somehow crossed the moat again, the score of wounded men would easily be swept away.

The shout from the battlements came a couple of hours later as Catin was carefully wrapping the damp dressing around Rowan's hand, his nervousness resumed by her proximity. Both remained silent as she tended to his wounds, the red blisters from the heat had already started to ooze puss and he felt like his palm was on fire but as he sat there and looked around him he felt lucky compared to the injuries of the others.

Since the bridge had been set alight there had been little sound from the besieging army. There was no sign of another wave of attacks, allowing a period of respite. So the call from the walls immediately caught the defenders attention. Anxiously men's faces looked towards the watchman in the north east tower whose call had been clear enough.

'Men are coming.' The remnants of the defenders looked at each other. 'Men are coming,' the unnecessary call came again.

No one dared speak and no one dared hope that the call could signal the appearance of reinforcements and he found himself unable to move as Sir Robert and Lord Fitz Warrin quickly strode across the courtyard to access the walls. It seemed an age before the two men appeared against the skyline looking far out towards the track that led down towards the castle. 'Please God. Let it be reinforcements,' he thought to himself. Around him anxious men stared upwards at the nobles waiting for them to communicate what fate had determined for them.

CHAPTER TWELVE

'Gods teeth!' William de Movran cursed and pushed against the men in the shadowed confines of the bridge. A feeling of intense claustrophobia hung over the tightly packed mass of soldiers who were not moving.

'Keep moving forward. Take the Castle!' he roared above the din.

He had watched the attack from the battlements and it had been going so well that he decided to join the attackers assaulting the gatehouse. It had now somehow stalled.

Among the press of men he could not see what had happened, knowing only that above the curses of the soldiers there had been a distinct crash of wood at the gateway ahead which had stopped any forward motion. The mass of attackers squeezed shoulder to shoulder meant that he now couldn't move and the intensity was becoming unbearable as the message had been passed back that the defenders had somehow managed to block the breach.

Then, suddenly, the wooden roof shuddered with the weight of a heavy object from above and the men looked up feeling vulnerable as the noise within increased. Another crash soon followed, shaking the timbered roof. Men began to push backwards as fear swept through them, exacerbated by not knowing what was happening above them and the fact they could no longer advance.

Their curses were then drowned out with the next impact of heavy stones. This time they smashed through the timbered roof causing chaos among the men.

Cries of pain and urgent calls of retreat were immediately taken up. William de Movran tried to stand his ground but found himself pushed back among the tide of men. There was now a gaping hole in the roof and he watched helplessly still facing towards the breach, his arms pinned to his side by the mass of men seeking safety from the heavy stones that had smashed bones, killing and injuring their comrades close to the battered drawbridge.

The oil and then the flash of flames that followed engulfed the front of the bridge and the screams of men, their flesh and clothing alight, quickly sent the attackers into panic. It was all he could do keep his feet as he joined the rest of the attackers as they forgot any thoughts of overcoming the barricade and surged back into the safety of the outer courtyard and its surrounding walls.

Fuming but also weary William de Movran had made his way back up to the barbican walls without even looking at those around him. He had watched as the flames licked greedily at the wooden structure, the protective roof covering giving off a thick smoke as the ingenuous bridge that the Irish engineer had been so proud of was turned into charred timber to match the scorched gateway. The evidence of their defeat was reflected in the bodies left lying among the debris and in the waters below.

That had been less than an hour ago and now he and the other knights were back at the inn. Their jovial mood of a few hours before had completely dissipated as the failure of the attack and the silence from their comrades hung heavy among the tired faces of the armoured men, many with dirt or smoke-streaked faces.

'I say we leave these English bastards to rot. What use is the castle anyway? It's not as though it will be a thorn in our side.' The words were spoken by a red tousled haired knight, his armour old and showing signs of repair. William de Movran recognised him as a particular confidant of the Welsh leader. 'We can leave a few men in the outer gatehouse so they're like rats in a trap.' His words were almost spat out.

He looked hard at Rhys Gethin who had called the council and who was listening to his knight and seemingly considering the advice which was supported by murmurs of agreement around the tables.

'Hold for a moment.' A large grizzled bear-like knight sporting a heavily bandaged thigh over his breeches held up his hands to silence the nobles and the noise within the inn subsided once more. 'I can understand the point but it isn't just the fact that it's a thorn in our side. It's still somewhere where the English can command our lands and I for one have had enough of these Marcher lords. There's got to be less than twenty men left inside against our hundreds. They obviously haven't got any arrows left and if the bridge isn't too badly burned we can still get across.'

Noises of assent accompanied the counter argument.

William de Movran silently assessed the authoritative knight in his vert and argent surcoat whose name he had learned was Ieuan ap Blethin. Moreover he had learned that the knight had apparently dragged the first ladder to the walls, inspiring the success of the attack two days before.

He was grateful for the soldier's interruption; he knew he couldn't continue to be seen as the only one intent on taking the castle and the knight was obviously respected among his countrymen, though it still seemed the views were split for the moment.

'Well, engineer, what is your assessment?' Rhys Gethin turned to the Irishman, ignoring the low conversations that continued among his men. William de Movran noted how the cheerful Seamus O'Breen showed no concern at addressing the company around him despite their status.

'I think it will hold unless they decide to throw more of the battlements at it.' If he was aggrieved at the destruction of his structure he didn't show it, simply shrugging his shoulders. 'If they do that then we'll make another one. It'll take a day or two and will depend on us getting the burned structure out of the way or we can pull down some of the houses and fill the ditch with rubble.'

That last comment provoked an increase in murmuring amongst the gathered men, many of whom disliked the destruction of homes and villages, while others saw it as a necessary evil in their struggle for independence.

William de Movran looked once more at the Welsh

commander who was seemingly happy for the arguments to continue and develop amongst Glyn Dwr's followers. It was only the sharp rap and immediate entrance of a worried looking captain that caused the noise in the filled room of the inn to recede. The eyes of the knights followed the captain's, including his own, as the man sought out and then recognised Rhys Gethin sitting at one of the largest tables.

'My lord, scouts have spotted a contingent of horses arriving.' The man was obviously nervous, his fingers playing with the handle of his sword as he spoke.

'What banner do they fly under?'

'The scouts report a quartered azure and gules banner with charges of lion and fish.'

Again a slight tremor in his voice belied his nervousness. Despite the detail the man was not sure of himself but the news of the arrival of another force was enough for the Welsh leader who looked around at his surrounding commanders.

'I think, men, that our assault on the castle is held for the moment until we have seen who our new visitors are.' His words were confident and were followed by the hasty scrape of chairs and helms being lifted from tables as the men left to assemble their units.

By the time the unknown horsemen arrived on the crest the besiegers were still hurriedly assembling, a battle of nearly three hundred men waited directly on the track facing the rise. They filled the space between the castle, some spilling onto the marshy ground to their right, constantly moving their feet to stop themselves sinking into the mire of mud and water. Others stood in front of the village buildings on the left flank, but all were looking up towards the small group of horsemen that had appeared.

Glancing back from his saddle, William de Movran could see that Rhys Gethin had placed a large number of archers and men-at-arms on the parapets of the barbican, and had even placed his own lion banner on the walls showing that they had at least partial control of the castle. Beneath him his destrier impatiently pawed at the dirt track beneath its iron shod hooves. Alongside, the other knights occasionally tugged at their bridles as the column seemed oblivious for the moment of the panorama that was before them and continued their slow approach down the track towards the host blocking their path.

He continued watching, expecting at any moment a line of soldiers to appear behind the small company who numbered no more than a dozen, though all appeared well armoured on big war horses with heavy colourful trappings, stout steel tipped lances held aloft, visors raised.

Eventually the leader held up his hand calling a halt when they were no more than two hundred yards away, well within bow range. For a moment that passed like minutes the unequal forces looked at each other silently before a detachment of three men broke off and slowly trotted down to meet Rhys Gethin and his knights, obviously intent on parley. Above the horsemen they held a quartered banner with rampant lions and three fish opposite each other which snapped in the light breeze, while the leader held a distinctive striped shield with a diagonal stripe, matching his surcoat.

William de Movran glanced at Rhys Gethin who seemed almost amused before returning the gaze. 'Well we'd best go and meet these brave English boys.'

It was clear he was invited to accompany the leader, so William de Movran put his stirrups to the flank of his war horse and followed the Welsh commander.

'Greetings to you my lord,' the tall, middle-aged English commander opened the conversation as the two parties halted their wary approach towards each other, the standard bearers that had accompanied them hanging back slightly.

'And to you too sire.' The Welsh leader replied politely.

'I see that you seem to be in a powerful position.' The knight's eyes had strayed from assessing the entourage towards the castle walls where the smoke continued to spiral lazily into the air behind them and the assembled mass of soldiers.

'We do that, I take it that you are not here as a relieving force.' Rhys Gethin replied confidently.

'Oh in God's name no, my good friend.' A grin spread across the knight's face. 'It is good to see you again, my lord, and you, William de Movran.'

William de Movran slightly nervous by the formality of the welcome relaxed and nodded in acknowledgement.

'You seem to have everything in hand here?' The knight continued.

'Indeed and were in fact just deliberating whether to finish them off.' Rhys Gethin answered cheerfully, though William de Movran thought that his voice betrayed a hint of annoyance, probably due to Sir John's arrival before they had captured the entire castle.

The messenger looked briefly at the walls again and the quartered banner of Fitz Warrin that still flew from the main ramparts, before returning his gaze to look at the two knights.

'There's no need to deliberate any further. I bring news from Sir Thomas Percy who has extricated himself from Shrewsbury and sent me to contact you and Lord Glyn Dwr. The forces are gathered and the cards are down.'

As the words were spoken William de Movran felt his heart beat faster. He had been nervous about whether this moment would come and anxious that the part he had played to date aligning himself with the opponents of King Henry and aiding the Welsh uprising may prove his downfall. Now it seemed that the collective rebellion was gathering pace.

'So be it but I'm afraid your assumptions might not be correct, Sir John. It's true we are despatched by Lord Glyn Dwr but he is still harrying the English in the south.'

The news brought a worried frown to Sir John Done who had been carrying messages between Thomas Percy's nephew and Owain Glyn Dwr for the past two years.

'That will come as a disappointment to my lord. Still, now is not the time to discuss it further and I am keen to discharge my responsibilities,' the knight replied, retaining his composure at what must have been unsuspected news judging by his expression and the trace of disappointment in his voice. 'Then there is all the more reason sir to make haste. My lord is assembling his army and will want news, and men.'

Sat astride his mount William de Movran was aware that the direction of the conversation meant the chance of capturing Whittington and staking his immediate claim was at risk of slipping away.

'But wouldn't it be better if the castle was to be taken? It would take no more than a day,' he ventured, looking at both men in turn.

'I'm afraid not. Even the men here will be valuable and could still be decisive. The appearance of some if not all of Owain Glyn Dwr's force would lend heart to the campaign which is why I was specifically despatched.'

With those words and a tug of the reins from the knights around him William de Movran knew he was beaten for the moment. There was a much bigger plan going on and his ambition would have to be served by patience. He turned in his saddle and looked at the castle walls, the banners of the Lord Fitz Warrin still hanging over them; ready to fall but not yet it seemed.

He departed with the army an hour later, leaving their dead in the valley behind them. They had lost over a sixth of the force and William de Movran nearly all of his men. There would be a reckoning, he swore, as he had rode up the track behind Sir John and Rhys Gethin, not able to resist looking back a last time as the soldiers disappeared over the crest and made their way northwards.

The column, slowed down by the foot soldiers, arrived at the rendezvous just to the north east of Chester two days later where an army was assembled. Even in his previous forays as part of Richard's army against the Welsh he had never seen such a force amassed. There must have been over five thousand men filling the valley outside the small village. Rows upon rows of tents had been erected either side of the main tracks that dissected the sprawling encampment so that not a patch of grass could be seen.

He, Rhys Gethin and Sir John with their standard bearers left the force from Whittington and kicked their horses onwards. They rode through the neat lines of the encampment that were alive with the sound and smells of soldiers packed together, the smell of food cooking and the clash of the practised swordplay.

Everywhere a variety of surcoats and shields were visible, showing that many nobles had thrown in their lot with the rebellion. The livery and banner of Rhys Gethin and his Lord Glyn Dwr brought some stares from the soldiers who looked up from their simmering pots of stews or from honing their weapons. Not all were welcoming but they stayed silent. Many had fought the Welsh on behalf of Richard including the veteran Cheshire archers still wearing his badge, the white hart embroidered on their jackets. If Rhys Gethin or Sir John noticed the stares they did not show it as they rode their big destriers through the camp, their heads held high as they headed towards the larger tents with their various banners flapping lazily in the early afternoon sun.

It took nearly five minutes for the small entourage to reach the centre of the camp where young squires took hold of the horses' bridles. The men dismounted in front of an arrangement of perhaps twenty tents, the shields and banners of their Lords showing who they belonged to. William de Movran recognised some of them including Hugh Leigh of Bowden and Thomas Hilford, both from the Cheshire guard who had served with Richard, and those of Arthur Davenport of Calverley and Sir Hugh Massey of Tatton whose colours he also recognised from campaign. It was a heady gathering of veterans and nobles and he felt confidence swell within as he waited, surrounded by the sights and sounds of the army.

Sir John entered a large canvas tent that had the renowned quartered lions and gules of the Percy family on a shield resting against the entrance. He and Rhys Gethin waited a moment before being ushered in, leaving the standard bearers behind.

'Welcome, welcome.' Sir Thomas, the Earl of Worcester, greeted the men happily, having already risen from his writing desk. He shook each of their hands in turn. 'Please take a seat.' He gestured to a set of campaign chairs to their right.

William de Movran sat down, immediate relief coursing through his muscles and bones from the long ride before the Earl continued.

'I'm glad to see Sir John here managed to rendezvous with you. It was a stroke of luck that the Earl of Stafford rode to Shrewsbury to seek aid. It was perfect.'

William de Movran's confused face must have shown for the Earl explained himself with a grin.

'I left Henry thinking I was going to relieve the castle while at the same time knowing exactly where Owain's vanguard was. I couldn't have hoped for a better excuse, though I had the devil's own job to dissuade Edmund from accompanying me. My God the Prince is going to get a shock,' he smiled.

William de Movran was almost jealous at the intricate web that was being woven and felt like congratulating himself on his choice of allegiance, feeling that victory and personal gain were finally in reach.

'My Lord, Rhys Gethin here has confirmed that his Lord's force is continuing to harass the borders to the South and is more than four days march away.'

The words from Sir John caused a flicker of surprise for a moment but, like the knight, he seemed to dismiss the news as no more than a disappointment as he assessed the words.

'No matter, it is good news you are here. My nephew Hotspur will be happy to see you.' Then, decisively, he grasped the handles of his chair and stood up with a sudden burst of energy that contradicted his sixty years. 'So let's go and see him.'

After threading their way past more guide ropes they found themselves waiting as Sir Thomas entered another large tent which could only be that of the commander of this massively arrayed force. Two men-at-arms wearing gules and or livery looked at the men warily, silently assessing them, their heavy poll axes prepared to prevent their entrance despite their chaperone, Thomas Percy, who reappeared a few minutes later gesturing for the men to follow.

Passing a clerk feverishly scribbling away at his desk who did not so much as glance up at the men, they entered a second large awning, well furnished with a large table dominating the space. A gleaming suit of armour stood in the corner by a rack of weapons and in the centre of the tent stood Sir Henry Hotspur Percy.

This was the first time William de Movran had met the famous Hotspur, the victor of the battle of Homildon Hill the previous year and previously a stalwart supporter of King Henry. He was a man who could gather supporters from across the country just by the mention of his name.

'Please come in, gentlemen.' The knight was perhaps thirty years old, not necessarily tall but his sparkling eyes exuded a confidence and air of authority as he raised his head from studying a map on the table. His smile was genuine as the men walked forwards. 'You must be Rhys Gethin. Owain speaks most highly of you, sir. It is a pleasure to meet you.'

'The pleasure is mine, Sir Henry,' the Welshman acknowledged, 'and my lord sends his respects.' Rhys Gethin bent slightly after offering his formal response.

'Aye, but we would have benefitted from bringing his whole force here.' The broad Scottish accent came from a heavy set, grey moustached knight who was stood slightly behind the Earl and who had been silently observing the newcomers.

William de Movran recognised a veteran when he saw one. This one was in the mould of Ieuan ap Blethin, he thought, judging by the patch over one scarred eye, the broken nose and the company in which he looked at ease.

'Gentlemen, may I introduce you to Earl Douglas. Please forgive him, we have often disagreed and not once have I succeeded in winning the argument, rather obtaining a peace settlement.' Hotspur chuckled good naturedly. It was quite clear the two were good friends. 'We are grateful to your lord for sending us your contingent at least and are pleased that he will continue to harry the King's garrisons in the south with Mortimer. Isn't that so, earl?'

'You know my feelings on the matter but, as ever, I will leave the planning to yourself and Sir John.'

'Quite so,' the English commander continued smiling as he turned back to Rhys Gethin. 'I know and respect your Lord Glyn Dwr and know we have the same outcome in mind. The appearance of your banner will be a welcome addition to our force. With your help and that of your lord we will be able to secure the throne to its rightful lineage.'

William de Movran listened to the words and knew that while men like Rhys Gethin and Sir Percy had noble thoughts and indeed he too wished for nothing more than King Richard to take the throne, he also had less noble priorities.

For a moment he felt as though his thoughts had somehow betrayed him as he was suddenly aware of the eyes of the charismatic commander focussed upon him.

'You must be William de Movran?'

'I am my lord,' and he found himself bending

forwards in deference to the noble.

'My thanks go to you too for I understand if it had not been for the unforeseen arrival of Earl Edmund you would have captured the castle at Whittington?'

'Indeed sire.'

'Well, there will be plenty of time for that and your loyalty will be rewarded once the King is persuaded to leave the throne.'

The words were like honey to William de Movran. He would have the Earl's support to take the castle and its lands and it was all he could do to stop himself from smiling.

'Now to business. I have already briefed my nobles as we are to break camp first thing tomorrow and you have arrived just in time. Now come and look at our plan.' Again the eyes lit up with excitement as Hotspur gestured for the men to step forward and peer over the map that was laid out on the wide table.

The detail and sweeping colours were of fine quality and William de Movran could easily make out the Marches and the rest of Wales with intricate pictures of castles clearly drawn. The main towns of Shrewsbury, Chester, Stafford, Worcester and Hereford were just as easily discernable and the illustration was bordered by the Pennines to the north east, Leicester to the east and Oxford to the south. He could not help but trace his fingers along the parchment feeling the brush strokes of the mountain ranges as his thoughts threatened to take him away.

'You like the map, William de Movran? I had the monks at Saint Chads in Shrewsbury draw it for me. They really do have some splendid skills as well as keeping our souls in check don't you think?'

William de Movran, never a pious man at the best of times but sensing the fervour of the Earl, nodded. 'Indeed they do my lord.'

The Earl once more turned his attention to the map, apparently satisfied by the knight's respectful manner. 'We know from our agents that the King is marching northwards via York to reinforce the Scottish borders, which is why we will be heading quickly south to Shrewsbury where I understand from my good uncle here that the Prince is still garrisoning himself.' The Earl pointed to the picture of the town on the map which showed it protected on nearly all sides by the curve of the river Severn while the narrow neck of land to the north was protected by Shrewsbury Castle itself.

'We are here, not more than forty miles away and can march straight down the Wem Road.' Hotspur continued sliding his finger slightly southwards. 'We know he now has half his men and in return we've increased our ranks by a thousand men-at-arms and archers thanks to my uncle, and your arrival has increased that number further.'

William de Movran looked at the knight as he spoke. He was creating a passion and enthusiasm among them that was contagious.

'It will be a shock for my good friend, Prince Henry, to see us before the walls and it should be enough to force him to surrender, God willing. After that we hold all the pieces. We will have Shrewsbury and the Prince, the support of Lord Glyn Dwr and my father, the Earl of Northumberland with his forces. Best of all, the King is marching northwards which means he is badly positioned, far from London and the throne.'

William de Movran was stunned for a moment, the enormity of the implications dawning upon him. He felt like congratulating himself once more on his choice of allegiance, it seemed that victory and personal gain were in reach.

The men were looking at each other with smiles spreading across their faces when the clerk they had passed so busily scribbling away at the parchment coughed politely. 'My lord, Sir Richard Venables is here to see you.'

The Earl nodded, returning their grins. 'You must forgive me for the moment gentlemen. I wish you well and my clerk here will pass on the order of march to you and make victualling arrangements for your camp tonight. I bid you good day.'

As they filed out of the tent and then rode through the encampment William de Movran could tell that the company, like himself, were buoyed by the meeting. In good spirits they made their way back to their men, taking in the sounds and smells of thousands of soldiers preparing for the next day's march.

CHAPTER THIRTEEN

Staring out across the stone battlements the exhausted defenders waited long after the dust from the marching feet had fallen back to earth before venturing out from the protection afforded by the scarred castle walls.

The few men-at-arms and archers able to walk and carry sword or halberds, cautiously led by Sir Robert, made their way across to the outer castle. The blackened and charred remains of the timbered bridge creaked in protest and the acrid smell of smoke caught in their throats as they crossed the stretch of moat. The bodies and weapons lay haphazardly on the muddied banks and in the still waters beneath, spent arrows sticking out like stalks of wheat.

Rowan held his sword cumbersomely in his bandaged right hand trying to ignore the pressure on his blisters, his buckler in his other hand, glancing anxiously at the ramparts above. The men stepped cautiously through the archway; the silence surrounding them was unnerving. At any moment Rowan expected to hear the screams of attackers but nothing came.

The scene within the barbican was ghostly quiet, filled with the debris of battle surrounded by the enclosing dark grey walls. Bodies hastily dragged back from the last onslaught across the bridge lay unceremoniously in the blood-stained dirt. It was an eerie feeling which was mixed with a strong sense of relief, making him feel almost light headed as it became clear the enemy had indeed abandoned their assault and left the valley.

Over the next few hours the exhausted archers began to collect whatever arrows they could find while the makeshift infirmary was busy with those who had previously shrugged off their injuries but now felt the deepness of their wounds, the urgency of battle no longer overcoming the pain. The women walked hurriedly between the baileys bringing bandages, water from the well and medicinal herbs from the garden. Soon the sound of sawing, hammering and masonry returned as the villagers came down from their hiding places in the forest. The carpenter worked to re-affix a new walkway and the mason began to repair the wall above the gatehouse, while others assessed the damage to their homes.

In the church grounds Rowan stood looking down at the mass grave that had hastily been dug by the attackers during their assault to prevent disease spreading rapidly in the hot climate. He tried to ignore the stench from the corpses which filled the air as he pulled out the small wooden cross from around his neck, thinking of his father. Leovald stood next to him and he knew the Welshman's son would also be lying among the dead. Among good company, he thought, thinking of his father and of the good-natured Eric. A local priest was reciting a psalm over the mass grave but he didn't hear the words, his thoughts were still dulled by the deaths, the ferocity of battle and the seemingly inevitable defeat.

There still remained a sense of disbelief among the inhabitants of the castle and village even though it had been less than a day since the enemy had left the valley. He felt a different person. His two best friends, Eric and his father, were now gone. He had experienced battle, the castle was once again secure, a bastion against the Welsh rebellion but what did that matter? His mother didn't know yet that she was a widow and if it was not for some unknown reason which had caused the attackers to cease their attack her son would also have surely perished.

With a heavy heart he looked back towards the castle where people busied themselves. He knew he couldn't just leave it there. He wasn't prepared to just let the matter rest; he neither wanted to remain part of the depleted garrison or return to his home. No orders had been given either way, the rebuilding and resupply of the castle was too urgent, but Rowan knew that he would follow the enemy and the cause of his sorrow. The faces of William de Movran and Bayard among the enemy were too easy to remember, seemingly unaccountable for the death and destruction their treachery had brought.

He tried to absorb himself in helping repair the battlements, collecting wood to make arrow shafts, shepherding the animals and horses back into their stalls and burying the dead from the last assault but still the pain remained raw. Over three quarters of the men had died defending the castle, while they estimated they had killed over a hundred of the enemy.

The next day Rowan, who by now was consciously aware that he continued to wallow in misery and bitterness and was unable to raise only the briefest and strained of grins in response to the efforts of his friends to encourage and cajole him, was called by Leovald to the Lord's chamber.

'Oi Rowan, come over here,' The Welshman was holding the door to the chamber half ajar, obviously inviting him inside.

He looked up, breathing heavily after pulling at the hoist to lift stones up to the battlements. Both shared each other's loss but had hardly spoken since the enemy had left the valley.

Rowan was puzzled and a little concerned; he had never entered the Lord's private quarters and never expected to. Self aware he pulled his tunic straight hoping, for he daren't look, that the sweat stains from the early rigours of the day were not too visible. He ran his fingers through his black hair before putting his hand to the pommel of his sword.

'Don't look so worried, me laddo,' Leovald gave a small smile as Rowan approached. 'His lordship and Sir Robert just want a word with you.'

Despite the few words he had shared with the nobles in the heat of battle, addressing them now in private made his stomach feel sick.

Passing the Welsh vintenar he ducked his head unnecessarily as he entered the dimly lit room. He could feel the blood rushing to his face as he looked to his right and saw Lord Fitz Warrin and Sir Robert standing around a finely constructed table, the wood smooth and a dark brown.

'There you are,' Sir Robert spoke first, a welcoming smile on his face. He was dressed in a plain linen tunic, much like Lord Fitz Warrin, although his was more ornate in its decoration. For now it seemed the trappings of war were not needed, although both retained a sword at their sides.

He bowed his head. 'My lords.' The words came out weakly, intimidated by the audience.

'The Lord and I have been pondering what we are to do about the rebels that have retreated.' Sir Robert looked at Lord Fitz Warrin briefly before continuing. 'We are in agreement that it would be a wasted opportunity to allow the enemy just to disappear. Particularly as it seems that there is much more afoot than we know about, if our eyes were not deceiving us.' The knight left the statement hanging in the air.

Rowan had learnt from one of the surviving garrison that the livery of the men-at-arms that had preceded the withdrawal of the enemy was of Sir John Done of Utkington, a visitor to the castle over a number of years and more disturbingly, that of the Earl of Worcester.

As this knowledge ran through his mind and he tried to understand what this meant to him and why he was here he suddenly realised he was being studied by both men. His eyes looked downwards at the rush covered floor self-consciously before looking back at the nobles.

'It is our intention to send a small group of men to shadow the enemy. If the rebellion is larger than we realise then there is a real threat to the King and we need to know what they are up to.' Sir Robert's eyes remained locked on him. 'Both the Lord and I know what you have been through and thank you for your efforts.' Another pause. 'And we have been made aware of your keenness to track the enemy.' At that the knight looked over Rowan's shoulder to Leovald who, by now, had come to stand just beside his young friend.

'Certainly it seems you have a persuasive friend.' The Lord Fitz Warrin interrupted in a disapproving tone before, to his surprise for it didn't seem in the young noble's demeanour, a slight grin spread across face. He glanced at Leovald who had obviously passed on his determination to pursue the enemy. 'It seems Sir Robert here is also keen that you track the enemy and even though I will likely regret the reasoning and know of your losses, your personal actions during the siege make it hard for me to refuse.'

Not for the first time Rowan considered the Lord's apparent distant demeanour but at the same time his ability to have an awareness of an individual soldier's troubles, much like Sir Robert.

Sensing the heightened seriousness of the conversation Sir Robert added, 'I wanted to tell you this personally, and Leovald here,' lifting his finger to point at his friend behind him, 'has also recommended that there may be comrades who may want to accompany you?'

'Yes sire.' His mood lightened slightly at the mention of his friends, even as he was already thinking about how fast he could gather the victuals together and saddle the horses.

'The tracks of hundreds of men won't be hard to

follow but the real question is where are they heading. Remember, I just need you to follow and observe.' Sir Robert held Rowan's arm tightly. The force in the man's grip was incredibly strong. 'You will have failed both of us and possibly even the King if you allow yourself to be captured or killed.'

The tone, the set faces of the two knights and the reference to the King left him in no doubt of the seriousness of the task nor the trust placed in him.

Martin received the news with relish and, despite the injury to his hand which was heavily bandaged and the various cuts and bruises, he declared himself fit and willing to pursue the attackers who had killed his friends. Jerrard on the other hand was distressed when he was informed he could not accompany them. His face was now a permanent grimace from the pain of his numerous wounds, particularly the one to his side, which Rosalind was certain would tear open if he rode too hard. The loss of Eric had affected him hardest and it was only the intervention of Sir Robert that eventually halted his resolve to accompany his friends.

On the other hand Rowan could tell Daniel was concerned about Rosalind despite his friend's willingness to journey with them. Even now, as he lifted a thick saddle cloth onto Constance, he could see his friend in deep conversation on the viewing mount overlooking the gardens, hand in hand with Rosalind.

'She'll be okay you know.'

He turned round to see the smiling face of Catin, a basket of herbs hung in the crook of her arm, obviously on her way back to the kitchens. Caught by surprise and immediately absorbed by her eyes he was lost for words.

'I hope you'll take care of him, and yourself.' She said softly.

The words slowly registered in his mind, particularly the last two. 'I will,' he replied lamely as her slim figure carried on towards the archway, but it was enough for him to see her turn back and give him a shy smile.

They left the walls of the castle behind two hours later, seen off by Leovald who led Rowan's mare through the outer bailey, her iron horseshoes resonating beneath the gateway. The Welshman had told Rowan that he was to remain, deemed now too valuable to the defence of the castle by Lord Fitz Warrin to allow him to pursue his son's killers.

'Remember your orders, Rowan. Make your father proud. I miss my son as much as you must miss your father but you must wait for revenge. It will come, boy.' Leovald had seemingly accepted the Lord's decision stoically, letting his emotions surface only briefly as he passed the reins up to him.

He gripped Leovald's wrist firmly, a physical acknowledgement of the words and their bond.

'God bless and good luck.'

With that Rowan tapped his heels gently against the flanks of the ever obedient Constance. Behind him Rosalind tenderly kissed Daniel's hand as above, Sir Robert and Lord Fitz Warrin watched from the battlements. Rowan looked briefly for the figure of Catin but saw no sign and tried to persuade himself that it didn't matter, for now all that mattered was that he find and follow the enemy.

They travelled hard for the remainder of the day, the tell-tale signs of the enemy march easy to discern; churned up earth from the boots of so many soldiers and the hoofs of their mounts made their direction of travel unarguable. Much of the ride was in silence, each man caught up in their own thoughts. The face of William de Movran and Bayard appeared constantly in Rowan's mind, despite efforts to shut them out.

The friends spent the first night hidden deep within the protective foliage of a wood, deciding not to light a fire in case the enemy were near and not suffering any great discomfort as the early July night remained warm.

'Where do you think they're heading?' Daniel whispered to Rowan as the friends tucked themselves under their blankets, weapons close and swords unsheathed. The whisper was indicative of the caution the group still felt.

'They look like they're heading northwards but we've probably only travelled fifteen miles,' he replied, pulling the coarse cloth of his cloak closer to his chin.

Sir Robert had suggested that the enemy may seek the relative safety of the Welsh mountains to link up with more of Glyn Dwr's followers, though that assertion had not been certain because of the arrival of Sir John and the Percy banner.

'If they're heading north they're risking it a bit with the garrisons at Shrewsbury and Chester,' interrupted Martin.

'Then what in God's almighty name are they up to?'

There was no mistaking Daniel's hostility which had begun to return as they had left behind the castle walls. He lifted his hand in the semi darkness under the trees, feeling the jagged scar which was the legacy of their first battle.

Rowan was thinking the same thing. He had heard that the Welsh rebels always used their home terrain effectively, fading away from any of the English expeditions that tried to bring them to battle. Now it seemed they were risking just that by their direction of march.

The friends fell silent, tiredness catching up with them and, with the fallen leaves as their mattress they wrapped themselves in their travelling cloaks and allowed sleep to overtake their weary minds and bodies.

They caught up with the enemy the next night having ridden hard but cautiously before catching the glow of campfires in the distance.

At once Rowan rolled off the saddle, his friends following suit, pulling their mounts anxiously towards each other.

'Looks like we've found them then,' Daniel whispered rhetorically, a bit too loudly for Rowans liking.

'They must have camped for the night otherwise they wouldn't have set fires.' Rowan couldn't discern the individual features of his friends but realised he had assumed command having been instructed by the nobles. Although slightly uncomfortable with this realisation he was determined to succeed in his mission.

'There seem to be a lot of campfires,' Martin interjected, for the sky over the low hills was glowing with shades of reds and oranges illuminating the night. Rowan could only imagine at the numbers of fires that could create such a glow and grasped for an explanation but none came.

'Well what do we do now then?' whispered Daniel, showing some impatience at the brief silence, his hand stroking the muzzle of his horse.

Rowan thought back to his first taste of battle when he had returned to the Earl with a less than convincing report and the disapproving scowl on Samuel Blacke, the Master-at-Arm's face. 'We need to see how many of them there are. There's no point us being sent if we can't really say what's happening or where they're going,' he said, hoping his tone sounded assured.

He knew what he was really saying. It meant that one or more of them would have to go forward towards the uncertain danger over the rise. 'I'll go and you lot keep hold of the horses here,' he said, after taking a deep breath.

'I'll go with you,' Daniel offered, followed by Martin.

Rowan held up his hand. 'There's less chance of being spotted if it's just one of us. I want to do it.' He wasn't sure he did but it felt the right thing to say.

Silently and determined he pulled his bow from its canvas sleeve, uncoiled the hemp string and notched first one end around the nock and then, with effort the second, feeling the stave bend before the string took the tension. He didn't bother with a spare sheave of arrows, relying on those in his arrow bag, thinking stealth would be the critical factor in success or failure. If he was going to be spotted, twenty or forty arrows against hundreds didn't sound good odds either way you looked at it.

He could feel the silent watching stares from his friends and made an attempt at a convincing farewell. 'Don't worry, lads, I'll be back before you know it,' and then, with a quick grasp of each man's wrist, he turned and jogged towards the fire-lit sky above the crest in front of him.

He was surprised at how long it took him to cross the meadow with its calf high grass and reach the foot of the rise which rose steadily. His breathing was already becoming laboured as he reached the bottom of the slope and lowered himself to crawl forwards, the wetness of the early morning dew on the grass beginning to soak the elbows of his jacket. The higher he crawled the more his unease grew until his eyes were able to look over the crest to gaze down at the camp below.

The fires that burned seemed to fill the valley, the tents and groups of men illuminated by the firelight. There were not four hundred men, nor a thousand, this was an entire army. Rowan had never seen the like. He was transfixed in that moment, the vision before him impeding his ability to think. All he could do was stare at the rows upon rows of tents, banners outside many, though he was too far away and it was too dark to discern any of the badges or coat of arms.

Like a sudden douse of cold water he was torn from his trance-like state, a shiver of fear coursed through his body as he heard the muttered whispers of a couple of unseen enemy soldiers close by. They were no more than thirty yards from his position slightly to his right on the reverse slope.

Panic threatened to overcome him as he felt his heart pound against his chest, while he tried to push his body deeper into the wet grass. He made himself still for a moment, resisting the urge to shuffle backwards, waiting, listening for the next sound that would betray the enemy movements.

There was nothing.

He couldn't tell if the soldiers were advancing towards him, somehow spotting his silhouette as he had crawled to the crest. Surely they couldn't have seen him? He had kept low but still he felt as though the enemy were somehow encircling him, knowing exactly where he was. Rowan looked quickly to his left and right and then, turning over on his back, looked back the way he had crawled. There was no sign of anyone.

Letting go of his bow he reached slowly and deliberately for the leather handle of his sword, not able to draw it in case there was the slightest of noise. Looking up to the stars he made a silent prayer, trying to steady his nerves.

With every sense tingling he must have waited a minute, though it felt a lifetime before he heard a chuckle, one of the sentries laughing at something said. The sound came from perhaps fifty yards away now, still to his right and much to his relief heading away from him. That was enough for him and, turning slowly back onto his front, he crawled backwards, dragging his bow with him. He didn't stop crawling even when he reached the foot of the slope still concerned that he would be spotted.

It was nearly an hour later when he reached his friends who had retreated into a small copse of trees.

'Where on this almighty earth have you been?' The words were accompanied by a slap on the back and betrayed Daniels relief at his return.

He took a proffered flask of water and gulped greedily before answering. 'There's a whole army over that rise which, by the way, is a heck of a way off. I've never seen so many men before in my life and from the banners it's not just a couple of knights, but plenty more.'

The two friends listened intently. 'How many do you think?'

'Thousands, the whole valley is full of them, I was lucky to get away.'

His last comment caused some concern from Martin. 'Did you get spotted?'

Rowan simply shook his head as he took a second gulp of the water from the flask.

'Thousands,' Daniel repeated the figure, 'are you sure?'

'Put it this way, by my reckoning there's enough men to fill Stafford's market square a hundred fold.'

The certainty in his words conveyed the enormity of their discovery.

'Mother of God, what do we do now then? Go back and inform Sir Robert?'

'Wait a bit. Let's think about this.' For some reason Rowan felt less disturbed than his two friends, even though he had seen the size of the enemy. 'If they had waited another day they could have captured Whittington, we all know it.' He looked up at his friends who neither agreed nor disagreed, 'but instead they chose to ride away and then meet up with this army.' He inclined his head towards the illuminated rise in the distance, made much more ominous now they knew what lay behind it.

'So what are you saying?' The question from Daniel was quietly asked, as if the enemy would hear somehow.

'I'm just saying we need to think about this a bit more.' Inwardly Rowan was intent on making his scouting report to Sir Robert much more valuable than his first effort all those weeks ago.

Despite Martin's obvious concern at the nearness of the enemy army he agreed with Rowan. 'He's right, you've got to admit there's a lot more to it.'

Rowan was grateful for his friend's support.

'Alright then,' there was no disguising Daniel's reluctant tone. 'What do you think is up then?'

He looked towards Martin, 'I think from what's been said and from what I've seen William de Movran and the Welsh have linked up with an army, probably Glyn Dwr's. Though God only knows where they're heading. My money would be on Shrewsbury.'

'But that would be stupid. Prince Henry is probably there as well as Earl Edmund.'

'Yes but think on it, why bother with Whittington when you could take Shrewsbury.'

Though Rowan had never visited the strategic Shropshire stronghold he knew it was seen in the same light as the great English border staging posts of

Chester, Worcester and Hereford.

'You're probably right. They must be heading somewhere and it has to suit the Welsh, and let's face it, if Prince Henry's there it wouldn't be a bad bargaining tool either.' Martin agreed.

'I think they're going to try and take Shrewsbury,' Rowan reaffirmed with more confidence this time following his friend's comment, the enveloping canopy of trees emphasising the significance of the words. He was in no mood to let the enemy continue to cause more deaths through their treachery and deceit.

'What in all our Holy Saints thoughts are we waiting for then?' Daniel, now convinced, broke into the brief deliberation his words had brought. 'If that's the case we've got to warn the garrison at Shrewsbury.'

Rowan was torn. His orders had been quite explicit and his assumption was just that, an assumption with no proof. He didn't want to look foolish in front of the Earl again. No, he was an archer and he would do as he had been told to do, he decided, as he and his friends hastily tightened the horses' girth straps and loaded their saddle bags.

CHAPTER FOURTEEN

William de Movran was impatient. He was with the vanguard of the army, nearly a thousand men while the rest of the four thousand troops were strung along the road from Wem. It felt to him that Hotspur was procrastinating in front of the castle walls by giving the Prince time to consider a response to their ultimatum. It was evident that, by displaying the banners of the earls and knights that had aligned themselves with the rebellion, Hotspur hoped that the King's heir would simply give up the walls of the town, recognising the forces against him.

Hotspur had decided to send Sir Thomas Percy, so recently the Prince's companion at Shrewsbury to negotiate but the response, when it came late in the afternoon, was unequivocal. It seemed that the appearance and defection of his recent ally and friend with nearly half the garrison had little effect upon the young Prince. In response Hotspur assembled his knights in his hastily erected command tent, north of the town and the castle walls behind.

'Well, we have our answer,' the commander said flatly. 'It is disappointing and I would have wished a peaceful settlement to our just cause. However if we have to take the town by force then so be it.' The comments were matter of fact, conveyed in such a way that the surety of the outcome was inevitable.

The assembled knights remained silent, those that knew the Prince were probably not surprised, mused William de Movran, who had heard of the young Henry's stubbornness.

'There's really only one way and that's straight through the town buildings at the fore gate. Once we've captured those we can begin to lay siege to the walls themselves. By then the rest of our force should have caught up with us and we can start our preparations proper. Speed, sirs, is what I want.'

William de Movran could feel the excitement in Hotspur's eyes, the energy that he transmitted passing among his knights as the commander looked into each face. At that moment he felt nothing could stop them. With the capture of the town many more of King Richard's supporters would surely flock to the cause, the fate of England would be changed and he knew his role in helping Hotspur would not be forgotten or go unrewarded.

The assault on the suburbs started less than half an hour later. One main battle was assembled, a third of the vanguard, over three hundred men a quarter of a mile distant from the assembly of wattle and daub houses below the castle walls.

Not for the first time he slid his rondel dagger in and out of its short leather-covered scabbard fastened at his belt. It would be bad in those narrow streets and he knew from experience that a knife could kill as easily as a heavy sword. Bayard as usual was by his side and he reflected on the usefulness of his sergeant who could stop him getting killed in fights like this.

Those thoughts were interrupted as the first of the trumpets sounded, signalling the advance. He resisted the temptation to snap his visor shut for now and, along with hundreds of men either side, he stepped forward for the first stage of the assault on the town and its castle.

He was to the left of the battle and because of his armour and status had put himself in the front ranks among men he neither knew nor cared to know. It was however where he and his few remaining men at arms would be noticed by Hotspur and so secure his favour when he put Richard on the throne.

The walk forward was unhurried and he hoped that the archers and men-at-arms he could see moving among the buildings would simply retreat behind the castle walls which stood impressively towering above the buildings below.

'Arrows!'

The shout came loud and clear. His hopes of an easy advance were dashed in that moment and he remembered the devastation wrought by just a few archers from the walls of Whittington. He quickly brought down his visor, reducing his vision to a quarter inch slit and amplifying his breathing in the metal confines. He bent his head downwards and focussed upon his armour encased feet, watching each step even as the first of the men began to cry in pain or just shock as the arrows whistled down upon them, the sounds muffled by his metal helm.

Moving his head left and right to make sure he was

not blithely carrying on while the attack stalled he was rewarded by the sight of hundreds of men still moving forward. The pace quickened as they sought to close with the deadly archers as soon as possible. He knew that the enemy were partly protected by the streets from which they flew but was grateful nevertheless to see more than one feather topped shaft imbed itself in the thatched roofs as their comrades behind attempted to provide covering fire.

The urge to curse the defenders increased as men overtook him in their lighter mail but he knew the words would be lost, better to keep his breath for the fight ahead. He guessed he still had one hundred yards to go before he was struck in the leg causing him to stumble, grateful the arrow hadn't pierced the cuisse plate.

'Damnation,' he cried out, his earlier resolution swiftly swept away as he regained his balance and followed the men that were now almost at the buildings. He avoided the bodies that lay on the ground, the familiar arrow shafts protruding from their torsos or necks.

The force of men crashed against the buildings like a wave, men almost fighting each other to enter the narrow streets, too many of them to squeeze through. They burst through closed doors, the sounds of splintering wood mixed with the shouts of men in front engaged with royalist men-at-arms.

He was now perhaps twenty men behind and could hear the clash of steel and the cries of men as they fought in the narrow confines of the streets and alleys. The concentration of men was too much and he lifted his visor taking in a deep gulp of air as he did so. Just in front of him Bayard was screaming insults, trying to push others aside as the madness of battle began to take over.

William de Movran allowed himself to be taken forwards by the tide of men. The defenders in front were definitely falling back and every so often he would feel an added crush against the bodies around him before they surged forward a few more feet.

Suddenly there was a cry from behind as, through a window, the needle-like point of a halberd spike skewered the neck of an attacker and blood sprayed the white washed walls of the house he had passed a few seconds ago. There was an incensed roar from the men around him who sought to stab at the aperture but already the defender had stepped back and then thrust the deadly point into the eye of another attacker with similar effect. Men pushed at each other to jab their blades at the new threat while others sought side alleys to kill the defenders.

Then a soldier next to him was thrown backwards, his sword spun in the air, the arrow that had hit him snapping in the same instant with a loud crack as metal point met bascinet. The arrow must have been fired from an upper storey, only the poor quality of the iron tip saving the man's life.

More arrows began to rain down on the crammed attackers and men injured or even killed were unable to fall to the ground because of the press of men. Around him panic began to take hold for there was little defence from the archers above. The confines of the streets and press of men meant only a lucky few could raise their shields, their arms soon aching as they were impacted by the arrowheads.

'Satan and his blood!' William de Movran uselessly cursed once more. This was like being a rat in a barrel. He started to push fellow attackers out of the way, heading back towards the outskirts of the buildings. It was evident to him that the enemy were playing a deadly game and though far less in number, were moving through the houses and streets like wraiths able to use their halberds and bows to deadly effect, disappearing before they had chance to break into the buildings.

So it was with relief when he was able to take off his helm after emerging at the edge of the suburbs, leaning his back against one of the buildings, closing his eyes as he drew in breaths of air.

'What in the Lord's name is going on?'

Opening his eyes he could see the words came from a knight wearing a rampant lion on his livery.

'I'll tell you what's going on, bloody murder is what's going on in those streets. There's too many of us. We're so many that we can't even raise a shield or shoot back. It's like target practice for Henry's men while we just wait to see who gets killed by the next arrow.' His anger was unchecked despite seeing Hotspur's badge.

The knight recognising his rage and seeing more men streaming out of the streets, many helping their comrades, didn't push him further.

And so Hotspur's forces fell back. At first it was those that were pressed within the streets unable to bring either sword or shield to bear but then men started to appear with cuts and gashes, dents in their armour showing they had managed to engage the defenders. William de Movran watched from where he had started almost half an hour ago and then glanced towards the group of nobles that had gathered, not expecting to see their forces retreat before they had even reached the castle walls.

'God's wounds,' he said to himself.

'Sire?' Bayard had returned unscathed along with his few remaining men–at-arms.

He didn't answer his subordinate as he looked at the inert bodies lying on the grass where they had been killed by the first few volleys of arrows. He could imagine the corpses lying in the dust and against the walls in the tight streets.

Hotspur was obviously not one to take an initial set back happily or endure delay and the next order, which came quickly, met with William de Movran's approval. Instead of sending in masses of men they would advance in small groups of no more than ten, each including archers. He silently cursed his own approval as he was given command of a group of surly men from the Cheshire Guard who regarded him critically. No matter, he thought to himself. He knew his business and they might not like him but better them than any amateurish levies, he thought.

Once again the trumpet sounded and across the front the groups advanced towards where their dead comrades had suffered so badly at the hands of the defenders sent to protect the buildings of the fore gate.

Again the arrows came, and again they marched resolutely on but this time not only had they the shields to protect them and the archers huddled closely beside but Hotspur had ordered a barrage of counter fire. Nearly two hundred bowmen had advanced behind the advancing sorties and now sent flocks of arrows high into the sky to plummet into the town.

Inevitably, despite the shields and the massed counter fire, some of the defenders' three foot long arrows found gaps and William de Movran heard beneath his helm an archer curse in pain as an arrow struck him. He knew that the injured bowman would try to keep up or probably be killed, exposed to the enemy archers but that was not his concern. His concern was to reach the buildings and head straight for the walls. Once there, he knew any enemy archer or man at arms would be trapped for there would be a killing ground beneath those walls. Either the enemy retreated before William de Movran and groups like him before they reached the edge of the buildings or they would be cut off and exposed to the rest of the vanguard behind. Knowing the casualties and fear the defenders had inflicted in the narrow passageways it would be an unpleasant fate.

More arrows thudded into the advancing shields despite the whistling barrage from Hotspurs archers that filled the sky overhead. The thuds as they smacked into the attackers were discernable even beneath his closed visor, the small group of men encouraging each other as they stepped forwards, trusting their shields and their armour as they increased the pace. Nevertheless another man was hit before they reached the buildings, cursing the defenders and their arrows even as he fell to the ground to die slowly on the turf.

William de Movran opened his visor with relief as they entered the collection of streets, his vision now widened and no longer having to hear his own breathing. The arrows ceased as he looked down the eight foot wide track bounded by one and two storey houses and workshops on either side. The enemy had fallen back as before and he looked at the open shutters, doorways and turnings suspiciously.

'Remember, keep your eyes peeled. Shields to the front and shoot any of the pox-ridden men that appear out of the windows.' He was still looking at the openings suspiciously expecting at any moment an arrow to come flying out of the interior. The archers and men-at-arms nodded grimly at his commands.

The next arrow came as they were halfway down the street. They had cautiously stepped forwards no more than fifty yards, passing two bodies lying in the dirt, bows drawn looking up at every window in front and behind before, with lightning speed, the blur of the arrow flight sped through the air and thudded into an upraised shield. An archer behind him instinctively fired back and the steel tip embedded itself into the wooden shutter.

The defender recklessly appeared again from the same window and, before he could let off a second arrow, two arrows flew at him, one taking him smack in the forehead, the enemy arrow clattering against the sill before falling to the dirt beneath where an archer picked it up almost cheerfully as they passed.

William de Movran could now hear the shouts from the other groups of men making their way down parallel streets towards the walls seemingly dealing with similar opposition as he pushed his group onwards.

Following the angle of the street he was confronted by a barricade that, judging from the bodies lying in front of it must have stopped the first advance. Again the shields went up just as arrows punched into them, one point almost tearing through the leather hide and no more than an inch from the face of a man-at-arms who looked up at his companions grinning with relief. William de Movran quickly shut his visor again so all he could see were the enemy in front and hurled a curse at them, pushing the men forwards. The street was wide enough for three men and they crashed into the barrier made from wooden boxes and a table. The defenders stepped back for it was hard to use weapons over barricades and they began kicking the wooden obstruction away before William de Movran hastily pulled them aside.

'Fire now.' It was the turn of the defenders to suffer from the lethal bodkins as three of the four archers let their arrows loose. At this range the steel tips were lethal. One man looked in disbelief as a point slid deep into his side piercing through the chain mail; another spun round as an arrow took him in the shoulder.

'Now get at them,' he was shouting, hauling one of his men back from the side of the wall and pushing him through the barricade, just as the point of a pike appeared from a window. It took one of his men-at-arms in the side, scraping across the plate and finding the gap between front and back plate, slipping into his flesh, through skin and muscle. He heard his man's screams but was fixed on getting past the barricade, leaving one of the archers to fire an arrow into the gloomy interior from where the point had come.

He yanked a box away, smashing the wood as he then kicked it aside, keeping his eyes on the defenders who wore the gules and azure livery of Henry and who were already stepping back, one helping his injured comrade. 'Fight, you villeins, fight!' he called out and suddenly he was free of the obstacles and rushing forwards, swinging his sword high over his head.

The first man tried to dodge away from the heavy blade rather than parry but William de Movran reacted quickly. He slashed downwards, the blade ringing out dully as it crumpled the thin plate of the soldier's armour, causing a cry of pain even as the man fell to the ground. Ignoring the man for now William de Movran moved forwards. Ahead the foot soldier helping his injured comrade stood to protect him, urging him backwards as he stood his ground, the halberd ready in his hands.

William de Movran could tell the man was nervous, his hands moving all the while as they gripped the shaft, unsure of his best defensive stance as he purposefully continued forward. He feinted right for a split second and saw the tip follow him before grabbing the pole with his left arm. The man held onto his weapon struggling for a moment even as he pulled him forwards and his heavy pommel smashed into his bascinet. The dazed man-at-arms was still gripping his weapon as he forced his sword through his mail collar to cut through his throat.

William de Movran was now breathing heavily and, sensing the immediate threat had gone, once more opened his visor. Around him there were two more bodies, one on either side. Turning back he could see one of his archers had despatched the man with the dented armour, an arrow thrust into his throat, while in front the injured comrade of the man he had just killed was now lying motionless on the ground.

He allowed the group a few moments of rest before they continued. All around them the small alleys resonated with the clash of metal and cries of men indicating similar heavy skirmishes were taking place. The pockets of attackers advanced towards the walls, causing William de Movran to warily peer around corners and alleys for the next surprise attack, constantly turning slowly as he stepped forwards forcing his small group onwards.

The next attack came almost from nowhere as he peered suspiciously into an open doorway. Two men launched themselves from a small alley just to their front taking the small group by surprise, gutting an archer before he could let go of his arrow. Suddenly the narrow street was a mass of sounds as chaos ensued. He instantly turned round at the threat just as two more defenders rushed out of the doorway he had just been peering into. A blow struck his helm heavily and he was thrown to the floor, his sword knocked from his grasp as the attackers ran past towards Bayard and the rest of his men. He grabbed at one of the men's legs and hauled him down into the dirt with him.

'Pagan's dog.' The Shropshire accent was clear as the man kicked out, the leather sole smashing into William de Movran's helm. He held on, pulling the man towards him while at the same time reaching for the dagger he had known he might need. The man kicked again and swung his sword cumbersomely. He twisted his body, allowing the sword to strike his shoulder plate before ripping the point up the inside of the man's leg towards his groin where he knew the mail skirt would offer little protection. The man's scream was piercing and warm blood gushed down William de Movran's hand and arm as the man like a caught fish wriggled in vain as he died almost sobbing.

Around him the sudden ambush had petered out even as the last attacker died with a blade pushed through his throat, another man holding him down. They were now down to just four men. In front, not more than a hundred yards away, he could see the dark grey stones of the castle.

As he looked billows of dark smoke were starting to obscure the walls, rising into the early evening air. The defenders had obviously set some of the buildings nearest the walls alight in an effort to stop their advance and he guessed the trumpet blasts from the walls were sounding for the defenders to fall back. A sense of satisfaction ran through him as wearily his fingers traced the dent in his pauldron left by the enemy's sword, knowing that he and his men had pushed back the stubborn defenders.

They advanced slowly until they could see and hear the crackling flames that had taken hold and it was clear there was nothing they could do. Still, he thought to himself, he had reached the walls and shown his commitment and now he would make sure that Hotspur saw his blood-splattered armour and know of the role he had played. As he continued watching the sparks rise lazily, a runner from the vanguard appeared, quickly taking in the bodies around the four men.

'The Lord asks that you fall back.'

'You what?' he responded curtly, reluctant to withdraw from the ground they had won, the flames for now not a threat.

'He asks that you fall back,' the man repeated, his breathing getting back to normal and knowing better than to get embroiled in a discussion with this blood-splattered knight

'Right, you men, stay here. I'll go and see what he wants.'

'Sire, he has requested all the men to fall back.'

He turned to the messenger accusingly as though he had issued the orders himself. 'You mean we get this bloody far and now we go back? God in heaven!'

The messenger shrugged meekly, shrinking under De Movran's anger.

'Come on then. Let's find out what's going on, but be careful there may still be some of Henry's men in the buildings.'

They warily retreated down the street, past the bodies, their blood already soaked into the dry dirt and staining the walls. As he led the group to the edge of the suburbs without incident he could see other men emerging who, like themselves, had battled through the network of streets. In front of them the massed ranks of the vanguard were re-deploying. In the centre he could see the distinct group of Hotspur and his entourage of knights all on their heavy war horses, looking and occasionally pointing eastwards.

Following their gaze, William de Movran looked to where the sun was beginning to set and to where a line of horsemen stood, though he couldn't discern their colours in the darkening sky.

Striding towards the still wheeling vanguard he caught sight of Rhys Gethin. 'What's going on?' he asked, taking a hold of the courser's bridle tugging the horse's enquiring head away.

The Welshman seemed to notice him for the first time, his eyes fixed on the line of men in the distance. 'We were wrong.'

'What do you mean we were wrong?' He was getting even angrier now. He had nearly been killed fighting through the streets in front of Shrewsbury's walls, then told to withdraw despite achieving what he had been asked to. Now the thousand or so men were apparently worried about a hundred horsemen at most.

'You don't understand,' the Welshmen replied looking down at him and reading his thoughts. 'They're the King's men, and behind them will be his army.'

With the arrival of King Henry's advance troop the mood among the men of the vanguard changed and it wasn't long before the inevitable order to withdraw came as Hotspur decided to abandon the assault for now, wary of the appearance of the King's horsemen.

It was as they rested at a small village called Berwick to the north west of the town no more than four miles away that William de Movran found himself sharing a poor meal of hastily boiled turnips in a thin potage with Rhys Gethin.

'What's the latest?' he enquired of the Welshman,

knowing he had been invited to Hotspur's tent half an hour earlier.

'He wanted to know if there was any chance of meeting up with my Lord Glyn Dwr's forces.'

'And?'

'I told him not. He will be too far south and Hotspur is thinking about heading northwards towards his father who is gathering forces in Northumberland.'

William de Movran's gloominess returned. Fate was playing tricks with him again and that gloominess turned to anger as the night passed and the morning came.

He saddled his horse and prepared to head northwards with the rest of the army, Hotspur having made up his mind during the night as had he. He had thought about leaving the mass of men and heading westwards and then possibly to France but as the noise of thousands of men around kept him awake he reasoned they were still a force to be reckoned with. If Hotspur did succeed as Rhys Gethin had suggested in meeting up with more men then there remained a good chance of success. This way he still kept his chance of gaining riches and power, and so he stayed with Hotspur's army.

CHAPTER FIFTEEN

Rowan, riding with his friends behind Sir Robert, was awestruck by the sight of the two massed forces facing each other. Thousands of steel tipped lances and banners were held aloft, filling the ridgeline to his left and a lower slope to his right. The shallow bowl of the valley was the only thing that separated the opposing masses. His scouting mission in the darkness hadn't prepared him for the vastness of the armies assembled in front him. The small group stared in silence astride their tired mounts which snorted heavily, tossing their heads in the early evening summer air, sensing the tense atmosphere that filled the valley.

It had been only two days ago that the nobles had listened to his nervous report following his and his friends' scouting mission after the assault on Whittington. His tentatively raised theory of the threat to Shrewsbury wasn't dismissed by the two nobles and he was surprised how readily they seemed to accept the scenario presented to them. Just as importantly to him and much to his relief there had been no rebuke for not warning the garrison of the town first.

Within hours Sir Robert had assembled a small troop of men to gallop towards the Shropshire stronghold to warn the Earl and Prince. Again, Rowan and his friends put themselves forwards to be part of this force including Jerrard who assured them his wounds were healing and who stood firm on his need to accompany the group. The remainder of the troop consisted of two of Sir Robert's less injured men-at-arms.

So it was that the small column had made their goodbyes again. Daniel and Rosalind shared a kiss and he shook hands with Leovald under the watchful gaze of Lord Fitz Warrin and the garrison. Only this time, as he had lifted himself onto the saddle, he turned to find Catin staring up at him. 'Be safe,' she said simply, her concern for him etched upon her face.

Without thought he had taken a hand from the reins and reached down to grip her hand, feeling the coolness of her palm as he gave her a reassuring smile. He had realised with a light heart that a special closeness was developing between them.

The order to move came at that moment and the company, led by the knight in his argent and sable surcoat, had ridden out of the barbican, the iron-shod hoofs echoing beneath the archway. Rowan had stared backwards, craning his neck to catch the last sight of her, before he turned Constance's head and headed up the track towards the ridge that led eastwards. This time a smile was on his face despite the seriousness of their errand.

They had ridden hard towards Shrewsbury to find that their assumption had been correct although it was immediately clear they had arrived too late to warn the garrison.

Townsfolk looked at them suspiciously as they guided their horses through the streets of the foregate. The signs of the skirmishes were still visible, the dark stains against the wattle and daub walls, broken doors, shutters coming from their hinges and, as they neared the walls, the blackened and burnt out buildings. Slowly they had ridden through the large open gates framed by towering bastions to find confirmation that the enemy had approached the walls only to fall back soon after.

Sir Robert had impatiently questioned an unfortunate man-at-arms who withered under the knight's rapid demands for information. Nervously the soldier, who was probably no more than twenty years of age and with a not too clean bandage wrapped around his head covering one eye, explained how the enemy army had arrived and then closed the walls despite a brief defence of the suburbs. The arrival of the King's forces was evidently as much of a surprise to the garrison as it was to the enemy, but the man could say little to explain this unexpected turn of events.

As the troop stared up at the soldiers on the battlements the unfortunate man had stuttered and stumbled under the knight's examination, confirming that the Prince with a large force had departed after the retreating enemy the previous day, determined to bring them to battle and followed by the King himself.

The men had waited patiently in the large courtyard as Sir Robert had ventured into the main hall to speak to the constable of the castle before reappearing and urging the men northwards, confirming that the King had indeed unexpectedly marched via the town of

Lichfield. Sir Robert was also able to confirm that the renowned Hotspur was now in charge of a rebellion which had been joined by Rhys Gethin.

Now Rowan and his friends were staring down at where the thousands of men under Hotspur's banner had decided to face the royal army. Squinting slightly because of the late afternoon sun that was setting behind the enemy, Rowan could now see that they were fixed on a shallow ridge, a mass of men arranged in ranks, too deep to count. The enemy numbered in their thousands, packed together so the steel hedge of points filled the slope, horsemen distinct behind the massed ranks, standards flying showing the knights that had come to support Hotspur's lion on its azure banner.

No less impressive were the thousands of King's men, rank upon rank of archers and men-at-arms assembled on the lower lying ground across the valley. Rowan could make out above the horsemen the gules and azure royal banner and swallow-tailed standard mixing with the livery of the King's entourage of knights and personal retinue in the central battle. He could see the royal forces were assembled in three distinct forces and above the nearest battle, on the left flank, he could see the same royal banners but this time with the three argent cadency bars, showing that these men were led by Prince Henry himself.

The closeness of the two opposing forces and the masses of men, no more than two thousand yards apart, suggested the inevitability of the slaughter to come, he thought, as he took in the thousands of soldiers. Any desire to look for the banner of Rhys Gethin was lost as his mind struggled to comprehend the size of the arrayed forces. His reverie, however, was broken as Sir Robert urged his horse into a canter, the hoofs immediately churning up the ground beneath, clods of earth tumbling into the air. Rowan followed, pulling at his own reins and heading towards the Prince's forces.

A few men-at-arms at the rear of the left battle turned round as the small group of men cantered towards them, the knight's surcoat and trappings of the heavy destrier making them step aside.

'The Earl of Stafford?' Sir Robert demanded from an unshaven sergeant, bringing his horse reluctantly to a stop, its head tossing from side to side in excitement.

The sergeant, wearing the quartered livery of the Prince and displaying a mouth that lacked a good number of teeth, pointed with his battered hide-covered shield towards the centre battle and the concentration of knights astride their big warhorses, distinct among the chain-mailed men at arms around them. So, urging their horses onwards, the group cantered across towards the rear of the centre battle before slowing their mounts to a walk.

Sir Robert and small company slowly guided their horses through the massed ranks who briefly looked up at the men before resuming their stare at the enemy in front and shuffled aside as best they could. The men eventually reached the edge of the King's personal retinue, all well armoured, wearing the distinct quartered royal livery and who were less deferential to the knight and what Rowan realised must have looked like a company of dishevelled soldiers.

'Make way, you devils!' The cheerful voice of Earl Edmund called out as he nudged his mount towards them, recognising Sir Robert and his own colours worn by Rowan and the other archers. A large smile crossed his face as he clasped arms with the knight.

'You made it then?' the young Earl's voice from beneath the open visor was welcoming. ' I thought we would have to leave you playing chess at Whittington all alone, while we dealt with these rebels.'

Rowan was conscious of his proximity to the noble, especially as he gave a quick glance in his direction, causing his skin to prickle nervously.

'I wouldn't want to miss out on this, sire,' Sir Robert responded happily, as though truly welcoming the battle to come and not bothering to explain the desperate defence of the castle since the Earl's departure.

'Don't worry, you haven't missed anything yet, just a poxy attempt to stall us. They sent a couple of squires with a manifesto but the King is having none of it. Mind you, in return he did send the Abbot of Shrewsbury to give them a chance to surrender instead but he had as much luck with that as you would expect from Hotspur. No, the die is cast I'm afraid.' The Earl gave a half-hearted smile just as trumpets pierced through the air. It was the sound of advance. 'Well here we go, no time for chatter it seems,' and he turned back to the front as the men in their ranks, accompanied by cries of 'archers forward' advanced in echelon.

'That's our men,' the Earl said proudly, pointing at the men in the leading right battle who were steadily advancing towards the ridgeline where the enemy waited patiently.

To Rowan it looked like the whole of the Stafford levy had gathered to join the retinue, at least two thousand bowmen and behind them another thousand men-at-arms.

The archers flowed forwards, spreading into the shallow valley as the centre and then the left battle also started advancing. The enemy on the slope stood silently, seemingly unconcerned for the moment at the approaching royal forces.

Rowan watched in silence, partly still awestruck but also anxious as the men advanced, letting out a breath of relief when the vintenars judging that they were nearing the enemies range ordered the men to increase their pace. They lost some of their cohesiveness, making the mass of men look even more numerous as they sought to close the distance before the enemy let go their arrows.

Glancing across the valley he saw that the experienced vintenars must have judged correctly because lines of archers purposefully stepped forwards from the enemy ranks on the ridge line. Bows were raised upwards preceding a wave of arrows that streaked up into the sky, hundreds and hundreds of them.

Rowan watched with a sense of horror as they reached their zenith and sped downwards towards his comrades below who were still running forwards. Only many of them were no longer running, they seemed to be tangled and almost grappling through fields of pea plants, as high as a man's waist and he could see men tripping and even resorting to drawing their swords and hacking at them.

Even as the men battled with the obstacles the arrows began to hammer down, piercing men's gambesons, jackets and mail, through arms and legs. It seemed to Rowan that no one could avoid being hit, men were knocked to the ground, others screamed with pain. The advance came abruptly to a stop, men too busy recovering from the first volley to shoot back even as the second enemy volley shot skywards, filling the sky with their dark shafts.

All along the ridgeline arrows were shooting skywards before plummeting towards the advancing men. Rowan could see and hear the damage that was being inflicted by the arrow storm on the archers. They were being badly mauled, and already it seemed like hundreds of men littered the ground or were staggering back to the lines with deep wounds, the ground around them bristling with those arrows that had not embedded themselves in flesh.

Somehow though, he could see the attacking archers were now bravely beginning to return fire. He could see men grasping for their own arrows and letting loose as quickly as possible, despite the deadly and seemingly unending barrage inflicted upon them.

He looked nervously at the King and his entourage who watched from their horses seemingly detached as the arrow duel continued unabated. The enemy, benefitting from their higher position and unimpeded ground, continued their lethal hail on the royal forces who returned fire as best they could, sending their arrows back towards the mass of archers fixed to the ridge. Nevertheless, more and more bodies filled the shallow dip and Rowan could see the most damage was being inflicted on the Earl's archers.

Rowan could sense their desperation as men who were not injured began to take steps back or looked to help their wounded comrades as a means to justify falling back, away from the storm of arrows which relentlessly continued causing such devastation.

The King seemed to sense the same concern about the carnage that was being wrought upon his men and, at that moment, gave the order to advance.

'Advance banners!'

The command was taken up across the lines and slowly, almost assuredly, the armoured swathes of men-at-arms advanced to give the enemy something else to think about and to relieve the pressure on the King's archers.

As the files of men passed either side of the royal entourage, the King and his horsemen dismounted and Sir Robert turned to his small company. 'Now is not the time for horses. Off you get and we'll advance on foot. Those arrows will murder them. You two go and tie up the horses,' he added, turning to Jerrard and Martin. He indicated towards the line of heavy wagons to their rear, off to the right flank behind where the Earl's retinue had started the day and where the King's squires were already leading their masters' horses.

Rowan saw his friend's disappointment, especially Jerrard's whose complexion remained pale from the pain caused during the ride, but the order was delivered in a manner that brokered no argument. The battle was now in full swing and the two pulled the skittish horses away, silently nodding their temporary farewells to Rowan and Daniel.

Rowan quickly patted the sweating flank of Constance, sharing her nervousness at the sounds and sights around them and wondering whether he would see her again. At that moment he also thought about Catin and fervently hoped he would survive and not be maimed.

Around him, the knights and men-at-arms were pulling their visors down if they had them, lifting up their shields or heavy halberds and beginning to move forwards grimly. Glancing into the faces of those advancing in the main battle, young and old, Rowan saw a mixture of determination and fear as they took their first steps towards the men on the ridge. The rattle of equipment and tramp of thousands of feet filled the air as they marched slowly and deliberately towards the enemy who continued to loose arrow after arrow.

He joined the advance following the Earl's banners, glancing nervously at Daniel and peering through the mass of armoured figures, steel points and banners distinct on the ridge in front from where arrows were now landing ferociously among the first ranks of foot soldiers. Curses and surprised cries of pain now added to the sounds of the battle as the needle-like points hammered into armour and shields, seeking to find weak spots that would wound and kill.

Still they marched on, the valley now turning into mud as they advanced, enduring the rain of arrows, thousands of men cursing, encouraging themselves and others, the cries of the wounded accompanying the thwack of steel tipped shafts.

It was the urgent and repeated blasts of a trumpet distinctively off to their right that caused the Earl immediately in front to stop and turn to Sir Robert, his back now to the enemy so he could lift his visor as men continuing to solidly stream past.

'For pity's sake, go and make sure our men hold if you would be so kind.' The Earl was obviously concerned that the urgent blasts signalled that his men were continuing to falter under the barrage of arrows. 'Take the standard and keep our flank secure. Rally them if need be, Robert. Rally them,' he urged as he gestured to a man-at-arms holding the swallow-tailed standard with the cross of Saint George firmly in his grip who passed it to one of the knight's men-at-arms.

'Sire,' the knight acknowledged, a professional tone in his response now taking over from the more familiar one of earlier, before he gestured to Rowan and his men to follow him.

Rowan was half relieved as he turned and began to fight against the tide of men, the standard visible, snaking between the advancing soldiers towards the embattled force on the right flank, for the moment no longer advancing towards the enemy arrows that were causing so much damage. Nevertheless he could not help hunching his shoulders and bending his head down hoping his steel bascinet would protect him. He felt vulnerable in his surcoat and chainmail compared to the armoured men-at-arms around him.

It took a good many minutes after pushing and bumping past the advancing soldiers until he emerged at the edge of the centre battle to see, a few hundred yards away, that the right flank was falling into disarray.

He could see that hundreds of unmoving bodies littered the ground, covering the valley floor while more of the surviving archers from Stafford were leaving their lines despite the advance of the Earl's men-at-arms. Those that fled headed towards the rear where the baggage train could be seen in the distance, but there were still many holding together, gradually stepping backwards in an ordered and systematic way.

The momentum though was with the enemy and, even as he watched, horsemen appeared on the ridgeline, advancing their big war horses slowly through their own archers. He could tell many of the Earl's archers and men-at-arms had also seen the feared mounted lances and more men began to stream backwards. The cries of 'horses' began to infect the hundreds of men so that the trickle of men became a flow, many of the disciplined groups now breaking up as their courage began to falter. Still the arrows came down.

The heavy horses of the enemy that had been walking ominously and steadily down the hill towards the faltering royal lines suddenly spurred forwards. Rowan could almost feel the wave of thundering hoofs as they carried their mounted knights down the slope towards the disorganised men, their lances lowered as they came, closing the distance rapidly. He was transfixed with horror as, in what felt like heartbeats the charging enemy picked their targets and without remorse pull their lance into their shoulders to spear the torsos of the retreating men.

No shield or armour could deflect the devastating force that broke upon them, and men were flung backwards, swords, shields and broken lances went spinning into the air, the crash of steel and bone horrendous in its intensity. The only ones that were saved were the groups of men who stood together a few yards back from the first impact, using halberds, poll axes, swords and shields to form a less easy target for the jubilant horsemen.

'Here, for God's sake, here!' The shout from Sir Robert was aimed at a mounted man-at-arms in the livery of the Earl who was urging his horse towards them, recognising the rallying standard.

Beneath the open bascinet Rowan could see the fear and urgency in the man's face as he pulled the leather reins back, his mount coming to a halt, its nostrils snorting as he made his report.

'Sire, Sir Browe has called for reinforcements from the centre. The battle, he fears, will not hold.' The report came in between gasps as the messenger struggled to control his breathing as well as his mount.

'Get off the horse,' Sir Robert responded authoritatively, not bothering to reply to the request. 'On our oaths we'll hold them alright. Help me up!' His last words were directed at Rowan who, caught off guard as he continued to stare at the bloodletting happening to his front, quickly cupped his hands, grunting aloud he heaved the knight onto the charger.

Sir Robert quickly grasped the reins and shouted 'bring the standard,' before putting his armoured spurs to the horse's flanks, urging the big destrier forward into a charge towards the enemy riders who continued to cause such havoc to the increasingly bewildered right battle.

This is madness!' Daniel shouted as he and Rowan followed the two men-at-arms forward towards the maelstrom of soldiers and horses, wheeling among the anxious and desperate archers and foot soldiers, threatening to destroy the King's flank.

Rowan had his bow strung but his arrows remained in his canvas bag and the sword still in his leather scabbard as he and the rest of the small group followed the knight, who now could be seen riding almost recklessly between the men on foot cutting savagely at the enemy horsemen.

The men steered towards the protection of a largish group of about twenty soldiers that had formed a protective schiltrom to deter the enemy horsemen from attacking and so go after easier prey. Easier prey, Rowan realised anxiously such as himself as an enemy man-at-arms spurred his horse forwards toward them.

The enemy horseman quickly succeeded in cutting them off from the protective hedge of blades, raising an already bloody sword in his right hand and guiding the sweat-lathered mount straight at the four men. The speed and size of the courser was horrific and the men veered in different directions as panic took hold, none raising their weapons, each trying desperately to get out of the maddened horse's way.

Rowan watched even as his legs carried him onwards, the slight change in direction as the rider steered the horse with his thighs and then the glint of steel rose high before sweeping down with all his force.

The mounted soldier chopped down through the

standard bearer's neck, splitting his hauberk and slicing into his windpipe, the cloth that had attracted the horseman falling to the floor before the enemy could grab it.

At that moment Rowan left reason behind and turned back to grasp the smooth ash shaft with the Earl's colours. At the same time the horsemen yanked at his horse's bridle turning the beast round swiftly. Immediately Rowan knew he had made a mistake.

He ran desperately once more for the schiltrom who were now cheering him on as he lifted his legs high, sprinting with all his will across the uneven ground, the standard in one bandaged hand and his bow gripped in the other. He could imagine the enemy kicking the horse forward and, sensing the man would reach him long before he found safety, fearfully chanced a glance backwards. That glance saved him as he tripped and stumbled forwards, the blade only tearing rather than splitting through the chainmail at his shoulder causing a cry of pain but saving him from a savage cut as the sword swept onwards.

Picking his feet up he carried on running towards the men, his heart pounding and breath ragged, amazed at his close escape. He registered Daniel and the remaining man-at-arms in front of him who, rather than seek their own security, threw themselves desperately at the horseman who whirled his horse once more to batter at the swords.

It was only when he reached the safety of the wall of halberds and swords, a small gap made for him so he could push past the blades that he was able to look back just in time to see another horsemen charging forwards.

His eyes registered helplessly as the man-at-arms turned round too late, much too late as a lance point pierced his mail, pushing straight through to appear in a burst of blood. The man's body carried forwards with the force of the impact, his face contorted with a mix of shock and pain, his screams mixing with noise of battle around him.

The man-at-arms grisly death left just Daniel facing the horsemen who had grabbed for the standard. Realising his predicament Daniel gave one last swing of his sword, smashing into one of the horse's forelegs causing the mount to rear up in pain unbalancing the rider and allowing him the time to sprint towards the group of men who roared him on, almost throwing himself into the defenders as they dared the horseman to try to break the hedge of steel points.

The mounted soldier and his comrade looked for a moment at the group of men before spitting on the floor in disgust and setting off to seek those men less disciplined with whom to slake their blood lust, of which there were still hundreds streaming away from the onslaught.

Gratefully leaning upon the standard Rowan allowed his breathing to slow as he looked around him. The sounds of battle were everywhere, the cries of pain, horses whinnying, men cursing, the sound of weapons against weapons but among his comrades there was a brief sense of relief.

'What in all the saint's glory are you doing with that standard?' The unmistakeable gruff voice of Samuel Blacke broke into his thoughts. The Master-at-Arms had brought the ragged group of men together and though he found his presence still intimidating, even in the heat of battle, he was reassured by the big professional soldier.

'Keep those points levelled for God's sake,' his next words showed the veteran had already dismissed Rowan from his thoughts, concentrating on keeping the men together. For a split second, despite the maddening crescendo around him, he found himself half smiling at the Master-at-Arms' back who was already shouting out more encouragement to the men around him.

CHAPTER SIXTEEN

It was no accident that William de Movran found himself on the left flank, swinging his sword with relish as the enemy crumpled under the charge of the heavy horses and haphazardly ran in all directions trying to avoid the three hundred horsemen that had sensed their fear.

He had led Bayard and his small retinue away from Rhys Gethin's forces and towards this flank, seeing the damage wrought by the Cheshire archers and sensing how close the men were to breaking the battle. Behind he could see the enticing baggage train of the royal forces but for now he would enjoy killing the enemy in front, the sight of the gules and or surcoats and badges of Stafford making him almost jubilant as he sought to exact his revenge on the Earl's men who had thrown his plans into confusion seemingly at every turn.

As he slashed backhanded he felt the blade smash into the face of another enemy archer as he rode past, laughing as he felt bone and teeth crack, imagining the man already clawing at the wreckage of his face, falling onto his back as though he had hit a stone wall. He pulled up his horse, lifting his visor for a moment, his gauntlet sticky with the blood of three dead archers.

Catching his breath he saw the bodies that littered

the floor, men on hands and knees, limbs too mangled to support them, eyes blinded, but still there were many more retreating, a few knots of men making a stand and fighting back. In the centre of such a group he caught sight of the split horizontal colours of the Earl's rallying flag and then shifting his gaze slightly caught sight of the sable and argent surcoat of Sir Robert who was calling for the men to stand. He was seemingly ignorant of the threat of the horsemen, swinging his sword in the air, his horse swirling round beneath him.

De Movran swore inwardly as he saw the knight's words and presence was having an effect, men were beginning to halt their retreat, looking round for companions as they heeded the rallying call. He was about to put his spurs to the flanks of his horse, determined to put an end to the noble's efforts just as he saw two horsemen turn their mounts, also attracted by the knight. He halted, pulling at his reins. Better to take a share in his ransom without risking his life, he thought, as he watched the men charge towards Sir Robert who belatedly saw the threat and turned his own mount with a firm twist of the reins to face his attackers, urging it forward and slapping his metal face plate down.

His men came on, the first fifty yards away and charging hard. The man held his mace out from his body so the deadly spiked ball hung vertically, ready to swing a crushing blow when the men met. They clashed, but not as his man had intended. Sir Robert angled his horse across the charging destrier, for a moment causing confusion so that the swing of the mace was unable to land a disarming blow, the momentum unchanged and unchecked even though the target had moved. Instead, Sir Robert struck the man's horse across the neck, causing it to shriek in pain, half rearing up and turning away. His enemy, now totally unbalanced, fell heavily to the ground while his mount reared away, the heavy spiked ball still smashed into the knight's pauldron, the shoulder plate buckling under the weight though with much less force than intended.

The second attacker, the visor of his helm now down had his charger at full gallop. It was clear he sought to exploit the knight's temporary injury and unpreparedness, his horse still wheeling and with no shield to protect him. William de Movran watched with professional interest knowing that the knight's vision would be extremely limited. Then, as he himself would have done, he saw Sir Robert thrust his visor up just in time to see the attacker whose sword was held straight and level bearing down on him. His man was now no more than ten feet away from the knight who was only now bringing his horse back under control. Sir Robert's reactions were fast as he kicked his feet from the leather stirrups, pushing himself from his mount at the same time deflecting the attacker's point harmlessly away with a ringing clash of steel.

Even as the knight fell, eyes seeking for the horseman, he was faced by his original assailant who had recovered his feet, his spiked ball and chain held menacingly. He advanced slowly, intent on injuring the knight. At the same time, the mounted man-at-arms wheeled his horse; all three men ignoring the melee happening all around them, intent on their own personal battle.

The knight moved quickly, stepping forwards and tempting the man to swing his weapon. To De Movran's disgust that's exactly what the attacker did and Sir Robert simply stepped backwards, letting the spikes miss his face by no more than an inch. It was time enough, however, to swing his heavy sword so it bit deep into the man's neck pulling it back quickly even as he watched the mounted horseman charge for the second time.

Sir Robert desperately threw himself aside, allowing the sword to swing harmlessly above him as the attacker charged past before hastily getting to his feet, his sword held warily in both hands. William de Movran saw the attacker learn from his mistake and slow his charge as he turned his horse for the third time. This time he was intent on battering his opponent into submission using his advantage on the large destrier and no longer giving his opponent the chance to avoid the blows. The sword was brought down time and time again. The mount was almost stationery now above Sir Robert who he could tell was now suffering badly from his exertions, raising his sword wearily as he tried to maintain his feet until he faltered, dropping to one knee. The man-at-arms smashed his blade downwards again and spun the noble round on his knees so he was defenceless.

It was at that moment an arrow ripped into the big destrier, piercing the heavy trappings and throwing the attacker off balance. Turning quickly he saw two men rushing forwards out of the nearby hastily formed schiltrom, men wearing the colours of the Earl. The dark haired archer who had fired was already notching another arrow as the other, roaring with rage, sprinted forwards with a banner in one hand and a sword in the other.

***

Screaming aloud, Rowan raced towards the conflict being played out within the massed melee around him, the undulating grass threatening more than once to cause him to trip but instead spurring him forwards, almost uncontrollably. He had watched with horror as Sir Robert flung himself to the ground, thinking he had been injured or even killed, and instinctively he had thrust his way through the men-at-arms. Daniel had followed behind him and had let an arrow fly. The missile had whipped past his head as Rowan charged, making him wonder why he had not had the sense to rely on his bow instead of drawing his sword. The arrow tip ripped deep into the horse's flank causing it to wheel in pain. It was all the horsemen could do to stop himself being thrown but Rowan made sure he lost his battle with the horse's grip by sweeping his sword into the man's side and sending him sprawling on the ground, landing heavily, his sword fallen from his grasp.

Sir Robert was the first to stumble over to the dazed attacker and he sat astride the enemy horsemen, pulling out a sharp dagger as he lifted up the visor to reveal the harshly lined face of Bayard.

For a moment Rowan felt his vision blur, his mind in turmoil at the turn of events as the knight, aware of the animosity between the two, turned his gaze towards him, the lethal tip of the dagger still held inches above the renegade's face. Bayard followed the gaze and their eyes locked.

No words were spoken even as Sir Robert, with no more hesitation, thrust the steel point hard and fast through the chain mail hauberk protecting the sergeant's neck and severed the artery. The blood immediately flowed from the wound as the knight got to his feet leaving Bayard vainly trying to stem the bright red flow with his hands. The sergeant made a choking sound, his eyes all the time on Rowan as slowly his heart stopped beating and they glazed over.

Rowan felt almost no remorse for his enemy, immediately taking in the fighting that continued all around him. Sir Robert had already resumed his rallying call, having retrieved his fallen sword, the bloodied dagger now back in its scabbard.

'To me, to me!' Sir Robert shouted, urging the men to stand.

He could see more and more of the battle heeding the call, many attracted by the standard Rowan still held, now planted in the turf even as he marvelled at the knight's energy.

The initial carnage wrought by the savage charge was descending into a vicious melee. While many defenders battled or sought to escape the whirling horses and their cursing attackers, others were left alone as some of the enemy horsemen continued their gallop heading onwards.

Those archers and men-at-arms realising that they had survived the lethal charge began to group together and those horsemen that had turned their mounts to slash and maim the defenders were soon beginning to find less desperate fugitives to run down. Instead snarling and cursing men with lethal blades and steel tipped arrows, their faces fixed with renewed determination began to drag them from their saddles to be remorselessly cut and hacked at.

***

William de Movran watched the knight crawl over his sergeant's prone body on the ground and slide the dagger into his windpipe without feeling. He certainly knew his business he thought to himself with grudging respect, though the appearance of the two archers had changed the outcome. By God he hated archers.

For a moment he thought about putting his spurs to the flank of his charger. Sir Robert still represented a good ransom and he had confidence in his own abilities to deal with both the archers and the unhorsed knight. To his right he could see the battle in the centre was going well, the cries for Sir Percy loud enough for him to hear as Hotspur's forces were cutting deep into the middle ranks of the enemy making straight for the royal colours. Even now he could see Hotspur himself and the unmistakeable figure of the Earl Douglas with his knights cutting swathes into the enemy as they launched their chargers into the mass of swinging swords and pikes beneath the rampant lion standard.

Switching back to the battle that ebbed and flowed around him, the Earl's men were beginning to resist where before it was a rout. He could see knots of men banding together even as the Cheshire archers and men-at-arms from the ridge surged down to press home the attack that had decimated many of the men from Stafford. Looking to his left he saw that those horsemen who had continued their charge, still chopping down relentlessly at the retreating archers and men-at-arms, were heading towards the baggage train. That made his mind up. There were easier pickings than Sir Robert.

Turning his horse sharply he kicked his heels, urging the mount on and following the galloping horsemen towards the assembly of wagons. He ignored the fleeing men of Stafford who, hearing the heavy hoofs behind them sped up, swerved, ducked and thanked their stars that the big horseman had not gutted them as he rode past.

He urged his black destrier onwards, its breathing heavy, its nostrils wide and its flanks white with sweat under the heavy trappings. Before him he saw one of the archers he had so recently cursed standing in his way among the retreating men, the bow drawn fully. He just had time to twist the reins harshly and tilt his body in the saddle as the arrow pierced the air inches from his face. Quickly regaining his balance he urged his mount into a charge, his sword in hand but simply aiming to ride the man down. The weight of his mount's hoofs would smash the archer's bones to pulp. His anger took over even as he saw the enemy drawing a second arrow.

The arrow sped between the rapidly closing distance and smacked into the leather barding of his horse but had little effect as he pushed the charger on, knowing the slim pale-faced man had no time draw a third arrow.

With relish he continued onwards, the hoofs of the destrier pounding across the ground beneath him. His eyes registered a second defender racing to the archer's aid, a curse on the lips of his bearded face but the knight didn't allow him to affect the direction of his charge.

He dug his spurs into the horse's flanks pressing it onwards while expertly swivelling in his saddle and smashing his blade down at an angle at the new defender, a satisfying feeling as the sword smashed through armour, flesh and bone. He knew he had cut deep as he let his horse literally ride the first archer to the floor. For a moment he slowed, tempted to make sure of his kills but, looking at the laden wagons, he could see that many of the horsemen had already reached the baggage train with their valuable loads. Without a backward glance he once more kicked his horse onwards, ignoring the battling men behind him.

Reaching the parked wagons he could see the riders milling round and, like him, ignoring those men who chose to flee past the heavy carts while clashing with the few guards that remained. All of them, like the man he had struck at moments earlier, seemed to be carrying one injury or other, either choosing to make a stand after retreating or not fit enough in the first place to stand in the royal lines. Well, they were in the front line now, he thought, as he watched one of the defenders nearby stagger backwards, his arm smashed by a mace. The scream of pain was piercing as the man turned and ran, weaving between the heavy wagons to escape.

That was enough for some of his closest comrades who backed away until they too could retreat between the carts seeking safety, but some still some fought on. He watched a man-at-arms suddenly appear from behind the chests piled high on top of a wagon and throw himself at one of the horsemen unseating him. The action caused the mount to tumble to the ground, whinnying loudly. A horseman next to him was forced to shy away from the kicking hoofs just as another defender emerged from the high wooden sides swinging his sword, a comrade by his side.

The man-at-arms was on the floor grappling with the now unhorsed knight even as the horse staggered up, shaking its head and snorting. The other horseman, who had managed to control his own mount, viciously stabbed down at one of his adversaries. The point speared through the man's mail and caused a fountain of blood to erupt just as his own armour deflected the blow from the other defender. William de Movran continued to watch as the attacker then simply turned his horse and swung at the second man who tumbled to the floor. Sensing flight was the sensible option he quickly dragged himself under the wagon.

On the ground the defender that had thrown himself at the horseman was now dead, despite his courage, a dagger buried deep in the centre of his chest piercing his padded gambeson. For the moment there were no more defenders around him and William de Movran, ignoring the brief suspicious looks from Hotspur's horsemen, took the opportunity to look back towards the battlefield.

***

On the valley floor Rowan could see that though the men around him had been given added resolve they were still largely disorganised, many taking the opportunity to gasp for breath. The sergeants were cursing and threatening the men, urging them to steady themselves as the tide of enemy foot soldiers, following behind the mounted charge raced towards them, intent on victory.

The forces met with the unmistakeable clash of sword and shields, war cries' pierced the air as soldiers launched themselves at each other, some physically cart-wheeling over outstretched shields or smashed aside to be despatched with thrusts of sharpened points through their mail.

The right flank, already chaotic from the enemy charge, quickly became a massed melee, a scene of mayhem as men found themselves assailed from different quarters. They were able to thrust their sword points unseen into an enemy's body as much as they were to receive it, the quick recognition of a man's livery or badge saving more than one defender from maiming another.

Among it all Rowan could tell men were drawn to the rallying flag which he clutched with fervour. Next to him the veteran knight in his sable and argent surcoat in the thick of the fighting acted as a human dam against the heaving and thrusting men-at-arms. A shield was now on his left arm, snatched from the ground where the dead owner now lay motionless, his own chain mail sticky with blood as the enemy continued to launch themselves forwards in the hope of seeking glory.

Swords swung, shields were rammed forwards, steel deflected blades and gaps were sought between armour plating as the men fought savagely. More than once Rowan was forced to step backwards as other members of the Earl's retinue in front of him were pressed hard and he found himself lunging forwards with the tip of his sword over their shoulders. It was a cumbersome move but it worked as he aimed for the enemy faces that naturally shied away.

The men continued to fight savagely on all sides as he glimpsed around him desperately. He caught sight of a large group of archers who were striking down the enemy with their arrows, stepping forwards as they did so, creating a bloody swathe of the writhing and the dead as they headed towards the Earl's banner. He recognised many of them but none were his closest friends as the group continued to draw their bows, snatching arrows from their belts and aiming their steel tips directly at the enemy a few yards away. At this proximity the force of the arrows was forcing the enemy backwards, sending many spinning to the ground, the bodkin heads sometimes even piercing clean through the breastplates before the men-at-arms could close with them.

Even as he watched, the deadly volley threw the closest attackers to the ground and he sensed around him the immediate battlefield was changing.

There were less isolated defenders now, either they had been cut down or had managed to find support from comrades and were fighting desperately in groups. The archers, like those that had sent the hail of arrows speeding towards the enemy, were now making a difference, taking a heavy toll regardless of which arrowheads they chose. All were lethal at short range and more and more bodies littered the grass, so that bodies lay on bodies, shafts protruding from their motionless forms. The attackers' momentum was slowing as the resolute defence began to exhaust both sides.

The numbers of the Earl's forces were now beginning to show against the smaller rebel force on the flank and despite his tiredness he was starting to feel exultant, surrounded by men-at-arms who were beginning to step purposefully forward, more and more of the enemy beginning to avoid their blades whilst being increasingly assailed by the barrage of arrows.

The immediate threat of a complete breakthrough on the flank had slackened for now and Sir Robert, sensing that the retinue was holding, turned back to face Rowan. Beneath the helm his face was bright red from his exertions, dirty trails showed where rivulets of sweat had flowed down his cheeks, his breathing laboured. 'Tell the Earl, in his and the King's name we will hold here. You know where to find him.' Rowan nodded as the knight pushed his visor back down not inviting further conversation as he once more turned to his front.

Looking round he grimly passed the standard to a surprised man-at-arms who was holding back from the fight due to a jagged tear in his mail on his left arm making it hang uselessly down by his side.

He set off at pace, dodging bodies that littered the ground and avoiding the hundreds still engaged in fighting, heading towards the centre battle who were similarly engaged.

He could see the main ranks of the enemy had now abandoned their fixed position all along the ridge and launched themselves forwards, most aimed at the centre battle. A surge in noise assailed Rowan's ears as they smashed their way into the Royal force intent on capturing or even killing the King and his household troops around him.

Rowan pushed his way through the men who were not engaged in combat, many of whom had already been dragged wounded away from the front lines. He caught glimpses of broken bones, bloodied gashes and severed limbs as he carried himself forwards to where the King's standard could plainly be seen swirling above the crush of fighting.

Dodging and weaving through the press of men engaged in combat he eventually got close enough to the royal banners to catch glimpses of the Earl beside the King engulfed in the full fury of battle.

Around them it was like a milling machine as men were being worn down. More and more of the loyalist forces were falling to the now muddy churned-up ground as the enemy, many in full suits of armour desperately sought to kill or capture the King. He, in turn, was fighting back desperately, his distinct surcoat with the three lions and the fleur de lis emblazoned on it was already dark with blood.

Bodies lay scattered by their feet, some trying to move, dragging themselves away from the fighting, attempting to avoid suffocating from the press of bodies above them, others lay still, their blood soaking into the mud.

Even as he continued squeezing his way through the ranks more trumpets sounded and the enemy parted for a moment as a charging phalanx of twenty well-armoured knights, on their heavy war horses, many in the azure and argent trappings of the Scottish nationalists crashed into the fray. Their banners including the rampant lion of Hotspur flew behind them as they smashed into the defenders, throwing men to the floor, their lances splintering against the punctured armour cutting a vicious swathe through the loyalist forces already battered from the assault.

The enemy foot soldiers closed behind them pushing forwards once more with renewed vigour and Rowan found himself abruptly among the front ranks.

Great roars came from the troops around the enemy knights as they saw them piercing into the heart of the royal troops. Cries of 'Percy, Percy' rang audibly above the din of the battle.

Suddenly they were beneath the royal banner and the King was being dragged among the enemy, his sword arm grasped tightly by a large brute of a knight on his charger despite the counter thrusts of the defenders. The sight of their King being carried away into the enemy lines caused a surge of anger among the loyalists and, with the Earl in the lead the defenders swung their swords in desperation.

Rowan was caught up in the uproar and, throwing his body forwards, he launched himself at the mounted knight dropping his sword and heaving with all his strength at the arm that still grasped the King's surcoat, hoping he would be protected by the desperate defenders as he did so. The knight, who was unwilling to loosen his grip on the King, lost his balance and toppled heavily onto the ground, bringing Rowan down with him. Instinctively Rowan grasped for a discarded mace nearby, its edges already shinning with the gloss of blood and lifting the heavy weight swung it down against the visor of the enemy, oblivious to the men around him, smashing down again and again until the steel edges of the eye slot were dented viciously inward.

Even as the bright red blood began to flow from the man's helm, a heavy strike made him cry out in pain as some unseen enemy swung their sword into his torso smashing into his left side throwing him sideways from the prone body beneath. Looking up desperately he waited for the expectant second blow, but instead his assailant wearing the now familiar lion of Hotspur was pushed backwards and he was unceremoniously dragged up under his shoulder by a mail gauntlet.

The Earl pulled him backwards, his visor lifted, encouraging his men who filled the gap he had left and continued to battle against the enemy onslaught.

Rowan stumbled back through the heaving bodies a few paces. The pain started to throb in his side and he pushed his right hand against it. Fresh blood had appeared on his bandaged hand but not in copious amounts and he hoped his mail beneath the dirt and blood splattered surcoat had done its job. As he tentatively felt his wound he noticed with relief that the King was back among his own men, the desperate rally fending off the enemy for now. Rowan could see that the royal troops had paid a heavy price, the tide of the attackers surging to the point where even the King's standard bearer now lay dead among the mass of men.

'Well done.' The words were accompanied by a slap on the back from the Earl. Suddenly Rowan remembered the message he had been sent to deliver.

'My lord, Sir Robert has sent me to inform you that your forces on the right flank are now holding.'

The words brought a grin across the noble's sweat soaked face. 'Good old Robert, he has my thanks. Now all we've got to do is sort these devils out here,' his eyes taking in the fighting all around.

The fight was tiring both sides. Swords seemed to swing less rapidly, shields raised slower to deflect the blows. Most of the horsemen so lethal and so nearly decisive could no longer be seen. Many of their riders were now fighting on foot or struck down as though they had never been there. Still the enemy kept pushing forwards, grinding relentlessly through the defenders.

As Rowan watched some of the men glanced backwards towards the King, his retreat, the slaying of the standard bearer, the roar of the enemy and the continued enemy surge starting to cause the first feelings of panic.

To Rowan it appeared that the battle was in the balance. He glanced quickly towards the King who was obviously exhausted, kneeling down, the Earl now once more by his side a hand on his Lord's shoulder as they exchanged words.

Rowan turned his attention back towards the battling men just a few feet away. With a deep gulp of air, he untied his buckler with blood-stained fingers and stepped forwards, seeking out a gap in the press of men. In the heat of the battle he was able to ignore, for now, his wound and he soon found himself among the front ranks facing the enemy.

An enemy foot soldier stepped forwards purposefully gauging his new advisory. Rowan immediately took the impetus and thrust his sword towards the man's armpit, remembering the words of Samuel Blacke to aim for the gaps in the plate armour. The strike wasn't true and his steel tip jarred and then scraped against the plate before glancing off. The man, slightly larger than him grinned as he swung his beaked war hammer. The razor sharp angled edges connected with Rowan's hastily raised buckler, wrenching heavily at his arm. The force of the blow half turned him just as the fresh cries of 'Saint George, Saint George' were taken up and the King in his royal surcoat launched himself back into the fray.

The attack caused a surge of men around him. The morale of the nearby defenders was at once reinstated. One of the King's retinue literally buried the broad blade of his halberd into the back of the foot soldier's knee cap. The strike sheared through the thin plate and bit deep into the bone and tendons making the man crumple to the ground with an anguished cry of pain. The man in the royal livery pulled quickly at the embedded blade before thrusting the foot-long steel point through the man's chain link aventail deep into his gullet. He nodded gratefully as Rowan swung his sword wildly trying to deter for a moment the dead man's vengeful comrades and swirling horsemen who sought to counter the surge.

Seconds later, from nowhere an unhorsed knight

wearing a distinctive azure and argent surcoat, a heart emblazoned in its centre, confidently stepped forwards and simply punched Rowan in the face with his sword hand. The metal gauntlet drove painfully into his nose. Blood sprayed everywhere as he fell backwards, registering the patch over one eye and bushy grey moustache of his attacker.

He was shaking his head trying to clear his vision, his mouth tasting blood as he saw the King swing his sword in a large arc down towards a knight who was battered sideways from the blow. At the same time another of Hotspurs knights took the opportunity to swing his own blade down with all his force. It smashed hard into the King's helm.

The blow caused the King to stagger and then fall to the floor. The enemy were clawing and stabbing at the fallen leader desperate for victory.

Rowan grasped at his fallen sword but too late to prevent the same knight who had viciously punched him to the floor from stamping ruthlessly down. The Kings helm seemed to sink into the churned up earth.

Cries began to sound out above the curses and clash of steel. 'Percy, King Percy!' The call was taken up and the enemy pushed forward so that Rowan had trouble seeing the motionless body beneath the royal surcoat. The enemy knight was standing above the lifeless body, urging the attackers onwards.

The death hit him as surely as a hammer blow. His face tightened as he scrambled to his feet, almost oblivious to the royal forces around him who were again beginning to take a step backwards. He swung his sword once again. His damaged buckler was held close to his body, protecting his injured side as a spear point was thrust at him. He dodged away and in the same movement swept the tip aside with his sword before thrusting the metal boss of his buckler towards the man's face. The man stepped back momentarily before the point of the spear was thrust forwards again. Anxiously Rowan tried to fend it off once more. But the enemy predicted and parried his swing and the counter blow caused him to drop his sword. He desperately threw his small shield forwards temporarily causing the man take a single step back. He knew he was in trouble.

'Hold, hold in the Kings name!' The shouts from behind him were loud enough over the noise of battle to cause him to glance round quickly in confusion hearing the confident cry.

The King, sensing the battle was turning against him, had returned to the fray. His helm was open so all could see it was Henry stepping forwards with his remaining household troops.

His re-appearance wrought similar confusion among the attackers as it had with the nearby defenders who had so recently thought him slain. The loyalist forces once more advanced as the tide of battle ebbed and flowed with alacrity.

Rowan, taking the opportunity for a moments respite looked towards the patch of ground where he had earlier seen the Earl in exhausted conversation with the King. He eagerly looked around for the distinctive chevron gules but there was no sign of the young noble. His heart sank as his mind grappled with what had happened.

Sharp blasts of a trumpet off to his left drew his attention back towards the bloodletting around him. Men continued to hack and batter at each other and the piercing sound seemed to re-energise the enemy. They once again threw themselves forwards, forging with added vigour into the heart of the centre of the battle.

He didn't know how long they could hold. The enemy knights still came forwards, and though all the armoured horsemen that had bit deep into the royal lines had now been killed or now fought on foot, their blades continued to do terrible damage. The defenders added their own counter blows and cuts. The din of battle had increased again as the enemy were enraged with the realisation that they had not killed the royal leader. They surged forwards once again within striking distance of the King.

Rowan's anger and sorrow was made worse from the death of the young Earl who he and his friends had looked up to in their formative years and who had worn the King's surcoat to rally his troops.

Now without his sword Rowan undid the buckles of his small dented shield and let it fall among the bodies that were littered around him. He reached round to pull his bow from his back, wincing at the pain from his side as he did so. All the time he kept a careful watch to his front in case the enemy broke through the thin screen of men-at-arms in front of him.

Fumbling with tiredness he pulled an arrow out from his belt. The white goose feathers were tainted by his blood as he notched the arrow. To his front the two forces remained heavily engaged. The cacophony of noise was all around as he focussed on the cluster of knights that were still forcing their way forwards, their armour, surcoats and banners heavily bloodied from the wounds they had inflicted.

He caught sight of the moustached figure of the Scottish noble with his distinct eye patch swinging his blade two handed and forcing a royal knight to bring up his guard hastily. Rowan, thinking of the Earl, lifted his bow and pulled back. The pain screaming from his left side and his hand fiery beneath the bandages as it tightened around the bow stave. With a determination of effort he pulled back a little more, battling the hurt and tiredness, ignoring the sickly taste of blood in his mouth and felt the string stretch at the bow a little more despite the short range.

Focussing between the melee and making himself count slowly, he aimed at the noble.

He released the string and watched intently as the arrow flew towards the Scotsman. It missed its mark. The knight had turned to attack another defender at that precise moment so the arrow whipped past him. Instead the arrow point ruthlessly embedded itself in a knight fighting by his side, piercing his chainmail.

Rowan's curse remained in his throat as the man was flung backwards by the steel bodkin tip. It had gone through the man's hauberk just beneath his chin, the knight's gauntleted hands grasping ineffectually at the dark shaft.

The attackers continued to surge forwards around him, forcing Rowan to take a step backwards notching another arrow onto his string as a cry began to call out over the clash of weapons.

'Percy slain. Percy slain.' The shout was quickly

taken up by men-at-arms around him. The knight he had felled in the distinct quartered surcoat with its blue rampant lions had disappeared from sight. Men gathered protectively around his victim as slowly he sensed a change in the ardour of the enemy.

It was a small thing at first. One of the kneeling knights close to his victim, looked up with sadness in his eyes, more men turned to look and then the slow steps backwards by the men in the front ranks. The cries became louder and were met with no counter claim.

The big Scottish knight was felled by a heavy poll axe, smashing him to his knees before he was unceremoniously booted to the floor. Suddenly space was opening up between the two forces, the attack faltering, the banners no longer advancing menacingly or with so much inevitably.

***

William de Movran watched warily as more and more men still poured back up the shallow slope. A ragged mass of men headed towards the baggage train despite many of the royal forces on the right flank now rallying. Defenders and attacker alike grasped at anything they could and taking the reins of the tethered horses before fleeing southwards.

It wasn't however the rallying royal forces that concerned him. It was the sight of Hotspur's own right flank being assailed by Prince Henry's force who had suddenly emerged from a sunken dip and threatened to surround the rebel lines.

From his vantage point sitting high astride his heavy

destrier he could make out Hotspurs rampant lion banner flying reassuringly in the front ranks pressing forwards singularly determined. The commander was no doubt swinging his sword below the heavy cloth despite the large force that was condensing his own men inwards.

He could see though that, despite the advance biting deep into the Royal centre, the tide of the battle was beginning to turn.

He quickly dismounted, pushing men roughly out of his way as he threaded between the parked carts, seeking out one with the personal royal livery painted on the heavy covering tarpaulin. Quickly pulling himself up and cutting back the cloth he hastily began to break open the various chests, discarding maps, robes, utensils until, with a grin spreading across his face, his eyes located a small iron bound chest. Eagerly he lifted the wooden box and felt the weight, hearing the tantalising clink of metal within. Hastily prising the lock with his dagger he was rewarded by the sight of what must have been hundreds of silver pounds. It was a small fortune.

As he straightened up, his mind already exploring what he would do with his new found riches and putting his heavy prize under his arm, an arrow suddenly thudded into one of the broken boxes protecting his lower torso, startling him. He hastily looked in the direction from where it had come, towards the rallying men of Stafford. He saw the pale-faced archer he had rode down earlier holding his bow and then glanced down at the protruding shaft.

There was now no doubt in his mind as to whether

he waited to see the final outcome of the battle. He quickly jumped down from the wooden boards, his feet planting themselves heavily on the floor before he buckled the small box to his saddle. He then led his horse through the parked wagons, making sure the he kept the obstacles between him and the archer. Nevertheless another arrow flew past as he rapidly rode southwards.

***

The centre battle, realising that the enemy were losing heart, forced home their advantage as cries that Hotspur Percy was dead began to communicate through the rebel lines. They had been fighting for perhaps two hours and the sun was now beginning to disappear to be replaced by the hues of the early evening. Both sides were weary but the cheers for Saint George and King Henry and then the cries for his son, the Prince, spurred the royal force forward. Vicious points of poll axes, halberds and swords were increasing inflicting casualties on Hotspurs forces. The rebels no longer protected each other's sides as they looked backwards searching for escape. For many there was none as the points found the gaps in their armour. The retreat was slow at first but as men began lose comrades and found themselves assailed by greater numbers the retreat gained an inexorable momentum.

Rowan watched exhaustedly as the enemy broke. The crescendo of cheers gained in volume as the King's forces chased the enemy towards the ridgeline still visible against the darkening sky as dusk finally began to settle.

Hotspur's rebels and their allies had been defeated and all that was left was to pursue them down. For now the kingdom was safe but instead of joy all Rowan could feel was weariness.

EPILOGUE

As night fell, Rowan knelt at the body of the Earl, the crushed helm and bloodstained royal surcoat with its golden lions now removed so that his armour flickered against the flames of the night time fires. His body had been lifted from the battlefield where it seemed that every blade of grass that was not covered by an injured man or corpse was stained dark red, the discarded weapons and broken shields telling the story. There were far too many dead for them to be buried yet and those men who had not continued to pursue the enemy and had remained on the battlefield were tired and weary.

Canvas tents had now been erected so that the few surgeons could care for the wounded nobles and knights, while it was left to comrades to tend to their friends as much as possible. Among the injured was the Prince who had suffered an arrow in the cheek, but was expected to survive. Rowan's own injuries had now stopped bleeding, clean pieces of linen now tied tightly round his wrist and side though the pain was constant causing him to wince every time he moved.

As he looked down on the noble's broken body he was conscious of an approaching group of men and wearily turning his head. He saw that it was Sir Robert, carrying the standard that had helped rally the Staffordshire troops, and behind him, his two friends, Martin and Daniel. His heart lightened as he saw that they had survived the battlefield though he could see even in the dimness of the night, their faces were dirty and drained.

Sir Robert strode purposefully forward his face saddened as he bent down to look at the body of his friend, Sir Edmund. He said nothing, the solemnity of the moment taking over.

'I heard you were at his side when he fell?' Sir Robert asked Rowan without looking up and eventually breaking the silence, his voice soft as he still looked upon the Earl's young face.

'Yes, sire, no more than a few yards away when he was killed.'

'I see and he died protecting the King?'

'Yes sire, in my humble opinion if it wasn't for him the battle may have been lost.'

A moment's pause followed.

'That's how he would have liked it,' said the knight as he pushed himself with effort to his feet. He looked Rowan straight in the face and studied the archer silently who instinctively lowered his head under the gaze. 'You have been through much, and you have carried yourself impeccably but I have some more bad news.'

He looked at the knight not understanding for the moment. His grief for the Earl hung heavily and then slowly his mind began to ask questions, his stomach muscles tightening as he turned to look at his friends.

Their faces were not just dirty and drained. He could

see against the flames from the nearby fires that they wore tear stains and sorrow on them.

'No.' he shook his head not wanting to realise the unspoken message.

His mind was numb, his body hung as though wearing a heavy harness as he looked down at Jerrard's body, the Earl's standard now in his hand, the gules and or swallow tail, its cross of Saint George and the knot and swan emblems now dirty and bloody.

He had stood silently taking in the news of another of his friends' deaths before Sir Robert had stepped forwards, a hand on his shoulder and proffered the banner. 'I would be glad if you would take this. Hold it and when we return to Stafford I would be grateful if you would consider becoming an esquire within my household retinue.'

For a moment the words had not sunk in, the grief too raw as he instinctively took hold of the proffered oak shaft.

'You have shown great character and fight, moreover you have shown the qualities one expects from a knight.'

The words had come through a haze. He had endured his first battles, had lost people he loved.

'There will be more battles to come, so I will have need of your services.'

That last comment came to him as he stood alone in the darkness of night staring at the bearded figure of his friend, Jerrard who had joined the exuberant Eric, the brave Willard, his beloved father and many more.

He felt tightness across his chest and could feel the

beat of his heart. He would take up the offer and, if God judged it so, would meet William de Movran in battle one more time.

He stared into the clear night sky and the stars above for a moment, picking the smooth wooden cross from under his jacket and feeling the reassuring smoothness of its grain before hefting the standard against his shoulder and heading back to the field with its shallow ridge. The campfires illuminated the survivors, injured and dead alike that had fought for a Kingdom.

Graham Nolan

AUTHORS NOTE

The story is fiction although I have sought to reflect the very real conflict and threat posed to the newly crowned King Henry of England by the Welsh forces led by Owain Glyn Dwr.

Ivo Fitz Warren, Lord of the castle at Whittington would indeed have been caught up in the rebellion of 1400 and have sought support from English garrisons. He was also discharged from the rest of his rent for the wardship of the lordship "in consideration of the wasting of the manor of Whittington in Wales by the rebels, so that he can receive no profit from it," though this was after the battle of Shrewsbury and against the backdrop of continuing Welsh resurgence.

The seizure of the throne and subsequent death years later of King Richard II by Sir Henry Bollingbroke with an overwhelming force, that included the support of the powerful Percy family, left many nobles cautious of the new King. This caution remained throughout his reign. The fictional William de Movran is based upon a good number of knights and men who remained loyal to King Richard II and would have found themselves cast adrift by the turn of events, seeking a new lord to serve.

Owain Glyn Dwr too was a casualty of the rise of the

new King. Lord Grey, one of King Henry's friends and closest allies became an enemy, enticed by the Welshman's holdings. He began a campaign that would ultimately lead the Welsh knight to rebellion. Unable to gain justice through the English courts for his land being stolen by Lord Grey, accused of being a traitor and encouraged by his patriotic countrymen who still faced prejudice from the English rule, Owain Glyn Dwr took the decision to march against Lord Grey and thus the English crown.

The catalyst for English rebellion came from Henry Bollingbroke's powerful once supporters, the Percy's, and in particular, Hotspur Percy. This was in the main due to the continued refusal by the King to pay the ransom for his friend Sir Edmund Mortimer. This was compounded by the King's own demands for the transfer of captured Scottish nobles, including the Earl Douglas from Hotspur's responsibility. Hotspur captured the Earl at the battle of Homildon Hill and became firm friends with the Scottish knight.

It seems that these events appear to have led to the charismatic Hotspur gathering an English force and marching towards Shrewsbury in the hope of capturing the strategic town, and perhaps even Prince Henry, aided by many of the former King Richard's followers.

Sir Thomas Percy did indeed extricate himself and half the garrison from Shrewsbury and it is unclear how this occurred without causing Prince Henry any concerns.

Similarly, why Owain Glyn Dwr's forces never joined before the battle of Shrewsbury has never really been decisively explained. Their arrival would have certainly made the outcome more questionable, especially with the rebel forces coming so close to success. Nevertheless I have sought to include at least part of Glyn Dwr's army in the form of one of his most renowned commanders, Rhys Gethin.

The Earl of Stafford accompanied the King's army northwards towards the Scottish borders rather than command an expedition towards mid Wales, while the local knight Sir Robert de Ferrier was actually recorded as a supporter of King Richard.

Now, though the battle of Shrewsbury is over, rebellion is still in the air. This time the Welsh will seek to benefit from their alliance with the French and their invasion into England where Rowan and his surviving friends will be called upon once more.

Graham Nolan

ACKNOWLEDGEMENTS

This book, my first would not have been achieved without support from some very fine people.

Top of the list has to be my wife for her understanding and patience. There are many times I have wondered if she was happy with someone who has enthusiastically charged up a steep hill to look at some castle ruins or continually talked about 'Retinue'.

There is my family of course. Especially I would like to mention my mother and father who are responsible for helping encourage my ambitions.

Thanks William for persevering with the book cover, not the normal level of help from a brother-in-law. My thanks also go to Sophie who has attempted to share her literary expertise with me.

Lastly but not least a massive acknowledgement to the regulars and bar staff at the Three Crowns in Stone, Staffordshire for not giving me too much stick - you know who you are!